RIFLES FOR WATIE

☆

☆

☆

☆

RIFLES FOR WATIE

by Harold Keith

HarperTrophy®
A Division of HarperCollinsPublishers

Harper Trophy® is a registered trademark
of HarperCollins Publishers Inc.

Copyright © 1957 by Harold Keith
For information address HarperCollins Children's Books,
a division of HarperCollins Publishers, 10 East 53rd Street,
New York, NY 10022.
Library of Congress Catalog Card Number: 57-10280
ISBN 0-690-70181-0
ISBN 0-06-447030-X (pbk.)

First Harper Trophy edition, 1987.

Contents

AUTHOR'S NOTE

Few Americans know how savagely the Civil War raged or how strange and varied were its issues in what is now Oklahoma and the neighboring states of Kansas, Missouri, and Arkansas. *Rifles for Watie* was faithfully written against the historical backdrop of the conflict in this seldom-publicized, Far-Western theater.

In my research, I drew heavily upon the sources of the region. I read the diaries and journals of Civil War veterans, most of them Union, in the State historical collections of Kansas, Missouri, Nebraska, Colorado, Oklahoma, Arkansas, and Tennessee, all of which I visited. I had access to the hundreds of personal letters written during the war by the mixed-blood Cherokees and now contained in the Frank Phillips Collection at the University of Oklahoma. My chief sources of published material were the *War of the Rebellion* series, *The Confederate Veteran*, Grant Foreman's *The Texas Road* and *A History of Oklahoma*, Wiley Britton's *The Union Indian Brigade in the Civil War*, Dr. Morris L. Wardell's *A Political History of the Cherokee Nation*, Mabel Washbourne Anderson's *The Life of General Stand Watie*, and Bell Irvin Wiley's *The Life of Billy Yank* and *The Life of Johnny Reb*. Jeff Bussey's flight on foot from Boggy Depot to Fort Gibson had its actual counterpart. Larry Lapsley, a Negro slave, escaped in 1864 from northern Texas to Fort Gibson over the same route. His account, later published in the Kansas Chronicles, was very useful. So was General James G. Blunt's account of his Civil War experiences, also published in the Kansas Chronicles.

Because I wanted an authentic flavor of the war in the Far West, I visited and interviewed in the summers of 1940 and 1941 twenty-two Confederate war veterans then living in Oklahoma and Arkansas, and wrote down their reminiscences. Two were in units commanded by General Stand Watie: Daniel Ross of Locust Grove, Oklahoma, Second Cherokee Mounted Rifles and Jim Long of Gravette, Arkansas, Company C, Arkansas Cavalry, attached to Watie's command. Besides Ross, the veterans from Oklahoma were George Frank Miller of Carmen, John W. Harvey of Okmulgee, James R. Arnn of Rush Springs, John A. Willis of Duncan, Frank B. Harrison of Ardmore, Josephus White of Bethany, Wiley Bearden of Sulphur, William H. Freeman of Wetumka, Burrell Nash of Sulphur, William B. Cantwell of Ada, William J. Briscoe of County Line, L. N. Gammell of Purcell, Joseph A. Chipman of Pauls Valley, John F. Trible of Sulphur, Marshall M. Clark of Duncan, J. L. Johnson of Foster, Charles H. Gordon of Ardmore, and Augustus Wilson of Ardmore. I also talked to Tom Wisdom of Mulberry, Arkansas, and Thomas Harris of Ozark, Arkansas. My obligation to all their memories is very deep.

While gathering information for my master's thesis in history at the University of Oklahoma, I talked several times to George W. Mayes of Pryor and Oklahoma City. He personally knew General Watie and his son, Saladin. He was a boy when the war began and made two attempts to join the Watie outfit, both frustrated by his father, Wash Mayes, who fought in the Watie brigade.

The eagerness of northern manufacturers to sell arms to the seceding states resulted in a traffic so common that it became a national scandal. For those who would like more information, I suggest an hour spent with *Firearms of the Confed-*

eracy, by Claud E. Fuller and Richard D. Steuart, printed by Standard Publications, Inc., Huntington, West Virginia; or a talk with my friend, Don Rickey, custodian of the Custer Monument, Crow Agency, Montana, who first called it to my attention. Repeating rifles, invented by Christopher Miner Spencer, got into the war late but they got in.

The plot is wholly fictional. I know of no attempt by General Watie to secure repeating rifles. I found it necessary to alter the lives of Generals Watie and James G. Blunt, Colonel William Penn Adair, and Major Elias Cornelius Boudinot only when they came into direct contact with my hero, Jeff Bussey. Noah Babbitt was a real-life itinerant printer and pedestrian of the early 1870's who occasionally wandered through Kansas, setting type for the *Wichita Eagle.* I do not know whether he fought in the Civil War. The other characters are almost totally imagined. They do, however, represent families and names typical of the region and the time. Incidentally, General Watie's name is pronounced as though it were spelled "weighty."

I am grateful to Dr. E. E. Dale, research professor emeritus of history at the University of Oklahoma and my teacher in the 1920's there, and to Dr. Edwin C. McReynolds, professor of history, for reading the galleys. Each took valuable time from a book he was writing to help with mine.

I am indebted to Virginia, my wife, for typing, for advice, and for tolerating our lack of social life as I tried to fit the five-year writing labor around my duties as sports publicist at the University of Oklahoma. I am also indebted to Mrs. Addie Lee Barker, my assistant in sports publicity at Oklahoma, and to Kathleen Keith, my daughter, for typing. Professor Dwight Swain, Mrs. Mary H. Marable, Dr. Jim Haddock, Bill Hoge, and Beatrice Frank all gave valuable assistance.

HAROLD KEITH

University of Oklahoma
January 10, 1957

RIFLES FOR WATIE

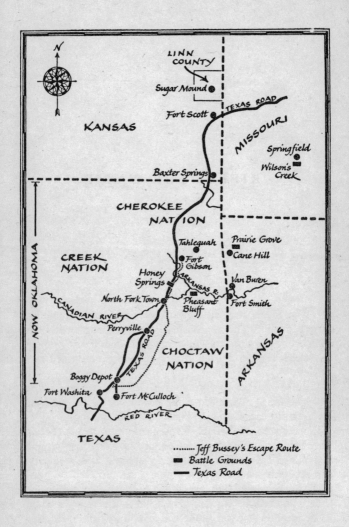

N

LINN
COUNTY

Sugar Mound •

TEXAS ROAD

Fort Scott •

KANSAS

MISSOURI

Springfield •

Wilson's
Creek •

Baxter Springs •

CHEROKEE
NATION

Prairie Grove •
Cane Hill •

Tahlequah •

CREEK
NATION

Fort
Gibson •

Honey
Springs

ARKANSAS R.

Van Buren •

North Fork Town •

Pheasant
Bluff •

Fort Smith •

NOW OKLAHOMA

CANADIAN RIVER

Perryville •

TEXAS ROAD

CHOCTAW
NATION

ARKANSAS

Boggy Depot •

Fort Washita •

Fort McCulloch •

RED RIVER

TEXAS

.... Jeff Bussey's Escape Route
■■■ Battle Grounds
——— Texas Road

☆ 1

Linn County, Kansas, 1861

The mules strained forward strongly, hoofs stomping, harness jingling. The iron blade of the plow sang joyously as it ripped up the moist, black Kansas earth with a soft, crunching sound, turning it over in long, smooth, root-veined rectangles.

Leather lines tied together over his left shoulder and under his right arm, Jeff trudged along behind the plow, watching the fresh dirt cascade off the blade and remembering.

Remembering the terrible Kansas drouth of the year before when it hadn't rained for sixteen long months. The ground had broken open in great cracks, springs and wells went dry, and no green plant would grow except the curly buffalo grass which never failed. That drouth had been hard on everybody.

Jeff clutched the wooden plow handles and thought about it. He recalled how starved he had been for wheat bread, and how his longing for it grew so acute that on Sundays he found

excuse to visit neighbor after neighbor in hopes of being invited to share a pan of hot biscuits, only to discover that they,
too, took their corn bread three times a day.

A drop of perspiration trickled down his tan, dusty face.
It was a pleasant face with a wide, generous mouth, a deep
dimple in the chin, and quick brown eyes that crinkled with
good humor. The sweat droplets ran uncomfortably into the
corner of his mouth, tasting salty and warm.

But now the drouth was broken. After plenty of snow and
rain, the new land was blooming again. Even his mother was
learning to accept Kansas. Edith Bussey had lived all her life
in Kentucky, with its gently rolling hills, its seas of bluegrass,
its stone fences festooned with honeysuckle, and its stately
homes with their tall white columns towering into the drowsy
air. No wonder she found the new Kansas country hard to
like.

She had called Kansas an erratic land. Jeff remembered she
had said it was like a child, happy and laughing one minute,
hateful and contrary the next. A land famous for its cyclones,
blizzards, grasshoppers, mortgages, and its violently opposed
political cliques.

Jeff ducked his head and wiped his mouth on the sleeve of
his homespun shirt, never taking his eyes off the mules. He
would never forget the scores of covered wagons he had seen,
during the drouth last fall, on the Marais des Cygnes road that
went past his father's farm as one-third of the hundred thousand people living in Kansas Territory gave up, abandoning
their claims and heading back to their wives' folks.

Curious, he had leaned on his father's corral fence of peeled
cottonwood logs and asked some of them where they were going.

"Back to Ellinoy," or "Back to Injeany," they replied in
their whining, singsong voices. "Don' wanta starve to death
here."

Although Jeff had felt sorry for them and their families,

his father, a veteran of the Mexican War, was disgusted with their faint-heartedness. Emory Bussey believed that in one respect the drouth had been a blessing to the new state.

"We got rid of the chronic croakers who never could see good in anything," he maintained. Emory was a Free State man in the raging guerilla warfare over slavery that had divided people on the Kansas-Missouri border into free and slave factions. It was a political dispute that was far more serious than the drouth.

Jeff yelled at the mules and whistled piercingly between his teeth to keep them going. He liked the new Kansas country. He meant not only to live and work in it but also to go to college in it. His father had told him that the first Kansas constitution, made in 1855, contained a provision saying that "The General Assembly may take measures for the establishment of a university." Jeff wondered if the drouth would delay its coming. At the end of the row he halted the mules.

He took off his hat to cool his brown head. His mother had made the hat from wheat straw she had platted with her own hands at night, shaping the crown to his head and lining it inside with cloth to keep it from being scratchy. While Jeff stood bareheaded, enjoying the warm breeze blowing through his hair, his dog Ring trotted up, panting, and nudged Jeff's leg affectionately.

Jeff reached down and pulled Ring's ears, and the big gray dog's plumed tail waved in slow half-circles of delight. Ring was half shepherd and half greyhound. He had big shoulder muscles and a white ring around his neck. Although the dog weighed almost ninety pounds now, Jeff recalled how six years ago he had brought him home in his coat pocket. His father and mother hadn't wanted him to have the dog; they already had a collie and a feist. But Jeff begged so hard that they relented on condition that he keep the animal at the barn.

However, that first night Jeff had heard the pup crying

lonesomely for its mother. He slipped out of bed in the dark, walked to the barn, and brought the pup back to his bedroom. The next morning his father and mother discovered the dog in bed with him. When they scolded him, Jeff hung his head and took his reprimand without speaking. Now he and Ring were such good friends that Jeff couldn't wrestle with the other boys at the three-months district school without Ring taking his part.

He put his hands back on the plow handles and looked around, smelling the freshly turned sod. The morning was alive with a soft stirring and a dewy crispness. Jeff heard the sharp, friendly whistle of a quail from the waving bluestem beyond the plowed space, and from somewhere in the warm south wind his nostrils caught the wild, intoxicating whiff of sand-plum blossoms. But the boy felt strangely out of tune with the beauty and freshness of the morning.

His mind was filled with a restlessness and a yearning. At breakfast his father had told him that six Southern states had seceded from the Union and that a war would probably be fought between the North and the South, a big war that might easily spread to Kansas.

Jeff's heart beat faster beneath his blue homespun shirt. If, by a miracle, a general war could be avoided, soldiers were still needed to halt the guerilla warfare in Kansas, brought on by the Missouri proslavery faction across the border. Jeff's dearest wish was to become a soldier.

It was all he talked about at home. He was small for his sixteen years but strong, wiry, cheerful, and not at all abashed in the presence of strangers. There was no doubt in his mind which army he wanted to enlist in.

He had known ever since that time he and his father had ridden horseback through the snow in the winter of 1859 to Leavenworth to hear Abraham Lincoln speak in behalf of his candidacy for the Presidency. Lincoln had just touched the northeast tip of the new Kansas Territory on his tour, speaking at Elwood, Troy, Doniphan, Atchison, Stockton and Leavenworth. Jeff never forgot him. He could still repeat from memory portions of Lincoln's speech he had heard.

The day was bitterly cold. Lincoln and his party had traveled in sleighs and were wrapped in buffalo robes.

Before the meeting Jeff saw Lincoln's kindly face and his rangy profile through the window of a Leavenworth barber shop. Conducted there by Kansas City newspapermen to get his hair cut, Lincoln was reading the New York and Chicago newspapers they had bought for him at the post-office news-stand while he waited his turn in the chair.

Later the cold prairie wind rocked the little bare-walled courthouse in which Lincoln spoke. Not more than forty people were present. Jeff was surprised when the tall lawyer from Illinois rose up behind a rough table and, with his long hands wandering awkwardly in and out of his pantaloon pockets, began, in a tenor voice freely punctuated with "jist" and "sich," not to orate but just to talk. At first Jeff had squirmed in his seat.

If the people of Illinois considered this a great man, their ideas must be peculiar. Despite his youth, Jeff knew a lot about slavery. It was all his father discussed at mealtime.

But as Lincoln talked on and on, Jeff began to change his mind about the gangling visitor from Illinois. Speaking as informally as though he and another man were exchanging thoughts while driving a buggy across the prairie, Lincoln discussed the question of slavery in the Territories with kindly but naked frankness. Although Jeff's father had told Jeff that Leavenworth was a slavery town, the frontier people there believed in fair play, and Jeff noticed that they listened courteously to Lincoln.

Jeff never forgot one thing Lincoln told the proslavery audience. "Your own statement of it is that if the Black Republicans elect a President, you won't stand it. You will break up the Union. Do you really think you are justified to break up the government? If you do, you are very unreasonable, and more reasonable men cannot and will not submit to you. If we shall constitutionally elect a President, it will be our duty to see that you submit. We have a means provided for expressing our belief in regard to slavery. It is through the ballot box, the peaceful method provided by the constitution. But no man, North or South, can approve of violence or crime."

Relaxing against the plow, Jeff frowned and fanned himself with his hat. Every family living along the Kansas-Missouri border knew all about the violence and crime that had arisen over slavery. Jeff was growing tired of it. Three years earlier a band of armed Missouri border ruffians had captured eleven Free State men, marched them to a gulch only eleven miles from the Bussey home, lined them up and fired a volley, killing five. Jeff's father had ridden over next day to help bury them. Jeff had begged to go along, but his mother wouldn't hear of it. That was known as the Marais des Cygnes Massacre.

Jeff put his hat back on his head and remembered the time two months ago his younger sisters Bess and Mary had ridden horseback to the trading post to buy an ounce of paregoric. Two miles from home they were surprised by five Missouri bushwhackers. The men took their horses, but the girls persuaded them to let them keep their light saddles. Later they arrived home, carrying the saddles. The stolen horses were the only ones the family possessed. One of them was Charley, Jeff's own three-year-old whom he had raised from a colt. In spite of Lincoln's speech, violence and crime over slavery still flared all along the border, just three miles from the Bussey home. And now there was going to be a war over it.

Jeff turned the mules, lifting the plow into alignment for the new furrow. He slapped the lines along the mules' backs and whistled shrilly. Crouching, the mules hit their collars together, leg muscles flexing. The leather traces tightened, creaked, strained. Grunting laboriously, they dug in and pulled hard, and Jeff felt the handles drawn almost out of his hands as the plow moved forward, hurling the black dirt off the moldboard and pulverizing it into the previous furrow.

The sun climbed higher and higher. He plowed for two more hours, then paused again to rest his team. He looked up, feeling strong pangs of hunger. Must be about noon. His home, half a mile away, was a handsome three-room log house with a lean-to barn and a sod smokehouse, nestling snugly in a clearing surrounded by oak, hickory, and blackjack. A column of gray smoke curled from the stone fireplace, and Jeff knew his mother was busy cooking among her pots and ovens there.

There would be fat bacon, corn bread in pone, dandelion greens, wild honey, and fried onions from the new garden. Jeff sighed resignedly. No dinner for him today. His mother had packed a big piece of cold corn pone and given him a bottle of water from the spring. But, boylike, he had eaten all the pone at ten o'clock in the morning and now he was hungry again.

Jeff was proud of his home. It had taken the family seven months to build it. Seven long months of hewing, beveling, chinking, daubing and plastering. Although Jeff had been small, he had helped, working long hours. So had his mother and his sisters. How pleased they all were to see the new house rising, log by log. They were tired of living in the dugout down by the creek. The new home was solidly constructed of hickory logs, warmly chinked with clay.

The floor was of split logs. The wall had been plastered cleanly with clay mud. The house was comfortable and weather-tight. Although his father referred to it as "my mud-dauber's nest," its oak-shake roof turned the hardest rains. Jeff thought it the finest home in Linn County.

However, lately he felt a vague fear and insecurity about it. His father's views on slavery were so pronounced that Jeff was afraid their home place might some day be the target for a raid by the proslavery bushwhackers from Missouri.

Jeff frowned. He wished the Missouri bushwhackers would live by the rule Mr. Lincoln had laid down in his speech at Leavenworth. He could remember almost word for word the President's counsel:

"If I might advise my Republican friends here, I would say to them, leave your Missouri neighbors alone. Have nothing whatever to do with their slaves. Have nothing whatever to do with the white people save in a friendly way. Drop past differences and so conduct yourselves that if you cannot be at peace with them, the fault shall be wholly theirs." But neither side had heeded Lincoln's gentle advice.

Jeff toed the warm black soil thoughtfully. If war came, he meant to join the Union volunteers already in training at Fort Leavenworth. He wanted to be in the cavalry, but David Gardner, a neighbor boy who, like Jeff, talked of little else but joining the Union volunteers, said you couldn't get into the cavalry unless you brought your own horse. Jeff frowned again. He didn't have a horse now. All he had was his father's mules, and that reminded him that he had better get on with the plowing.

All afternoon he hustled the mules and steered the plow. With pride and satisfaction he saw the tilled space behind him bulge larger and larger. Soon the sun began to slant toward the west and Jeff saw his shadow lengthen across the field. Ring had long since stopped following him and was lying in the shade of a fresh furrow, waiting for him to make another round of the field. When the plow passed, Ring got up, whined, and followed for a few steps. Then he went back and lay in the shade.

Suddenly Jeff's ears caught a sound that made him jerk the mules to a stop in the middle of the field. It was the thin, muted toot of his father's large sea horn. It was only blown in an emergency.

Worried, Jeff thought he saw men and horses in the yard. A chill of fear ran through him. Bushwhackers!

Quickly he unhooked the traces, leaving the plow in the field. With Ring following at a puzzled lope, Jeff turned the harnessed mules homeward, driving them ahead of him at a trot, and holding onto the lines as he ran behind.

 2

Bushwhackers

Jeff guided the mules into the corral and, without removing their harness, quickly looped the gate's homemade leather clasp over the cottonwood post and hurried to the house.

He saw his father coming with his awkward limp from the garden. Two years before, Emory had dropped an anvil on his foot, laming it permanently. That was why Jeff was doing the plowing.

Jeff's mother, small, frightened, and pretty, was standing on the rock porch with two rough-looking whiskery strangers who carried sawed-off Enfield muskets. Blue ribbons were fastened to their hats and fluttered from the bridles of their horses. Bess, elder of Jeff's sisters, had slipped out the front door and blown the sea horn.

"Good morning," said the smaller and dirtier of the two

strangers, although it was then late in the afternoon. "Is this
the Emory Bussey place?"

Jeff's father nodded curtly. "I'm Emory Bussey."

The smaller man looked significantly at his companion,
as though to say, "This is our man." Then he whipped his
brown eyes back upon Jeff's father, regarding him insolently
from head to foot.

"We're two of Cy Gordon's Union Home Guards. We want
something to eat," he said. Emory Bussey stood in his back
yard, his legs apart, staring coldly at them.

"That's a lie," he said boldly. "You're not Union. But I
never turn anybody away that's hungry. Go on into the
house, and I'll have 'em get you something."

Jeff caught his breath. He was proud of his father's fear-
lessness but afraid of what it might bring. With a start, he
thought of the family rifle but remembered it was standing
unloaded in the corner of the house.

The small man's jaw sagged with surprise. Again he
stared at Emory, and this time there was rude cunning in his
rough face. The larger man stood silently behind him.

Without a word Jeff's mother and the girls stepped inside
to prepare the meal.

Emory said coolly, "Jeff, better go unharness the mules."
Then he turned to the strangers and, with a brief motion of his
head, gestured toward the door, indicating they should go
inside.

Spurs clanking, the men tied their horses to a small cottonwood tree and strode inside the house, still carrying their guns
and wearing their hats. Emory hobbled after them.

Uneasy, Jeff watched them over his shoulder as he walked
to the barn. He didn't trust them. Trembling with helplessness,
he wished he had the rifle. He feared for his father's life. But
obedience was strong within him. His father had told him to
unharness the mules.

All the time he worked, his mind was in a turmoil. He

wished with all his heart he could think of some way to help. But he was too excited to think. He picked up the mules' halter ropes and tied them to the stalls while they ate.

He was halfway out the barn door when he heard Bess scream and saw her run from the house and climb over the wooden style they had erected so the women could cross the fence. She was crying hysterically.

"They're going to shoot Father!" she gasped.

Jeff looked at her, feeling his body go rigid. He began running toward the house. Bess flung herself upon him, holding him. Although she was only fourteen, she was strong.

"No, Jeff," she begged. "They'll kill you too."

Jeff jerked roughly away from her. "I'll follow them even if they crawl into a hole," he vowed hoarsely. As he passed the barn, he grabbed a small curved haying hook off a wooden peg.

Ring was close on his heels, a low growl in his throat. Jeff burst into the house. His mother and Mary were cowering along the wall.

With a gasp of thankfulness he realized his father was still unharmed. Emory Bussey was sitting in a chair, defiantly facing the two strangers who stood pointing their guns at his breast. Jeff's mother was pleading with them not to shoot him.

"You're under arrest," the small man growled menacingly. "Come on outdoors."

Emory Bussey shook his head firmly. He said, "If you want to kill me, you'll have to do it right here in my own house because I'm not going with you."

Jeff felt his breathing quicken. He gripped the haying hook in his right hand.

"Let him alone!" he warned, with hoarse fierceness. The big bushwhacker swung his musket around, covering Jeff.

The smaller bushwhacker took a threatening step forward. His musket still covered Emory's breast.

"Git up on yer feet!" he ordered, striking Emory roughly on the shoulder with one hand and nodding with his head toward the door.

Emory braced himself in his chair and looked defiantly at them. The two bushwhackers glanced uncertainly at each other, as if debating their next move.

Suddenly hoofbeats clattered in the back yard, rang down the kite-track, and were gone.

Scornfully Emory glared at the Missouri border ruffians. "That's my daughter Bess. She's gone for help. In five minutes' time there'll be a dozen Free State men hot on your trail. I wouldn't give a nickel for your chances."

Jeff wondered where Bess had summoned the courage to ride one of the wild Bussey mules bareback.

An insane glow burned in the face of the smaller man. Holding his rusty musket at hip level, he pulled the trigger. But there was only a loud metallic snap as the cartridge refused to fire.

Jeff yelled in a strangled voice and hurled the sharp haying hook at the man with all his strength. Struck in the chest, the bushwhacker dropped his gun.

Before he could pick it up, the boy leaped clear across the room and flung himself upon the man, striking him in the face with doubled fists, flooding him with sharp punches. Jeff was the best bare-knuckle fighter in his school, and the spat-spat-spat of his quick blows staggered his adversary.

But now the other bushwhacker came forward. Using his gun barrel as a club, he stepped behind Jeff and swung it viciously downward across the boy's head. *Clonk!* A thousand colored lights exploded in Jeff's skull. With a low groan he collapsed unconscious on the floor. Now the whole Bussey family entered the fight.

Jeff's mother reached for a plate of boiled greens and hurled them at the smaller man. The dish and its contents stained his shirt green and flowed down his rough trousers.

Emory Bussey stood and, brandishing a small stool, advanced around the table. Both bushwhackers retreated.

A sudden howl of pain broke from the larger man as Mary, Jeff's twelve-year-old sister, snatched up a pan of hot dishwater from the fireplace and threw it on him. They stumbled out the back door. But their troubles weren't over.

As they emerged from the house, the dog Ring, growling fiercely, fastened his strong teeth onto the seat of the bigger man's trousers.

With a superhuman effort the man got one foot in the stirrup of his excited horse and tried to mount with the ninety-pound dog anchored to his pants. Luckily for him, the cloth ripped noisily and when Ring fell to the ground on his back, both men were able to gain their saddles.

"We'll be back!" the smaller one threatened. "There's thirty men in our band, and they're close by. We'll burn your house down and string you all up by the necks, you Free State scum . . ."

But the rest of his threat was lost as Ring, scrambling to his feet, threw himself so fiercely at the heels of the horses that the frightened animals stampeded down the kite-track with their riders hard-pressed to stay in their saddles. The Busseys could tell by Ring's gradually diminishing cries that the dog chased them nearly a quarter-mile down the road.

When Jeff awakened, he was lying on a hard dirt floor. Wrinkling his nose, he thought he smelled smoked bacon. It was a nice smell, salty and pungent. He could hear water dripping faintly onto a metal pan. The sound was familiar and he finally recognized it. It was cold water from the spring striking the pan covering the cream crock. Then Jeff knew he was in the smokehouse. His mother kept her milk and butter there. Sighing, he relaxed. It was dark and cool on the smokehouse floor.

Opening his eyes, he saw the whole family clustered anxiously around him. His mother was bathing his face with cold water from the spring. His father's arm was under his neck as, with another cold cloth, he made a compress for the long red welt across Jeff's scalp.

"Ugh!" Jeff groaned. "Water's running down inside my ear." Relieved to hear his voice, the Bussey family began to laugh and chatter.

Jeff thought he heard horses whinnying and pawing the ground outside. When he could focus his eyes better, he looked around and saw not only his own family, but also a couple of Free State neighbors standing in the background, rifles in their hands. Bess had summoned them with her plucky ride.

He grinned weakly at her. "Thanks, Sis," he mumbled. "You did even better than Paul Revere. He didn't have to ride no mule."

Taking a long breath, the boy sat up and looked at his father, his face serious and determined.

"Pa," Jeff said, earnestly, "the Missourians aren't going to let us alone. I'm sick and tired of their meanness—stealing our horses from Bess and Mary—trying to kill you in your own home—belting me over the head with a gun. We've got to organize and fight 'em or give 'em the whole country. And I'm tired of fighting 'em with just a hay sickle. Pa, I want to go to Fort Leavenworth tomorrow and join the volunteers."

Emory Bussey looked fondly at his son. His eyes blurred, and he stared dully out the smokehouse door at the log home they had built with their own hands and the fields they had broken and planted at such hard labor. This was reality to him. All he had in the world was here. His farm, his family, and his son. Especially his son.

Emory swallowed hard. He much preferred going to war himself. Then he dropped his eyes helplessly to his crippled foot.

"All right, son. I'll write out my consent. You shall go tomorrow."

Quietly Jeff's mother began to sob. Rising, she stumbled toward the door, dabbing at her eyes with her apron. It was hard to give up one's first-born. Jeff had come into the world back in Kentucky when she was a girl-wife of seventeen. With him to care for, life on the new Kansas farm hadn't been so lonely when Emory was gone all day working in the field. With all the tenderness a mother could muster, she had fed, bathed, and cared for Jeff, loving his bright, cheerful ways, nursing him through his boyhood diseases, teaching him the Biblical precepts of decency and kindness. And now he was to be wrenched from her.

"Don't cry, Mama," Jeff said, embarrassed at her tears in front of the neighbors. "I won't be gone long. This war's just a breakfast spell. I don't want it to end before I get there."

Bess moved quietly to her mother's side, put her arms around her and tried to comfort her as they walked together to the house.

☆ 3

Fort Leavenworth

Jeff walked briskly up the wagon road toward Fort Leavenworth. It was early in the morning and much of the dewy trail still lay in shadow. Beneath his dusty brogans the road was like a treadmill holding him back. It seemed to him he kept passing the same clumps of sumac and hearing the same crickets chirping from the bluestem. He was bursting to get to the fort.

Soon the land became lower and flatter and rockier. Ahead of him Jeff saw the Chadwick farm with its small log barn, its lean-to smithy and the smoke from its breakfast fire coiling from the small rock chimney of the two-room slab-sided cabin where the family lived.

Big John Chadwick was standing by the family woodpile, his arms full of small blackjack logs. His black hair was awry.

Jeff waved at him, hoping John wouldn't delay him by wanting to stop and talk. But John stared with amazement at the light bandage running over Jeff's head and under his chin.

"What's that—toothache?"

Jeff laughed. "Bushwhackers," he corrected. "Two of them raided us last night. Big one busted me over the head with the barrel of his musket."

John whistled in astonishment. Still carrying his armful of wood, he walked alongside Jeff, staring with fascination at the bandage. "Don't it hurt?" he asked.

"Naw," laughed Jeff. "My head's hard. He's lucky he didn't bust his gun barrel."

"How's all your folks? Anybody get hurt?" Shaking his head, Jeff related the whole incident. He concluded by telling John he was on his way to Fort Leavenworth to enlist.

John puckered his mouth to whistle a second time, then closed it as an idea came to him. Excited, he began to blink his china-blue eyes.

Cautiously he looked back over his shoulder at his home. "Believe I'll go with you, Jeff. I was going to enlist at Sugar Mound anyhow, but I'd rather go with you."

Jeff was glad to have company. Then his face clouded. "Yes, but how about your folks? Aren't you going to tell them?"

John squared his chin defiantly. "They'll know I've gone to the army when I don't bring back the wood. We've been fussing about it for the last six weeks. Pa says he'll tan me if I ask him again. So I'll jest go without askin' him. He don't need me here nohow. He's got my two brothers to help him lay by the crops. I'm eighteen year old now an' I want to see the world. I'm agoin'!" And dropping the armful of wood on the chip-strewn ground at his feet, he brushed the shavings off his shirt and joined Jeff on the military road.

They walked half a mile. The rising sun began to warm them a little. The road became crooked and rocky. Soon they passed the humble home of David Gardner, whose place was located in a woodsy area near the stone quarry. David lived with his mother and three smaller brothers and sisters. His father had died three years earlier from typhoid. Their lot was hard.

David was hoeing the runtish corn that grew so reluctantly in the flinty soil. He was freckled and red-haired save for his heavy eyebrows, which were white as corn silk.

David stared too at the light bandage plainly visible under Jeff's chin.

"Goshallmighty, Jeff. What happened?" he asked, leaning on his hoe.

"Bushwhackers," Jeff replied. "Two of them raided us last night. Big one hit me over the head with his musket." He was eager to be on his way.

David almost dropped the hoe. "You mean he fetched you a full clout with his gun barrel and you're still alive?"

Jeff grinned. "My head's hard. You ought to see the gun barrel. They had to put splints on it."

"Goshallmighty!" David exclaimed again and begged for more details. Patiently Jeff explained everything that happened.

When he told David that he and John were on their way to Fort Leavenworth to join the Kansas Volunteers, David promptly tossed his hoe back into the field. It hit on the end of its long handle and bounced high into the air.

"I'm goin' too," David announced, stepping to Jeff's side. "I'm sixteen, Jeff, same as you. That's old enough."

Jeff blinked. At the rate he was recruiting, he would have
himself a regiment before he ever reached the fort. He eased
his pack. It contained the lunch his mother had fixed and the
extra shirts and pants she had washed and ironed after he
went to bed. His father had given him a silver dollar, all the
cash money he had in the world.

"Corn, Dave. Aren't you going to tell your mother?" Jeff
asked. He knew that if David went to war, Mrs. Gardner
would have to plow, plant, and harvest in the fields as well as
milk the cow and do her housework.

"Naw," David replied scornfully, throwing a careless look
over his shoulder at the mean little one-roomed log home.
"If I told her, she wouldn't let me go. She says I'm too young."

Jeff still didn't think it was right. "The least you can do is
let her know. She needs you on the farm. Besides, the woods
are full of bushwhackers prowling around. She'll think they
caught you and hung you in the bushes."

"Let her," David replied unfeelingly. "Le's go. This is the
only way I'll ever get to leave. Le's go by the spring first an' get
a drink."

They walked under the trees. When they reached the
Gardner spring, they came up behind Bobby, David's six-
year-old brother. He was on his knees busily shaping mud pies
at the plashy edge of the water. David knelt beside him.

"Good-by, Bobby. Tell Ma I've gone to Fort Leavenworth
to enlist in the volunteers."

Bobby never looked up. With dirty hands he scooped up
another double handful of mud and began calmly to fashion
another pie.

"Ma'll skin you, Davy!" he warned suddenly in his shrill,
quavering, old man's voice. "You're not old enough to go to
war. You'll git killed an' we'll find your bones bleachin' on the
prairie."

David snorted. Standing, he looked at Jeff and John, his
face red with embarrassment.

"Come on," he said impatiently. They walked on. Jeff didn't see how David could be so indifferent.

His own family leave-taking that morning had been more painful. His mother had cried again. Although Jeff wanted to go to war worse than he had ever wanted anything else in his life, he even felt a little like crying himself. Until he got out of sight of the house.

That took more time than he had counted on. Ring kept trying to follow, and it was hard to refuse him. Twice Jeff sent him back, but each time the faithful dog returned, showing his savage teeth in a loving grin and frisking all around, as though they were playing a game. In a hurry to get started, Jeff had finally thrown rocks at Ring to scare him home. But the dog still hadn't understood.

Picking up the rocks in his mouth, he brought them dutifully to Jeff, laid them at his feet, and looked up, tail wagging, waiting for Jeff to pet him. Jeff finally had to take him back and lock him in the barn. Bess volunteered to release him in an hour.

"But I may turn him loose sooner," she warned, sniffing bravely as her tear-stained face broke into a wan smile. "Then you'd have to bring him back, and I'd get to see you again."

Jeff felt sorry for Bess and the lonely, humdrum existence his sister would have to live on the farm. He was glad now that David and John were going with him. He hadn't relished the long trip alone.

They walked fifteen miles on the military road. Then they rested, eating most of the cold corn pone and potatoes Jeff's mother had sent.

In the afternoon they caught two different rides with settlers going northward for provisions, and after sleeping that night at the home of a hospitable farmer, they arrived the next afternoon at Fort Leavenworth, riding the last twenty miles in an army teamster's wagon.

A husky sentinel stopped them at the fort's stone gate, his

gun held diagonally across his chest. The three country boys stared with awe at his trim uniform. He wore a blue coat with brass buttons, blue trousers with a yellow braid down the sides and on his head a little, sloping, flat-topped blue cap. Jeff could hardly wait to get one himself.

They told him who they were and that they wanted to join the Kansas Volunteers. The sentry admitted them and told them to go to the enrollment officer in Barracks "K."

The fort, an orderly cluster of neat white buildings, was beautifully situated on rising ground near the southern shore of the Missouri River. Bounded on both sides by dark green strips of woodland, the river flowed southeastward in oceanic grandeur. From his high vantage point Jeff could see the distant ferry rafts moving slowly across the river, like bugs crawling slowly in the sand. Beyond the river the light green sweep of the prairie ran endlessly.

After being sworn in, the three Linn County boys were sent to the military hospital to take their physical examinations. On the way they passed hundreds of soldiers in blue blouses marching on the spacious green drill fields. Bugles were tooting. Officers crossing the parade grounds saluted smartly as they passed one another. Jeff watched with excitement. Apparently everybody was getting ready to fight.

As Jeff, John, and David turned the corner of a barracks building, they heard a thunder of hoofbeats and were almost run down by a squadron of cavalry. Spurs jingling, sabers rattling, and the oaken butts of their carbines resting against their thighs, they thundered past grandly with a drumming of horses' hoofs and a creak of leather. It was quite a sight for a boy fresh from the plow handles. Jeff could smell the horses' sweat and see the metal ring bits on their bridles flashing in the bright Kansas sunshine. He wished he were joining the cavalry intead of the infantry. But the bushwhackers had stolen his horse.

At the hospital the three boys were asked to strip to the

waist while a gruff old army doctor with a fat paunch and tired eyes examined them. Jeff lined up with the scores of other men and boys awaiting their turns.

"Come on, kid," the old doctor said, finally beckoning to Jeff, "you shall have all the war you want."

"Yes, sir!" said Jeff. His father had carefully coached him never to forget that "sir" as long as he was in the army.

"Humph!" grunted the old doctor as he worked. "Lots of fellers nowdays can't wait to put on some blue clothes and go out and shoot at perfect strangers." Noisily he spat a stream of brown tobacco juice all over a brass spittoon on the floor behind him and looked suddenly at Jeff. "Are you one of 'em?"

"Yes, sir," said Jeff, promptly. "I want to shoot at them before they shoot at me."

The doctor tapped Jeff's chest roughly with his dirty, horny knuckles and grunted again. "Humph! That's a pretty good chest."

Jeff beamed modestly.

"Jest right for the rebels to shoot Minie balls through," the old doctor added. Jeff stared at him, feeling strangely depressed.

Later, when they put their blouses back on, Jeff told John and David, "Far as I'm concerned, he could have left out that last remark."

They were surprised still more when they reported to the enlistment officer and one of the first questions he asked was, "Where do you want your pay sent if you are captured?"

Pondering the question, Jeff felt better. He had been afraid the rebels would surrender and the war end before he could get into the fighting. And here was this fellow, suggesting he might be captured. Maybe he was going to see some action after all.

As they stood in line before the quartermaster, Jeff strained his neck trying to get a look at the new Federal uniforms he was sure would be issued to them, like the handsome blue outfit he had seen on the sentry at the fort's gate. But all they got was one light blue blouse, one pair of cotton socks, and one pair of drawers each.

The new recruits fell to talking about why they had enlisted.

"I came all the way from Seward County, down near Injun Territory," said one. "My family's Union. Mammy didn't want me to go to no war. But we knowed the bushwhackers was hid out in the brush, stealin' money and hosses and chokin' boys my age when they found 'em. I didn't wanta git choked. So I runned away. I wanted to run away sooner."

"I jined up fer a frolic," laughed a tall fellow from Republic County with warts on his face. He turned to his messmate, a blond boy from Fort Scott. "Why did you come in?"

"Wal, by Jack, because I thought the rebels was gonna take over the whole country."

"I joined up because they told me the rebels was cuttin' out Union folks' tongues and killin' their babies. After I got here, I found out all it was over was wantin' to free the niggers," complained another, disgustedly.

"I decided I'd jest as well be in the army as out in the bresh. Now I'm about to decide I'd druther be in the bresh," snorted another. They were nearly all frowsy-headed, boot-shod, and lonely-looking, fresh from the new state's farms, ranches, and raw young prairie towns. Before the war ended, Kansas furnished more men and boys to the Union forces in proportion to its population than any other state. And all of them were volunteers.

Jeff smiled to himself and went on eating. He had heard his father discuss the issues so often that he knew them forward and backward. But he saw no need for injecting them into the conversation here. Besides, he was too busy with his supper. The food was good, and there was lots of it.

In bed that night in the barracks, Jeff turned on his stomach and sighed with satisfaction. At last he was in the army.

☆ 4

Captain Asa Clardy

Next morning the bugle awakened them early. After breakfast they were assembled and taken to the drill field. Each man was issued an Enfield rifle and a bayonet.

Through an error, Jeff, David, John, and the other late arrivals were assigned to fill out a company that, unknown to them, had already received several days' instruction.

"The captain's a terror," warned the man standing next to Jeff, in a whisper. "Name's Asa Clardy. He fought in the Mexican War and hates being outranked here by volunteer officers who were farmers a few weeks ago. He takes it out on us volunteer soldiers."

Jeff dropped the butt of his rifle onto the ground. His father had fought in the Mexican War. Perhaps he knew Clardy. Jeff resolved to ask him next time he wrote home.

"Fix bayonets!" roared Captain Clardy. He was a tall, spare-built man with gray sideburns and a long irregular scar on his left cheek. The sides of his black shoes were wet with dew. He had the look of a fellow who was always angry about something.

Mystified by this command, Jeff, John, David, and the other new recruits never moved.

The captain glared and stepped in front of Jeff. Jeff looked at him and felt a quiet shudder. What had he done wrong? On the man's face was a savage, gloating expression.

"Didn't you hear me say fix bayonets?" he demanded.

"Yes, sir," Jeff replied, innocently, "but mine isn't broken, sir."

A roar of laughter ran down the line. Jeff reddened with shame.

"Silence!" shouted the captain curtly, "or I'll run you all around the compound."

The officer scourged Jeff with another searching glare.

"What's your name?"

"Jefferson Davis Bussey, sir," Jeff replied, speaking in a loud, clear voice as his father had taught him.

This time the laughter was more subdued but again it was plainly audible.

The captain's face almost purpled with rage.

"Then change your name!" he roared. "Jefferson Davis is the president of the traitorous Southern Confederacy we are now at war with."

Jeff felt the hair rising on the back of his neck. He neither liked the remark nor the man who delivered it.

"Sir," he said, looking the captain fearlessly in the eye and continuing to speak loudly, "I won't change it. My father gave me that name. He knew Jefferson Davis before the Mexican War. He fought in Jefferson Davis' regiment at the Battle of Buena Vista. Both were serving then under the Stars and Stripes."

Captain Clardy looked as if he was about to explode.

"Fall out!" he roared at Jeff. "I'll teach you to be impertinent. You volunteers never did know your places. You ought to be stripped, lashed to the wheel of a cannon and flogged with a mule whip."

Jeff stepped forward obediently, supposing he was about to receive the punishment the captain had described. To his surprise, he was punished in a different way. At the captain's order, a private from the regular army escorted Jeff to the main kitchen, where for an entire week he was to wash pots and kettles, peel potatoes, and empty swill after he had spent all day at the drill field.

Next afternoon Jeff was made to peel potatoes for Captain Clardy's own mess. As usual the kitchen workers were discussing the officers in an uncomplimentary light.

"Are you close to Captain Clardy?" one of them asked, cautiously.

Jeff laughed. "I'll say! I peel the same potatoes he eats. Why?"

The man looked evasive and fell silent. But later one of the cooks, a muscular man with an American flag tattooed gaudily in red and blue on the inside of his right arm, came up to Jeff when the others had gone. His name was Sparrow.

"What are you bein' punished for?" he asked.

Jeff told him about the incident on the drill field.

Sparrow sneered. "Clardy knows he wouldn't dare talk like that to me or—"

"Or what?" Jeff asked curiously.

A cunning look came into Sparrow's swarthy face. "I'm not gonna shoot off my mouth but I could tell you somethin' about Asa Clardy that he wouldn't want you ner nobody else to know. I knew him back in Morris County."

Jeff was curious to hear more, but Captain Clardy himself walked up, frowning, and Sparrow scuttled back to the kitchen.

Fifteen minutes before the supper call each night, Captain Clardy came on an inspection tour. The surly officer liked the tasty bean soup that was served regularly at the evening meal. Twice that week as Jeff was carrying the heavy soup kettle out of the kitchen, Clardy stopped him and, picking up a big metal spoon, lifted the lid of the kettle, scooped up a full spoonful of the delicious soup, and ate it.

Next evening Jeff was careful to be carrying a soup kettle just as Clardy came into the kitchen. As usual Clardy stepped in front of him, blocking his way.

"Here, you!" Clardy growled. "Give me a taste of that."

"Yes, *sir!*" said Jeff with enthusiasm. Holding the bail of the heavy kettle in his left hand, he saluted smartly with his right. Selecting a large spoon and dipping deeply into the kettle, Clardy greedily downed the contents of the spoon. Quickly he gagged and spat it out upon the floor.

"Do you call that stuff soup?" Clardy roared, glaring angrily at Jeff.

"No, sir," said Jeff, with pretended innocence, "that's dishwater."

Clardy stamped out of the kitchen without a word.

The cooks all looked alarmed. "Lad, you'd best steer clear of that bucko," one old fellow warned Jeff, kindly. "He's cruel and vindictive. He'll never forget that, long as he lives."

"No, I suppose not," Jeff replied. "Thank you for warning me." But as he performed his duties about the kitchen, Jeff felt repaid for the captain's slur on his name.

He did his work so well that on the sixth day he was dismissed an hour early and wandered down to the stables to see the horses.

There he saw an old teamster leading half a dozen fine-looking cavalry mounts around and around the corral. The old man wore a white undershirt and blue army pants with scarlet stripes down the sides. He was muttering angrily to himself. The horses looked jaded, as if they had been ridden hard.

Suddenly a gust of wind whipped a piece of paper across the corral. Frightened, one of the animals jerked loose from the man and started running for the open gate, his long rein dragging in the dust.

"Ho! You black dog!" shouted the old teamster, but the horse paid no attention. The gate was near Jeff. Quickly he ran in front of it, raising his arms and calling to the horse soothingly. The animal plunged to a stop, eyeing Jeff distrustfully. Still talking to him, Jeff was able to recover the rein and return the horse to the teamster.

"Sir," said Jeff, saluting, "I was raised on a farm and know something about horses. I'll be glad to help you walk 'em. Why are they in such a lather?"

The old teamster must have been impressed by that "sir" and also the salute. He handed Jeff three of the halter reins.

"These dom stable boys are no account," the sergeant growled in his rich dialect. "If I send them to the crick to wather the horses, they bile the wather in them on their way back."

As they walked along, Jeff stole a sidelong look at his companion and saw that the teamster was small, wiry, and had lots of wrinkles in the corners of his eyes. His face was covered with black whiskers, as though he hadn't shaved in a week. Jeff judged him to be nearly sixty years of age.

Later Jeff helped Mike Dempsey, for that was the teamster's name, to rub down the animals, return them to their stalls, and feed them. As they worked, he told Mike all about himself and about his run-in with Captain Clardy.

Mike chuckled when Jeff related what he had said when ordered to "Fix bayonets." Without a word, the old Irishman carefully knocked the ashes out of his cob pipe and stuffed it into his side pocket.

Walking into his small office in the harness room, he came out with a bayonet and an old, well-oiled rifle. He showed Jeff every command involving bayonets in the manual of arms, then gave him the gun and bayonet and began to drill him. Jeff soon got the hang of it.

"After this, me boy, you fix it whin he says to, whither it's broke or not," counseled Mike.

In spite of his good intentions, Jeff found out next day that a volunteer soldier serving under volunteer officers has a lot to learn about military etiquette. Henry Slaughter, a neighbor

from Linn County, had joined up earlier than Jeff and secured
a commission. He approached Jeff on the drill field and handed
him a letter from home.

Jeff knew Slaughter well. They had hunted rabbits together
many times in the Bussey cornfield.

Grateful, Jeff blurted, "Thanks, Henry." Slaughter drew
himself up haughtily and cursed Jeff roundly for his familiar-
ity. And Jeff learned that two neighbors of yesterday could
today be separated by an impassable gulf when two bits'
worth of tinsel was pinned on the shoulders of one and not the
other.

When the men in Jeff's outfit elected their own noncom-
missioned officers, they chose for sergeant Pete Millholland,
a big, broad-beamed farmer with white hair and blue eyes,
who had homesteaded along the Kaw River, near Lawrence.
Jeff was surprised at the choice, since Millholland was green
as a gourd about military procedure and wore his uniform
in a slipshod manner.

As a drillmaster, he must have been the worst in the regiment. His squad marched with their rifles down or held over
the wrong shoulder. Their coats were unbuttoned, their pants
legs stuck out of their boots. And when they attempted the
bayonet drill, they stuck each other repeatedly.

For three weeks the Kansas Volunteers marched and drilled
at the fort. Jeff was afraid the war would be over before the
First Kansas Regiment of Infantry would reach the battleground. His fear grew each day.

Finally on the first of July, 1861, the command was suffi-
ciently trained to cross the Missouri River on the military ferry
and bivouac in the big timber beyond. There Jeff liked the
hard, rugged training in the open. It was getting him nearer
his first battle.

But David Gardner liked no part of it. He never seemed
to understand the commands. The officers scolded him constantly, and the other recruits hazed him. Soon he became the

loneliest volunteer in camp. Jeff helped him all he could. But David never seemed to adjust to army life.

One night Jeff found him sobbing in his bunk.

"I'm lonesome," David blurted, miserably. "I want to go home and see Ma. Goshallmighty, Jeff, I ain't cut out to be no soldier. I was a fool to ever leave the farm."

"Corn, Dave," Jeff said, in alarm, "you can't just walk off from the army once you've joined it. That's desertion. You know the penalty for desertion. They'll stand you up against a wall and shoot you."

David's pinched face looked pale. His eyes were red. He clenched his teeth with desperation. "I'm jist about homesick enough to chance it," he said, defiantly. Then his mood softened. "It's just about time to harvest the wheat at home. How's Ma gonna manage with me gone? Onless I'm there to help her, they'll likely starve, come winter."

"No, they won't, Dave," argued Jeff. "Pa will help her. And so will the other Free State families." David stopped sniffing, but he didn't seem comforted.

At night the soldiers had lots of time on their hands. The veterans, who had already drawn their pay, gambled it away. There were all kinds of card-playing, foot-racing, long-jumping and side-hold wrestling.

Bill Earle, a corporal in Jeff's company, had a rich tenor voice. He was from Bluemont Central College, a Methodist school at Manhattan. He would sing to the boys whenever they asked him after supper. Once they discovered an open-air revival in progress behind a small sod schoolhouse near the bivouac spot. Most of Jeff's outfit attended, and several of the boys became converted, including all the tough ones.

Because of the hard daytime training in the woods and on the prairie, the soldiers never seemed to get enough to eat. They were served bacon, beans, hardtack, and coffee three times a day but soon began to yearn for more variety.

One hot night in mid-July they discovered a large patch

of ripe watermelons in an open field. Unfortunately, a soldier stood guard over them. For nearly a week Jeff's company marched back and forth past the field, their mouths watering.

One of the men in Jeff's outfit was Noah Babbitt, a tramp printer from Illinois. He was a tall, droll fellow, whose skin was tanned dark as mahogany from his long travels in the open. He had set type in newspaper offices all the way from Illinois to San Antonio, Texas, traveling by foot across Indian Territory. Even the longest marches failed to tire him. He was always soaking his long, gnarled feet in salt water to toughen the skin for the long jaunts. He read everything he could get his hands on.

"Boys, I've got it," Noah said, late one hot afternoon after they had been dismissed from maneuvers. "Get ready to eat those watermelons."

"I've been ready for a week," said Jeff, dropping his knapsack and canteen into the sand by his feet. Pulling off his shoes, he lay on his back in the shade, wriggling his bare toes in the cool south breeze.

"How we gonna git past thet guard?" asked a private from Lecompton.

Babbitt lowered his voice, looking cautiously around him. "Tonight I'll go on guard myself in the melon field. One of you can hide in the brush along the fence. I'll roll the melons out to you."

"Yup," frowned Ford Ivey, "but the field's already got a guard. What you gonna do about him?"

Babbitt ignored the remark. He said, "I've got to have help. Who'll volunteer to snake the melons out from under the fence to the timber after I roll 'em out of the field under the fence? It'll be open moonlight." Everybody looked at everybody else but nobody answered.

"How about Jeff?" somebody proposed.

"Shore. He's jist the man."

"Jeff's little. They'll never see him."

Jeff rolled suddenly to a sitting position. "Now wait, boys," he protested. "You can't do this to me. It's against the articles of war. It's against the constitution." But they persuaded him.

After dark they all walked quietly to the melon field. The moon was so bright that Jeff could see the light stripes on the big green melons as they lay amid the vines in the sandy soil.

Babbitt advanced on the uniformed guard, climbing boldly over the wooden fence.

"Halt! Who are you? I'm on guard here," challenged the sentry, raising his weapon.

Babbitt's deep voice answered in demanding tones, "Whose command do you belong to?"

"To Graham's battery," the man answered.

"That's funny," grumbled Babbitt, pretending to be confused. "Wonder why they need two guards? I'm from McGregor's company. I'm assigned here for guard duty, too. Well, you watch that end. I'll watch this." The first guard grunted an assent and moved to the upper end of the field.

Soon Babbitt was rolling several big melons under the fence to Jeff, who transported them, crawling, to the fringe of the nearby woods, where hungry hands reached for them in the dark.

Later they cut and divided the tasty booty and all went quietly to bed. The incident convinced Jeff that privates were as capable of strategy as officers.

Next morning they were told that after one more week of training, they would depart for Missouri. There General Sterling Price had organized thousands of Missouri state troops into a rebel army. It was reported Price had gone into Arkansas to meet the Confederate General Ben McCulloch and urge him to aid the Missouri Confederate cause. Jeff was elated by the news.

A short furlough had been granted the volunteers living

within seventy-five miles of the fort. That meant David and Jeff could make a quick trip home to see their families. John Chadwick decided to stay at the fort.

"If I go home, I'll just have another big brawl with Pa over joinin' up, and he'll whop me," John grumbled.

Two days before the furlough began, Jeff awoke early. He drew in a long, luxurious breath. He liked the pungent, early-morning smell of the sandbar willows and the tamaracks. He liked to see the white river mist crawling slowly along the surface of the water.

He looked at David's bed and felt a vague alarm. David wasn't there. His clothing was gone. His army knapsack and canteen lay on his folded bedding. His rifle, brightly polished, was neatly stacked.

Something white was pinned to the bed. It was a torn-off fragment of notebook paper. On it rudely printed in pencil was this note: "jeff i cant stand it no longer i have goned home to see ma. david."

Jeff was stunned. How could David leave the army and its excitement, its promise of glorious adventure? Where was he now? As Jeff hurriedly thrust his legs into his pants, he tried to calculate. David would probably travel alone, swimming the river and skirting the fort until he encountered the military road leading south to Linn County.

Jeff resolved not to report him. That way they wouldn't miss him until after the morning roll call, and he would have at least two hours' head start toward home.

"I don't understand why he didn't wait," he told John Chadwick. "We were both going home in two more days. I just don't understand."

☆ 5

Furlough

"Jeff!"

His younger sister was the first to see him as he strode wearily into the yard just before sundown. Barefoot, she was sweeping the rock porch. She threw down her straw broom and with a glad shout ran to the house to tell the rest of the family. Then she returned, slamming the door behind her, to throw both arms around Jeff's waist and hide her brown head under his arm.

Bess and his mother ran out to join the happy homecoming and found Ring leaping and bounding all over Jeff. The big gray dog was so glad to see his young master that he grasped a cottonwood stick in his mouth and, whining and moaning with pleasure, ran around and around the woodpile with it, scattering the chips and kicking up small clouds of dust.

Mary shouted with laughter. Emory Bussey hurried up from the barn. Grinning, he held out his hand.

They sat up that night until nine o'clock while Jeff told them all about his new life in the army. To Jeff's surprise, his father remembered Clardy from the Mexican War.

"He had the makings of a good officer, but he was a strange, vindictive fellow whom nobody trusted," Emory recalled. "He turned very bitter when his own regiment, the Mississippi Volunteer Rifles, elected Jeff Davis colonel. Clardy wanted the job. He had set his heart on it. When they elected Davis,

Clardy left the regiment and moved away from the South forever." Jeff leaned forward, listening carefully. So that was why Clardy hated the mention of anything Southern.

The family had more news for him. David Gardner wasn't home. Jeff's heart missed a tick when he heard that. Had David drowned, trying to swim back across the wide Missouri? Had he been captured by the soldiers or murdered by the bush-whackers?

For supper that night, Jeff's mother fried wheat biscuits in a pan and roasted sweet potatoes in the fireplace ashes. Best of all, she baked a delicious green-grape cobbler in her fire-place oven. For breakfast next morning they had "sweet toast," home-baked wheat bread toasted in a pan over the fireplace coals. There was hot milk to cover it, and butter, salt, and sugar to add for taste.

"Mama, the army hasn't got any cooks near as good as you," Jeff told her loyally between gulps.

She looked anxiously at him. "I don't see how you can tell. You're eating too fast to taste the food."

Jeff said, "I'm tasting it when it goes down."

His brief leave of one day and two nights at home passed all too quickly. He spent the morning helping his father thresh the wheat by hand, using two hickory clubs tied together with buckskin and letting the wind blow out the chaff. Early in the afternoon he helped Bess pack the eggs in bran, so they would be ready to take to the trading post. He went to the spring-house with Mary and helped her skim the cream off the cool milk and churn the butter. He helped his mother plait lamp-wicks and fry refuse pork, out of which to make the fuel oil for the lamps.

Although all four of them were putting up a great show of being brave, Jeff couldn't help noticing how they kept stealing pensive sidelong glances at him, as though they didn't want to forget what he looked like. He wished he had thought to have a daguerreotype made at the gallery in Leavenworth so he could give it to them. Neither he, nor Bess, nor Mary had ever had their pictures made.

Just before bedtime, Jeff took a short walk outdoors with Ring. He looked thoughtfully at each well-known object as it lay sleeping in the bright Kansas moonlight: the little creek where he had trapped skunk and muskrat, his duck blind on the riverbank, the big oak tree where he had twisted the rabbit out with a forked stick. Now they seemed unimportant and far-away, like a child's toys.

A coyote's melancholy wail floated in from across the river. Jeff saw the hair rise on Ring's back. The big dog growled deep in his tawny throat, then whined and looked inquiringly at Jeff. But Jeff just reached down and patted him, then turned back toward the house. There wasn't time for a hunt now.

Next morning at sunup he was back on the military road, headed for Fort Leavenworth. As he passed John Chadwick's place, he saw gray smoke curling from the chimney.

Old Man Chadwick and one of his boys were yoking the oxen to the tar-hubbed wagon. Probably getting ready to go to the trading post, Jeff thought. He stopped a minute to tell them how John was getting along.

John's mother was anxious for news and gave Jeff a big drink of cold clabber milk. But the rest of the family seemed to regard him coldly, as though he had persuaded John to join up. He was glad to be back on the road again.

Then the road became rockier, and the soil lighter and thinner. He was approaching the Gardner place. The brown corn had made a fair stand and was nodding in the warm wind. But the rows were so crooked you could tell that a woman had done the planting. Jeff glanced at the mean one-room log house and thought he heard voices. Then he stopped in surprise.

David and his mother were standing in the yard. Mrs. Gardner looked tired. Apparently her faded blue sunbonnet failed to protect her plain, florid face from the sun. Like David and all the rest of her homely brood, she was red-haired, with splashes of orange freckles running over her face, neck, and arms.

Glad that David was home safely, Jeff ran beneath the trees toward the house. As he came closer, he saw that David's face was dirty and tear-begrimed, and his clothing torn, as though he had been living in the brush. Apparently he had just arrived.

Mrs. Gardner was looking fiercely determined. Her red face was flushed, her mouth a tight line. Two of her children stood behind her, listening with curious concentration. Bobby was playing in the mud by the horse trough. Nobody paid any attention to Jeff.

Mrs. Gardner said to David, "You walked sixty miles away from me to enlist and now you come crawlin' back to tell me thet you're tired of it and thet you wanta come back home. Well, it's too late now to come back home. You're in the army. That's what you always wanted, so go on back to the army."

David's blond brows wrinkled with anger.

"I won't go back," he almost screamed. "I'll go up into the hills an' live before I'll go back to the fort agin."

His mother put her hands on her hips and stared at him with disgust. "You'll go up into the hills!" she mimicked him scornfully. "You couldn't live a week by yoreself up there. You'd starve or you'd get homesick. Or somebody'd turn you in as a deserter jest to make the thirty dollars the government would pay to anybody turning you in. Or the bushwhackers'd find you an' kill you like a dog."

David sniffed and wiped his red eyes with the knuckles of both his dirty hands. His manner changed from defiance to pleading.

"Please let me stay here, Ma," he begged. "I don' wanta go to war. I git too homesick."

She shook her head and pointed to the road. "If yore brave enough to leave us and run off an' join the army, then yore brave enough to go on back to the army. There's the road. Take it."

The wretched boy looked at her incredulously, then broke into a fresh torrent of tears.

"You're agin me, Ma," he bawled bitterly. "I never thought my own ma'd go agin me like that."

Jeff felt sorry for David, felt sorry for them all. But he was glad to see that David had somehow reached home safely. He walked slowly up to them, feeling embarrassed to interrupt.

"Howdy, Dave," he said. "Howdy, Miz Gardner."

Both of them looked at him, but neither spoke. Jeff walked a step closer.

"You can go back with me, David," he offered. "I'm on my way to Leavenworth now. If you came back with me, they might let you off light. I'll sure talk to them about it. Pretty soon the lonesomeness will all wear off, and then you'll like it in the army, David. I know."

David looked once at Jeff, then at his mother.

"I guess I'll have to go with you, Jeff," he said brokenly, his voice still rough with anger. "Nothin' else I can do."

Again he looked accusingly at his mother. Calmly but firmly she met his look and conquered it.

"Better go down to the crick, Davey, and wash yoreself," she said, her voice softer but still stern. "Then you can come to th' house, ef you want. It's a long walk to the fort. You'll need a fresh change of clothes. I'll cook you some breakfast an' pack you a lunch fer the trip."

Obediently David turned and trudged off dejectedly toward the creek.

For a moment a look of tender compassion crossed her face. He was her own flesh and blood, the only man she had left in the world. Jeff swallowed as he watched her. He knew

how hard it must be for her to send David back to the war. But
Kate Gardner never hesitated. Chin up, she walked with a firm
stride back into the house and began rattling the pots and
pans.

While David washed and ate in silence, Jeff dropped his
bundle and pitched into the Gardner chores. He finished
milking the cow and toted the filled pails to the springhouse.
He turned the cow out and cleaned her stall with a pitchfork,
scattering fresh straw on the hard, dirt floor.

Half an hour later he and David were again on the road.
This time there was little talk between them.

☆ 6

March

A week later they broke camp and began the long battle
march from Fort Leavenworth to Springfield, Missouri.

The bugles blew at three o'clock in the morning. Jeff didn't
hear them but when the orderly sergeant shook him, he got
right up, washed his eyes in cold water, and began to pack.

Tents were pulled down and rolled up and, with mess boxes
and camp kettles, packed into the baggage wagons. Mules
were fed and harnessed, horses saddled, cannon and ammunition trucks backed into line. Soldiers hurried to the creek,
filling their canteens with fresh water.

"Fall in!" barked Millholland, the sergeant, pointing with his arm to indicate the right of the line. Shortest man in his squad, Jeff went automatically to the left end of the line. He had learned long ago that the tall men always took their places on the right and the short ones on the left, so it was easier for each to find his place.

"Count off! Remember your numbers! Don't swap places!"

The night was black and still. A cloud bank was rising in the west and when fiery threads of lightning veined suddenly across it, Jeff saw them reflect dimly off the cannon, some of the guns showing black, others brassy bright. Behind him, the artillery gun drivers had their teams hitched and were standing patiently at attention, ready to mount at the word. Jeff felt a flush of excitement. Unlike the bivouac in the Missouri river bottoms, this was the real thing.

At Grand River the Kansas Volunteers were to join General Nathaniel Lyon. Their combined force of a little more than five thousand men was the only Federal command between Rolla and the new state of Kansas, representing the forlorn hopes of all the Union people in that vast area.

Jeff knew very well what was at stake. Lyon was hurrying to Springfield to meet the rebel armies of Price and McCulloch. If the Southern force of ten thousand men won a decisive victory, Missouri would fall to them, with its rich middle portion from which valuable supplies could be had and thousands of men recruited for the rebel cause.

Jeff felt a grim satisfaction. It seemed good to be moving aggressively into Missouri for a change, instead of always waiting for the bushwhackers to come across the border and hit them first. But for half an hour the infantry stood in line, waiting.

Impatient, Jeff twisted and squirmed in his tracks. Corn! What were they waiting for? He would explode if there was further delay.

Daylight came finally, and the eastern sky was laced with

pearl and orange. The cloud bank in the west was receding. The wind blew up softly from the south, carrying upon it the musty odors of the creek bottoms; Jeff could feel its cool flush on his face and see it gently bend the buck brush and the prairie grass close by. But still the column didn't move.

Suddenly he heard a cavalry bugle blowing *Prepare to Mount*. It wouldn't be long now. He saw each trooper grasp his reins in his left hand and put one boot in the stirrup. At the bugle's single toot ordering *Mount!* they all swung into the saddle as one, their rumps slapping the leather seats almost in unison. A dapper little lieutenant up front dropped his arm violently downward, and the cavalry moved out in single file.

Quickly the infantry received its marching summons too, and amid the muffled tread of thousands of feet, they were off at last. Jeff heard the creak of harness, the jingle of chains, the chucking of cannon wheels and the pounding of hundreds of hoofs as the horses and mules plunged obediently to obey the shouting, cursing teamsters and the cruel popping of their long black bull whips.

It was fine to be marching in the cool of the morning. As Jeff marched he squinted suspiciously out of the corner of his eye at Pete Millholland, the big lout of a sergeant who plodded along out of step beside the squad. Millholland was bowlegged and walked with an awkward roll, as if he were following a plow on his dirt farm back in Douglas County. Nothing he wore seemed to fit him. His shirt sleeves were too short. His wafer of a cap perched on the side of his blond head, and its bill fell almost over one ear. He seldom spoke, preferring to enforce discipline with a stern half-scowl. Despite his inaptitude for military life, the new sergeant was trying to better himself. Each night Jeff saw him laboriously studying a well-thumbed army manual by the light of a campfire. At times he seemed like a fairly decent fellow. But he was an officer, and Jeff didn't like officers.

Jeff thought it was a great sight to see the army, like a

gigantic bull-snake, serpentining through the countryside in a long, loosely jointed column a mile in length, the cavalry leading, the infantry in the middle, and the artillery riding behind. His heart beat high. They were leaving the last jumping-off place, going farther and farther away from the security of the fort. Every mile they traveled took them nearer to battle.

The sun rose higher and higher in their faces, and the morning grew hotter. Now the exhilaration was gone, and the marching became hard work. Sweat began to drop off the tip of his nose, and he was conscious of black gnats crawling into the hairs on his arms.

He plodded steadily forward, his footsteps blending with thousands of others ringing off the hard pike. Grasshoppers snapped noisily in zigzag flight, bounced on the hot ground, and were upended in the dust. Cicadas sang from the roadside elms. The heat was so great the trees were losing their leaves; it reminded Jeff of his mother's hens dropping their feathers as they molted.

The men began to murmur. One complained he couldn't go a step farther. Millholland wiped the sweat off his nose with his sleeve and gave him a dirty look.

"Sure you can," he growled. "You can always go farther than you think you can. This is pretty hard, but we can stand it."

The sergeant was right. Jeff had learned in his training marches across the Missouri that fatigue is mostly mental. Browned by the Kansas sunshine, his body was wiry and tough. He felt as if he could keep going all day.

Every time the column stopped to rest, Millholland reached over and, with a powerful tug of his right hand, helped ease the heavy pack off Jeff's small back. Each soldier was carrying about forty pounds—his musket, canteen of water, haversack of rations, a twenty-pound knapsack and forty rounds of ammunition, besides the heavy shoes on his feet and the clothes on his back. Jeff should have been grateful for the assistance. Instead, he felt embarrassed.

"Thank you, sir," he told the sergeant. "I can heft it." Millholland gave him such a dark, glowering look that from then on he accepted the sergeant's aid in resentful silence.

"Wisht I had me a cavalry hoss," John Chadwick said enviously. "Them fly-slicers shore got it easy."

"Not as easy as the batterymen," said Ford Ivey, switching his rifle from his right hand to his left. "Them wagon sojers always gits to ride." The back of Ford's blue cotton shirt was stained dark with perspiration. Ivey upped his canteen and took a long pull of the water. His Adam's apple oscillated as he drank.

Tramp, tramp, tramp, tramp. Soon the sun was almost directly overhead. The heat was searing. Jeff felt every tissue in his body was being wrung dry. He knew the horses must need water, too, but they hadn't passed a pond or stream for miles. Tramp, tramp, tramp. Now their marching footsteps were slower. The sun began to slant westerly, behind them and over their right shoulders. They passed a meadowlark sitting on a rail fence, gasping with its bill open. The heat came up through the soles of Jeff's brogans, burning his feet. In the hot south wind the roadside grass rippled in long waves. Wheels rolled, wagons creaked. Canteens flashed in the burning sunshine as the men drank heavily during the rest stops.

They seemed to suffer more from drinking too much water than from lack of it.

"Jest take a sip," advised Millholland. "Don't drink too much. It'll make you sick."

But not all the thirsty Kansans accepted his counsel. Three boys in Jeff's company guzzled too deeply and had to drop out and be picked up by the ambulances. It was on the third day of the march that Jeff discovered with surprise how much water a single company could drink.

"Here's water," somebody had called, and without waiting for the officers to give the command, the soldiers broke ranks, hurrying through the dusty woods. Carrying little ropes and buckets, they crowded around a farmer's stone well near the road.

Jeff got one good drink and filled his canteen, then watched incredulously as his company scooped water so busily that soon all splashing ceased, and all he could hear was their empty buckets scraping the well's rock bottom. It was the first time he had ever seen a well drained in fifteen minutes.

Refreshed, the crawling column again was put in motion. Jeff noticed that Noah Babbitt, the tramp printer walking next to him, swung along easily and effortlessly and seemed to be standing the heat quite well.

"How come you like to walk so well, Noah? Don't you ever get a hankering to straddle a horse?" he asked.

Babbitt shook his shaggy head. "Ridin' makes my head dizzy and my feet sore. I'd rather walk. I like to touch the earth, eat haws, smell the wheat, an' mingle with the quails, bluejays, and woodpeckers in God's great outdoors."

Jeff blinked with surprise. Noah was certainly an odd one. Always pausing to finger and study the leaves of some tree he did not know, or stooping to inspect some wild flower, or glancing keenly into the bushes at a strange bird. But Jeff liked him. Noah was easy to get along with. And he knew more geography and natural history than all the rest of the company put together.

"What's the fartherest you ever walked on one trip?" Jeff asked.

Noah gazed abstractedly at the parched ground passing beneath their feet. Then his white teeth flashed briefly in his tanned, leathery face.

"I guess it was two years ago when I hiked from Topeka, Kansas, to Galveston, Texas. Why?"

Jeff shrugged. "Oh, no particular reason. I just wondered."

They tramped fifty yards more in the broiling sunshine.

"How come you walked clear from Kansas to Galveston?"

Noah turned his somber face seriously toward Jeff. "You probobly won't believe me, youngster, but I wanted to see the magnolias in bloom."

Jeff caught his breath in surprise. Estimating fast, he reckoned it was roughly about nine hundred miles from Topeka to Galveston. If a fellow could stand all that walking, it would take about a month and a half to hoof it down there and another month and a half to hoof it back. Eighteen hundred miles just to see some flowers. Jeff stole another look at Noah. If anybody would do it, Noah Babbitt would be the man.

Jeff said simply, "I believe you. Did you get to see them?"

Noah nodded solemnly. "Shore did. An' they was worth every foot of the trip."

At Grand River, Lyon and his three thousand Missourians and Iowans were waiting for them. Quickly two columns were formed side by side and the march resumed. Jeff gazed with interest at his new comrades. The only Missourians he had ever seen were the bushwhackers. He had supposed that everybody in Missouri was for the rebels. But these men were unmistakably Union. They were outfitted much more completely than the Kansas Volunteers.

Their blue uniforms were newer, and they carried rubber blankets, bayonet scabbards and Springfield muskets. Their officers were equipped with Colt six-shooting revolvers. The Iowans sang while they marched and wanted to go swimming in every creek they crossed.

As they marched along together, one of the Missourians, weighed down by his pack, staggered a little in the torrid heat and nearly dropped his gun. Looking closer, Jeff saw a boy even smaller than himself. He had big blue eyes and a mop of curly black hair.

"Here, I'll help you," Jeff offered, reaching for the gun.

But the lad refused the assistance, clinging tightly to the weapon.

"Thankee," he mumbled, doggedly. "I can make it."

Jeff handed his own gun to Ford Ivey. Stooping, he picked up a handful of dead grass and turned to the boy.

"Give me your cap a minute. I'll show you a way to turn the heat."

Obediently the lad handed it over. Jeff put the dried grass in the crown, poured water from his canteen over it, and handed it back to its owner. It was a trick he had learned with his own straw hat while plowing. The boy clapped the cap gratefully onto his black curls.

"Thankee," he said, shyly. "That's real cool."

Trudging along, Jeff asked the Missouri boy, "What's your name?"

"Jimmy Lear. What's yours?"

Jeff told him, and they fell to talking. Jimmy was from St. Louis and belonged to Lyon's army. He had walked all the way except for a short boat ride near Boonville. He told Jeff he had belonged to a military club in St. Louis, organized by Frank P. Blair, a leader there of the unconditional Union men. They had drilled for weeks without guns. When war was declared, they had promptly joined the Union army. Riding in steamboats, they had already been in a couple of skirmishes at Jefferson City and Boonville, breaking up small concentrations of state troops that were being pointed for service with the rebels. Jeff listened enviously. Nothing so exciting had yet happened to him.

They were deep in Missouri now, and Jeff stared with curiosity at everything he saw. Everything here seemed so different from Kansas. The houses were much older, and the country more heavily populated.

All afternoon long, Jeff had felt something itching under his arms and in the edge of his hair. He thought it was gnats or heat rash until after supper, when he walked to the persimmon grove where the Missouri troops were camped and hunted up Jimmy Lear.

Instantly Jimmy clapped his eyes on Jeff's arm. Reaching over, he began to pick several small gray-looking objects off Jeff's skin.

"Look!" Jimmy blurted. "You got graybacks."

Jeff's forehead wrinkled in puzzlement.

With a quick motion of his right hand, Jimmy captured another of the tiny insects. "Boy, you got 'em, all right!"

"So have you," said Jeff. With thumb and forefinger, he trapped one on Jimmy's forehead. For a moment the two boys stood toe to toe, pulling the insects from each other's skin. Finally Jeff asked, "What are graybacks?"

"Lice," said Jimmy. "Only we calls 'em Arkansas lizards. Lookie here. I'll show you how to make 'em kill each other." He put two of the small insects together on a piece of white cartridge paper, and they began fighting fiercely.

"Corn!" marveled Jeff. "Watch 'em go after each other. Just like hogs fighting."

Later that evening both boys stripped and Jimmy showed Jeff how to shake his clothing over the campfire. When the lice dropped into the flames, they popped like salt. But the soldiers never seemed to be entirely rid of them.

Day after day they marched, usually covering twenty to twenty-five miles from morning to dusk. The more they marched, the more they got used to it. Now the heat didn't bother them so much. The flat land began to give way to hillier country, and they encountered more streams and saw more trees, mostly hickory and oak and persimmon. Each night they tried to camp beside a small river, and when everybody but the mess cooks stripped off and went swimming, the stream would be so full of naked men that Jeff couldn't see the water. As they dressed he could smell the smoke from the campfires and hear the hiss of the bacon frying.

One night Jeff wrote to his parents, "We eat breakfast early and supper late to lose the flies. But at noon the flies get as much of it as we do." He hoped to mail the letter when they reached Springfield. The government stage would take it back to Fort Leavenworth and it would go south from there by mule train to Sugar Mound, near Jeff's home, where his folks would get it when they came to buy supplies.

After the meal the men usually sat around smoking and resting. Some washed their socks, shirts, and drawers in the river. Others submitted to the shears and razors of the several regimental barbers who traveled with Lyon's army from St. Louis. General Lyon had even brought along a twenty-piece regimental band that played each night. Ever since the Missourians had joined them at Grand River, Jeff had watched the perspiring German musicians striding along stoically in the heat, carrying their brass horns on their thick red necks or under their fat muscular arms.

One night after supper, Jeff walked over to the Missouri troops' camp to visit Jimmy. He found him shaving under a small persimmon tree. Jimmy had placed a small broken piece of mirror in the crotch of the tree and, straight-edge in hand, was peering into it. He had lathered one side of his face and was scraping it with the razor when a husky sergeant, hairy and pug-nosed, walked up. Standing behind Jimmy, he watched him suspiciously.

Jimmy must have seen the sergeant in his mirror because his hand was trembling.

"How old are ye?" the sergeant asked, stepping around in front of Jimmy and looking at him accusingly.

Jimmy's face blanched. He looked sheepish. "Sixteen, sir."

"That's a lie," the sergeant snorted. "Likely you're nearer thirteen." He looked shrewdly at Jimmy. "Why are you shavin' atall? They ain't no whiskers on either side of yer face. They ain't even any goose down." With a dirty forefinger he reached up suddenly and wiped the soap off one side of the boy's face, exposing a cheek as smooth as a girl's.

Jimmy stood silent, still holding the open razor.

The sergeant growled, "Come with me. I wish I knew what recruitin' officer signed ye. He'd get a court-martial and a dismissal, forfeitin' all pay and allowances."

Jimmy's face was tragic. Jeff saw him swallow helplessly and wished there was something he could do.

Jimmy found his voice. "Sir, they won't kick me out of the army for this, will they? I'm fourteen but I'm big for my age." His big blue eyes stared beseechingly at the sergeant.

The sergeant said, "They otta make ye walk clear back to wherever ye came from." Still scowling, he marched Jimmy off to see the captain. Jeff was flabbergasted. No wonder Jimmy had trouble standing the long, hard march.

Next evening they camped twenty-five miles north of Springfield and Lyon ordered vedettes and guards posted and sent out scouts.

"We're gettin' close," Millholland told them. "Captain says the rebels are comin' up fast from the South. Looks like we're gonna have a battle, all right."

Elated, Jeff got up and took his rifle into the woods to clean it and replace the old load with a new one. If there was going to be a fight, he aimed to be ready. Pointing his gun at the sky, he fired it off so he could clean the breech.

A sentry came running up, frowning with excitement. "Did you fire that gun?"

Jeff nodded.

"Did your captain give you permission?"

Jeff stared at him innocently. "No, sir. I didn't know I needed permission. I just shot it off so I could clean it. When I go hunting in the woods at home and want to clean my gun, I always shoot it off like that. Why? Is it against the rules?"

The sentry raised his own rifle across his chest. "You're under arrest," he said sternly. "Come with me."

Jeff was taken before Captain Clardy. Clardy stared coldly

at him. When he recognized Jeff, the long scar on his left cheek turned livid. For a full moment his wild green eyes darted over Jeff. His look was like a whip. Feeling it, Jeff writhed uncomfortably.

"Put him on all-night sentry duty," Clardy snarled and turned his back on them.

Although he had marched all day in the torrid heat, Jeff walked sentry all night. At nine o'clock his eyes began to feel heavy, at eleven he was nodding, at midnight he was dozing on his feet and went to the cook's mess to get a cup of hot coffee so he could stay awake, helping himself to the pot on the fire. As he stood drinking, he heard the cooks snoring loudly as they slept on quilts under the stars. Then he heard a voice, calling his name.

Jeff went closer and saw Sparrow, the cook, sitting up in his bunk. He reeked of alcohol.

"Bussey . . . you're a fool," Sparrow mumbled thickly. "Nex' time he gits rough with you . . . ask him how the widow Spaulding died . . . back at Os'watomie . . . an' where her eight hundert dollars went."

Jeff's jaw dropped. "Who you talking about?"

Sparrow winked at him owlishly. "Ask him . . . who bashed her skull in th' night o' th' storm . . . I saw him slip up to her house . . . I wash fishin' fer flatheads an' went inter her barn to get outa th' rain . . . He better not . . . git rough . . . with me." Falling back on his bunk, Sparrow began to snore.

There was something familiar about the cook's mumbled threat. Jeff remembered his words in the army kitchen back at Leavenworth: "Clardy knows he wouldn't dare talk like that to me. I could tell you something about Asa Clardy that he wouldn't want you ner nobody else to know."

Thunderstruck, Jeff walked back to his post. Was Sparrow talking about Clardy? Had there been a murder or was the cook babbling from a drunken dream?

Just thinking about it the rest of the night helped keep him awake. Relieved at four o'clock in the morning, he slept in his uniform a couple of hours before the army started marching again. Noah awakened him ten minutes before they lined up. Jeff was tired and logy. He just had time to wash his eyes in cold water and swallow some cold bacon and fried potatoes Noah had saved for him when he heard the cavalry bugles.

That night they camped four miles north of Springfield. Jeff heard the staccato beat of a drum, coming from the Missourians' mess. Suddenly he saw Jimmy, surrounded by German bandsmen.

One was teaching him to beat the various calls. A parade drum hung from a strap around his shoulders. A pair of polished drumsticks was in his hands. When he saw Jeff, he beamed with pleasure.

"General Lyon says I won't have to go home," Jimmy said joyfully. "I'm going to be a drummer. They're gonna let me hone the surgical instruments, draw maps, and carry water to the barbers. When I reach sixteen I get to go back into the army."

The next morning they marched into the edge of Springfield. Laborers in Union blouses were digging earthworks around the town. As one of the workers raised his pick, he looked familiar. With a glad shout Jeff ran to his side.

"David!"

David Gardner stared up wearily, despair written all over his freckled boyish face. His clothing was sweaty and dirt-begrimed, his hands dirty, calloused, and raw with blisters.

A rough-looking guard with a sandy hawk-wing mustache stepped threateningly in front of Jeff.

"Move on," he commanded. "These is deserters. Cap'n says nobody's to talk to 'em."

Jeff said, "He's from my home county over in Kansas. If I could just speak a word to him . . ."

The guard looked ugly and showed his teeth. "I don' care if he's yore long-lost brother! Move on or I'll run you in."

Reluctantly Jeff moved on. As he walked he sighed with relief. At least David hadn't been shot. When they had got back to Leavenworth from Linn County, Jeff had gone with David to Millholland, explaining that David was returning voluntarily to his outfit. Millholland had promised to pass on that information to the regimental court-martial handling David's case. Apparently the sergeant had done as he promised.

When the army marched into the streets of Springfield just before noon, the town was in a near panic. It was August 9, 1861. Everybody knew a battle would soon be fought. The whole town seemed frightened. All afternoon Jeff watched the excitement and the confusion, while the soldiers lay resting on the grass beneath several gigantic oak trees in the shady town square. Merchandise and household goods were being loaded into wagons, ready for flight. People were cooping their chickens, harnessing their teams, calling to their children. Storekeepers and citizens presented food and tobacco lavishly to the soldiers. Everybody was afraid that if the rebels won, they would ravish the town.

A merchant's wife gave Jeff two pairs of socks and a small sack of apples. Surprised, Jeff stammered his thanks.

"Good luck," the woman said. Then she added, "My, but yore awfully leetle and younglike to be fighting in a war. You ought to be home with your mammy."

After giving Jeff a long soulful look, she began sniffing and dabbing at her eyes with the bottom of her blue calico apron.

Jeff didn't like her pessimism. "Corn," he told himself disgustedly. "She acts like we're all going to be killed by the rebels. We can take care of ourselves."

General Lyon rode up on a big gray horse and, without

dismounting, began to talk to the Kansas Volunteers. He was a short, slender, bony man of about forty-five, with a rough, homely face. A coarse reddish-brown beard ran up past his ears into his thick sandy hair. He wore a blue uniform with heavy yellow epaulets concealing his frail shoulders. Jeff knew that he had fought with honor in the Mexican War and against the Indians.

The general said, "Men, we're going to have a battle. We're going to march out and try to hit 'em before they know we're comin'. Don't shoot until you are given orders. Wait until they get close. Fire low—don't aim higher than their knees. And don't get scared. It's no part of a soldier's duty to get scared."

Scared? Who was scared? Jeff felt a gay excitement. His chance to strike a blow for his new state had come at last. He reached toward the left side of his belt, feeling for his bayonet. It was there. His pack was on his back, and his musket was in his hand. He was impatient to get started.

The thin, sweet trill of a bugle pealed in the early twilight. A dozen drums began to beat. An officer shouted, "Fo'wud mawtch!"

Thousands of feet began to stamp the hard, dusty ground in unison. The soldiers' heads rose and fell as one as they marched four abreast at quick step. The long blue column moved southward.

☆ 7

Battle of Wilson's Creek

General Lyon had decided upon a bold plan of battle. His smaller Union army had no reinforcements. Their provisions were running low. A superior force was in front of them and General William J. Hardee with nine thousand more rebels was reported marching to cut off their communications. Retreat seemed wise. But Lyon didn't propose to retreat and be closely pursued all the way back to St. Louis. Boldly he decided to attack and hurt the enemy so he could not follow them.

His plan was to march secretly at night the twelve miles to where Price's and McCulloch's rebel army was encamped, and strike at daybreak in a surprise onslaught. Lyon with thirty-eight hundred men and two batteries would hit the rebels from the north. Colonel Franz Sigel with twelve hundred men and one battery was to fall upon the Confederates from the south.

As the infantry swung along briskly, clouds covered the western sky, and Jeff thought he could smell rain in the air. Millholland raised his bearded chin, eyeing the heavens hopefully.

"A rain ud be jist right for us," he said. "Might cause 'em to draw in their pickets. If they do, we'll give 'em a real surprise."

"Wonder what them rebels looks like?" quavered a frightened boy in the ranks.

Jake Lonegan, the grizzled sergeant from Junction City,

snorted. "They wear horns," he croaked. "A common article o' diet among 'em is young an' tender babies."

As they moved nearer the enemy, there was silence in the ranks. The road grew rockier. Fearing that the enemy could hear them approaching, they stopped to bind the cannon's wheels in blankets and the horses' hoofs in sacks, then resumed the march. Jeff's company, commanded by Clardy, was stationed near the rear. Behind them were the horse-drawn ambulances, their shelves filled with bottles and drugs, and the doctors and medical orderlies with their cases of sharp surgical instruments.

The men were solemn, now that the hour of battle approached. Jeff could sense it in their white, wistful faces and hear it in their hushed whispering. They exchanged messages to be delivered to relatives and sweethearts back in Kansas in the event they were killed.

Jim Veatch, a Westport boy who liked to play cards, tossed his deck into the sumac bushes at the side of the road and grimly resumed his marching. In the dim light, the white faces of the cards settled slowly over one bush, decorating it gaily.

Puzzled, Jeff nudged Noah Babbitt, marching next to him. "Noah, why did he do that?"

"He probably doesn't want to be killed in battle with playing cards on him," Noah said, gravely. "It's a superstition lots of soldiers have. They've been told in church that it's wrong to play cards. They're afraid if they get killed with playing cards on them, they won't go to heaven."

Then Jeff saw Neeley North, a breezy recruit from Shawnee Mission, stoop and carefully pick up the cards Veatch had thrown away, pocketing them.

"Neeley's not so superstitious," Noah explained. "He'll probably sell Veatch's cards back to him if they both live through the battle."

If they both lived through the battle! Jeff stepped around a limestone outcropping in the dusty road, scoffing inwardly.

They had been told back at the fort that very few soldiers were killed in proportion to those who fought. What made everybody so gloomy? War was a lark, an adventure made for men.

Swinging blithely along, he felt Noah's steady gray eyes on him.

"How do you feel, youngster?" Noah asked. "Haven't you got scared yet?"

Jeff shook his head. "I've been waiting a long time for this night."

The Kansas Volunteers were the worst-dressed troops Jeff had ever seen. The war had just begun, and much of the new equipment hadn't yet arrived from the Northern factories. Jeff was wearing the civilian pants and shoes that had been furnished him at the fort, and army drawers, blouse, and socks. On his head was the same hat his mother had plaited from Linn County wheat straw.

With a clatter of hoofs, the Sixth Kansas Cavalry galloped past on its way to the head of the column. A big, swarthy cavalryman clad in a black suit rode with them. He was bareheaded and his curly chestnut hair was fluttering in the breeze.

"That's Rufe Forney of Atchison," Jeff overheard somebody say in the next squad. "He's a corporal in the cavalry. He jest got spliced at Leavenworth before we left. Got himself a purty gal, too—the blacksmith's daughter. He's still wearin' his wedding suit."

Suddenly a muffled gunshot, followed by a scream of agony, rang out ahead. The column was thrown temporarily into confusion and slowed to a halt. Captain Clardy came running past from the rear, his sword swinging and bouncing noisily at his side, his stern face dark with displeasure. A medical orderly sprinted close behind him.

"Keep marching, you fools! Nobody ordered you to stop," Clardy roared. Then he disappeared up ahead, plunging through the brush as he skirted the column.

"Route step! Keep marchin'!" Millholland barked. "Hup! Hup! Hup!"

Swallowing hard, Jeff tried to march on tiptoe so he could see better. For the first time he felt a slight panic. He looked at Noah, then at Millholland, but they were staring stonily ahead as they marched. Soon he heard voices and somebody weeping loudly with pain.

Captain Clardy and the medical orderly appeared. Between them limped Walter Van Orstrand, a Douglas County boy from their own company. His weak face twisted with suffering, he was blubbering and sniffing. His left hand was wrapped in a bloody white bandage which he held tightly clutched in his right hand.

"Captain, I tell you it was an accident," the boy kept pleading and sobbing.

"You're a liar," Clardy stormed, his face black with rage. "You deliberately shot it off so you'd get a discharge. Well, it won't work. I'll have you court-martialed for cowardice. You're yellow as a dandelion." His rough voice rang with scorn.

"No, Captain, no," the boy whimpered piteously. "Honest I'm not. My gun jest went off while I was marching." He gave another howl of pain. "Oh, it hurts, awful!"

"Shut up your sniveling!" roared Clardy. "You were carrying the gun over your shoulder. It's a long gun. You couldn't have shot off your finger unless you stuck it over the muzzle. You're jest a yellow-bellied coward, that's all!" Their arguing became fainter and fainter as they passed toward the ambulances in the rear.

The men began to mutter to one another in low voices as they marched.

"What happened? What happened?" everybody asked, although everybody had a pretty good idea now.

Jake Lonegan grunted, shifting the pack on his back with a single swagger of his powerful shoulders. "Cappen's prob'bly

right. The man prob'bly got so scared that he shot off his own
finger jest to git a discharge. They do it in every war."

Leave the army, when they were just heading into their
first battle? Jeff could hardly believe his ears.

Jeff looked at Lonegan and sighed. He envied the brawny
sergeant who had bulging muscles and weighed two hundred
thirty pounds. In their training bivouac, Lonegan had shown
a perfect mastery of the manual of arms and could throw
down any man in the company. In the election of officers he
had been the almost unanimous choice of his squad.

The night deepened. The pace slowed. The road wound up
and down several small, rocky hills covered with timber. Once
Jeff saw the dark outline of a log house, although all the
windows were dark and no dog barked. He felt thirsty and,
without slackening his marching pace, took a drink out of his
canteen. The water tasted cool and sweet. It was surprising
how well you could see after you got used to the darkness.

At one o'clock in the morning by Millholland's big silver
watch, they stopped in the roadside grass and rested a couple
of hours. Jeff checked the priming and the hammer on his
musket, then lay down on the rough ground and slept. At three
o'clock he felt a hand shaking his shoulder and heard the
sergeant's voice whispering in his ear.

"Fall in and keep silent. We're mighty close to the enemy."

It was cool on the ground. As Jeff got quickly to his feet, he
could hear the June bugs droning sleepily from the grass roots.
Their song sounded plaintive, almost hushed. Reaching into
his pocket, he drew out a small package containing the last of
his rations, a strip of cold bacon, some stale corn pone, and
two apples from the sack the lady storekeeper had given him at
Springfield. He had given all the other apples away. He was
too excited to eat much.

A flash of lightning illuminated the scene, and Jeff saw
that Zed Tinney, a quiet, religious boy who lived near Wa-

baunsee, was clutching in one hand a small Bible bound in black leather. Fear and despair ruled his face. Resigned to being killed in battle, he was praying quietly to himself. Lonegan saw him and stepped across the intervening space.

"Hello, Parson," he taunted. "What time does the revival start?"

Millholland walked up to Lonegan, scowling fiercely. In a low voice he said, "You shut up an' git back over thar with your own outfit. Iffen anybody in my squad wants to pray, he shore can, an' nobody's gonna laugh at him, neither. You hear me?"

For a moment the two big sergeants glared at each other. Then, to Jeff's surprise, Lonegan walked obediently back to his own squad. And Millholland went up several notches in Jeff's estimation.

Tinney paid no attention to the incident. His mind seemed far away. "I'm glad I've always lived a good life," Jeff heard him whisper. "I'm glad that I've never knowingly harmed a soul."

Again the army was put in motion. It now marched southeast in column by companies, the batteries by section, and a line of skirmishers in front. Disappointed because his company wasn't selected for duty with the skirmishers, Jeff felt a cool moisture on his face and looked up.

A fine drizzle of rain that was little more than mist had started. Word came back from the skirmishers that apparently no rebel pickets were out.

Jeff was elated. He wanted to get on with the fighting. If they could win this battle, the war might be over in Missouri, and they could go somewhere else and fight. He was in the second line of advance. He knew that the advance line, which had drawn the honor of hitting the Southerners first, was somewhere ahead. He wished fervently that he was with it.

They left the road and climbed silently up a rocky slope.

He could feel the wet brush pulling at his trouser legs and thighs. When they finally crested the ridge, they halted, panting silently. Despite the inky darkness, Jeff knew through some sixth sense that they were on an elevation.

Breathlessly he squinted over John Chadwick's thick shoulder and felt a cold chill run along his spine. In the valley below lay the sleeping rebel camp. He could see the sheen of their dying campfires and hear their mules braying faintly in choruses.

A half hour passed. The night wore on toward a gray dawn. Jeff was on the north hill with Lyon. Sigel was on the south hill. Between the two hills flowed the spring-fed waters of Wilson's Creek. The Confederates were camped along both its brushy banks. The slow rain stopped, and the stars began to shine brightly between broken patches of clouds.

"Fix bayonets," came a whispered command. As Jeff groped at his belt, he heard faint clicks all around him and knew that the Kansas Volunteers were clamping the long steel knives onto the tips of their musket barrels.

It was almost daybreak. The country was open, and here and there Jeff could begin to see dark objects. Excited, he felt no fatigue whatever from the twelve-mile march, although he knew he should have been dog-tired. He looked around at his comrades.

"I don't mind going," somebody whispered. "The thing I dread most is parting with Mother."

Jeff frowned impatiently in the dark. Why be so gloomy?

"The hardest thing for me to part with will be my g-g-g-graybacks," Bill Earle whispered, trying to take away some of the sting of death.

The stars paled. Birds began to twitter. Now Jeff could see the live-oak trees taking shape all around him and smell the cool, musty odors of the woods. His bare hand brushed accidently the leaf of a dwarf oak and came away wet. Everything was dripping.

Suddenly away off to the south they heard a dull, heavy "Pum!" It seemed to come from the direction of Sigel's ridge. Crouching in the sodden brush, Jeff glanced at Millholland, who was down on his knees next to him, peering intently through the leaves of a buckeye bush.

"What was that, Sergeant?"

Calmly Millholland checked the cartridge box fastened to his belt and listened.

"Cannon," he whispered hoarsely. "Probably Sigel."

The Kansas Volunteers caught their breath, braced themselves, and looked inquiringly at one another.

The distant booming began to come faster and faster. Soon it was answered by the much louder "Brrom! Brrom!" of an awakening rebel battery from the creek below. Long ropes of orange flame streaked from the dark woods of the rebel-held creek.

"Blam!"

The deafening roar came from a Union battery located two hundred yards behind them. Jeff ducked and heard the grape-shot rushing noisily through the quiet air over his head, as though projected by a giant slingshot. His eardrums throbbed, and the ground beneath his feet trembled.

Now the guns were all speaking boisterously together. "Pum! Brrom! Blam!" Both ridges and the valley between were alive with long, slow lines of fire. The Battle of Wilson's Creek, Missouri, had begun.

A wild burst of cheering rang out one hundred yards below as Lyon's first line of attack hurled itself down the ridge and across a small field filled with wheat shocks and onto the brown- and gray-clad Confederates who were trying frantically to form a battle line in front of their tents.

Just before the two lines met and fused, there came a different sound, a menacing mutter and snarl, like thousands of beans being dropped into hundreds of tin pans. Jeff knew what that was—musket fire. Drawing in his breath, with solemn wonder he watched the Union line strike the Confederate one, bending it backward and driving it in confusion toward the creek.

Feeling a wild thrill at the solid charge of the first Union advance, he yelled joyfully at the top of his lungs. It was time for the second line of advance—his line—to join the battle.

Hoofbeats sounded behind him. A mounted staff officer in full uniform galloped up full tilt, jerking on his reins. As the bay horse slid to a stop, it kicked up a shower of small rocks and gravel. On the shoulders of his blue uniform coat, the officer wore the chevrons of a major. There was an urgent expression on his handsome face.

"Got your line formed, boys?" he called stridently. "Be ready. We'll give you the word in a minute." He kept looking back impatiently over his shoulder. Then his nervous eyes swept up and down the line of men before him and fell on Jeff, the smallest one in the platoon.

"Boy!" he barked, pointing with his gloved hand. "Something has happened to delay the quartermaster. Go to the rear and find him. Tell him to join us on the double. Hurry!"

Jeff recoiled. "Sir," he protested, saluting weakly, "can't you please send somebody else? I want to stay with the boys here."

The major stared harshly at Jeff while he tried to control his plunging horse. Then he saw Jeff's stricken face and his own countenance softened perceptibly.

"Do as I tell you," he ordered firmly. "Another time you shall have your chance to fight in battle. What's your name?"

Jeff swallowed miserably. He was the most disappointed man in Lyon's army.

"Bussey, sir," he replied tonelessly. "Jefferson Davis Bussey."

The officer looked at him sharply, then recovered himself. "Very good, Bussey. Better start at once." Wheeling his horse around, he galloped off along the ridge.

Wild with anger, Jeff stood and watched him ride out of

sight. Recklessly he considered ignoring the command. Then
Millholland stepped quietly to his side.

"You heared him, kid. Like it or not, it's a order. Better git
started."

Jeff looked defiantly at the sergeant. Millholland looked
right back at him.

Throwing one last yearning glance at his comrades, most
of whom looked as if they would enjoy changing places with
him, Jeff stepped back out of line. Still clutching his bayoneted
musket, he trudged to the rear, descending the same slope they
had marched up. Behind him the cannon were booming like
thunderclaps, and he could hear the salvos of musket fire and
the wild, frenzied shouting of the second line of advance, *his*
line, as it charged down the ridge without him.

Hot tears of disappointment stung his eyes. Twice he
walked blindly into trees. Never again, he told himself, would
he obey an order that took him away from his comrades.

"Bussey!"

Jeff stopped abruptly and looked up. Before him in the
growing daylight stood Captain Clardy, saber in hand. He
broke into a volley of abuse.

"Get back into line, you little yellow-bellied cur," he
stormed.

Jeff's patience, already threadbare, snapped. He matched
Clardy, glare for glare.

"I know where the line is," he shouted back. "I don't need
no old grouch like you to help me find it."

Clardy seemed to gasp and explode, all in one motion.
Raising his saber and waving it threateningly, he took a step
toward Jeff. Jeff cocked the hammer on his rifle and coolly
pointed the bayoneted gun at his captain's commissary department.

With his finger on the trigger, Jeff looked Clardy squarely
in the eye.

"What are you doing back here yourself, so far away from

the fighting?" Jeff asked. "At least I've got an excuse. A major just ordered me back to find the quartermaster. I didn't want to come, but he ordered me to."

Hand tightening whitely on his saber, Clardy fixed Jeff with a look of hatred. Now Jeff's own anger was rising and he felt a rash, uncontrollable urge to nettle the bullying officer, shocking him out of his attitude of arrogant authority.

"What's your excuse for being here instead of on the front?" Jeff taunted grimly. "Are you looking for some other widow's eight hundred dollars?"

Clardy's face drained and turned a sickly yellow. Fear leaped into his face, and his right hand shook so badly that he almost dropped his saber. His breath began to come in little wheezing gasps. Jeff saw that he had shaken him clear down to the toes of his immaculately blackened shoes. It *was* Clardy whom Sparrow had been talking about!

Clardy's green eyes swept Jeff with murderous cunning.

"Who told you that?" he snarled.

"A little bird," Jeff twitted him. "A little bird who flew into the widow's barn when the rainstorm struck, and saw a wolf sneaking toward her house."

Clardy's face glittered, suddenly triumphant. His voice went high and shrill, like a woman's. He panted, "Sparrow! You must mean Sparrow. He's the only man in my company from Osawatomie. You've been talking to Sparrow, haven't you?"

"Remember the storm, Captain? How the rain came down blindingly? It blinded everybody, even the Miami County sheriff."

Deliberately Clardy sheathed his saber. Still panting, he was very white now and spoke with terrible earnestness. "Better keep your mouth shut, boy, if you value your life."

Jeff felt the hair prickling on the back of his neck. He knew a deadly threat when he heard one.

Clardy went on, "Never talk to me again as you have today, boy. Never talk to anybody else about me, either. You look like a sensible lad. I've been a little hard on you, I know. But I see no reason why we can't be friends."

Keeping his bayonet in the captain's belly, Jeff shook his head decisively. Clardy couldn't buy him off with a cheap promise of favor in the future.

"Why not?" Clardy asked, a flicker of surprise coming into his face.

Jeff said flatly, "Because I don't want any kind of a deal with you."

The anger came back into Clardy's face, leaving it bloodless again. With a final murderous glare at Jeff, he moved off through the gray light of dawn toward the front.

Jeff was careful not to turn his back on him until he passed from sight in the timber. Laughing grimly to himself, he relaxed a little. Now that he had told Clardy off, he felt a little better.

After wasting half the morning looking for the quartermaster, Jeff finally found him replacing a broken wagon wheel three miles in the rear. Quickly he relayed the major's order to him and rode back with him in one of the wagons, hoping to find his outfit and still participate in the battle. But as they advanced along the road, they began to meet Union soldiers hurrying to the rear.

Many of the men had lost their hats and their guns. Some were hurt and walked with wounds untended and still bleeding. Others wore crude bandages and used their rifles as crutches. All looked sick, defeated, and very tired.

Astonished, Jeff jumped down from the quartermaster's wagon.

"How's the battle going?" he asked anxiously. He didn't understand their haste and he saw no rebel prisoners among them. He put the question to man after man, but they just looked at him with glazed eyes and kept walking.

"They whopped us," one lanky fellow said, finally. "Lyon

got killed an' Sigel got lost. Hundreds of our boys got shot."

Another quavered, "No use fightin' no more. We air done up the spout."

Shocked, Jeff could scarcely believe his ears. "Why, we were winning it when I left," he said with disbelief. "What happened?"

"They was too many of 'em. We drove 'em back at fust, and I thought we had 'em licked. But they kept coming on, regiment after regiment, all on the double quick, until they had as many as three lines agin' us in some places. Mister, you wouldn't have a smoke on you, would you?"

Jeff shook his head dully. It was a calamity. The army—his army—had been licked. He felt like bawling. Sobered by the bad news, he groped on, trying to find comrades from his own squad in each cluster of weary, discouraged men he encountered. Finally he discovered part of his company walking northward, through a potato field.

Dirty and exhausted, they wore a dazed, disenchanted look on their smoke-blackened faces that suggested they had come straight from hell. John Chadwick was the first one Jeff recognized. A bloody bandage was wrapped around his left arm, where a rebel Minie ball had struck him. Pete Millholland had torn off most of his own shirt to dress the wound.

"What happened?" Jeff asked.

John just looked at him bleakly and, without answering, hurried on toward the rear as though to put as much distance as possible between himself and the horror he had seen. Noah followed, carrying John's gun. He had lost his cap. There was dirt on his face and a long, red welt across his neck.

"Zed Tinney got killed," Noah reported briefly. "Shot in the forehead when our line charged. Ford Ivey was probably killed, too. He fell when we were retreating. Several of our boys got hit. We were lucky to be in the second advance line. Our first line lost almost one third killed."

Zed Tinney dead. The news sobered Jeff. Blinking, he

thought of Zed's last words. "I'm glad I've always lived a good life."

Quickly Jeff fell into step beside Noah. He took John Chadwick's gun and carried it himself. He would miss Ford Ivey, too.

Pete Millholland lumbered wearily into view, carrying three muskets under one brawny arm. There was a dark circle around his mouth where the black powder had spilled as he tore open cartridge after cartridge with his teeth. He spat out his tobacco, wiped off his chin with his free hand, then wiped his hand on the leg of his homespun trousers.

"We'da whipped 'em if we'd had more men," the big sergeant growled. "We chewed 'em purty good anyhow, I think. Your friend Jimmy the drummer boy is a cool 'un," he told Jeff. "At the first rebel volley, Jake Lonegan threw down his rifle and run like a rabbit. Jimmy dropped his drum, picked up Jake's musket with the bayonet on it, and charged right on with our boys. I saw him later an' he asked about you."

Ashamed, Jeff felt his ears reddening. His bitterness returned. What must the men think of him! Desolate, he jammed his hat down over his eyes and fell in behind the others.

They hiked all the way back to Springfield. Walking wearily into the town at dusk, they read their defeat in the frightened faces of the people staring at them on the streets. They didn't look much like an army any more and they knew it. Disorganized, they would have been easy prey for a rebel pursuit. But the Southern army, as Millholland had said, and as Lyon had planned, was itself too badly battered to follow up its victory.

Later Jeff found Jimmy gulping cold water from a well behind a tavern. He still had Jake Lonegan's musket with him. Despite his heroism, his boyish face was crestfallen.

"I lost my new drum, Jeffy," he said mournfully. "Jist when I was learnin' to beat it good, too. Now that General Lyon's dead, do you think they'll send me clear back to St.

Louis fer losin' it? It was a fifteen-dollar drum. Made in Boston, Massachusetts."

Jeff dropped his head. His old misery returned. He couldn't speak. Although Jimmy was only fourteen, he had already won the respect of all the men. Jeff envied him profoundly.

It was growing dark. After they had eaten the remainder of the corn pone and the apples Jeff had in his pocket, they went out into the horse lot behind the tavern. Jeff's legs ached. He felt he could sleep for a month. Lying down, they pulled an old tent over them.

Just before they dozed off, Jimmy said fervently, "Jeffy, I hope I never have to hear another gun go off, long as I live."

Jeff tucked a corner of the canvas around his shoulder. What was the matter with Jimmy and all the others? He wished with all his heart that there would be another battle tomorrow. But he knew there wouldn't be. The army was licked.

 ☆ 8

Hard Lessons

At daybreak next morning, Jeff awakened to feel something hard toeing him in the ribs. Rolling over, he saw a rough black shoe covered with gray Missouri mud.

Slowly his eyes traveled upward. Above the shoe and the dirt-begrimed ankle was a blue pants leg; tucked in the waist of the pants was a faded blue blouse. The man wearing the shoe, the pants, and the blouse was holding his musket in both hands. He was obviously a sentry. Jeff recognized Ben Gerdeon, a Franklin boy in his own outfit. Behind him, Jimmy had thrown off the canvas coverlet and was staring sleepily about him.

"We're marchin' in thirty minutes," Ben told Jimmy. "Your mess is t'other side o' the tavern yonder."

Jeff wiped the sleep out of one eye with his ragged sleeve. Bracing himself on one elbow, he sat up. A pale, sickly glow had begun to illuminate the eastern horizon. Against it the sharply angled tavern roof was silhouetted black as ink. He smelled sowbelly frying and felt a fierce hunger. He hadn't had a square meal since he'd been home on furlough. And he probably wouldn't get another one for longer than that. You never did in the army. Jeff yawned and squinted inquiringly at the guard.

"Where we goin', Ben?"

Ben looked down at Jeff pityingly. "You ain't goin' nowheres. Cap'n Clardy has got you down fer duty with the ambulances. You gotta report to the field hospital in twenty minutes. Jeepers, Jeff, the cap'n sure must hate you. What did you ever do to him to rate thet stinkin' duty?"

Jeff blinked uneasily and didn't answer. Clardy hadn't lost any time. He pulled his legs up under him and climbed to his feet. His legs still felt dead. Six hours' sleep wasn't nearly enough after you'd marched twenty-seven miles in a day and a night.

Jimmy, sitting up groggily, his eyes half shut, was trying to pull on his shoes.

"Where's he and you and the army going?" Jeff asked the guard.

Ben shouldered his gun. "To Rolla," he said. "An' then the Ioway an' Missouri troops may ride on the steamcars to St. Louey. Got orders to march to the Gasconade River an' ford it at the mouth o' Little Piney. Guess where they found Sigel last night! Asleep in bed right here in Springfield! He's in command, now that Lyon's dead, but some o' the other brass don't like it. They think we mighta won the battle yestiddy if Sigel had done what he was supposed to." And clenching his jaws angrily, Ben walked off.

After breakfast, Jeff told Jimmy good-by and reported to the field hospital half a mile south of Springfield. After the battle, the ambulances had picked up the most dangerously wounded and transported them there.

Jeff never forgot that day. The field hospital proved to be two large, gray Sibley tents thrown together in a clump of big-boled oak trees. Cows were still grazing peacefully in the pasture. Jeff's detail carried those who had bad leg wounds to and from the amputation tent, where the tired surgeons who had already worked all night were destined to labor all day as well.

Finally only a dozen men were left. They lay on litters under the trees, awaiting the surgeon's saw. Their groans and cries of agony wrenched Jeff's heart. With wet eyes he passed among them, brushing flies and gnats off them, moving them into the shade, carrying water to them.

"Jeff!"

He spun around. Somebody had called his name. Carefully he scanned the litters on the ground. Then he saw a familiar figure stretched out on a pile of yellow straw. One long leg was rudely swathed in bloodstained bandages. The face was haggard and stubbled with beard. Suddenly Jeff recognized him. Ford Ivey!

"Ford," Jeff gasped joyfully. "They told me you had been killed."

The tall boy with warts on his face clutched Jeff's hand thankfully in both of his and looked nervously at the amputation tent nearby. One flap of it was turned back. Inside Jeff could see the surgeons, bareheaded and with sleeves rolled up, frowning as they toiled busily in the semidarkness. Ford's hands trembled.

"Don't let 'em cut off my leg, Jeff," Ford begged. There was fear in his eyes. Big crystal drops of sweat beaded his pale face. Then the pain of his mangled leg struck him.

"Oh!" he moaned, gripping Jeff's hand with all his strength. "It hurts awful. I can't stand it!"

"Easy, Slim," counseled an older, sandy-haired fellow from an adjoining litter. "This is gonna be lots better than dyin' with gangrene." Although his leg, too, was encased in bloody bandages, he was calmly smoking a shuck cigarette.

Jeff got them both a fresh drink from the ambulance barrel.

"Corn, Ford, I'm sure glad you're alive. When they told me you'd been killed, I gave up on you."

Ford shut his eyes and swallowed painfully, then turned his head slightly toward Jeff.

"Naw," he said, with a touch of bravado. "I got it in the leg as we retreated."

Ford's eyes kept leaping wildly from Jeff to the amputation tent. "Some Missouri boys was carryin' me to the rear, but the rebels was firin' so fast they had to drop me an' run. The rebel advance skirmishers found me. They stole my money an' my watch but a major made 'em give it all back. I laid all afternoon in the sun on the battlefield until one of our ambulances picked me up last night. Jeff, it was awful out there alone, listenin' to the wounded an' the dyin' ashriekin' an' cussin' an' prayin' an' nobody there to help 'em."

A tired-looking surgeon in a bloodstained coat stuck his head out of the tent. He was trying to thread a needle with silk thread, so he could tie blood vessels. Unable to thread the needle, he moistened the end of the silk strand with his tongue and rolled it between dirty fingers. He pointed with the needle to the sandy-haired man at Ford's side.

"Bring him in next," he mumbled wearily to Jeff and the litter detail. Gently they picked up the litter. The sandy-haired man took one long, deep draw on his cigarette and exhaled the smoke noisily.

"So long, Slim," he told Ford, almost gaily. "Next time you see me, my dancin' days will be over forever."

Jeff and the litter bearers carried him inside the tent and lifted him carefully onto a table. Jeff looked around him with awe. The surgeons and medical orderlies hardly had room to work. A disgusting stench assailed his nostrils. The place reeked with the sweet odor of chloroform. Two army lanterns dangled from a wooden ceiling crosspiece, furnishing some light. Jeff saw one of the medical orderlies washing a catling in a pail of dirty, dark-colored liquid. The other was cleaning human bone fragments from a small saw. When one of the surgeons motioned him outside, Jeff was glad to leave.

"So long, kid," the sandy-haired man called after him. Then noticing Jeff's stricken face, he added apologetically, "I don't care, kid. I never could dance worth a darn anyhow." An orderly plucked the cigarette rudely out of the man's mouth.

All too soon the surgeon appeared at the tent flap and gestured toward the unhappy Ford.

"Your turn next," he said roughly. Ford's face turned chalk white. A single convulsive shudder shook his long frame. His horror-stricken eyes sought Jeff's.

"Don't let 'em cut off my leg, Jeff," he pleaded.

"It won't hurt you, Ford," Jeff tried to comfort him as they lifted his litter. Ford was so lanky that his bare feet slopped over the end. Jeff went on, "You won't even feel it. They have to do it to save your life."

"Soon you'll be all through with war, son," somebody else said as they carried Ford inside and laid him on the table.

"I don't want to live if I hafta be a hopeless cripple for life," Ford screamed, thrashing about wildly. "Please, Jeff, for God's sake don't let 'em do it!" Ford grabbed Jeff's hand and held on. Wearily the surgeon gestured Jeff outside.

Ford saw the gesture. "No!" he pleaded, half rising on his litter. "Don't go, Jeff. Please don't leave me."

Jeff halted indecisively, his heart in turmoil. His stomach

felt weak and his throat dry. Impatiently the surgeon motioned him outside again.

Tears stinging his eyes, he took one last look at his friend, then gently detached his hand from Ford's despairing grip. The boy stared at Jeff in wonder, turned his face helplessly to the tent wall, and began to sob bitterly. Jeff ducked beneath the tent flap and went outside. He had no time to find out how the operation went, for immediately his detail was assigned to burying dead Union soldiers. Using pick and shovel, they dug shallow trenches in the hot sunshine.

The dead had fallen in long windrows, as though shot down by volleys. They lay in queer convulsive positions with all sorts of expressions on their faces. They seemed almost equally made up of Kansas Volunteers and Lyon's Missourians.

With a start Jeff recognized the first victim they buried as the big Kansas cavalryman he had seen riding merrily into battle in his black wedding suit. Hit in the side by artillery fire, the man apparently had died during the night, his face twisted grotesquely under his shoulder.

When it came time to put him into the rocky Missouri hillside that was to be his final resting place, Jeff wondered whether the bride had been notified. Casualty reports traveled horseback or by stage and usually required weeks to deliver. After he helped ease the body into the shallow trench, he stood back, a weight in his throat, and thought how awful it was to be buried without any identification or without even a song or a prayer. The sergeant roughly flipped the corner of the blanket over the dead man's face.

Later Jeff's detail was ordered back to the Wilson's Creek battlefield with an ambulance to claim the body of General Lyon. There they saw several rebel Negro burial parties busily interring the dead, a duty that usually fell to the side winning the battle.

They also found a mourner. In a small thicket of blackjack where the savage cannon fire had gutted the tops of the trees, a handsome shepherd dog sat in the broiling sun near the corpse of a fallen rebel lieutenant. The lieutenant lay with his arms flung out. His hat was still on his head and his eyes were open.

The dog kept licking the face of her dead master and whining piteously. When the Negro detail came to bury him, the dog growled and refused to let them touch him. They had to drive her away with their shovels. Jeff saw that she was a brown shepherd, two or three years old, and that she looked very thin.

"Here, girl," he called kindly. Whistling to her, he bent down and held out his hand.

The dog walked over to him and paused, regarding him gravely. Jeff began talking to her, using the same gentle, coaxing language he used on Ring at home. He had never seen a strange dog he couldn't make up to.

She came closer, permitting him to fondle her ears. Later, when his detail picked up the body of the general and headed back toward Rolla, Jeff whistled to her and she followed the ambulance. At the evening mess Jeff persuaded the cook to give him a piece of beef.

He held it out to her. Despite her hunger, she came gracefully to her feet, accepted it gently from his hand, and then ate it slowly. Her beautifully plumed tail waved in gratitude.

She was obviously a lady. That night they were such good friends that Jeff lifted her into the moving ambulance, and she slept at his feet all the way back to Rolla. He decided to call her Dixie.

Upon rejoining his outfit, Jeff lost no time telling his comrades that Ford Ivey was still alive and had had his leg amputated. Pete Millholland's blue eyes swept the group authoritatively.

"Ford's got a long siege ahead of him at the hospital in Springfield," he said. "If anybody ever gits thar agin, be sure to stop an' see him."

After reveille and roll call next morning, new uniforms were

issued to everybody by the quartermaster. Jeff's eyes shone
when he saw the trim blue coats and the bright brass buttons.
However, the first uniform he tried on was much too big for
him.

Bending over in front, he peered with dismay back between
his legs at the sagging seat of his new trousers.

"How do you like 'em?" beamed the quartermaster.

"Sir, I think I'd like 'em smaller," Jeff said forlornly. "If you
took about two inches off the waist and a gallon and a half out
of the seat, I think they might fit."

A pair of trousers was finally found that did fit reasonably
well, and fifteen minutes later Jeff walked out for guard mounting, wearing his new uniform proudly.

At the regimental parade grounds he found Noah sweeping
one of the company's earthen streets. He told him about Ford
Ivey and he also told him about his encounter with Clardy
behind the battle lines.

Noah stopped sweeping. Leaning on the broom, he looked
at Jeff intently, his keen eyes clear and unblinking. For the
first time Jeff thought he saw fear in Noah's usually placid face.

Noah said anxiously, "Youngster, you talk too rough and
too plain to the officers. Now don't misunderstand me. I think
in every army they otta fire about ninety per cent of the officers
just to diminish the general confusion. But this fellow's different. You'd best watch him like you would a snake. It's probably his strategy to keep turning you in for this and that, so
if you ever do inform on him, he can discredit your charges
by pointing to your long record as a troublemaker in the army
and say that you were just trying to get even with him for
enforcing discipline. Don't ever turn your back on him in battle.
He probably wouldn't hesitate to take your life."

Jeff felt a tiny shiver running up his spine. Then he laughed
bitterly.

"Don't ever turn my back on him in battle? Corn! It doesn't
look like I'm ever going to get in a battle."

That night Jeff hung his new uniform carefully on the tent pole. Although he usually slept in his woolen uniform pants and shirt for warmth, he broke the custom that night. He didn't want to wrinkle his new blue pants with the handsome light blue stripes down the sides.

It was good to be back with his own outfit, although he felt awfully left out when they began talking about their experiences in the battle. And that was all they seemed to want to talk about. Moodily he turned over on his side and tried to sleep.

Next morning he awoke at daybreak to find Noah's cold hand shaking him.

"Get up and dress quickly, youngster," Noah whispered hoarsely. "I want to show you something." There was a strange urgency in his voice.

He led Jeff a hundred yards away to the camp's outskirts. Suddenly Jeff's body goose-pimpled with horror. A crowd of soldiers had formed silently around a body lying in the brush, a body with a knife sticking up out of its back. It was Sparrow, the cook. Apparently he had been stabbed during the night while on sentry duty.

Captain Clardy had been summoned and, not taking time to dress fully, had thrown a long blue overcoat and cape over his gray woolen drawers.

He stooped and examined the body, shaking his head. Then he rose and looked straight at Jeff.

"You must all be more careful," he warned, his voice suddenly soft and silky. "The enemy has stray patrols all around us. What happened to Sparrow here might well happen to any of you who are not prudent."

Jeff felt his stomach puckering. It was plain to him now that Sparrow had died at the hands, or orders, of the captain. Suddenly a strong remorse punished him.

"Noah, I feel awful," Jeff confessed, as they walked soberly back to their tent. "If I hadn't got mad and deviled the captain about the widow's murder, poor Sparrow might still be alive today." Overwhelmed with grief, he sat down on the ground inside the tent and began sobbing.

He felt Noah's big hand on his shoulder. "You didn't mean to hurt him. Clardy would probably have got him anyhow, sooner or later. Sparrow was the type who couldn't keep a secret. He would have had to tell somebody, some day."

After a supper of hardtack and beans Jeff began to feel a little better. The army, recovering from its exhaustion and its casualties, seemed almost normal again. Noah was soaking his big feet carefully in salt water. From somewhere in the woods Bill Earle's clear tenor was singing "Aura Lee" and Jeff knew Bill was probably surrounded by a group of young soldiers, all of them homesick. Jeff thought of his own family and wished with all his heart that he could see them tonight.

Jim Veatch and half a dozen comrades played cards by the light of the smoldering campfire. Jim was dealing from the same deck he had thrown away on the battle march to Wilson's Creek. Jeff grinned in the dark. Apparently Neeley North had sold the cards back to Jim after the army had returned to Rolla.

Finally Jeff stretched and lay down outside the tent on the single cotton quilt that was his bed.

He heard a slight rustle and saw the dog, Dixie, stand, turn around once, and then deposit herself in a neat brown bundle at his feet. She was careful not to lie on his bedding, and again he smiled. Her manners were perfect. Somebody, probably her dead master, had trained her well.

Soon Jeff fell asleep. He began to dream. He dreamed that he saw Clardy, at the head of a gang of cutthroats, creeping stealthily toward his bed. Each man was carrying a dagger. He awoke in a cold sweat of fear. After tossing and tumbling another hour, he finally dropped off to sleep again. But he kept having nightmares.

He kept seeing Sparrow lying in the brush with the knife in

his back, the surprised, questioning look on his pain-glazed face.

Finally he began to breathe more regularly. But the lonely dog who had changed armies only that afternoon stayed awake a long time, her head lying across her paws, her eyes wide open. Whenever she heard a strange noise in the sleeping camp or the dark woods, her ears would point alertly, the fur would bristle along her back and a quiet growl would issue from her throat as she guarded the fitful slumbers of her new master.

☆ 9

Light Bread and Apple Butter

Summer passed, and with the coming of autumn the Kansas troops at Rolla were issued warm woolen gloves and long blue overcoats. Jeff was satisfied with everything but the food. He would always be hungry, he reckoned. They never got enough to eat.

He was issued three days' rations during a march and could have eaten it all in one day. And now that cooler weather had arrived, his appetite had burst its fetters. He was hungrier than a woodpecker with a headache.

One Sunday afternoon in October, after inspection, he took Dixie for a walk down the leaf-strewn road to the clay pits, hoping to find some ripe persimmons. It was good to be out in the tingling air.

The north wind held just enough of a sting in it that his

short coat felt comfortable. From somewhere back in the quiet
timber he heard the splintering thud of an ax. His nose caught
the sour, winy odor of a cider press. A sharp pleasure came
over him. It was good to get away from the camp, where for
three long hours the officers had kept him busy cleaning his
quarters and scrubbing his buttons and buckles with a fresh
corncob in advance of the brigade commander's weekly inspection visit.

The Missouri woods reminded him of his mother's brilliantly colored rag rug that lay on the split-log floor beside
her bed, back in Linn County. The blackjack seedlings seemed
aflame in the genial sunshine. The young hickories glowed
in livid gold. The oaks couldn't seem to agree on an appropriate color; some wore a subdued foliage of yellow and pale
green, others were gay in bronze and bright red. A cardinal
flew leisurely out of a tall, coppery sweet gum, and Jeff thought
at first it was a falling leaf. Dixie trotted along contentedly
at his side.

Soon they came to a rude clearing and Jeff saw a small, un-
painted clapboard house with crude leather hinges on the door.
Behind the house were several apple trees, heavy with fruit.
A small patch of big orange pumpkins lay in a garden nearby.

The red apples looked so tempting that for a moment Jeff
hesitated. It would be easy to help himself. Curbing his fierce
appetite, he decided to ask first and, walking up a small pas-
sageway of pulverized white rock, knocked vigorously on the
thin-planked door.

A woman opened it, frowning suspiciously at his blue uniform. With a gnarled hand she raked the black hair out of her
eyes. Jeff snatched off his army cap.

"Mam," said Jeff, twisting the cap in his hands bashfully,
"I'm real hungry. Could I have some of those apples yonder?"
With his cap, he pointed at the fruit trees nearby. He saw a
small boy's white, scrubbed face peering curiously at him from
behind the woman's skirts.

"Begone with ye," the woman snapped, in a tired, strained voice. "Iffen I feed one of ye, ye'd come back tomorrey, an' bring the whole army with you. We ain't got enough fer ourselves." She started to shut the door.

Jeff stepped back, disappointment in his face. "Mam," he said politely, "I wouldn't bring the army down on you. And I'll be glad to work for the apples. I was raised on a farm in Kansas. You got any man's work needs to be done around here? Anything you want lifted, any fence to fix?"

Now it was the woman's turn to look surprised. Hopefully Jeff watched her. When she glanced at his blue uniform she scowled. But when she looked into his boyish face, her hard features began to soften and her distrust to fade.

"I reckon it's all right," she whined, wearily. "Jest help yo'sef to the apples. Ye don't need to work fer 'em. Most soldiers woulda jest taken 'em and not even bothered to knock."

Relief flooded Jeff, like a warm shaft of sunshine.

"Yes, mam," he said, "I come pretty near doing that myself, mam, I was so famished."

She seemed pleased with his honesty and opened the door wider. A small girl with curly yellow hair thrust her head bashfully around the jamb. When Jeff smiled at the children, the boy opened his mouth and smiled back and Jeff saw he had two upper front teeth missing.

"Ye don't look like a soldier nohow," the woman said. "Ye look more like a schoolboy. Ye orter be home with yer mother."

"Yes, mam," grinned Jeff.

That grin must have done something to her, because now she stepped back. "Why don't ye come in?" she invited. "Sit down. We ain't got much ourselves but mebbe we can do better fer ye than jest raw apples."

She indicated a kitchen table covered with oilcloth. "Sit thar." She went back into the shed room. Gratefully Jeff stepped inside and sat down.

"Do ye like light bread and apple butter?" she called from somewhere inside the house.

Jeff could feel his mouth puckering with hunger. "I sure do, mam. I'd like it even if it had bugs on it."

She came back carrying a stone jar of apple butter, part of a round loaf of fresh light bread and a tall blue-glass bottle of cold milk. "It ain't much. But it ain't got no bugs on it. Hep yersef."

"Yes, *mam*. Thank you, mam."

With a long, sharp, bone-handled knife, she planed off three slices of the bread. Jeff could smell the fragrant yeast. With an effort he restrained himself.

"Mam," he said, "may I give my dog some of this? I'll bet she's almost as hungry as me."

The woman said, "You jist go ahead, now, and eat yore vittles. I'll feed yore dog."

"Yes, mam," Jeff said. "Thank you, mam."

Overjoyed at his good fortune, he ate ravenously while the two children, fingers in mouth, stared shyly at him.

"My name's McComas," the woman said, returning and sitting at the other side of the table. "We're lucky to hev any food at all these days. One army or t'other's on us all the time."

"We get rations," Jeff explained between bites, "but they aren't much. Just a little bacon and corn meal and coffee."

"Ye talk different than us," the woman said. "Where'bouts was ye raised?"

"In Linn County, Kansas, mam, close to the Missouri border," Jeff said. "My mother was a schoolteacher back in Kentucky before she got married. She taught all of us our speech." He told them all about his home, his family, and the bushwhackers.

The woman's eyes grew hard at the mention of the bushwhackers. "There's bushwhackers in both no'th an' south," she said, smoothing her faded gray apron over her knee. "I got a sister livin' near Neosho, close to the Kansas border. They was raided twict by Montgomery's Jayhawkers from Kansas an' got cleaned out both times. Bushwhackers, no matter which side they's on, is the lowest critters on God's green earth."

"Yes, mam," agreed Jeff. With the back of his hand he wiped the bread crumbs off his mouth. Feeling full for the first time in weeks, he arose to go.

"Mam, are you sure you haven't got some chores or something I could help you with around here? I've a little time before I have to go back."

Appreciative, she showed him an ax and several long blackjack logs piled together in the yard. Taking off his coat, Jeff picked up the ax and began to swing it in the crisp fall air. He enjoyed the exercise. He hadn't used an ax since he had left home. Soon he had cut enough wood to keep the fireplace going several days. He carried part of it inside for her, stacking it neatly on the hearth.

She thanked him, wiping her rough hands on her apron. "Thet'll last us a week. My man's in the army. It's hard to keep going without him."

"Mam," said Jeff, just before he left, "could I take a blouseful of those apples back to my messmates in camp? I'd take the ones on the ground. And I wouldn't tell them where I got them. They're hungry, too."

She gave him an old tow sack. Jeff filled it with windfalls.

As he and Dixie walked away, he looked back and saw them all three standing in the doorway watching him. He waved. The boy and the girl waved back.

Back at camp, Jeff's bunk mates bit hungrily into the apples.

"You're the best rustler in the whole outfit," Bill Earle praised, bearded cheek full, and chewing noisily. "After this, we'll send you out to do all our foragin'. You're so small and boyish, the farm wives all take pity on you."

Next afternoon, Captain Clardy assembled the company and

asked for ten volunteers for what he called "important duty." Still one battle behind everybody else and eager for any kind of action, Jeff stepped promptly forward two steps. As he did so, he heard Noah Babbitt whisper urgently "No, youngster, no." But it was too late.

Others volunteered until soon a detail was formed. As it marched down the pike, Spruce Baird, the sergeant in command, told them they were on their way to visit the homes of rebel soldiers who had violated their paroles by returning to the Confederate army. Captured at Wilson's Creek, they had promised under oath that they would stay out of the fighting until the war ended.

"It's a tough duty," the little sergeant bellowed in his heavy, coarse voice that utterly belied his small frame. "We're ordered to punish their families."

Jeff blinked. "Sir," he asked, uneasily, "how do we punish them?"

Baird cleared his throat noisily. "We confiscate their livestock an' their property an' take the stuff back to camp with us."

Jeff was appalled. He brushed a horsefly from his ear. Surely the government, President Lincoln's government, didn't rob the innocent and the helpless. "But, sir, if the men are gone away to war, won't the women and children need all the worse what we're going to take away from them?"

"Aye," growled Sergeant Baird, nodding, "that they will. An' now, youngster, lay off askin' your searchin' questions. Orders is orders. I don't like 'em no better than you. But I don't make 'em. All I do is enforce 'em." He kicked savagely at a rock in the road and added, "It's a tough duty."

It was, indeed. Before the hard day ended, Jeff wished a score of times that he was back in camp. Some of the Confederate women accepted the confiscation coolly. Others wept, pleading for their cows and for their children's pets. Some became angry and cursed like men as Jeff and the soldiers rounded up cows, calves, horses, sheep and hogs and drove them down the road ahead of them toward Rolla.

"Only one more place," barked the sergeant gruffly. "Let's come up on it through the woods so's they won't see us comin'." Leaving the road, they cut into the timber. The sergeant had sent all the livestock back to camp by five of the men. Only Jeff and three others remained with him. It was just turning dusk.

After they walked half a mile, a small house loomed ahead. They could smell the smoke from its fireplace chimney. Breaking ranks, they hand-vaulted a rail fence and approached the place from a path through the woods. Ahead of them, Jeff heard the familiar sound of milk spurting against the bottom of an empty metal bucket and knew somebody had started the milking.

As he flipped up the back of his collar, he saw several apple trees and then a small field of pumpkins, their orange faces pale and eerie in the twilight.

Cold fear gripped him. The McComas place!

They surprised Mrs. McComas milking a black and white spotted cow in the barn. Startled, she gave a squeal of fright and rose clumsily, spilling part of the milk on the ground and on the threadbare coat she was wearing. Alarmed, the cow plunged to one side.

Baird hauled out his paper and, clearing his throat huskily, read the confiscation summons. When the unhappy woman saw Jeff among the soldiers, she was furious.

"This is what a body gits fer goin' soft an' feedin' a Yankee swine." She spat at him, bitterly. "Ye brought 'em here, jist liken I said ye would."

She turned wildly on the sergeant. "Sure, my man's a rebel! What's wrong with thet? So is the husbands of thousan's of other wimmen all over Missouri. Sure, he broke his parole! He couldn't bear standin' round doin' nothin' when his state was bein' invaded by a passel of furriners."

Panicked by the noise, the cow started to lumber out the door. Jeff ducked quickly and picked up the frazzled fragment of rope that was fastened around the beast's neck.

"Ho, bossy!" he commanded gently.

"Take her on back to camp," Baird ordered, motioning with his hands toward the road.

Jeff's face fell. "Yes, sir," he said, wishing the sergeant had given the task to somebody else.

He looked imploringly at Mrs. McComas. "Mam, please believe me. I didn't have nothin' to do with bringin' 'em here." He pointed to the other soldiers. "Ask 'em, mam. None of us likes this kind of duty."

The woman scourged him with an angry look.

"Liar!" she said, clawing the black hair out of her eyes. "Yankee liar!" Scornfully she turned on Baird. "Ye'r a brave crew, th' lot o' yer. Took five of ye to capture one woman's cow."

Sheepishly they marched the cow back to the camp at Rolla and put her in the corral with the other confiscated animals. As he fastened the gate's catch, the little sergeant took off his cap and shook his shaggy black head with disgust. "It's a tough duty," he croaked for the tenth time and dismissed them.

Bitterness in his heart, Jeff returned to his winter quarters, a shelter tent superimposed on a hickory log base. It was heated by a stick and clay fireplace. Four bunks, two built above and two below, extended from wall to wall in the rear. In the foreground was a table constructed ingeniously from an inverted hardtack case mounted on legs. A sign hung over the door. Printed in Bill Earle's rude scrawl, it said "The Astor House."

Noah Babbitt looked up from his seat on the fireplace where he was writing letters off a shingle on his knee. "How'd it go, youngster?"

Jeff hung his head. Slumping to a seat on one of the lower bunks, he stared at the earthen floor, covered with yellow straw.

"I feel low down as a snake," he said and told Noah and the others all about it.

"Don't volunteer like that for extra duty," Noah warned, looking up soberly from his shingle. "Far as that's concerned, don't ever volunteer for nothin'! I tried to warn you, but you moved too fast for me."

Miserable, Jeff kept shaking his head. "That cow was all the livestock they had," he said. "Now those children won't have any milk to drink." He was thinking of the tall blue-glass bottle of cold milk he had drained back in the McComas kitchen.

John Chadwick whistled incredulously. "You mean, this is the same family that sent us the apples?"

Jeff nodded, glumly.

Bill Earle, squatted on his heels, shook his brown head in bafflement. "War's hard," he said, philosophically. "I wished they was something we could do about it. But they ain't nothin' we can do. Not a gol darned thing."

Jeff glared at him, an idea forming in his mind, a bold, crazy idea that didn't make sense at all. Maybe he couldn't do anything about it. But he could try. The McComases had fed him and given him apples for his comrades, despite the fact he was an enemy. And this was how they were repaid. Impatiently he crawled to his feet. It was still an hour before bedtime.

He looked at Noah, sudden decision in his face. "Who's the sentry down at the corral tonight?"

Noah peered up at Jeff. "Oscar Earnshaw. Why?"

Jeff looked at Noah meaningfully, without replying. He knew he could trust Noah. And Bill and John, too, for that matter. He put on his coat. He felt lots better about it, now that he had made up his mind.

"Careful, youngster," Noah warned in a low voice as Jeff went out. "It's after retreat, you know."

Jeff found Oscar Earnshaw standing behind a tree in the corral, blowing on his hands. Oscar was a fleshy fellow with long brown sideburns that came clear down to the lobes of his ears. He had leaned his musket against the corral fence.

Oscar peered uncertainly at Jeff in the dark, reaching for his gun.

Jeff hastened to identify himself. "It's me. Jeff Bussey. I want to talk to you a minute." Suspicious, Oscar kept his musket in the hollow of his arm and thrust his hands into the sleeves of his greatcoat for warmth. "Whad'ye want to talk about? I was hopin' you was comin' to relieve me. It's cold out here as a well-digger's bloomers."

"Oscar," whispered Jeff, "how'd you like those apples I brought you yesterday afternoon?"

Oscar looked sharply at Jeff. "You didn't come way out here in the frost jest to ask me that. You know how well I liked 'em. Best winesaps I ever et. Only thing, they wasn't enough of 'em. Why?"

Jeff went straight to the point. "Look, Oscar, if I bring you a big slice of home-baked light bread with apple butter smeared all over it, would you do something for me?"

Oscar took his hands out of his sleeves and thrust them under his armpits to warm them. He looked inscrutably at Jeff.

"Depends," he said. "You know I'd do murder fer a feast like that. But where you gonna git any light bread and apple butter round here, let alone this time o' night? This is an army camp. All we got to eat here is buckwheat an' beans."

Jeff told him about the McComases. "Oscar," he concluded boldly, "I want you to look the other way while I take that black-and-white heifer out of the corral and drive her back to the McComas farm."

Oscar's eyes twinkled shrewdly. He stared thoughtfully at Jeff. "What d'yuh mean, look the other way? I'll help you cut her out myself. The corral's full o' cows. They'll never miss one."

As Jeff moved off, driving the cow ahead of him, Oscar

warned in low tones, "Be sure to come back through my sentry position. An' bring the bread and jelly."

Jeff nodded, herding the cow off the road into the dark woods. The beast went willingly enough, as though she knew the path. As he walked, Jeff could feel the damp cold shutting down on him.

An hour later he drove the animal quietly into the Mc-Comas corral and locked the gate. A big smoky moon, yellow as brass, was rising through the branches of the apple trees. The house and the barn stood silent in its glow.

Jeff took the milk bucket off the oaken peg, rinsed it at the well, and finished milking the heifer. Walking up to the back door with the half-filled bucket in his hand, he knocked and called out guardedly, "Mrs. McComas." After he had called several times, he heard a noise inside and somebody stirring.

Mrs. McComas opened the back door cautiously. She was holding a hog-fat lamp in one hand. It splashed faint pools of light here and there in the yard. She looked frightened and sleepy.

Jeff said, "It's me, mam. I brought your cow back. Sentry helped me smuggle her out of the corral. I just now finished milking her for you. Here's the milk." He thrust the bucket toward her.

Puzzled, she set the lamp down on the table. Brushing the hair out of her eyes, she accepted the bucket with a look of astonishment. Quickly Jeff told her about the confiscation detail and how they had all volunteered for it without knowing what it was.

Ten minutes later he was on his way back to camp, carrying a couple of fresh apple-butter sandwiches in his blouse for Oscar Earnshaw and gorging another she had given him for himself.

Three months later he wasn't so fortunate. On a balmy day in January, Captain Clardy ordered all guns cleaned for a noon inspection.

Walking a short distance into the woods, Jeff raised his old-style musket to shoot it off preparatory to cleaning the barrel. An unpleasant memory stayed him. Remembering his arrest and punishment for doing this same thing on the march to Springfield, he lowered the weapon. He decided it would be more discreet to go to Clardy and get his permission.

Ushered by a sentry, he found Clardy inside his quarters in the officers' barracks. A fire burned cozily in his "California" type furnace, a hole dug in the ground and covered with a removable stone. The smoke was tunneled to an outside flue. A long blue overcoat, a cape, and a pair of gray woolen drawers hung from pegs in the wall. Clardy's glistening black head was bent low over his reports. They were alone. The captain didn't look up.

Jeff saluted briskly. "Sir, may I have permission to fire off the load in my musket so I can clean it? It'll take too long to draw the load with a ball screw."

Clardy's probing eyes rose slowly and deliberately over the feathered end of the quill with which he was writing. He transfixed Jeff with a cold, naked stare, letting him stand for a whole minute with his question unanswered. Finally the captain seemed to tire of his sport. He dropped his gaze back upon his reports.

He nodded curtly. "Permission granted."

"Thank you, sir." Feeling relieved, Jeff backed out. He walked two hundred yards into the woods, fired into a sand-bank, and had hardly begun to clean the barrel when a patrol swooped down upon him, arresting him by the order of the colonel.

Jeff claimed the permission of Captain Clardy. Deciding to check, the sergeant took him before Clardy and asked if he had given Jeff the permission.

Clardy snarled, "Of course I didn't. This man did the same thing on the march to Wilson's Creek when we were only a few miles from the enemy. I had to punish him."

Enraged, Jeff turned on Clardy, forgetting all caution. "Sir," he said hotly, "you gave me the permission yourself right here only five minutes ago, and you know it."

Shocked by Jeff's effrontery, the sergeant fell back a pace. Confusion in his face, he looked uncertainly from one to the other.

Clardy sprang to his feet, his face livid with anger. "Arrest that man!" he howled. "You hear me? Take him to the guardhouse. I'm tired of his eternal impertinence. This time I'm going to teach him a lesson he'll never forget."

Jeff spent one day in the guardhouse, a guarded tent. For two weeks he was assigned to the most disagreeable tasks the captain could contrive, marching about the camp carrying a knapsack filled with rocks, digging stumps, burying dead horses, digging latrines. Finally he was switched to a shovel crew that was busily constructing breastworks around the southern approaches of the camp. It was hard work. The ground, rocky and frozen, had to be broken first with a pick. The more Jeff labored, the more his hate for Clardy grew.

One day he passed a husky, brown-faced young workman carrying a big stone. When the workman saw Jeff, he looked so astonished he almost dropped his boulder.

"Jeff!"

It was David Gardner. Overjoyed, David threw down his stone, ran to Jeff's side, and began to pound him on the back. Then he saw the shovel in Jeff's hands and the dark look on Jeff's face.

"Goshallmighty, Jeff," he stammered. "What are you doin' on the ditch crew? Did you desert, too?"

That night Jeff lay quietly on his cold pallet, trying to think. All around him he could hear the snores of the other prisoners and smell the stench of their unwashed bodies. Slowly his mind began to go back over the last few weeks. They had been difficult weeks for him, thanks to Clardy's tyranny.

Turning on his side, he shut his eyes and clenched his teeth.

Although he still hadn't lost his desire to fight in battle, he was torn with loathing for all the cruelty and tyranny that accompanied war. Sleep didn't come to him until nearly midnight.

Next morning, after he had awakened and had breakfast, he felt better and began again to dream his old dream, looking forward to the day when he would get off the trench-digging detail and back onto the battle line, where he could settle his old score with the rebel Missourians. With the coming of spring, Jeff knew there would be more fighting.

He was right. In May, 1862, two months after he won his emancipation from the road crew, he was transferred to Fort Scott, Kansas, and became a part of a Federal invasion force of six thousand men under Colonel William Weer. Weer was a soldierly-looking fellow who had commanded a band of Jayhawkers in territorial days and had been a lawyer at Wyandotte, Kansas. Leaving Fort Scott in June, Weer's army moved down the old military road into the Cherokee Indian nation.

Its mission was to restore to their homes the loyal refugee Indian families who had fled into Southern Kansas early in the war. Also, it was to form a protective cover for Kansas and Southwest Missouri, operating against small enemy forces in the vicinity of Tahlequah and Fort Gibson.

Jeff could hardly wait to start. Nearly thirteen months in the army and he still hadn't fired a shot in combat!

☆ 10

Foraging in the Cherokee Country

The expedition started in early June, crossing the Kansas state line below Baxter Springs and moving down the Grand River into the Cherokee Indian nation. Pickets were posted every night, for now they were in enemy country and small parties of rebel Indians prowled all around them.

It had been a dry spring and they were plagued by lack of water every mile of the march. The only running water was in Grand River itself. However, it did not cross their route often, so they had to rely on the stagnant pools in the bottoms of the dried-up creeks, where small herds of brown Indian cattle stood in the muddy sinkholes, switching their tails and shaking their heads to protect their legs from the large green-headed flies that attacked them constantly.

When Jeff saw the army cooks drive the cattle out of the creeks and scoop up the greenish ooze with their big government buckets and camp kettles, he lost all his thirst and resolved not to take another drink until autumn. However, the cooks kept boiling the muddy liquid and skimming it through clean white dish towels until finally it was usable. He was surprised what good coffee it made, and coffee was all he drank until they veered alongside the river every three or four days and refilled their canteens.

With them were two regiments of newly organized Union Indian Home Guards, mostly Creeks and Seminoles armed with antiquated long-barreled Indian rifles. Jeff had never seen soldiers like them. Their small blue military caps looked ridiculous on their bushy heads. Every night they made medicine for the coming battles by singing their weird war songs. The backbone of the expedition consisted of two white regiments of Kansas and Wisconsin infantry, three of Kansas and Ohio cavalry, and batteries from Kansas and Indiana. Behind the army in creaking wagons rode thousands of Indian refugees, women, children, and aged men, and it seemed to Jeff that every child in the caravan had a pet puppy. Destitute, they were returning to their homes after being driven out by the rebels in the early days of the war. Jeff walked. Although the rocky miles stretched endlessly and his feet hurt, he was glad to be back with the infantry. Anything was better than the road gang.

As they kept trudging southwestward along the old military road, the weather became unseasonably warm. Although it was spring, no rain had fallen, and the grass was dry enough to burn. The winds blew so hot and searing that the birds stopped singing. Tempers began to grow short, and the men to grumble.

"Nothin' here but rocks and dead grass," one protested.

"This is Stand Watie's home stompin' grounds," another sulked. "I didn't jine up jist to fight Injuns. I thought we was gonna fight the rebels."

Jeff had heard of Stand Watie, a warlike Cherokee of mixed blood, who owned slaves and commanded a small, hard-riding rebel cavalry unit that had begun to raid, boldly and sharply, the comfortable homes, fields, and livestock of the Union Indian sympathizers who had not yet left the country. Cherokees, Choctaws, Chickasaws, Seminoles, and Creeks—most of them were now fighting actively with the South. He had also heard that some of the rebel Indian troops at Pea Ridge, armed with nothing better than bow and arrow and tomahawk, had scalped dead Union soldiers on the field.

Pea Ridge. Jeff felt his face and neck redden angrily, even in the stifling heat. Clardy had kept him so long on the road crew at Rolla that he had missed the Battle of Pea Ridge in northwestern Arkansas. His company had fought in it, and it had been the first Federal victory of the war in the far West.

Herds of brown Indian cattle grazed on the Cherokee prairies, which stretched for miles. Only an occasional clump of blackjack or post oak interrupted the long grassy flatness. One morning the brassy sky became overcast, and Jeff looked expectantly for rain.

"Rain no come," an Indian boy told him.

Impatient with the standard military attire, the Indian boy had thrown away his cap and coat, cut off his blue army pants below the knee and was marching barefoot with the Union Indian Home Guards. An ear of corn, half its yellow kernels chewed away, swung from a string at his waist. He was carrying a long-barreled Indian rifle. The furry hilt of a hunting knife showed at his belt.

Jeff asked, "How do you know?"

"Before rain come, lots of sign. Sky all red before sunrise, no early dew on ground. Flies thick and stay close to your hands, fish jump out of water to catch bugs in air, hickory leaves curl. You can smell the woods better, hear noises better. Campfire smoke stay close to ground. None of these signs here now."

Jeff was impressed. "What's your name?" he asked.

"Joe Grayson. I Cherokee. Not many Cherokees in Indian Home Guards now. By and by many other Cherokees join up, I think. Most of Home Guards now Creeks, Seminoles."

Jeff pointed back over his shoulder at the long line of Indian refugees, some walking, others riding in wagons. "What tribe are they?"

"Mostly Creek. Some Seminole, Cherokee, too. Ever' day, more Cherokees desert rebels, join us."

Jeff motioned toward Joe's bare feet. "Don't you get tired marching all day barefoot?"

An expression of quiet pride came over Joe's smooth brown face. "When I get tired I think of time my mother told me how she walk barefoot all way behind their wagon from Georgia when Jackson's soldiers took our Georgia land away from us twenty—twenty-five years ago. If she could walk eight hundert mile, I walk this hundert'n fifty easy."

Three days later they began to pass occasional log cabins and see rude brand marks on the flanks of grazing horses, cattle, and hogs.

"Full-bloods," Joe grunted, scornfully. "They lazy. All they wanta do is live like old-time Indians. They raise little mess corn so family have corn meal and hominy to eat and swill for hogs. That all. They jest wanta hunt and eat."

As they penetrated deeper and deeper into the Cherokee country, the farms became bigger, and the homes alongside the trail larger. Many of the houses were two-story with tall corner fireplaces and wide porches. The valleys were filled with waving corn. Orchards of peach, apple, plum, and quince grew behind the big homes, and the broad lawns were shaded by gigantic oaks enclosed by plank fences, neatly white-washed. Jeff had never seen anything like this in Kansas.

"Mixed-bloods and intermarried whites," explained Joe proudly. "They run things in the nation. They not like brush Indians. They know how to live."

In midafternoon they passed the blackened ruins of a large home destroyed by fire. The desolation was complete. The fences had been wrecked, and the long cedar lane leading to the front door had been chopped down wantonly. Even the springhouse and barns had been burned to the ground. As he saw it, Joe's smooth brown face grew hard.

"That was Clem Vann's home. Watie men burned it down,

I think. Vann was Union man. All his boys go north to fight. I used to play with his son John. They had a pet cub bear. We'd wrestle with it." Joe fought to regain his composure.

Finally he turned to Jeff. "Rebel Cherokees and Union Cherokees hate each other. Handful of rebel Cherokees, mixed-blood families led by old Major Ridge, sign treaty back in Georgia giving up all our tribal land there. Watie sign it, too. They had no right do that. Chief John Ross and most of tribe protested, wanted stay in Georgia. But old Andy Jackson, United States President, got his Senate ratify the false treaty. United States government took our Georgia lands and homes away from us. Jackson's soldiers came and made us move to this country. Hunderts our people died on the long, hard trip. We call that trip 'Trail of Tears' because they have stop ever' few miles and bury somebody. Ever since, Ross Cherokees hate Watie Cherokees. Lots of assassinations, killings."

Jeff turned incredulously. "You mean the United States took your homes away from you?"

Joe nodded gloomily. An expression of long-seated resentment came into his dark face. "My family's home was two-story brick, prettiest in whole Georgia country. It had hand-carved mantelpiece, circular staircase, big pine trees growin' all around. My mother loved every brick in it. It had belong in her family hundert years. She live in it since she little girl. She got married in it. One day Jackson's soldiers come to take the home and drive Mother and family away. Mother stand in yard look at them. She asked them give her half hour. She take broom, sweep whole house lovingly, burn broom for good luck. Without looking back, she walk out of house and start long walk to this country. She never see her house again."

Sobered by Joe's simple telling of the dramatic event, Jeff marched in silence. He wondered at Joe Grayson's loyalty to the Union after such infamous treatment. How could the United States have done such a terrible thing?

That night they camped near Cabin Creek. Noah, a shuck cigarette dangling from a corner of his mouth, stooped over the creek bank to scour his knife and fork. He plunged them into the gray soil and wiped them clean on his pants leg. Bill Earle, sprawled indolently on the grass, was rolling himself a cigarette out of a tiny square of newspaper.

"Noah, why we goin' to this Godforsaken Indian country?" Bill asked.

A bird whistled from a nearby button bush. Noah listened, trying to identify it. "To return the Indian refugees follerin' us to their homes. An' to impress the Cherokees aroun' Tahlequah and Fort Gibson with our strength, now that we're mobilized. Lots of Cherokees aroun' Tahlequah had to join the rebels against their will. When we show up, some of 'em might wanta change their minds and come back to our side." He saw that Bill's cigarette was unlit. "Gotta match?"

Bill growled, "Naw! All I got's the habit." Noah took a quick pull from the burning cigarette in his own mouth. With a long arm, he thrust the hot end of it toward Bill so Bill could ignite his.

Bill blew twin puffs of gray smoke out of his nostrils. "While we're trying to impress 'em, what's to stop another rebel army from comin' up from Texas with twice as many men as us and givin' us a good scobbin'?"

"Our commanders probably know there ain't no large rebel force in the Indian country now."

"How do they know?" Jeff asked. He was folding his blanket carefully. The visiting inspector today was Colonel Salomon of the Ninth Wisconsin Infantry. He knew how to run an inspection.

"Our scouts and spies probably told 'em," explained Noah. "Each side has got plenty of spies in the other's army."

Jeff was aghast. Maybe he'd been marching alongside rebel spies in his own outfit that very afternoon.

He stammered, "Corn, Noah. Don't spies ever get caught?"

Noah nodded, placing his knife and fork carefully in his knapsack.

"What happens to 'em?"

Noah ran his long finger expressively across his throat and went on packing.

"Corn!" Jeff said again and decided it must take an awfully brave man to be a spy.

A slow rumble of wagon wheels was heard. A wagon hauled by a yoke of oxen and driven by an old Arkansas farmer lumbered into view. Halting his wagon in the midst of the soldiers, the farmer moved to the rear, untied one of the sacks, and began selling big green Henry Clay apples to the soldiers.

Jeff hadn't tasted an apple for months. Holding aloft his "shin plaster" currency as all the others were doing, he eagerly joined the mob clamoring to be waited upon. The whole transaction moved so slowly that Bill Earle climbed jocularly into the front end of the wagon, cut a sack string, and began helping the boys right and left. The farmer hurriedly pushed Bill out.

But while he was retying that sack, Noah and John Chadwick lifted out the open sack in the rear and began handing out apples to everybody. At the same time, somebody belted the oxen across the rump with a brush and they began running, the soldiers hopping alongside, yelling like Indians. Several clambered into the wagon and, despite the farmer's efforts to prevent them, threw all the sacks of apples overboard. Nearly every man in camp got at least one apple, and everybody was laughing.

As Jeff bit juicily into his and found it delicious, he could hear the farmer still shouting helplessly, "Captain! Captain!" But no captain came, and finally the old man drove off with an empty wagon.

Gradually Jeff was beginning to learn the army's careless regard for the private property of civilians, especially food. Petty stealing in camp was dealt with harshly. At Rolla, Jeff had seen the punishment of a Missourian who had stolen $12.50 from a comrade. He was made to stand on a stump with placards marked THIEF hanging from him, front and back. His head had been shaved and he had to forfeit all his pay. Moreover, all the other soldiers seemed to think the punishment was deserved. Yet here was the whole company participating cheerfully in the pilfering of a farmer's harvest of apples and regarding it as a great lark.

The weather stayed hot, the trail dusty, the rations short. Some said they were going to Fort Gibson, others said to Fort Smith. Many times it seemed to Jeff that they were marching for no other reason than just to keep up the motion. Everybody was complaining about the wretched army food.

One night when they were still camped on Cabin Creek awaiting the arrival of the supply train from Fort Scott, a bareheaded soldier walked up to their campfire after they had finished eating. He was a moody-looking fellow. His curly, uncombed hair was red as strawberry jam. His piercing blue eyes glinted fretfully, as if he were nursing a grievance against somebody.

He glanced hungrily at the pittance of bacon gravy left in the bottom of their camp skillet. Suddenly he reached one hand back toward his coat pocket, as though to draw a pistol. Jeff ducked behind Noah's broad back. Food was now so scarce that some messes waited until dark, then forcibly took food away from other messes. But instead of a pistol, the stranger's hand came away holding a great piece of cold corn bread. He looked shyly at them.

"I would like to wallop my dodger in that there gravy, if you hain't no objection." With a dirty forefinger he pointed to the skillet.

They had no objection. After he had "walloped," he wasn't long letting them know why he wore that peeved look. He told them he was Stuart Mitchell of Council Grove, Kansas, and that he knew all about the Watie outfit, having been their prisoner several months.

Mitchell talked with the loquacious annoyance of a man who wants to get something unpleasant off his mind. The war had caught him visiting friends in Texas. Trying to escape to the north, he had been captured by Watie's men near Boggy Depot. They compelled him to be their body servant. They made him walk seven miles a day to cut wood for their fires. All he got to eat was a pint of mush and a small piece of beef daily. At night he slept in a tent. If he stuck his head out, they shot at him.

At first he had got along well with them and thought they were a pretty good lot. They told him about the battles they had won. But when he tried to tell them about the battles the Union had won, they wouldn't let him talk.

One of Watie's rebel corporals threatened to cut off Mitchell's red curls and send them to his rebel sweetheart near Webbers Falls "so she'd think he was flirtin' with a little redheaded gal in Dixie." They threatened to make him sit on a cake of ice to cool his hot northern blood.

As Mitchell talked, his blue eyes flashed angrily. Hating the Watie men passionately, he had finally escaped. "And iffen I ever meet up with them Cherokee devils agin, I'll never show 'em any mercy or take a single prisoner," he swore in conclusion. Fascinated with his firsthand account of the enemy, they invited him to join their mess. It was a gesture of social significance only.

The food became so intolerable that a week later they formed a protest committee and called on Millholland. It was dusk. The army had pitched camp where it had stopped along the deeply rutted road. The men were sitting or lying in the gray smoke of the small fires that flickered everywhere, cursing the flies and gnats and wondering how things were going back home.

Noah saluted and explained the situation.

Bill Earle added, "Sir, we been cookin' carrots with a squirrel's head, but yesterday we loaned the squirrel's head to Joe Danning's mess an' they cooked it with cabbage an' ruined it."

"Sir, we're so hungry we could eat old Watie off his horse and snap at the stirrups," said Jeff.

Mitchell held up one of the thick army crackers he had been issued. "Sergeant, if you hain't no objection, sir, these here crackers is so hard I can't break one off in my hands without gettin' a pry on somethin'."

Millholland squinted thoughtfully at the cracker Mitchell was holding. He knew as well as anybody that the food stank.

"Well," he said, with honest practicality, "regulations forbid it, but we can't starve. If you wanta to do some foragin' o' nights, go ahead. But try to take it from families that's got plenty. We'll try it awhile an' see what happens." Grasping his belt between his forefinger and thumb, he pulled it six inches away from his stomach, staring mournfully at the gap caused by his lost weight.

Bill Earle grinned gratefully. "Thankee, Sergeant. We'll be careful."

At first the pickings were good. In the daytime they marched; at night they raided smokehouses and hen roosts, carrying off chickens, ducks, geese, eggs, milk, and cheese. Once they found a bee tree. It was a tall ash. Noah chopped it down with an ax. They camped on the spot, building a fire and scooping up the golden honey in dishes and camp kettles.

Noah had found several ears of corn in a rebel crib, and Mitchell, who had been a baker at Council Grove, knew what to do. Using the butt of his musket, he pounded the corn into a pulpy meal, adding a little flour, water, and an egg. He spread his black oilcloth cloak on the ground, rolled up his sleeves and, adding salt to the batter, made a dough so delicious-looking that Jeff's eyes stuck out like marbles as he watched the wet cakes drop from Mitchell's freckled fingers onto the hot pan over the fire. He was sure he had never eaten anything half so good as that hot corn bread and the fresh honey they spread over it.

The bountiful Cherokee farms gave up many a hog and a chicken to the small but hungry Union army of Colonel Weer. The first thing the soldiers did after pitching camp in the evening was to visit the nearby barnyards. Gunshots were heard, then the soldiers returned to camp, carrying game over their shoulders or safely gigged on their bayonets. Although Colonel Weer threatened to punish anybody caught foraging, the pickets usually yawned and looked the other way as the army, tired of the wormy hardtack and the tasteless salt horse, rustled its own provisions.

One day the army camped early. Mike Dempsey, the old Irish teamster who had befriended Jeff at Fort Leavenworth, went foraging with Jeff and Bill Earle.

Jeff filled his pockets with beets and onions. Bill Earle was straining under the weight of half a sack of last year's sweet potatoes, and Mike had speared a large gray goose with his bayonet. On their way to camp, they passed a deserted log house in the midst of a thicket of black cedars. The waters of a small creek sang sweetly nearby.

Jeff halted, looking curiously at the old cabin. Rose and lavender from the dying Cherokee sunset reflected faintly off its broken windowpanes. "Let's see what's inside," he proposed.

"Aw, let it go, Jeff," Bill urged. "We already got all we can carry. Nothin' there, anyhow."

"Might be," said Jeff. Entering the open door, he explored the dark interior but found nothing. Just as he was leaving, he heard a plaintive meow and a large yellow tomcat followed him out into the warm dusk, pausing to arch its back and stretch its toes on the hot ground.

Jeff stooped to rub its back and the fur felt warm to his

touch. "All they left was the house cat," he reported. He picked up the cat and started back to camp.

"Hey!" protested Bill, frowning. "Whad'ya wanta take a cat back with us for?"

Jeff said, innocently, "I don't know. To keep the enemy from getting him, I guess."

Disgust showed plainly in Bill's face. "Jeez!" he snorted.

Although they waited until dark to enter camp, they had the bad luck almost to collide with a detail of soldiers. A firm voice command, "Halt! Fetch a light, somebody."

Jeff could feel the sweat crawling down his neck. He knew the penalty for pillaging—two days' hard labor digging up stumps. He knew that in his own case Clardy would cheerfully double it and, on the grounds that Jeff was an old offender, probably make him stand all night on his tiptoes with his thumbs tied together over an overhanging tree branch.

A torch flashed in their faces. They were half-blinded by its sudden glare.

"You men know the regulations against stealing from civilians," a lieutenant scolded sternly.

Jeff blinked and swallowed nervously. "Sir," he protested helplessly. "We didn't steal it. We just took it."

Hearing the lieutenant's voice, Mike Dempsey glanced keenly at the officer's face.

"It's Lootenant Sor-rely, isn't it, sor?" he said, dropping the goose so he could salute. Its heavy carcass thumped noisily into the weeds at his feet.

Surprise creased the lieutenant's whiskered face, vaguely visible in the torchlight. "Is that you, Dempsey?" His voice sounded a little more conciliatory.

Mike began to chuckle in his hoarse growl. "It is, sor. Bedad, sor, I can explain everyt'ing. I've got a dead goose on the ground here that I had to kill. Me frinds here and I was goin' along paceably whin this goose dar-rted out of the brush and hissed at the Amer-rican flag. An so bejabez, I speared him on the spot. What else could I do, sor?"

"Meow," purred the cat in Jeff's arms.

The lieutenant's head jerked about. Ignoring the vegetables in Jeff's possession, he looked with amusement at the cat riding on his shoulder. Jeff began to feel better.

With rough amiability the officer barked, "What you got there, mister? A pussycat? I know nothing in regulations forbidding the confiscation of a rebel pussycat. Detail dismissed!" Tossing his torch into a nearby fire, he walked off into the gloom.

"Whew!" panted Bill Earle. "That was close." He turned to Jeff. "That cat saved our necks. And it was my big mouth that tried to talk you outa bringin' him." Picking up their booty, they began walking again, hugging the shadows.

Jeff whispered to Mike, "Who was he?"

Mike was still chuckling. "Lootenant Sorely. His father and I were boys togither in County Roscommon, back in west Ireland. Tim Sorely and I used to play Gaelic football togither with an old leather ball fulla straw. When the lootenant was a laddie, I held him on me knee many a time."

Bill Earle said, "The good Lord was sure holdin' all three of us by the hand t'night."

"Amen," Jeff said heartily.

"Meow," said the cat, and that seemed to make it unanimous.

Three days later the command moved on down the military road toward Flat Rock, twelve miles north of Fort Gibson. Again the northern troops sweltered in the almost tropical heat. No rain had fallen since the expedition had entered the Indian country. The cavalry had constant brushes with small bands of Stand Watie's rebel horsemen, who raided busily on both flanks. Jeff's outfit had missed the defeat of Clarkson and Watie and the capture of some of their supplies by the Union Creek Home Guards at Locust Grove.

"Just my luck," Jeff muttered to Noah Babbitt. "I'll never get in a real fight."

Noah was chewing a blade of grass. "That's what I'd call good luck, youngster." But Jeff didn't see it that way.

"All I ever get to fight are these dad-gummed body lice," he complained. He began to look along the roadside for red pokeberries. Joe Grayson had told him that if you'd boil up a kettle of pokeberry roots and bathe yourself and wash your clothes in the juice, it would kill all the body lice in creation.

They kept walking. The day became hotter and the ground rockier. The straps on the heavy pack chafed Jeff's back. The warm sweat ran down his neck and chest. His rifle barrel felt hot to the touch.

Stuart Mitchell drawled laconically, "This country is two rocks to one dirt."

Dixie trotted alongside Jeff, her pink tongue vibrating as she panted. Despite the universal dryness, Jeff had never seen finer cattle country, nor more cattle. He could always look up while marching and see a bunch of beef grazing somewhere. The yellowing bluestem grew stirrup high to a big horse. Occasionally coyotes galloped through it, only the tips of their tails visible.

Bill Earle sighed and changed hands on his musket. "Cripes!" he panted in his high voice. "If this keeps up, it otta take the frost outa the ground."

They were patrolling the right flank of the main column so they could forage as they marched. They hadn't had anything to eat all day save a prod of ham John Chadwick had found in the ashes of a cold campfire that morning. Noah said the fire had probably been made the day before by Watie's men. Jeff had found a quarter of a pail of sorghum in a smokehouse and filled his canteen with it.

Late in the afternoon they flushed a young beef out of the brush. Herding it to the edge of the woods, they shot it. As it lay kicking, its eyes glazed in death, John thrust his knife into its throat and a column of blood gushed over the hot grass. After the animal had bled, Millholland flipped the carcass over on its back, carefully turning the head under the shoulder to balance it. He drew his knife and began skinning. Jeff watched with admiration.

The sergeant certainly knew what he was doing. Quickly Millholland straddled the carcass and, working down the belly, slit the hide from chin to tail. Then he slit each leg from the heel to the belly. Grasping the hide with his strong hands, he peeled it off, laying it back so the meat could be cut up on the inside of the hide instead of on the dusty ground. After he had carved off several steaks, Millholland dropped them in Noah's camp skillet.

He wiped the knife clean on his pants legs. The ragged men stared with hungry fascination at the fresh meat.

John Chadwick blurted, "Le's stop right here and broil 'em. We can join the main column later." Everybody looked at Millholland. The sergeant squinted at the sun and nodded, and Jeff's heart leaped with joy. Bill Earle and Mitchell began breaking off dead tree limbs for a fire. It was Jeff's day to cook.

The red meat looked fresh and tender. Jeff's mouth drooled hungrily.

He tenderized the steaks by pounding them with the butt of his musket. Noah produced a skin bag filled with white salt, and Jeff salted the meat carefully. Borrowing John's knife, he cut some green switches from a dogwood growing nearby. After the fire burned down, he threaded the steaks on spits over the live coals. Noah wrapped the remainder of the carcass into a slicker.

While the steaks were broiling, Jeff found some red pokeberries, dug up the roots with his bayonet and, borrowing some water from Mitchell's canteen, placed the roots on the fire in a stew kettle to boil. He began pulling off his clothes. So did Mitchell. They were going after those body lice.

As Jeff struggled with a knotted shoelace, he could smell

the aroma of the broiling veal and hear the steaks sizzle as juice from them dropped into the fire. The smell was maddening. He yanked off his shoes and socks.

Mitchell peeled off his drawers and, standing naked by the fire, dropped them into the open kettle. Huge splotches of pink freckles covered his entire body.

"Look," he said, glancing up. "There's riders."

Jeff straightened, shading his eyes with his hand. A dozen men, all mounted, rode into the clearing. They wore boots and slouch hats. All were heavily armed. Jeff shifted his bare feet on the rocky ground, studying them. They were probably from Judson's Sixth Kansas Cavalry.

A long, piercing yell, shrill as a wildcat's scream, rent the air. A rifle cracked, and Jeff ducked instinctively as a bullet cut through the trees over his head and twigs and leaves fell in a cascade around him. He stared incredulously at the cavalry. Darned fools! Couldn't they see the blue pants of the infantrymen?

"Rebels!" Mitchell shrieked the hated word in mingled alarm and rage. Astonished at the reckless boldness of enemy riders striking so close to Weer's main column, Jeff stood rooted to the spot. Then he heard the swift drumming of hostile hoofbeats and the Confederates were on them, yelling fiendishly and firing pistols.

Cut off from his rifle, which lay against a small hickory where they had skinned the beef, Jeff dived barefooted into a nearby thicket. Dixie was at his heels, her tail between her legs and her ears flattened out. Pistol reports rang out loudly behind him, the noise spanging into the woods, arousing echoes. It seemed the whole rebel army was shooting at him.

Letting out his last notch of speed, he ran with all his strength between the trees, scarcely noticing the rocks tearing the soles of his bare feet. It seemed that the concussion of the rebel fire was pushing him along, lending him wings.

He felt something wet flowing down his left leg and saw

that his pants were sodden with a red stain. Blood! Wildly he realized he must have been hit, but there wasn't time to stop. The gray-clad riders were yelling fiercely as he doubled and dodged ahead of them. Puffing loudly, he stumbled, fell, and rolled over and over on the rough ground, feeling sharp stabs of pain where the rocks gashed his bare skin. Then he noticed that the shooting and yelling had stopped.

Dizzily he sat up and stared frantically behind him, his breath coming in dry sobs. Apparently the rebels had fled, fearing pursuit because they were so close to the main Federal column. As quickly as it had happened, it was over.

Still panting, Jeff scrambled to his feet and began to search for his wound. He couldn't find it. He wiggled his arms and legs but felt no pain. He grasped his canteen, which had slipped around in front of him, and noticed that it felt wet and slippery. The last of his precious sorghum was oozing out of a jagged bullet hole.

Sheepishly he realized he hadn't been shot.

Instead, his canteen had been hit and the sorghum had flowed out through the bullet hole and down his leg.

His feet were bruised and bloody from the rocks. Brushing off the dirt, he looked cautiously through the trees. The rebels had disappeared into the timber.

One by one, Jeff's patrol began to appear. Noah's tall form showed first. He had lost his cap. Blood was dripping from a cut under his right arm. A rebel saber had slashed him.

"Where'd they come from? Who were they?"

"Watie men!" Mitchell spat out the word venomously, his blue eyes alive with hate.

Naked as a jaybird, he emerged from the woods and limped up to the fire. His nude body was reddened from running through the shrubbery. His bare feet were cut and bleeding. Then he saw Noah trying to stanch his wound with his bare hand.

Mitchell limped to his haversack, hanging on a nearby bush.

Reaching into it, he drew out a pint bottle a quarter full of brown whisky. Without a word, he handed the bottle to Noah.

Noah poured whisky into the hollow of one hand, flung the raw liquor onto the wound, winced, rubbed it in, then put the bottle to his lips and drained it.

John Chadwick crawled out of a nearby hazel thicket. Eyes transfixed, he stared at the fire. He began to curse, pronouncing each syllable slowly and vehemently.

"The dirty, low-down so's and so's! Stole our steaks."

Blinking, Jeff pressed forward to look, his face dull and set. It was true. Every spit was bare. Then he brightened.

"We still have the carcass," he remembered, joyfully. "We can still cut us off some more meat."

"No we can't," contradicted John. "They stole that too." He pointed to where Noah had laid it in the slicker. Gone.

The sun was hot. Glumly Jeff found his hat and put it on. Then he drew on his shoes and stockings. He ignored the boiling kettle of pokeberry roots. The stolen steaks were all he could think about.

"They waited until our meat was just about done before they rushed us," John said. "Probably been watching us the last hour with a field glass from the woods."

"Where's Earle and Millholland?" Noah asked suddenly.

Jeff looked at Noah with a premonition of disaster. The rebels had fired a lot of shots. It would be a miracle if all the patrol had escaped.

John called loudly several times, but nobody answered. With dread, they scattered and began to search the premises. In the tall grass to his right, Jeff saw an odd depression. The long grass lay flat, as though a weight had fallen on it.

Staring, his body went rigid. Forcing himself, he walked closer. A blue-clad form sprawled face downward, the legs spread awkwardly. One black shoe was half twisted off the left foot. How crumpled and flattened out and still the body looked. Jeff's breath began to come in gulps. He knew it was a dead body. Whose?

A few more faltering steps and he saw the sergeant's chevrons on the sleeve of the dark blue blouse. Millholland! From a small black hole between the sergeant's shoulder blades, fresh blood seeped slowly and darkly, staining the long green grass.

Numb with shock, Jeff grasped the body by the belt and turned it over gently. The sergeant still wore his tiny cap with the sloping crown protruding ludicrously over one ear. His eyes, wide open, stared unblinking into the sun.

Jeff groped for Millholland's wrist, feeling for his pulse. There was none. His throat tightened and he felt a deep and abiding grief for his friend and a wild, uncompromising hate for those who had slain him. Dropping to his knees on the ground, he began to sob.

Shoes grated on gravel. The others were coming up. Dully, Jeff stood so they would see him. He couldn't find his voice. He saw that Bill Earle was with them now.

When they saw the sergeant, shock showed in all their faces. They had great respect for this big Kansas farmer who was fast becoming a leader despite his lack of military bearing.

"You murderin' Indian thieves!" Across the stillness of the hot afternoon Stuart Mitchell's screeching voice lashed like a whip. He began to curse the Watie riders slowly, roundly, and fluently as he buttoned his faded blue shirt over the mat of flaming red hair on his chest.

Depressed, Jeff began preparing supper. He had no enthusiasm for cooking. As he rattled the pots and pans, he could hear Bill Earle's and John Chadwick's shovels biting softly into the rocky earth as they dug Millholland's grave a few feet from where he had fallen. Bill and John had hurried back to the main column to borrow the shovels and report the incident, hitch-hiking rides with a patrol of Union cavalry they encountered.

Noah sat glumly on a log, trying to compose a letter to Millholland's wife, back in Kansas.

Later, a patrol from the Sixth Kansas Cavalry, the yellow stripes down their pant legs gleaming in the sunshine, cantered past, raising the dust in sultry clouds as they began the hopeless task of tracking down the rebel raiders. Jeff knew it would be like chasing a heat mirage on the prairie.

Ignoring the pain of his bruised feet, he tossed dry wood on the fire. Rice from their rations was all they had to eat. Mechanically he reached for it. He had never cooked rice before, but he knew you had to boil it. As he poured water into a gallon stew kettle, he still felt stunned. You marched with a guy for a whole year, ate with him, bunked with him, learned to like him, learned to obey his orders. And then suddenly he was shot in the back, and you buried him and marched away, leaving him lying forever alone in the soil of a hostile land.

The water began to bubble. Listlessly he poured in the rice. They had pooled their rations, but he was afraid there wouldn't be enough.

Soon the rice began to boil over and spill down the sides of the kettle. With a big spoon, Jeff tried to salvage the bubbling white overflow. But it was rising and swelling faster than he could ladle it out. Hurriedly he spread an old saddle blanket near the fire and, with his tin plate, scooped the cooked rice onto it. It made a big snowy pile.

The others plodded up wearily, found their camp plates, and gathered silently around the fire, looking loathingly at the rice. Jeff knew they were thinking about the stolen steaks.

"For them that don't like rice, supper's over," Jeff said.

Ignoring their plates, they ate it off the blanket with their spoons.

☆ 11

Lucy Washbourne

Jeff stood on a rocky bluff and gazed through the shimmering distance at Tahlequah, capital of the Cherokee Indian Nation that had joined the Southern Confederacy in the war.

Surprise ruled his face. He thought the Cherokees were blanket Indians, like the Potawatomi and Miami near his Kansas home, and that Tahlequah would be a city of teepees scattered over the grassy prairie. Instead, he saw a good-sized town, much bigger than Sugar Mound and almost as big as Leavenworth. It was located among low, green-timbered hills at a picturesque spot near the Illinois River. Many of its town buildings were of brown stone and red brick. And instead of teepees, there were log houses chinked with red clay and chimneys of rock and mud. Spirals of gray smoke twisted lazily into the hot blue sky.

"Now lissen, you foot-sloggers!" bellowed Jim Pike, the new sergeant. "We're comin' into town. Cap'n Greeno says we're to impress 'em with our sodjery bearin'. So smarten up! March good. No profanity. No talkin' to civilians. No swipin' fruit ner vegetables. Close ranks! March!"

Loyal to Millholland and slow to give his allegiance to any new officer, Jeff didn't like Pike, a tall, flint-eyed, thin-shouldered fellow of nearly forty who spent much of his free time boasting about his experiences in the Mexican War. But Jeff marched "good," as the new sergeant ordered.

It was one week after the death and burial of Millholland.

As they plodded along, it seemed to Jeff that the town was slumbering and nobody in Tahlequah knew there was a war.

On the road winding southwest to Fort Gibson, a freighter's wagon, hooped over with gray canvas, crawled through the sand like a June bug. Adjusting his eyes to the distance, Jeff saw what looked like a mail hack crossing the Illinois River at Beane's Ford, the sun reflecting the tiny splashes of water kicked up by the wheels. A solitary Indian boy, humped forward in the saddle, jogged ponyback on a lonesome-looking trail that led toward the hills. Jeff wondered who he was and where he was going.

Jeff lengthened his stride to match the man ahead of him. Noah had told him their march had something to do with making a good impression on the Tahlequah people so that the hundreds of Cherokees who had been compelled to join the rebel army might want to come back to the Union side.

As the trim blue column tramped slowly into the outskirts and on to the town square, Jeff saw Indian people, mostly women and children but also some men, standing in their well-trimmed yards, curiosity and fear in their brown faces. Most of them were dressed like white people.

They looked like white people, too, and Jeff remembered what Joe Grayson had told him about the Cherokee mixed-bloods who governed the nation. They had two legislative houses elected by the people and a school system that surpassed that of many of the states. Colonel Weer had given strict orders that anybody caught stealing or looting private property would forfeit a month's pay and have to work thirty days on fortifications.

Jeff stood beneath a big elm tree on the town square, fanning himself with his cap. He enjoyed being in a big town again. The horses around the shady capitol square fought off swarms of dog gnats with their tails and pawed the plank fence to which they were tethered. People milled about, talking and visiting in musical, low-pitched Cherokee voices. There was the clank of boots on the board sidewalks, the creak and jingle of harness, the measured ringing of a blacksmith's anvil, the snarling of strange dogs meeting in the street, the mingled odor of fresh horse droppings and baking bread, and the whoop and laughter of children playing.

Jeff was assigned to a small escort that accompanied Captain Clardy and some of the Union officers. They wanted to find a house where meals might be procured. As they walked along the street, frightened faces watched them from around the edges of window curtains. Dogs walked up stiff-legged to accost Dixie, but she stayed close to Jeff's heels and paid no attention to any of them.

In the middle of town they approached a handsome log house shaded by several majestic sycamores. Obviously its owner was a man of considerable wealth. They turned into its ornate front gate with wrought-iron hinges and walked up a path of gray chat bordered by bushes of yellow roses. Jeff saw that the rafters of the house were of peeled pine poles held together with wooden pegs. Behind the property were slave houses and a barn.

Ignoring the property's magnificence, Clardy clumped boldly onto the wide front porch and, flanked by Jeff's patrol, rapped sharply with his knuckles on the heavy oaken door.

The door opened from the inside and revealed a girl, a very pretty girl. Her black sun-streaked hair was caught in a dark green bow. She was carrying a big white Persian cat which at the sight of Dixie began to swell up angrily like a peacock.

Jeff's mouth flopped open and he got a weak feeling in the pit of his stomach as though thousands of butterflies were beating their wings madly inside him. Although the girl's skin had a brownish cast, her complexion was lovelier than wild strawberries. Breathless, he wondered what any girl that pretty was doing in this far-off Indian town.

When she saw the blue-clad Union soldiers, the girl shrank

back quickly. Her small round mouth parted with surprise and displeasure.

"My officers and I are hungry," Clardy growled. His sly, nervous eyes darted past her into the house. "Order your servants to fix us some supper." As usual, his tone was surly and domineering.

The girl raised her oval chin a trifle and looked fearlessly back at him.

"Since you freed all the Negroes, we're not even cooking dinner for ourselves," she said. "We're all rebels—to the backbone." Proudly she gestured behind her. "My mother and two sisters live here. They all have husbands in the rebel army." Her voice was melodious and low-pitched.

Jeff saw that despite her hostility, she was a girl who went well with July, even a hot, drouth-stricken July. She was wearing a long cotton dress of light green and looked as fresh and clean as a green shrub after a rain.

Clardy's face purpled. "I'll brook none of your rebel impertinence," he roared in bullying tones. "Which will it be? Supper for us or must I burn your house down and set an example to the rest of this yappy Indian town?"

The girl didn't back up an inch.

"I've no doubt, sir, that if any white man would stoop to that sort of barbarism, you'd be completely capable of it," she said. Clardy stood on the porch sputtering helplessly.

A Union officer who wore the gold shoulder bars of a major on his blue dress coat stepped forward, smiling courteously.

"Firing the house won't be necessary, Captain, I'm sure." He faced the girl, sweeping off his black hat and bowing gracefully from the waist. "May I speak to your mother, please?" He was Major Thompson of the Ninth Wisconsin.

The girl's stormy brown eyes settled on the major. She said, coolly, "Wait here, please."

But as she started to withdraw, the big white cat in her

arms flattened his ears and began to moan threateningly way back in his throat. Jeff's dog Dixie, who had wandered up to the door, started calmly to follow the girl inside the rebel home, as though she had lived there all her life.

With an angry yowl, the cat jumped out of the girl's arms and landed on Dixie's back. Quickly he discovered he had overmatched himself. In an instant dog and cat swept past the girl and, vanishing into the dark interior, began a running battle through the house. With a little gasp of dismay, the girl ran after them.

Appalled, Jeff could hear the crash of china, the soprano screams and protestations of the women, the incessant barking and growling of Dixie, and the wrathful snarling of the cat. The soldiers on the porch were laughing uproariously.

Jeff stepped forward and looked imploringly at Major Thompson. He saluted. "Sir, that's my dog. May I go get her —before she tears the place up?"

The major nodded. Jeff darted inside and felt his dusty brogans sink into the deep pile of a rug. Looking quickly about, he discovered the room was elegantly furnished with armchairs and divans upholstered in blue. The combatants weren't there, but Jeff could tell they had been. A small candle stand with slender, tapered legs had been overturned. A tall spinning wheel, wound with orange yarn, lay on its side on the floor, still whirling round and round.

Jeff followed the uproar through a dining room and into the kitchen, where Dixie had cornered the cat atop a food cupboard. He snatched her up the quickest way he could, backward, her head behind him and her tail in front. Two other women, both young and well dressed, were chattering hysterically as they cringed along the wall. The girl was with them.

Jeff swept off his infantry cap. "Mam, I'm awfully sorry," he apologized, backing out of the room with Dixie under one arm. As the dog squirmed to free herself so she could renew the battle, her tail kept swinging around and swabbing Jeff in the mouth.

Like a statue of cold fury, the girl stood. Her eyes were blazing.

"You—you—Yankee!" she began, unable to find the words she wanted. "Get out!"

"Yes, mam," said Jeff. As he bore Dixie back through the elegant parlor, he saw lying on a table a large Bible bound in blue leather with the name "Levi Washbourne" engraved on it in silver. He blinked. He had never seen anything like this in Kansas. It seemed strange that he had to come clear to the Indian country to see a home as plush as this one. As he carried Dixie out the front door, her excited barking rang noisily through the halls.

Finally a young woman came to the door. She had the same proud lift of chin as the girl but looked older and seemed to have better control of her emotions. She told them that she was Mrs. Adair, an older sister. She looked pale and frightened.

Major Thompson swept off his hat and bowed. "I'm sorry to discommode you, mam, but my officers and I haven't dined today. Is there anybody here who could fix us some dinner?"

"There isn't any firewood," she answered. "We have plenty of food but no fuel."

The major told her that he would see that she got plenty of firewood. "And I'll post a guard around your premises to see that you aren't harmed," he promised, noting the uneasy look she gave the soldiers. He turned to Clardy.

"Captain, may I borrow your escort as wood procurers and also for temporary guard duty?"

Clardy had no reason for refusal. He nodded and turned toward Jeff. Jeff knew Clardy was going to order him to cut the wood. He hoped he would. He wasn't afraid of Clardy. He wasn't afraid of work, either. Besides, the work might give him a chance to see that pretty rebel girl again.

"Bussey, here, will cut your wood," Clardy said to the woman at the door. "And if you've any other odd jobs to do, like peelin' potatoes or emptyin' swill or diggin' stumps or diggin' graves, Bussey will be glad to do them, too. He's had lots of experience. Haven't you, Bussey?"

Jeff straightened, popped his heels together, and saluted briskly.

"Yes, sir." He didn't mind Clardy's abuse any more. While he was cutting the wood outside the town limits, he learned from a Negro passing by that Levi Washbourne was a captain in Stand Watie's Confederate Cherokee cavalry and that the girl was his sixteen-year-old daughter, Lucy.

Just before supper Jeff drove a wagon, heavily loaded with the chopped wood, up to the house. He knocked on the back door. The young woman who had identified herself as Mrs. Adair opened it a few inches. She carried a saucepan in one hand.

Jeff swept off his cap. "Mam, I've fetched the stovewood. Where would you like me to stack it?"

The woman seemed surprised at Jeff's kindness. She showed him where to put the wood in the yard.

"Mam," offered Jeff, "do you have a woodbox in the kitchen? If you want me to, I'll be glad to fill it for you." She hesitated, then nodded. When Jeff returned with his first armful, she showed him where to stack it. Two women with aprons tied about their waists were busily cooking supper for the officers. In an adjoining room he saw a big, heavy-legged dining table of oak spread with plates and silver. His jaw dropped. They ate in a different room than they cooked in.

Jeff could hear ham frying. He smelled what he thought were hot, mealy Irish potatoes roasting in a pan set in the fireplace ashes. He hadn't tasted a roasted Irish potato in months.

"Thank you, mam," he said, trying to hide his hunger as he

backed out of the house after filling the box. He hadn't seen the girl, although he knew she must be there.

Major Thompson, Clardy, and three other Union officers knocked on the front door. They were admitted. Jeff, on duty outside, could hear them talking and laughing. He heard the rattle of the crockery and the jingle of the silver. Later, when his nose caught the whiff of cigar smoke, he knew they had finished eating.

Glumly Jeff sat on the rock fence that ran around the property. He wondered if Lucy had helped serve them? For the first time in his life he envied the officers. They had the privilege of at least meeting her.

Corn, but he was hungry! Dad-gummed officers. It never occurred to them that their guard might be hungry, too.

Just before dusk the back door squeaked, and Lucy came out of the kitchen with a pail on her arm. Jeff's heart leaped happily. He guessed she had come to do the evening milking.

The rest of the soldiers who comprised the Union guard were lounging against the fence. When the girl walked by, they strained their necks and eyeballed her from head to toe.

One of them whistled seductively and catcalled, "Yuh know, I hain't hugged a gal fer so long I'm outa practice."

The girl looked uneasy. At first Jeff thought it was because of the men. Then he found out that wasn't the only reason.

With an assurance she apparently was far from feeling, she went to the barn, emerged with an armful of prairie hay, and dropped it awkwardly in a corner of the lot. Then she drove a brindle cow into the lot.

Jeff watched her with foreboding. Even before she sat down on the stool, he doubted she had ever milked a cow in her life. And when she sat down on the wrong side of the cow, he was sure of it.

A titter of amusement went up from the guard. The girl blushed scarlet. Jeff felt sorry for her, even if she was a rebel.

He got down off the fence and walked up to her. She saw the dog and recognized him.

As he drew near, Jeff felt dizzy. Again he had the peculiar butterfly feeling in the pit of his stomach. Dad gum! She was pretty as a basketful of red monkeys, twice as pretty as any girl he had ever seen before.

He took off his cap. For a fleeting moment he looked into large brown eyes that were fringed with the longest, blackest eyelashes he had ever seen.

"Mam, you're supposed to milk from the cow's right side, not her left. I've lived on a farm all my life. Why don't you let me milk her for you?"

Angrily she arose, grasping the bail of the empty bucket in her hand and drawing it back threateningly as though she were going to belt Jeff over the head.

"Get out or I'll call the major!" she breathed furiously. "Take your old Yankee dog and get out."

Jeff stopped dead in his tracks. "All right, mam. Only she's not a Yankee dog. She's a Confederate dog."

Back on the fence, his chin in his hands, he watched her gloomily. Corn! She was the sauciest girl he had ever seen. Why couldn't she forget the war long enough to let him help her milk the cow?

The rebel girl was dead game, even before an enemy audience. This time she began to milk from the correct side. The blue-clad guard applauded with handclaps and more cat-calls.

No matter how hard she worked, very little milk came from the cow's udder. Finally, after she had labored twenty minutes and had drawn about twenty teaspoons of milk, she went into the house, pursued by the jibes of the soldiers.

Vaulting the fence, Jeff walked into the stone smokehouse and found a small wooden pail with an upright stave as a handle. Although it looked clean, he drew fresh water from the

well and washed it. Then he milked the cow and, carrying
the milk to the back door of the house, he knocked. The door
was opened by a third Washbourne daughter.

"Mam, here's the rest of your milk," Jeff said.

The young woman was taken aback. She stared at the
piggin and the fresh, warm, bubbly milk in it.

"It's clean, mam," Jeff assured her. "I scrubbed the bucket
carefully in your smokehouse."

"We're very beholden to you," she told him and accepted
it. "We've always had slaves to do our milking and, now that
they're gone, my mother has been doing it. But she didn't
feel up to it tonight, so Lucy said she'd try."

She smiled a little and looked back over her shoulder at
Lucy, who was washing the dishes in a large gray porcelain
pan on the cupboard. Lucy blushed but didn't say anything.

"You look most too young to be in a war," the young woman
continued, more kindly. "You ought to be home with your
mother."

Now it was Jeff's turn to blush. His face flamed crimson.
His hands tightened on his blue cap. If all the women in the
country, both Union and rebel, kept telling him he looked
like a schoolboy, it must be true.

"How old are you?"

"Seventeen, mam," Jeff replied. What would Lucy Washbourne think of him now!

He smelled the odor of food in the big candle-lit kitchen. In
spite of all he could do, his eyes kept wandering to the cooking
fireplace of native rock where he saw several large, fluffy,
brown-topped biscuits languishing in an open Dutch oven. He
could tell from their height that they were sourdoughs, his
favorite back home.

Lucy Washbourne spoke from the cupboard. "Liz, maybe
he's hungry."

Astonished, Jeff could scarcely believe his ears. Lucy's

voice, if he had heard it correctly, was gentle, sympathetic, kind. He shot a grateful look at her, but she bit her lip and kept her eyes glued on the dishpan.

"How long has it been since you've dined?" Liz asked solicitously.

Jeff felt his insides trembling. He kept big-eyeing the biscuits.

"Mam—do you mean—how long since I've set down at table to a square meal?"

She nodded.

"About a year, mam."

Liz gave a little gasp of surprise. Stepping back, she looked around uncertainly at the other Washbourne women, as if hesitating to invite an enemy soldier into the kitchen where the family usually ate their meals. Jeff understood her reluctance. This was war. He was a Yankee soldier and might be shooting at her rebel husband tomorrow. She stood silent, her lips compressed. Jeff's heart almost stopped beating, he was so afraid she'd say no. But her natural instinct for hospitality triumphed.

She stepped back from the door. "Won't you come in? We've all had dinner. We ate after we served your officers. We have plenty left."

"Yes, *mam*," said Jeff enthusiastically. "Thank you, mam." He almost leaped inside, closing the door behind him.

It was a nice kitchen. Besides the wide fireplace, there were tall cupboards with glass doors and a large oak table covered with a red linen cloth. The chairs were of oak and had leather backs. The long walls had been sheathed in oak paneling and painted brown. Overhead, the rafters were stained blue with yellow undersides. He wished his mother could see it.

The food was good. As Jeff ate ravenously, the women busied themselves elsewhere, leaving him alone at the big table. But each time his glass of milk was empty, Lucy ap-

peared quietly at his elbow to refill it. She also replenished the
empty biscuit plate beside him and put two more roasted potatoes on his plate.

Jeff wanted to talk to her but he didn't know what to say.
He was afraid he might say the wrong thing.

He brushed the crumbs from his mouth and looked up at
her. "Mam, I'm sorry my dog disgraced herself this morning by
fighting with your cat. Was there a lot of damage in the house?"

Lucy's chin lifted indignantly. She didn't speak. Carrying
the pitcher back to the cupboard, she went on washing the
dishes. Jeff felt his ears reddening.

Miffed, he finished his meal and arose to leave. What was
the matter with her?

He thanked the woman named Liz. "Mam, may I give some
of those leftover scraps to my dog? She hasn't eaten all day."

She raked them into a paper sack. "Thank you for doing the
milking for Lucy," she said.

"I didn't do it for her, mam. I did it for the cow. It hurts a
cow not to be milked."

Chin up, he walked proudly out the back door. He didn't
want that rebel girl to think she could wipe her feet on
him. . . .

Weer's Union army didn't stay long in the Cherokee nation. The weather continued hot, the grass burned to a crisp,
and the supply train from Kansas was long overdue. Weer put
the army on half rations, without vegetables. Alarmed, most of
the officers wanted to return to Kansas. Weer not only opposed
them but became intoxicated and abusive.

Finally Colonel Salomon, the next ranking officer, arrested
Weer and took command. He marched most of the expedition,
including Jeff's company, back to Fort Scott.

Jeff had never seen such a sorry-looking array. The cavalry
looked the shabbiest of all. Forage was so scarce that when
the horses were picketed, they ate off each other's manes and
tails. Most of the strong little ponies of the Indian Home

Guard scouts were unshod and totally unfit for use after galloping over the rocky, flinty Cherokee land.

With the coming of winter, Jeff hoped he would be allowed
to go home on furlough. But the Department of Kansas had
other plans. They had decided upon a bold penetration of
Western Arkansas. Jeff's company was to be part of the in-
vading Union army.

Jeff didn't know it, but he was destined to fight in a real
shooting battle at last.

☆ 12

Battle of Prairie Grove

Rebels ahead!

Twelve miles south of Fayetteville, in northwestern Arkansas, Jeff and the Kansas Volunteers overtook the main
force of the enemy at the crossing of Illinois Creek. General
T. C. Hindman, the rebel commander, had the stronger position. His fourteen thousand rebels—mostly Arkansawyers,
Texans, and Missourians—were defending a heavily timbered
ridge known as Prairie Grove. The Union army was stationed
in open fields.

Suddenly they heard the booming of cannon.

John Chadwick's china-blue eyes were popping with fear.
"Hark!" he called nervously. "What's that?"

Oscar Earnshaw snorted in fright and blew his nose. "It ain't
duck hunters."

"Wish to God it was," quavered somebody else.

It was two o'clock. Jeff didn't know it was Sunday until he dug the tiny calendar memorandum out of his shirt pocket. December 7, 1862, it read. Impatiently he peered hard ahead into the timber held by the Confederates. All he could see was trees.

Bill Earle changed his rifle to his left hand and, lifting one foot, looked at it wearily.

"Ow!" he complained in his high, clear voice. "This blister's killin' me."

A recruit from Leavenworth raised his canteen with both hands and drank deeply. Bright drops of water ran down his smooth cheek.

"Darn," he gulped, coming up for air. "Our new commander sure likes these forced marches."

Bill Earle scowled at his sore foot. "He don't jest like 'em. He loves 'em. Twenty-five mile from Babcock to Cane Hill. Then twelve mile chasing that rebel general, Marmaduke, all over the Boston Mountains. Then fourteen more today on top of that. That's better'n fifty mile I've walked in the last three days. Back home, the fartherest I ever walked was from the back door to the barn. Shucks, I'm too tired to fight." He squinted disgustedly at his scuffed army brogans. Both soles were loose and flapping.

They had marched all night to reach the battleground. It had been a dark, cloudy night, too. Several times the new commander had halted the column to scratch a match on his saber guard so he could see his compass and set their course anew.

Although the calves of his legs felt heavy, Jeff hadn't minded the last fourteen-mile hitch in the warm, balmy weather. He liked the blue haze of the Arkansas mountain country.

He had even liked the quiet mountain shower they had passed through yesterday. They had seen it coming across the valley, the falling, lifting clouds wrapping the mountain's piny shoulders in gray shawls of rain while the thunder rolled and growled majestically. Unlike the rains in Kansas, there was no wind. Everything was so still that long before the rain struck the marching blue columns, Jeff could hear it whispering softly on the fallen leaves a quarter of a mile away as it approached. Wearing overcoats and slickers or covering themselves with blankets and squares of oilcloth, the infantry had taken the drenching like stock in the field. Afterward the smell of the wet pines was everywhere, and a small herd of cows, their clean-washed red and brindle sides gleaming in the bright sunshine, spread out over a roadside pasture.

Today the sun was shining, and Jeff could hardly wait for the fighting to start. For the twentieth time he checked the priming on his rifle and the cap box in his belt.

"What's the new commander's name?" he asked, curiously.

Earle snorted. "I don't know his name. I sure hope he knows somethin' about fightin'."

A tousle-headed private from Shawnee Mission looked apprehensively to the southeast, where the rumbling of the guns began to grow louder. "We'll soon find out if he does."

Noah, who had set type on newspapers and seemed always to know everything, eased the pack off his broad back with his left hand while still holding his rifle in his right. "His name's Blunt. He's a doctor from Maine. Used to be a sea captain before that. Moved out to Anderson County, Kansas, in 1856. Been practicing medicine at Greeley ever since."

A grizzled private from Minneola spat a brown spray of tobacco juice onto the tan prairie grass. "Gawsh!" he swore disgustedly. "Commanded by a bloody sawbones! What'll the politicians think of next?"

"Wonder if he's a foot doctor?" Bill Earle asked, hopefully.

The new sergeant glared belligerently at everybody. "Stow the gab!" he barked. "We're liable to be in action any minute now."

Pike waved one long arm in the direction of the Confederates. "Those fellows over there mean business. They think

they're fightin' for their homes, their wimmen, an' their kids.
If you don't think they're ready to take you apart, lissen to this.
It's a circular Hindman issued three days ago to every man
in his command. Our cavalry took 'em offa prisoners this
mornin'."

He drew a sheet of yellow paper from his blouse and thrust
it triumphantly into Noah's placid face. "Here, Babbitt. You
repeat it to 'em. I cain't read."

Planting his size twelves wide apart in the prairie grass,
Noah began slowly to read the rebel general's statement to his
soldiers:

"Remember that the enemy you engage has no feeling of
mercy or kindness toward you. His ranks are made up of Pin
Indians, free Negroes, Southern Tories, Kansas Jayhawkers
and hired Dutch cutthroats. These bloody ruffians have invaded your country, stolen and destroyed your property,
murdered your neighbors, outraged your women, driven your
children from their homes, and defiled the graves of your
kindred. If each man of you will do what I have here urged
upon you, we will entirely destroy them. We can do this; we
must do it; our country will be ruined if we fail. A just God
will strengthen our arms and give us a glorious victory."

The men were stunned. Jeff was wonderstruck. It was his
first contact with propaganda.

"Gosh, Noah," he blurted incredulously. "Is he talking
about us?"

Noah nodded soberly. "He shore is."

Now the rumbling of the cannon came from all around
them. Jeff was surprised that they were campaigning at all
in winter. Usually both armies seemed to have an unwritten
agreement that after the first frost each would go into winter
quarters and not molest the other until spring. Apparently
Blunt, their new commander, was an ignorant chap who had
not been schooled in the accepted military customs.

Jeff wiped an arm across his face. At that, he believed he

preferred campaigning in winter. Especially the clear winy winters of Western Arkansas. Their last commander, a general named Schofield, didn't believe in winter fighting. Noah had found a St. Louis newspaper in a fence corner while they were chasing Marmaduke. In it was a dispatch from Schofield's army correspondent saying, "The Army of the Frontier has fulfilled its mission and has gone into winter quarters near Springfield, Missouri. General Schofield is about to leave for St. Louis to recruit his health, which has been shattered by long and arduous duties in the field."

"Humph!" Noah grunted. "There's nothing wrong with Schofield's health. He probably went to St. Louis to try to get a promotion to major general."

From the woods ahead, a drumming of hoofbeats. A squadron of Union cavalry, wearing long gauntlets, came riding helter-skelter out of the trees. It looked as if they had been used roughly. Some had lost their hats and carbines, others had had their horses shot out from under them and were riding double. They had ridden into the timber, found the enemy, determined his position, drawn his fire. Now it was the infantry's job to go in and clean up, if it could.

Noah spat on the ground in disgust. "Buttermilk Rangers!" he said scornfully. Jeff didn't understand why Noah held the cavalry in such contempt.

Mitchell jeered the cavalry openly: "Better get on back to the rear, boys. Yous stirred up a fuss. We'll settle it for yous. Go on back to the rear and git yous some more buttermilk."

Jeff saw a tiny, circular puff of white smoke blossom above the trees. Then suddenly on the prairie some fifty yards in front of their line, a dash of dust, and something whizzed noisily over their heads, buzzing like a monster bee.

"Blam!"

Jeff dove flat on his stomach. He felt a painful jar as several of his comrades jumped in on top of him to escape the glancing rebel cannon ball.

"Boys, if I ain't flat enough, won't some o' you please jump on me and mash me flatter?" Bill Earle said weakly from the bottom of the pile.

"Git back into line!" Clardy roared sternly. "Eyes front! Stop your cowardly dodging! Any man leaving his station again will be shot!" With the flat of his sword, Clardy spanked a timid recruit in the seat of his pants and pushed another roughly into position.

Sheepishly they re-formed their line. Jeff felt his breathing quicken. He saw another tiny spiral of smoke appear above the tops of the trees. This time a charge of grape came flying overhead, screeching like forty locomotives. Again the men ducked instinctively, but this time only a few left the line.

"It's all right, boys," Jeff heard Bill giggle in his nervous tenor. "Just dodge the biggest of 'em."

Jeff felt a hysterical urge to laugh but discovered that he couldn't. For some strange reason, his throat had gone dry as a bone. The insides of his palms itched, and he could hear his pulse pounding. Again he checked the load in his rifle and was angry at himself. He knew there was nothing wrong with the rifle load.

Furious because he couldn't control his odd behavior, he clenched his jaws and shook his head vigorously. He had looked forward so long to his first battle. And now that the long-awaited moment had finally come, he discovered that some queer species of paralysis had gripped his legs. His chest felt heavy, as if a blacksmith's anvil was weighing it down. It was hard for him to breathe.

Noah looked at him anxiously. "What's the matter, youngster?"

Jeff licked his lips and swallowed once. Perplexed, he shook his brown head. "I don't know. My stomach feels bashful." Embarrassed, he looked around, hoping nobody would get the wrong idea and impute this accursed nervousness to cowardice. He was fiercely determined not to disgrace his family or his county.

Suddenly the Union drums began to roll, loudly and ominously. The noise was startling. Jeff's lips flattened on his teeth. He squinted down the line of infantry at the nearest drummer boy. To his surprise, he saw Jimmy Lear. Then Jeff remembered that there were Missouri troops in action. General Herron's two divisions had marched gallantly more than one hundred miles from Wilson's Creek, Missouri, to support them. Varnished drumsticks whirring in his hands, Jimmy was staring sternly straight ahead and stepping lightly up and down as his feet marked the time, a look of concentrated duty on his boyish face.

"Flam-a-dee-dee-dee! Flam-a-dee-dee-dee!" rang the drums weirdly and vibrantly. Jeff stretched his neck, trying to catch Jimmy's eye, so he could wave at him. But Jimmy was keeping his mind on his business.

"Fall in!"

Obediently Jeff backed into line, dressing up on Noah's tall form next to him. A spiteful crackle of rifle fire, punctuated by the deeper roar of cannon, broke suddenly from the woods. Now the stinking, acrid odor of gunpowder was on the air. A rebel bombshell screeched over their heads, hunting for them. Jeff imagined he could hear it say, "Where-is-yuh, where-is-yuh, where-is-yuh—booooom!"

He began to hear tiny thuds here and there in the ground. They reminded him of the first, isolated dropping of hailstones during a spring storm on the Kansas prairies. Tardily he realized they were rebel rifle bullets.

"Fix bayonets!" Mechanically Jeff groped for the scabbard at his belt. Fingers shaking, he managed to clamp the long knife over the muzzle of his rifle. He shot a quick look at Noah. It was good to have Noah next to him.

"Be ready, youngster! We're goin' in after 'em!" Noah

yelled. Jeff pulled a couple of long breaths and felt the goose bumps rising on his arms.

He heard Clardy cursing. Big Jake Lonegan had thrown down his musket and run in terror to the rear. Jeff felt a powerful urge to follow him. He could hear the officers shouting threats, too, but they failed to stop the big sergeant or even to slow him down.

"Eyes front!" bellowed Clardy. "Any man leaving his position will be shot!"

Swallowing nervously, Jeff found he could not keep his thoughts on the coming battle. Oddly, they kept wandering back to Linn County. It was a Sunday afternoon, and his family had probably just returned from church in the rock mission at Sugar Mound. He could see his mother, busy over her fireplace ovens, cooking the Sunday dinner, with Bess and Mary both helping, each careful not to soil the Sunday dresses they had not yet taken off. He could see his father unhitching Jack and Beck from the buckboard and Ring crouching mischievously by the gooseberry bushes, waiting to give the mules a run when they were liberated through the corral gate.

Tears stung Jeff's eyes. Angry at himself for showing emotion, he winked them off. What in the world was the matter with him? The rebel fire grew hotter. What funny music the rebel Minie balls made. Some of them mewed like kittens. Others hummed like angry hornets or whined like ricocheting nails.

A soldier on Jeff's right went down with a strangled moan, clutching and raking at his stomach. Jeff began to pray hard, straight from the heart. He hadn't dreamed that war was anything like this. He vowed that if by some miracle he came out alive, he would always go to church thereafter.

"Forward march!" Jeff barely heard the command above the battle's din. But every man obeyed. Bayoneted muskets carried at the ready, they strode blindly forward to whatever fate awaited them. Angrily Jeff thought of how little control a soldier in the ranks had over his own destiny.

It was a soldier's business to starve to death, take the guff from the officers, march all night, and be shot to pieces in the daytime without ever opening his mouth in protest. Suddenly he felt a violent anger. The officers had him, coming or going. He was like the farmer's dog trotting to town beneath his master's wagon. If he stood and fought, the town dogs all ganged him and whipped the whey out of him. If he turned and ran for home, they chewed his tail from behind. Either way they had him.

Bullets zipped all about them. Jeff wondered how it felt to be hit by a musket ball; whether it stung or whether it burned. He wondered why their own artillery hadn't begun shooting.

Looking to both right and left, he found himself part of a long blue line of soldiers moving at a quick walk toward the woods ahead. Men all around him were taking off their coats and dropping them on the prairie. Jeff peeled off his, flung it to the ground and felt a little better. He wouldn't need it anyhow because he expected to be killed.

"Flam-a-dee! Flam-a-dee! Flam-a-dee-dee!" rattled the drums, sounding their doleful call to death. They entered the woods. A wounded horse screamed in agony. Stifling an impulse to turn and run, he clenched his teeth and kept advancing, dreading what lay ahead because he couldn't see it, nor imagine what it was like.

Although it was December, sweat ran down the tip of his nose. The winter sun gleamed brightly off his steel bayonet.

Noah, tall, gaunt, looking grim as death, was walking in a low crouch, his bayonet-tipped musket held in front of him. Jeff felt a little better. Just being close to Noah helped. The presence of the other men helped, too.

He stumbled over a fallen log but kept going. His mind

was sharp now. He began to recall all the mean things he had ever done and how he might never have time to atone for them. Life was running out on him. He wasn't ready to die. He didn't want to be rushed into it. He needed more time to think about it. After all, a person died just once. Anybody who let himself get killed was just plain stupid. The world was a wonderful place to live. No matter how revered he was in life, a dead person was so completely out of things. Even his own relatives soon forgot him and quickly reshaped their lives without him.

"Ba-loom! Ba-loom!"

A sudden rush of air passed overhead, and Jeff's heart leaped thankfully. Casting a startled look back over his shoulder, he saw streaks of orange-gold flame burst from Blunt's forward guns as the Union batteries, elevating their cannon, fired over the heads of their infantry, using two-second fuses. For the first time he appreciated how dependent the infantry and artillery were upon each other.

"Charge bayonets!"

With a wild yell the long blue line leaped forward. Sprinting at breakneck speed, Jeff yelled at the top of his lungs, too. Their little red and white striped flag with the blue patch in the corner was going along with them at a jerky motion. There was a steady rattle of musket fire ahead. Gaps were torn in the line by the rebel volleys. They began to run through clouds of sulphurous smoke. It stank and made his eyes smart.

Thud! Down went a man at Jeff's elbow. *Thud! Thud!* Men were dropping all around him.

Now they had reached the fringe of the timber and were stumbling through the brush. *Thud! Thud! Thud!* Jeff saw comrade after comrade pitch to the ground, but Noah was still at his right elbow, panting and grunting as he plowed laboriously through the greenbrier and the shinnery.

With mounting rage Jeff wondered when they would be

allowed to fire, retaliating to the volleys that were mowing them down like oat stalks before the sickle. He felt a wild impulse to fire anyhow.

Still running, he looked ahead through the trees, and there the rebels were, a long line of men clad in mingled brown and gray, partly obscured by powder smoke. Wearing tan campaign hats, they were standing shoulder to shoulder, shooting muskets held at face level. When the advancing Union line saw them, they pulled up and raised their guns for a volley.

"Fire!"

From one end of the long blue line to the other, red spouts of flame leaped from the bayonet-tipped muskets of the Kansas Volunteers. As his finger tightened on the trigger, and the gun recoiled against his shoulder with the first shot, Jeff felt a vast relief.

With both armies now at full fire power, he was conscious only of the awful thunderclap of battle. There were no clear thoughts in his head. Breathless, he thought neither of victory nor defeat but rather that the end of the world was coming and he was only a small, unimportant part of this tremendous spectacle that was a swift prelude to it.

A rebel bullet sheared off a branch a yard away. Jeff dove to his knees, furious at the stupidity of both armies standing in line and shooting at one another like duelists at ten paces. On his right, he saw Noah firing carefully off one knee. That still wasn't low enough for Jeff.

Flat on his belly, he began firing as fast as he could. Loading a single-shot musket was an intricate operation. Rolling over on his back, he bit off the end of the paper cartridge, thrust it in the gun, poured powder into the muzzle, withdrew his iron ramrod from the groove beneath the barrel, and rammed the charge and the bullet down the barrel. Then he pulled the hammer back with his thumb and stuck a percussion cap on the nipple. After that, all he had to do was draw a bead on the enemy and press the trigger. With the firing of the shot, smoke and fire from the black gunpowder belched into his face, and then he had the whole thing to do over.

Each time he fired, Jeff scrambled to his feet, ran forward a few steps, then dropped again to reload. He bit the cartridges off so fast that he swallowed some of the spilled powder. It tasted bitter. He wanted to rinse his mouth. But he couldn't. His canteen had been full of good, cold Arkansas spring water but he had foolishly thrown it away with his coat. Hot with battle now, he felt only that he wanted to encounter the worst and get it over as quickly as possible.

Then with shrill yells and screams and do-or-die expressions, they met the rebels hand-to-hand in the dark gloom of the trees, using clubbed muskets, fists, knives, stones, anything they could get hold of. Jeff hurled himself upon a big fellow in brown, shrieking at the top of his lungs and thrusting upward with his bayonet.

He felt a sharp stab of pain across the knuckles of his left hand as his opponent parried the thrust with such force that both muskets were knocked to the ground.

Scowling, the rebel crouched to recover his musket. Jeff rushed him fiercely, tackling him by the legs. As the man fell, he snatched a long, wicked hunting knife from his belt and tried to slash his way free. He began kicking violently. Jeff dodged the knife and tried with all his might to hang on to the rebel's legs.

Suddenly his view was blocked by a blue pant leg as somebody stepped close to his face. He looked up in time to see his benefactor swing his rifle downward, like an ax.

Clonk! The sound reminded him of the squashing noise a melon makes when it is dropped onto a stone walk. The thrashing legs in his grasp trembled violently and grew still.

"On your feet, youngster!"

Noah, his brown face looking unnaturally ferocious in the gray gloom, reached down and, with one mighty jerk, lifted Jeff to a standing position. His mouth was smeared with black powder, as though he had been eating it. As Jeff bent over to pick up his musket, he saw the brown line of rebels retreating through the woods, loading as they backed away.

"Wait!" Noah yelled hoarsely, glancing through the smoke at his right. A slow panic blossomed in his powder-begrimed countenance. "Lookie thar! Millions of 'em!"

Jeff looked, and his jaw fell open with alarm. An entire rebel regiment, the men swarming like ants, had completely turned the right anchor of the Union line and, boiling out upon the prairie, was threatening to outflank them. They were after a Federal artillery unit that had just arrived and was running up its long black guns.

The rebels were tearing the top logs off a rail fence so they could clamber over, charge the Union guns, and capture them.

"Let's go help 'em!" Noah proposed. Jeff didn't think much of the idea but he did not hesitate. By that time he would have followed Noah anywhere.

Noah ran with long awkward strides, Jeff at his heels. A tall battery lieutenant with red stripes on his tattered blue pants and tiny crossed cannons on his cap lumbered awkwardly to meet them. He cast frantic looks over his shoulder at the rebels forming behind the rail fence, only three hundred yards away.

"Will you fellows help us?" he pleaded. "My cannoneer deserted. One of our crews is short-handed."

Quickly he showed Jeff how to carry the heavy tin cans of canister, each charged with eighty-five round lead balls weighing an ounce, from the ammunition wagon to the guns, which were muzzle-loading Parrots on two wheels. It never occurred to Jeff that if a rebel shell made a direct hit upon the ammo wagon, they would all be blown to Kingdom Come. A long ram with a sheepskin swab on the end was thrust hurriedly into Noah's hands.

Hoofbeats thudded behind them. A stubby, scowling, thick-set man, with a heavy black mustache and small beardlet, rode up on a bay horse, accompanied by several Federal cavalrymen. He took one look at the menacing rebel movements, then began barking orders in a raspy growl. Noah stole one sharp glance at him.

"That's Blunt," he told Jeff. "That must be his personal staff an' bodyguard with him."

The Greeley doctor seemed to know his business. Quickly he moved the battery by right flank, reforming it until it faced the oncoming Confederates. Then he dismounted his bodyguard and staff, forming them in protective support to the battery.

"In battery action left—load with canister! Fire at will!" roared Blunt.

The lieutenant set off the brass gun by dealing the pin in the touch hole a clout with the butt of his pistol. It seemed to jump two feet into the air.

"Balooie!" thundered the gun. "Balooie! Balooie! Balooie!" thundered companion pieces nearby. Jeff felt a painful pressure on his eardrums and was nearly knocked off his feet by the concussion. Doggedly he tried to ignore the awful noise and concentrate on his new job.

"Ram her!" the tall lieutenant shouted, frowning fiercely. Noah leaped forward, thrust his ram in the gun's muzzle, and with one scythelike sweep of his long arm, quickly completed the operation.

"Swab her!" the lieutenant roared. Noah stuck the sheepskin end of his ram into a box of water and again thrust it down the gun's maw, cooling it. Now the lieutenant fixed his compelling eyes upon Jeff.

"Load her!" he yelled. Jeff ran to the gun, pushed home his cartridge can, and jumped back. Again the tall lieutenant stepped forward and swung his pistol butt.

"Balooie!" Now the guns were firing so rapidly, and the ground was shaking so badly, that Jeff had to stand on tiptoe.

He couldn't take the terrible concussion flat-footed. His ears were throbbing from the continual roar. The black smoke from the cannon drifted everywhere, exuding a sour stench.

Jeff heard a shriek of horror and saw that one Southern shell had wiped out a complete Federal battery unit. One man had both legs sheared off below the knee. He was yelling at the top of his lungs with agony. Jeff knew the rebel sharpshooters had moved up. Deadly marksmen, they were picking off the Union gunners one by one.

Rebel Minie balls began to pepper around them, but Jeff kept feeding canister into the big gun. He saw an enemy ball brush off the lieutenant's cap. Other balls skipped noisily off the barrels and wheels of the cannon. The battery horses whinnied in terror. General Blunt and his staff officers moved in closer, firing at the rebel sharpshooters. The noise of the cannonading was so great that each time Noah completed his swabbing duty, he would scamper away several yards and crouch in the brush, a finger stuck into each ear. But he always returned to the gun.

Jeff shot a worried look at the advancing rebels and saw that they were wavering. Shoulder to shoulder, six and seven men deep, they were a target the Union battery couldn't miss. The rebel dead and wounded were lying in long, still swaths. The woods behind them were ablaze with fire.

"Alf!" somebody shouted to the tall lieutenant.

Something was wrong with the off-side wheel-driver of the near-side gun, an Indian with a smooth face and long black hair sticking out from under his campaign hat. There was a puzzled, vacant stare in his black eyes. Without saying a word, he sat down weakly. Reaching behind him, he placed his hand on the ground and lay down as quietly as though he were going to sleep. The swing driver next to him went coolly to his side and examined him. Straightening up, he turned both thumbs down expressively. Jeff knew the man was dead.

Suddenly the Southern fire slackened. Jeff was relieved to

see the rebels falling back into the woods. The tall lieutenant, his brown hair bared to the breeze, swung his guns around on the Confederate artillery and quickly got the range. After ordering half a dozen more rounds fired, he waved both long arms, a jubilant smile on his face.

"Cease firing!" he shouted and cocked his head, listening. The rebel batteries did not answer. All he heard was the rattle of the Confederate gun carriages retreating over the rocky ridges. Everywhere the fighting had stopped.

Jeff was surprised to see the sun sinking in a welter of purple clouds. It was dusk. What had seemed to him like an hour and a half had in reality been the whole of the afternoon.

His dirty face beaming, the lieutenant asked for Jeff's and Noah's names, scribbled them on a dirty piece of cartridge paper, and thanked them profusely. He said proudly, "We fought 'em flank an' rear an' licked 'em ever' clatter."

Dazed, Jeff sank down onto the grass. Miraculously he was still alive. His ears still rang from the battle din. His eyes were red and smarting from the dust and the cannon smoke. His knuckles ached from his bout with the big rebel infantryman in the woods. He felt indescribably tired and dirty.

From all around he could hear the pleading moans and cries of the wounded as the ambulances of both armies gathered up the worst hurt. Already burial details, hoisting little white flags on sticks, were digging long trenches in the flinty, clay soil. Jeff was shocked at the rough, indifferent manner in which the dead were rolled into the trenches, and the clay and gravel shoveled on top of them.

Noah towered over him like a tall wraith, his brown eyes grave.

"Well, youngster. You joined up to fight in battle. Now that you've been in one, how'ja like it?"

Jeff raised an ashen face and shook his head positively. "Noah, anybody that ever joins anything is crazy. I'll lay in the woods until the moss grows on my back a foot long before

I'll ever join anything again." He felt that being alive was the biggest miracle in the world.

Thirsty, they began walking, looking for water.

It seemed that everybody else was thirsty, too. Soon they came to a little creek thronged on both sides by ragged, exhausted men in blue. Men and horses were drinking thirstily, side by side. There were so many men that soon they stopped the creek from running as they tried to scoop the muddy water into their mouths. Jeff and Noah decided to wait until morning.

Dark was falling. It was growing colder, too. Now they were sorry they had thrown away their coats. Union soldiers were breaking up fence rails to feed their fires. The firelight flared brightly in the soft Arkansas dusk. At the rate the rails were disappearing, Jeff knew the entire fence would be gone before midnight.

"I'm hungry," Noah said, "but the commissary wagons probably won't be here until morning. Guess we better fergit about food and find us a place to sleep."

Jeff nodded dully. He was dead tired all over. He was hungry and thirsty, too, but his fatigue overbalanced everything else. He looked up. There were still a few streaks of lilac in the western sky.

Finally they found a strawstack. Burrowing into it, they went quickly to sleep, lying close together, spoon fashion, for warmth.

☆ 13

Expedition to Van Buren

Jeff lay on his back in the long grass, one army blanket under him and another over him. It was pleasant basking in the Arkansas sunshine. Bone-tired, he felt as if he never wanted to get up. The ridge broke the breeze, and he could feel the sun's rays warming him through the blanket. It felt as though somebody were stroking the outside of the blanket with a hot iron.

After sleeping all night in the haystack, Jeff and Noah had walked fourteen miles without any breakfast before they reached Rhea's Mills. There they found Blunt's baggage trains and mess wagons awaiting them. Gratefully they devoured the hot coffee, fried salt horse, and cold hardtack, and had their lost equipment resupplied by the quartermaster. Then they flopped down in the warm December sun. Jeff would have liked a bath but he was too tired to strip off his sour clothing.

He lay in a comfortable stupor, reviewing with awe the battle he had survived. Among the dead were two men he knew from Wyandotte and also Spruce Baird, the crusty little sergeant who had commanded the confiscation detail that had raided the McComas home.

Baird had been hit in the side by an exploding rebel bombshell. They had buried him on the battlefield. Using the bottom of a stew kettle for a desk, Noah was writing the sad tidings to Baird's family. He sat hunched over in the sun, a blanket draped about his broad shoulders.

Jeff felt a twinge of pain in his left hand. Beneath his fingernails, blue with dirt, the bruised knuckles were swollen frightfully. He had heated water in a stew kettle and soaked them, but the pain was still there. Jeff was thankful to be alive; his puffed hand seemed of small importance. He thought Rhea's Mills the most peaceful spot he had ever seen.

A blue mountain stream, tumbling over a ledge of greenish moss-grown rocks, rushed through a log flume onto a large wooden water wheel. Revolving slowly with a musical swish and creak, the wheel furnished the power for the nearby mill. The mill itself was a weather-beaten edifice of hand-hewn boards. Its roof sagged crazily. The miller's cottage and a country store stood nearby on a gently sloping hillside. Jeff could hear the redbirds whistling sharply from the tall black walnut trees. It sounded as if they were saying, "Ker-soop! Ker-soop! Ker-soop!" Sighing with pleasure, he lay back down, wishing they could spend the entire winter there.

Instead they stayed only nine days. Blunt was still acting as though he had never heard of winter quarters. His scouts informed him that General Hindman and his defeated rebel force were camped at Van Buren, forty miles southward. He and General Herron decided to take eight thousand picked infantry, cavalry and artillery, cross the mountains in two columns and attack the Southern forces before they could have time to prepare defensive fieldworks.

The day before the army left Rhea's Mills, Jeff was surprised to hear his name called while the company was lined up at a morning inspection. Noah's name was called too. Obediently each took two steps forward and saluted. With a measured stamping of feet on the drill ground, half a dozen officers approached. Out of the corner of one eye, Jeff spied Clardy among them. Recoiling, he felt his insides tighten. What had he done now?

The tramping stopped. A big man with black whiskers and two curved rows of brass buttons on the front of his blue dress coat, ambled up to Jeff and Noah. He was short and heavyset, with a thick neck and sloping shoulders. He walked with a roll, swaying his hips and planting his feet carefully, like a sea captain. In one hairy hand he carried a piece of paper. Everybody saluted. Then Jeff recognized General Blunt. Dumfounded, he wondered what it was all about.

In a bass voice sonorous as a bell, Blunt began reading from the document in his hand: ". . . for gallantry beyond the call of duty . . . distinguished themselves conspicuously at the risk of life . . . voluntarily assisted a battery that was hard pressed, although it was their first experience with artillery and they had already participated intrepidly in the infantry charge . . . the Medal of Honor, presented in the name of Congress." As the general continued reading, Jeff watched with fascination the small beardlet beneath his lower lip bob up and down.

Then the general stepped so close that Jeff could smell the pomade on his thick black hair. Leaning forward, he passed a ribbon around Jeff's neck and underneath his collar. Suspended from the ribbon was a tiny piece of red, white, and blue fabric. And dangling from the fabric was a shiny bronze star and eagle that flashed more brilliantly in the sunshine than even the general's gold shoulder bars.

Noah got one, too. Just as Jeff began to realize that he and Noah were being decorated, the general was shaking hands stiffly with each of them.

Jeff couldn't hide the embarrassment and unbelief in his face. Somebody had made a mistake. He hadn't done anything in the battle but follow Noah. If this was the way the army handed out decorations, then something was wrong with the system.

"Shoot, General," Jeff blurted in protest, "all we did was load her and swab her."

He looked at Noah for confirmation. But Noah, usually the most articulate man in the company, was strangely tongue-tied. He just stood there, ramrod stiff, staring straight ahead, his long neck pink as a peony.

Several of the officers looked displeased at Jeff's boldness. Blunt smiled faintly behind his heavy black mustache.

"Your name is Bussey?"

"Jefferson Davis Bussey, sir," corrected Jeff in a loud, clear voice, and waited for his usual reprimand. But Blunt only looked at him curiously and turned away.

Later Jeff wondered how the general knew who they were. As usual, Noah had the answer. "Remember the tall artillery lieutenant that axed us our names soon as the battle ended?" Jeff nodded.

On the next day, which was Christmas, Jeff's company began marching southward. Meanwhile the warmish weather changed. It grew much colder. The wind blew from the north and the sky was heavily overcast.

At noon they reached Cane Hill, where a month earlier a battle had been fought. They were told there would be a short rest and that they might visit the rebel hospital, if they wished.

Jeff looked about him with dazed wonder. War had made a shambles of the quiet little college town. Homes were looted and laid waste, outbuildings burned, stables pulled down, fences destroyed, shrubbery and fruit trees ruined. Dead domestic animals lay in the streets, stinking up the scene. Jeff wondered how the inhabitants bore the awful stench. The whole town was one vast hospital. Most of the wounded were concentrated in the Methodist church.

As Jeff entered the church, rain began pelting the roof overhead. The wooden pews had been carried outside to make room for the rebel wounded, and his nostrils caught the sickening odor of morphine. The cots of the wounded had been placed in a long line the length of the building. Their whiskery faces were contorted with pain. Jeff heard their smothered groans and wanted to talk to them, but something restrained him, something hard and inflexible as iron. These men were his enemies.

They belonged to the side that had tried to take his father's life. They had begun the war, killed Pete Millholland and wounded Ford Ivey so badly that his leg had to be amputated. Tight-lipped and silent, he moved slowly and cautiously about the straw-strewn floor, looking with horror at what he saw and marveling again and again at the divine Providence that had enabled him to survive the battle and escape such a terrible fate.

A French harp moaned from somewhere within the dark gloom, playing the same dreary tune over and over, until a long, heart-wrenching cry echoed through the church. Then it fell silent. Overhead the rain swelled from a patter to a deluge.

A doctor carrying a small surgical valise of reddish-brown leather bent wearily over the last bed in the ward. Jeff paused, peering through the dim light. A Sister of Mercy, her gray gown brown-stained and disheveled, stood near the doctor, ready to assist him.

Seeing Jeff's blue uniform, she looked from him to the patient on the cot.

"He's just a lad but he's going to die," she said in a low voice to Jeff. "He's one of your own bluecoat boys. Got run over by a caisson at Prairie Grove. It broke both his legs and hurt him internally. He's barely conscious."

Jeff looked pityingly at the patient. Then he caught his breath with surprise. The boy on the cot was Jimmy Lear!

With rough, well-meant kindness, the tired doctor was saying, "Jimmy, you are very badly hurt and will have to die. It's impossible for us to do anything more for you."

Jimmy's big blue eyes blinked with shock as he read in the doctor's face the certainty of his going. Jeff never forgot that look. Of all the poignant expressions he would see on men's faces during the war, none matched the desperate, cheated look of this young Missouri lad who had just been told his life on earth was ebbing.

Jimmy mumbled, "Doctor, I don't want to die. I'm not ready to die." There was a look of wild frustration on his youthful, pallid face, flushed with fever.

Jeff stepped forward, grasping both of Jimmy's hands in his own. "Jimmy, it's me. Jeff. Don't you recognize me?"

The boy peered at Jeff, his breath coming in short, uneven gasps. Then a faint, glad flicker of recognition lit up his eyes.

"Jeffy," he murmured, "don't leave me. I don't want to die."

Jeff felt tears stinging his own eyes.

"Jimmy, I'd help you if I could. I don't know what to do for you." Beseechingly he looked up at the Sister of Mercy, his eyes pleading for some slight sign of encouragement. But she shook her head slowly. Then she and the doctor moved on to care for the other men.

"Pray for me, Jeffy," Jimmy said.

Jeff swallowed, overcome with grief. "Jimmy, do you know who Jesus is?"

Jimmy shook his curly black head faintly. "No. Who is he?"

"Jimmy, only Jesus is able to save you."

"Well, where is he?" Jimmy whispered, looking very tired. Jeff told him as best he could. Jimmy listened silently, then stared reflectively at the dull gray wall.

"I wouldn't mind leavin' if I could jest come back sometime," he said.

"Jimmy, what's your mother's name and where does she live? I'll write to her."

"She's dead. So's my father. I ain't got no kinfolks."

Jeff felt an overwhelming compassion and sympathy. He reached down and smoothed Jimmy's hair. His skin felt hot and sweaty to the touch.

The doctor came back and gave Jimmy a strong opiate. His eyes fluttered sleepily.

"Jeffy," Jimmy whispered, "lean over." Jeff did, his ear close to Jimmy's mouth.

"Jeffy, my new drum's under the bed. You can have it when I die. Treat it good, Jeffy. Always keep it in a dry place so the vellum head will stay tight."

Jeff nodded. Blinking, he tried to swallow the lump in his throat. He remembered that Jimmy's drum was his dearest possession. He looked out a nearby window and saw snow-flakes sifting down thickly. The Arkansas weather couldn't seem to make up its mind.

Jimmy stirred restlessly, a frown of pain on his boyish face. "I wouldn't mind leaving, Jeff, if I could jest come back some-time," he said again. "But my father and mother ain't never come back. None of my relatives or friends that's died has ever come back, either—or writ any letters back—or sent any word."

A shadow fell across the bed. "Time's up, Bussey!" some-body barked gruffly. Jeff looked up. It was Sergeant Pike.

"I'll hurry, Sergeant."

The Sergeant moved off.

A shaft of winter sunshine, clean and warm, fell across Jimmy's rude coverlet, then faded away. A sudden gust of wind shook the old church. Jeff talked a minute to the Sister of Mercy. She promised to keep Jimmy's drum for Jeff until he returned from Van Buren. He felt awful about leaving. He wished with all his heart that he could stay.

"Jeff, I don't wanta die while I'm asleep. Hold up my hand so Jesus will see it when he comes," Jimmy murmured feebly.

Jeff propped his hand up with the bedclothing as best he could, and sobbing softly to himself, tiptoed silently out of the church.

The march to Van Buren was miserable. How awful it must be to die when you are only fifteen years old. Every time he thought of Jimmy, Jeff felt as if something was pinching his throat. His eyes became so misty that twice he stepped in road-side puddles and felt the icy water rise in his brogans and wet his socks. Darkness was descending on the land. There was still snow on the north sides of the mountains. Thin sheets of ice were forming on the puddles in the road.

He pulled up the collar on his long coat and tried to walk around the puddles. As usual, it didn't look good for the infantry. However, as they kept moving southward, there was less and less snow until soon it had all disappeared and the roads became firmer and smoother. They marched until midnight, rested until dawn, and after a breakfast of hot coffee, cold bacon and the hated hardtack, began walking again.

But now a new species of torture awaited them. About ten o'clock in the morning they struck the head of Cove Creek. The stream grew wider and deeper as the snow melting in the mountains emptied hundreds of noisy rivulets into it, and meandered in so many loops and curves that the road crossed it thirty-seven times.

The first time they forded it, the water was only ankle-deep and they ran through it with loud whoops. Then it got deeper, and their pants were soaked a little higher. Soon it was belly-deep on the horses. That was fine for the cavalry but tough on the infantry. Holding their muskets and packs shoulder-high, the men plunged into the icy, milk-hued water up to their armpits.

As an ambulance with Clardy aboard crossed a ford, lurching, bumping, and floating, the driver cracking his whip and yelling shrilly at the swimming mules, Bill Earle grasped an iron rail on the rear, hoping to be towed across the stream.

Snarling, Clardy brought his heel down hard on Bill's hand. Uttering a cry of pain, Bill released his grip on the rail and with a big splash disappeared beneath the swift water. When he bobbed up a few feet downstream without his cap, his wet blond hair plastered to his head, Jeff plunged in after him, extending his musket at arm's length. Clasping the barrel tightly, Bill was towed to shore, his face blue with cold, his teeth chattering as he cursed Clardy with every breath he drew.

Jeff was surprised how well the infantry bore the frequent wettings. It was amazing how much you could stand when you had to. The constant marching with the wind to their backs kept them from growing chilled. They marched until ten o'clock that night, then built great log fires on the bank to dry their wet clothing. The bugles sounded reveille at three o'clock next morning, and after a breakfast of dried peas and hot coffee, they resumed the punishing trek. They plodded through the noon hour without food. The valley had widened now, and the road crossed the creek less often. Hunger was their main discomfort.

"I'm so famished I'm gut-shrunk," Stuart Mitchell confessed, weakly.

Without breaking stride, Bill Earle took a long pull from his canteen. Smacking his lips, he growled, "Dried peas for breakfust an' water fer dinner. I guess I'll jest swell up fer supper." Soon they heard cannonading ahead. Jeff figured the Union cavalry and battery ahead must be encountering rebels.

Half an hour later they came to the top of a high bluff overlooking the Arkansas River.

"Lookie thar!" somebody sputtered in awe. Below them a town of considerable size sprawled at the foot of the bluff on their side of the river. Jeff looked inquiringly at Noah.

"Van Buren?"

Noah nodded. "Must be."

Jeff sighed wearily. They had walked forty miles to reach it. Even if they took it, what would they have accomplished?

He was impressed by how far he could see from the top of the bluff. The wide river stretched away for miles. Beyond it, the brown woods dominated the landscape, growing uphill toward a range of blue mountains in the distance. Jeff could see the sun's rays slanting obliquely off the distant mountain peaks. Union cannon were booming. Across the sandy river half a mile away, a regiment of rebel infantry fled the city, scurrying for safety beneath a belt of cottonwood trees. Van Buren was theirs.

They marched into it down a wide road gullied by recent rains. Orders were passed along the line to stop talking, brace up, and present a soldierly appearance. Jeff was proud of how trim and orderly the army looked despite its hardships. The guidons were fluttering, and flags of the infantry and the battery were unfurled. As the long blue lines entered the streets of the rebel town in platoon formation, the band struck up "The Star-Spangled Banner."

Hearing the stirring music, Jeff was prouder than ever. He guessed that starving and fighting all day and being marched to death all night was what made a good soldier out of you.

"Let's show 'em what a real army looks like," Bill Earle challenged, straightening his body.

"Yeah, an' a winnin' army," growled Stuart Mitchell, picking up his big, muddy feet.

"Yeah, and a wet one," said Jeff, throwing back his shoulders. As they swung smartly into town, their ragged shoes smacking the ground in unison with the rattle of parade drums, Jeff heard people along the sidewalks say in admiration, "They look like sure soldiers."

The army was ravenously hungry. They had been marching without food since three o'clock in the morning. Soon they broke ranks, and four thousand Union soldiers were helping themselves to whatever they could find. Jeff, Noah, Bill, and Stuart Mitchell, foraging in a side street, had immediate luck. They ran into a Negro who had emerged from a deserted brick store, carrying a large ham.

Noah stepped suddenly in front of him, and the Negro stopped, the whites of his eyes rolling in fright. Seeing the yearning looks of the soldiers, he thrust the meat behind him. But Jeff could smell it anyhow.

Noah licked his lips, motioning toward the ham. "Any more like that in there?"

The Negro's white teeth flashed in a relieved smile. "Yassuh! Yassuh! Plenty hams in theah, suh."

"Wal, you go on back and git you another 'un," Noah said roughly. And to Jeff's astonishment, he took the ham bodily away from the Negro. Quickly they all jerked out their knives and carved off a piece.

Jeff bit greedily into the tender meat. "Gosh, Noah," he said, his mouth full, "what would you have done if he hadn't given it to you?"

Noah lowered his shank of pink meat and, with the back of one hand, wiped the grease from his mouth.

"I 'spect I'da shot him, youngster." Noah looked as though he would have, too. Jeff's jaw slacked. It was funny how war changed men.

Nearly every store in town was plundered by the soldiers. A big cavalryman swaggered out of a grocery store, his hat filled with oats. Carefully he poured the oats on the wooden sidewalk, so his half-starved horse, tethered to an iron post nearby, could reach it. The horse nickered hungrily, lowered its head, and thrust out its thick lips.

The cavalryman saw the infantrymen and grinned. With a sweeping gesture of his arm, he pointed at the store.

"Pitch in, boys!" he invited. "It's all ours."

It was indeed. As Noah led them inside, they met other soldiers coming out, their arms filled with all sorts of merchandise. Noah concentrated on tobacco, filling a sack with twist after twist. He also pocketed several boxes of sulphur matches.

From the back of the store, they heard Bill Earle whoop exultantly in his high voice. Triumphantly he held up a pair of shiny black shoes and a pair of thick woolen socks. Sitting down on the floor, he kicked off his old, tattered brogans and laced on the new ones.

Jeff looked at him enviously. "What size are they?"

Bill chuckled, gaily, "I used to wear an eight but a nine felt so good that I jest took me a ten."

"If you hain't no objection, git me a pair, too," Stuart Mitchell called in a muffled voice from the front of the store. His head was out of sight in a-hogshead of raw brown sugar.

"What size you wear?" Bill called.

Mitchell came up for air, sugar all over his freckled face. "I don't care," he bellowed amiably, "jest hand me a pair."

Although the owner of the store had fled, inviting looting, Jeff couldn't bring himself to take the heavy merchandise on the shelves. He nibbled tentatively at a piece of rock candy somebody had dropped on the counter. Stuart assured him that the store-owners were all rebels anyhow and therefore their goods were subject to confiscation. Mitchell and Earle led Jeff over to the shoe counter and made him try on several pairs, but they were all too large.

Mitchell shook his red head disappointedly. "You got feet like a deer."

Two hours and three stores later, the bugles sounded and they were pressed into duty as a guard for several rebel cavalrymen who had been captured and brought in by the Sixth Kansas Cavalry. Some of the rebel prisoners were laughing and joking and asking how far it was to the "Lincoln coffee." The South had no coffee and was using a vile-tasting substitute brewed from roasted bran. But Jeff noticed that all the rebels looked unhappy when they were parted from their horses, brought with them from their homes. Now that they were prisoners, they knew they would never see their pets again. When they dismounted they hesitated a minute to bestow a fond look and a final pat. Jeff respected them for that, even if they were rebels.

Three of the dismounted rebels were assigned to Jeff. He had never been given custody of a prisoner before. Gingerly, he felt over each of them for weapons, then ordered them to sit down on the curb. Then he noticed that the oldest man, a captain wearing a big felt hat with a plume, had on a pair of handsome new riding boots, polished and hand-stitched. They looked just Jeff's size.

Fascinated, Jeff couldn't take his eyes off them. The rebel captain saw him staring. Frowning, he drew his feet up under him. He was a big, important-looking fellow with a sandy, cowhorn mustache. Jeff thought if the rebel officer had been half smart, he would have daubed mud all over those new boots so they wouldn't look so inviting. Jeff glanced once at his own crumbling footwear, then back at the captain.

"What size are they?" Jeff asked boldly.

"They don't have any size. They are custom-built."

Jeff was tempted. "You won't need 'em anyway where you're going."

The rebel officer's face flushed with indignation. "Young man," he said, sternly, "that's highway robbery."

Jeff laughed. "Well, if that's the way you look at it, keep 'em. I won't take 'em. But the boys down the line will." He walked the three prisoners to the prison compound, an abandoned school building of native stone, and turned them over to the guards.

Five minutes later Jeff passed the prison compound again and heard somebody calling, "Young man. Young man."

The same rebel captain came hobbling to the log fence and hailed him. Jeff saw that he had lost both his pretty brown boots and his plumed hat. In their place, he wore a cast-off pair of union brogans, his toes protruding; and on his head was an old straw hat that looked as if the Arkansas crows had been nesting in it all winter. But he was beaming.

"Young man, you're the only gentleman in camp," he told Jeff, his cowhorn mustache bobbing excitedly up and down as he talked. "Before you got out of sight, they took my boots and watch, and swapped hats with me. They're nothin' but a lot of thieves."

Jeff grinned. He thought of the stories he had heard about Watie's raiders. There were looters in both armies.

Suddenly the fresh booming of cannon was heard. A two-story red brick building half a block down the street began to twist and buckle. With a shivering roar, it toppled and collapsed. Bricks flew in every direction. A rebel shell had made a direct hit.

A lieutenant sprinted down the middle of the street, one hand on his clanking sword to keep it from tripping him. As he ran, he muttered, "That crazy, dumb Hindman! Shelling his own town!"

Bugles sounded and drums rolled. Jeff ran to join his company, and they were sent to rescue the wounded from the ruins. Among the dead were three Union soldiers. One of the worst hurt was a rebel prisoner whom the three dead men had been escorting to the prison compound. He was old and whiteheaded. Unarmed and painfully wounded in the shoulder, he was lying on his back in the street, yelling at the top of his lungs.

The wounded man's screaming seemed to enrage Clardy, who was standing nearby. Drawing his saber, he ran over to where the rebel was lying.

"Shut your trap!" he roared, his face livid with anger. Cursing, Clardy raised his right boot and, stamping powerfully downward, deliberately ground his heel into the helpless rebel's eye. The dying man's mouth flopped open. There was a slow rattling in his throat, and his hands clawed and twitched. Then he lay quiet.

Every man in the company saw it. Sickened by the brutal act, Jeff rushed at Clardy, his eyes blazing with anger. Paying no attention to the drawn saber, he pushed Clardy backward roughly with both hands.

"You're not fit to be an officer!" he told him, hotly.

Stuart Mitchell thrust his bearded chin into Clardy's face. "You cowardly swine! Why don't you try rammin' your heel in my eye?"

"Yeah—or mine!" growled an artilleryman, stepping on his feet.

"Here's my eye. Let's see you stomp it!"

"Here's mine."

Jostled by his own furious soldiers, Clardy might have been mauled badly had not the cannon fire begun again. Sullenly the men formed a line. This time the firing came from across the river, but a Union battery quickly got the range of the rebel gun and silenced it.

"Let's give the cowardly so-and-so the treatment," somebody proposed after the firing stopped.

Quickly they lined up behind one another, fifty of them. Jeff fell in line with the others and learned for the first time how soldiers punished an unpopular officer.

As they passed Clardy, one at a time, each man saluted briskly. Mechanically, Clardy saluted back. The line grew longer as some of the soldiers ran from the head to the foot so they could pass him two or three times. Clardy's right arm grew heavy from the exercise. Soon he could hardly lift it.

Soon Clardy guessed their purpose. Although he returned the salutes, a sneer was on his lips, and his eyes flashed vengefully.

Jeff looked again at the prisoner. He lay motionless in the dusty street. Jeff's fists clenched in helpless anger. Upset by the incident, he rejected an invitation to accompany Stuart and Bill and Noah on a tour of the town, and turned off alone to walk along the river levee.

He had gone a short way when he was accosted by a Negro slave. Hat in hand, the Negro asked whether he would be kind enough to come to a cabin close by to see an old man who was dying. He said the old man, a former slave, loved freedom and had prayed to live long enough to see a "Linkum soldier."

"It he last chance, young massa," the slave entreated. "He goin' fast."

Touched, Jeff followed him through the dusk to a small shack built on stilts. The slave opened the door, and Jeff stepped inside, taking off his cap. The poorly furnished room was illuminated dimly by candlelight. A fire of cottonwood logs crackled faintly from the mud fireplace, casting weird, dancing shadows on the rude plank walls.

Beneath a patched and faded quilt on the only bed in the room lay an old Negro. Eyes shut, he looked as limp as a piece of rope. In the eerie light, the black skin on his wrinkled face looked the same texture as document paper. Several other Negroes stood around the foot of the bed, regarding Jeff wonderingly.

As they raised him gently to a sitting position and pointed toward Jeff, the old man opened his eyes and whimpered, "Whar? I don' see nuffin."

He was turned facing Jeff. When his old eyes fell on Jeff's blue uniform, he raised his hands. In a deep voice he murmured, reverently and brokenly, "I bress God," and fell back dead.

Deeply moved, Jeff walked quietly outside. This was part of what they were fighting for. Freedom meant a great deal to many Southern people, too. Behind him he heard the Negroes praying in the room where the old fellow lay.

When the slave came out the door to thank Jeff for coming, he said that the old man was one hundred years old, "an' maybe mo'."

He walked back toward the Union camp on the bluff. It was dark now, save for a faint smear of orange low in the west. Overhead the first stars were twinkling timidly. He could smell the river mud and hear the gentle wash of the current. His mind was busy with the events of the last two days. Never had so much happened in so little time.

He thought gloomily of his own family back in Kansas. Would he ever live to see them again? He thought of Lucy Washbourne, the proud, mettlesome rebel girl back in Tahlequah and wondered what she was doing tonight? Probably holding hands with some rebel sweetheart. A girl that beautiful was sure to have her front porch full of suitors.

Back in camp he had the bad luck to run into the orderly

sergeant and was detailed to stand picket guard on the road
leading from Van Buren to the Union camp at the top of the
bluff. His instructions were to commandeer all the liquor the
men might try to bring. The Second Kansas Cavalry had captured three rebel steamboats. Hundreds of Blunt's cavalrymen
had swarmed into the galleys and helped themselves to the
cold corn pone, spareribs, pies, candied yams, and to un-
limited quantities of bottled liquor.

Soon the men came straggling back. Many of them were
intoxicated. Ignoring their arguments and protestations, Jeff
made them pile the liquor on the ground until soon he was
standing guard over samples of whisky, gin, brandy, wine,
rum, cordials, and such local products as moonshine and
home-brewed beer. Despite his careful surveillance, some of
the liquor got through.

For want of anything better to do, he began to pull the
corks from the various bottles and jugs and to sniff them. He
thought most of it pretty horrible until he came to a small
basket flask that smelled exactly like the delicious apple cider
his father concocted. Carefully he emptied the water out of
his canteen and poured in the cider.

At one o'clock he was relieved and crawled between his
blankets high on the bluff overlooking the town. Most of the
soldiers were sleeping Behind him Jeff could hear their snores
and their measured, heavy breathing. He was just dozing
off when somebody shook his shoulder roughly.

"Pardon me," a thick voice said. It was Baldwin, a big,
quiet, sour-faced infantryman who rarely spoke and never
laughed or smiled, until he became intoxicated, whereupon his
black eyes would dilate with good humor, his mouth expand
hospitably, and he was a whole circus by himself. But this
time he wasn't by himself. With him was a small private whom
Jeff didn't know. The small man wore a black beard.

"Pardon me," Baldwin burped, politely, "I want you to
meet General Blunt."

With an expansive sweep of his hand, he indicated his small companion, who came forward unsteadily and, in a very dignified manner, bowed so low that he almost fell into the nearby campfire.

Amused, Jeff got to his feet and, with a salute and a handshake, acknowledged the introduction. Then Baldwin and "Blunt" left him and began waking up other soldiers and going through the same routine.

Unable to go back to sleep, Jeff yawned and, turning on his side, looked down upon Van Buren. The ruby glow of a big fire blazed from the distant river levee. He heard returning soldiers say that it was a large brick warehouse filled with rebel supplies. He sat up in his blankets so he could see it better and felt the hard bulge of his canteen under him.

Uncapping it, he sniffed the cider. It still smelled good. He decided to taste it. Tilting the canteen, he drank a couple of swallows, smacking his lips. Although it stung his tongue a little, he liked the smooth apple flavor. It tasted even better than the cider back home. Soon he began to feel very cheerful.

He got to his feet, only to discover that the sky, brightly spangled with stars, was swimming around and around. He reached for a small black gum tree nearby to steady himself but, owing to some strange confusion, there were now three trees instead of one. Missing all three, he fell back down upon his bed.

There was a mumble of familiar voices. Noah, Mitchell, and Bill Earle were returning from town. They greeted him noisily and began to spread their blankets. Jeff pushed his canteen, still uncapped, over toward Noah.

"That's—stronghest—cider I ever drank," he mumbled, his tongue feeling thick and furry. "I donwananymore." He pulled a blanket over his head.

Noah looked at him queerly, then stooped and picked up the canteen, sniffing at it suspiciously. He grunted, "That's not cider, youngster. That's high-proof applejack."

Jeff felt Noah stuffing the blankets around his hips.

"Lor' Noah," Jeff said, miserably, "you'll ner—get me—take 'nother drink."

Noah said amiably, "I don't remember anybody asking you to take this one."

Noah sat down and began to unlace Jeff's shoes. He pulled them off and, looking at them in the flickering firelight, frowned and shook his shaggy head. The boy was practically barefoot. And they were heading back to Cane Hill in the morning. Forty miles over stony roads and through thirty-seven fordings of Cove Creek.

When the bugles sounded reveille at daybreak, Jeff sat up in his blankets. He smelled smoke. A campfire burned merrily in the gray light close by. He felt tired and worn-out as though he were taking a cold.

Noah towered over him, a bottle of whisky in one hand. "Come on, youngster," he said and led him to the creek. When Jeff saw the whisky, he shook his head positively, hanging back.

"I don't want ary, Noah."

Noah's white teeth shone in one of his rare grins.

"Take off your shirt," he said.

Jeff fumbled with the buttons. A lavender flush lay along the eastern horizon. The early morning air was sharp. Pulling off his shirt, he looked down off the bluff. Most of the sandy river plain below was hidden by a long low cloud of fluffy white vapor that hugged the valley floor for miles, clinging to the water and the low places. Only the fuzzy tops of a few tall cottonwoods and willows showed. It was half an hour yet until sunup.

Noah made Jeff plunge his head into a bucket of water, then handed him part of an old blanket to dry it on. He jerked the cork out of the bottle with his teeth and began rubbing the whisky vigorously over Jeff's upper body.

Jeff wrinkled his nose. "Whew!" he said. "I smell like a distillery."

When he dressed and got back to the fire, Noah was frying thick slabs of ham in a skillet. It was the same ham he had taken away from the Negro. Mitchell was mixing flapjacks in a new white enamel washpan he had found in one of the Van Buren stores. The price "5¢" was still crayoned on it in a purple scrawl. A big can of coffee was bubbling on the coals.

Both the coffee and the ham smelled wonderful to Jeff. Invigorated by the cold water and the rubdown, he felt better. As he turned to pack his bedding, he felt so good that he didn't mind at all the forty-mile hike back to Cane Hill.

☆ 14

The Cow Lot

It was spring in the Cherokee Nation. As Jeff tramped along with the infantry on the road from Three Forks to Tahlequah, he took a long pull of the pine-scented morning air.

On the slopes needle points of greenness were thrusting through the gray earth. Wild onion, verbena, and buffalo burr nodded from the sandy trailside, and Noah said the dogwood blossoms would soon appear, looking like enormous coverlets of white lace spread here and there in the woods. Down in the bottoms the new grass was out. Sweet, damp smells of new life came from the ground, and the April sun warmed the air.

They struck a sandy path that cattle had trodden. Obeying a sudden impulse, Jeff sat down and pulled off his shoes and stockings. Knotting the laces together, he swung the shoes around his neck and began walking barefoot in the cool, moist earth. Bill Earle eyed him with amazement.

"One of us must be crazy, and I feel all right."

Jeff laughed. He felt as bouncy and frolicsome as a biting shoat. He swung along, feeling the cool gray sand sift between his toes. Soon they would be in Tahlequah. Maybe he would see Lucy Washbourne again.

Dixie was exploring the field nearby. The top of her head was wet where she had been nosing in the dewy brush. Mike Dempsey had kept her for Jeff during the long march to Van Buren.

Soon Jeff smelled willows and water and river sand. He stopped to draw on his shoes and stockings. They came up to the Neosho River and a small, deserted crosswoods store built near the ferry landing.

Jeff dropped out of the column to get a drink, Dixie at his heels. A flash of blue in the brush behind the store arrested his attention. Squinting curiously between the branches, he almost stepped on a little old woman wearing a sunbonnet and a man's coat that was much too large for her. She was seated on a small wooden barrel, fishing from the riverbank. In her wrinkled hands was a short willow pole.

Startled, she jumped. "Look out, thar, soldier boy. You scairt me!" she shrilled in a burst of high, thin laughter. "Well, well! So yer bluecoats. On your way to Tahlequah, I bet. Couple, three days ago a bunch o' Watie's grays rode their hosses acrost thet very ford, right thar. They was goin' to Tahlequah, too. How'd you aliked to met up with 'em, soldier boy?"

Watie men! Jeff's hands tightened whitely on his musket. He had already met the Watie men.

Tucking her linsey skirt around her thin ankles, the old

woman jerked her line out of the water and flipped it neatly
into a different riffle.

"I lived fifteen year in Tahlequah," she said, proudly. "Andy
Jackson's soldiers made me hoof it thar all the way from
Rome, Georgia. Rome's whar Stand Watie was born. But I'm
not a rebel, even iffen I am from Stand's home town. I got
grandsons in both armies."

Jeff took off his cap. "Mam, may I have a drink and fill
my canteen here? I'm dry as a gourd."

With a gnarled forefinger she pointed to the spring behind
her. "Thank you, mam," Jeff said and buried his face in the
cool water, drinking deeply.

"Jeepers, soldier boy, I tried to enlist in both armies, but
neither one 'ud have me. I'd be useful to an army. I can cook,
sew, wash, and doctor. And fish! Man, I could ketch enough
fish on these h'yar crawdads to feed old Blunt's whole outfit."

"I know one family in Tahlequah," said Jeff, coming up
for air. "Our officers boarded at their house last summer. It
was the Levi Washbournes."

The old woman's face lit up. She pushed a scraggly wisp
of gray hair out of her eyes. "Levi Washbournes? Why, I've
knowed 'em fer years. They ain't no finer people anywhars
than them Washbournes. They owned niggers and treated 'em
good, too. They got one boy and three gals, two of 'em married. They're all rebels an' they'll come right out and tell you
so, too. Youngest gal, Lucy, went to the academy at Cane Hill
until the war started an' the college quit."

At the mention of Lucy, Jeff jerked his face out of the
spring again, listening eagerly. The water ran off his chin and
dripped down onto his shirt front.

The old lady ran on like a bubbling mill race. "Lucy thinks
the world of her brother Lee. He's with Watie. So's her pappy.
Why, soldier boy, I know everybody in Tahlequah. I can
borrey coffee an' sugar anywhar's in thet thar town."

Thoughtfully Jeff filled his canteen and corked it.

"I'll bet Miss Lucy's got rebel beaux swarming all around her, hasn't she, mam?"

"Like flies aroun' a sugar bowl, soldier boy," the old woman cackled merrily.

Discouraged, Jeff put on his cap and picked up his rifle. He wanted to ask the old woman more about Lucy but he had to catch up with the column. "Thank you, mam, for the drink."

"Jeepers, don't thank me, soldier boy!" she chuckled gaily. "Water ain't mine. That thar spring b'longs to th' whole Cherokee Indian Nation. Thank John Ross. Or Stand Watie. They's both good men but they can't decide which one is gonna run things. They's been lots o' people killed aroun' here, but this ford is a safe place. Nobody'll bother old Belle. I live too close to the fort. I don't run my store no more. Can't keep it stocked."

Jeff swung down the Tahlequah road.

"Come back after the war an' see me, soldier boy," she called after him quaveringly. "I'll have the store goin' then. Come back an' buy a plug o' chewin' tobaccy an' I'll throw in a thousand pounds o' sugar."

But Jeff didn't hear her. All he could think about was getting to Tahlequah.

He found Tahlequah full of Union soldiers. Besides their own small force, there were several hundred men from Colonel W. A. Phillips' Union Indian brigade camped in tents along the Illinois River, some of them Cherokee mixed-bloods who had defected to the Union side. In spite of the fact their uniforms fitted poorly, they were good soldiers and not at all in sympathy with Stand Watie's rebel Cherokee cavalry. Their mission in the nation was to protect the thousands of Cherokees who had lately revoked their alliance with the Confederacy and come back to the Union side.

When Jeff finally got liberty, it was late in the afternoon. He tried to persuade Noah to come with him, but Noah

wanted to go down to the *Cherokee Advocate* office instead.
He said he had always had a hankering to see a plant that
printed a newspaper in two languages.

"I don't think they can do it," Noah marveled. "Every time
they dropped a form that had both English and Cherokee type
in it, it would take six months to sort it out."

Jeff brushed his buttons and buckles with a corncob and
cleaned the mud off his shoes with a sharp twig. He scrubbed
his face and combed his hair. Excited and nervous, he walked
to the Washbourne home. Would they receive him this time?
The tall sycamores were gay with new leaves. The yellow rose-
bushes that bounded the gray chat walk were pruned back
neatly. Jeff heard voices back by the barn. He walked anxiously toward them.

The Washbourne women were standing in the cow lot,
looking worried. The same brindle that Lucy had tried vainly
to milk was bellowing obstinately. On the opposite side of the
lot a new calf staggered unsteadily on its bandy legs.

Jeff saw at once what the trouble was. Brandishing her
horns threateningly, the cow wouldn't let her own calf nurse
her. Lucy, her girlish figure hidden in a short coat, tugged
at a rope around the cow's head. She was trying vainly to
lead the cow to its calf.

"Haw! Haw! She's a Union calf. No wonder she won't suck
a rebel cow," jaunted a Union Indian soldier who had wandered in from the road.

"Or have nothin' to do with rebel females," another jeered.

"Why don't ye spoon-feed it?" mocked a third.

Jeff hand-vaulted the rock fence and approached the
women. They cowered back against the barn, not recognizing
him, afraid of his blue uniform.

"Mam, have you tried salting its back?" Jeff asked kindly,
taking off his cap.

Mrs. Adair gave a little gasp of surprise. "Why, it's the
little Kansas soldier who milked the cow for Lucy," she said.

The other sister came forward shyly, and they introduced Jeff to their mother.

Mrs. Washbourne was large and motherly and, like all of them, carried herself with dignity and poise.

Heels dug into the soft dirt of the cow lot, Lucy had been pulling the rope with all her strength but hadn't moved the obstinate cow an inch. She looked hot and angry and very determined. A wisp of her soft black hair had fallen into her face. Blowing it aside, she peered at Jeff. Recognizing him, she let the rope slacken.

"Good evening, mam," Jeff said politely. Even in a cow lot, Lucy Washbourne's beauty was breath-fetching.

With a startled little nod, she acknowledged his greeting. Jeff's heart pumped wildly.

Pulses singing with pleasure, he turned to Mrs. Adair. "Mam, if you'll fetch me a cup of table salt, I'll show you how to make the cow take her calf."

In another moment he had the salt and rubbed it on the calf's back. Thereupon the cow came forward and, mooing gently, began to lick it. Soon the calf was nudging at its mother's swollen udder. The Washbournes looked at Jeff as though he were a magician. Jeff laughed.

"Corn, mam. Any Kansas farm boy knows how to do that."

"So yer from Kansas," snarled one of the soldiers, climbing over the fence and coming forward truculently. "Then how come yer consortin' with these bum-blistered Secesh wimmen? Which side ye on in this war, anyhow?" His hard eyes glared belligerently beneath his blue cap. Big and beefy, with bearded cheeks, he was obviously irked because Jeff had spoiled their rough badgering of the women.

Jeff felt prickles of anger running up and down his spine. Who did this stupid fool think he was?

"Why don't you go off on down the road and let these people be? I don't want any trouble with you."

The big soldier sneered. He had a red face and coal-black

hair. Obviously he had some Indian blood, probably Cherokee. Jeff could smell liquor on him.

"Of course ye don't want trouble with me, you little bugger," he mocked. "Yer dad-gasted right, yer don't! What ye
hangin' round these rebel wimmen fer?" A cunning gleam
came into his eye. "Yer sweet on the youngest 'un, ain't ye?"
He moved closer, glaring at Jeff with his black bloodshot eyes
and sticking out his long chin.

Jeff's patience snapped. Leaping into action, he swung with
all his strength, hitting the out-thrust chin with a short right-
handed punch that cracked like a bull whip.

The man reeled but didn't go down. Feeling a savage and
unfamiliar exhilaration, Jeff sprang after him, fisting him
furiously, punching him so fast with both hands that the
staccato spat of his fists sounded like a barber stropping a
razor. The fellow's surprised, florid features began to redden
and bleed. He went down limply in the dry cow dung, batting
his eyes and shaking his head groggily.

Suddenly Jeff felt his arms pinioned powerfully from behind. One of the other soldiers, a drunken, black-headed
fellow, had slipped up on him.

"No ye don't, me bucko!" he snarled triumphantly, blowing
whisky fumes in Jeff's face. "Come on, Chilly! Bash in his
purty face whiles I holds him! Shell out his purty white teeth!"

The third soldier obediently doubled his horny hands into
fists and charged. Jeff heard Lucy scream, "Stop it! You'll
hurt him!" He struggled vainly to free himself. This one didn't
look so drunk. Probably more dangerous than the others. He
stopped struggling and waited.

Kicking out suddenly, he buried his right foot in the oncoming stomach. *Whoosh!* With a sharp exhalation, the fellow
tumbled to his knees, sobbing for the breath that had been
driven out of him. Grasping his belly with both hands, he
groveled in the dirt, making queer, strangling noises in his
throat. Two down. One to go.

Jeff was astonished to feel the soldier holding his arms spring spasmodically into the air.

"Aa-gh!" A hoarse yell of pain escaped him.

Surprised, he twisted free, spun round and nailed the man with a punch high on the cheekbone, dazing him. Pouring out the last of his youthful strength, he drove him reeling backward with a flurry of sharp, fast hitting that spread him helplessly against the barn door.

Lucy, a pitchfork in her hands, jabbed again at the man's blue trousers. The fellow yelled in fright, dodging desperately, escaped the sharp tines by inches.

Clambering hurriedly over the fence, he began to run clumsily up the road. His two friends staggered after him. Lucy shot Jeff a look of such pity and concern that he was flabbergasted with surprise and joy. He looked with wonder at the gentle-born rebel girl who had come to his aid.

"Thanks, mam. I reckon—they'd have worked me over good—if you hadn't used that pitchfork." He blew on his skinned knuckles, cooling them.

Recovering her composure, Lucy slipped back into her mood of proud aloofness.

"You deserved my assistance," she said, matter-of-factly. "You were helping us with the cow when your own soldiers attacked you. I would try to help anybody beset by three such ruffians under those circumstances."

She calmly leaned the fork against the barn, its sharp tines downward. Bitterly Jeff felt almost as if she had plunged them into his heart.

Why did she call them his soldiers? He had never seen them before. He wanted to remind her that they had been *her* soldiers. At least until they had deserted the Confederacy and, with their colonel John Drew, had come over to the Union in a body.

But he didn't. Leaning over, he brushed the wrinkles out

of his pants. He smoothed his coat and ran his fingers through his mussed hair. He was still panting in big gulps.

The women, who with the start of the fighting had retreated to the house, came forward timidly. They looked at Jeff with new respect, as though wondering how one so young could fight so well.

"We're grateful to you, sir," Mrs. Adair said, "for helping us with the calf. We're sorry if we've involved you with our troubles. This is the third time this week those men have stopped and annoyed us. How do you feel?"

"All right, I guess, mam, although my knuckles feel driven up into my wrists." He was getting his breath back.

"I don't believe we've ever asked what your name is," said the young woman called Liz.

"It's Bussey, mam. Jefferson Davis Bussey." Seeing Lucy's eyes go bright with surprise, Jeff told them how his father had fought with the Confederate president at Buena Vista seventeen years earlier.

Mrs. Washbourne gave a little gasp of motherly solicitude. "Your cheek is bleeding. Won't you let me dress it for you?" She spoke gently. Her voice was low and melodious, like Lucy's.

"And you've ripped two buttons off your coat," Liz added. "While mother fixes up your cheek, Lucy can sew on your buttons. She sews better than anbody else in the family."

Lucy colored and looked provoked. But she went obediently into the house, and Jeff guessed she had gone after her needle and thread.

At the front porch there was a moment of awkward hesitation. The three older women looked uncertainly at one another, as though debating the propriety of asking an enemy soldier into their home. Then Mrs. Washbourne laughed, a low, musical laugh.

"Won't you come in, Mr. Bussey?" she invited pleasantly.

"We won't let Lucy bite you. Naturally we all feel pretty strongly about the war. My husband and also the husbands of my two daughters here are all in the Cherokee Mounted Rifles with Colonel Watie. So is my son Lee." She spoke slowly and deliberately, selecting her words with care.

Jeff liked her. He liked her honesty, too. He said, "Thank you, mam."

He followed them inside the house, seeing again the rich carpet on the floors, the paneled walls, the glow of china. He thought of his own modest log home back in Linn County and wished that this home wasn't so big and elegant and taste-fully furnished.

Mrs. Washbourne seated him on a stool in the kitchen while she washed his cut with soap and water and dressed it with arnica salve. Then she led him to the parlor.

Lucy, skirts rustling, entered the room with her sewing basket. There was a tiny silver thimble on her middle finger. Immediately Jeff felt the tension between them.

Without speaking, he took off his blue coat and handed it to her. As his fingers touched hers, a shiver of pleasure shot up his arm. He looked at her, but she sat down silently on a settee. He sank uninvited into a chair opposite her. The other women went about their tasks in other parts of the house.

While she was busy selecting her thread, the large white Persian cat padded in silently and rubbed against Jeff's legs. He reached down and stroked its back.

"Where's your dog, Mr. Bussey?" Lucy asked with a cool politeness that Jeff found maddening. She peered at him over the needle's eye and then threaded it swiftly.

"Mam, I tied her to a tent pole back in camp. I didn't want her to fight your cat."

The corners of Lucy's small, oval mouth seemed to want to turn upward in a smile but with an effort she stifled it. She said primly, "I believe you told me last summer that she was a Confederate dog."

"That's right, mam," said Jeff and he told her about finding Dixie at Wilson's Creek. Although she tried not to show it, he knew she was listening carefully.

Lucy held up his blue coat. A shaft of late afternoon sunshine struck the cloth and the dark blue suddenly became lighter. An expression of strong emotion crossed the girl's face, as though the coat had aroused some unpleasant memory.

"I have no Union buttons," she said, staring coldly at him. "All I have are some leftover buttons off my father's first uniform coat. Would wearing Southern buttons violate your Northern scruples, Mr. Bussey?"

Jeff said gently, "Mam, they'll do fine. I'll gladly wear them." He felt vaguely uneasy. She looked as if she wanted to quarrel.

With a quick, deft motion of her right hand, Lucy knotted the end of the light blue thread and looked at him with thinly veiled hostility.

"Why do you make war on us?" she asked, looking him squarely in the eye.

Jeff was taken back by her directness. Then he felt a strange relief. At last some of the trouble between them was out in the open. Maybe at least she'd talk.

He took his time, feeling his way carefully and trying to stay calm.

"Mam, I think we make war upon the South for the sole purpose of restoring it to the Union. I know slavery's involved, too, but President Lincoln made it plain before he was ever elected that he didn't want to interfere with slavery where it now exists."

She bit the thread off with her small, sharp teeth.

"But why won't Lincoln let the South have slavery in the new Western territory? After all, we helped win that country in the Mexican War. What's right about that? Why shouldn't the territories themselves decide what they want to do about slavery?"

"Because, mam, the Declaration of Independence itself forbids slavery. And the declaration is what we're supposed to live by in this country."

"Not in my country," she corrected him. "You're not in the United States now, Mr. Bussey. You're in the Cherokee Indian Nation. We have our own system of government here and you are bound by treaty to respect it. And anyway, what in your Declaration of Independence or your Constitution prohibits slavery?"

Warming to the argument, Jeff sat up straighter. He was sure of his ground here. "Mam, the declaration says that all men, and that includes Negroes as well as whites, are created equal. It says that they are endowed by their Creator with certain inalienable rights, among them life, liberty, and the pursuit of happiness. It doesn't say, mam, that just the rich man, or the white man, or the Anglo-Saxon white man, or the Kansas white man, is entitled to liberty. It says *all* men. Mam, no man or woman in slavery has any liberty." Jeff saw her wince and a small shadow of doubt cross her eyes.

"But it doesn't specifically say we can't have slavery," she argued stiffly. "There was slave trade in both north and south when your Declaration of Independence was written. And ever since it was written, slavery has existed and Congress hasn't tried to stop it. Can you quote me anything from it that comes right out and says that slavery shall not exist?"

"No, mam," acknowledged Jeff truthfully, "not in the final draft. But did you know, mam, that in the original draft, the slave trade was called 'an execrable commerce,' 'a piratical warfare,' and 'a cruel war against human nature'?"

Jeff had no trouble quoting the words accurately. He had heard his father repeat them scores of times. They were clearly engraved upon his memory as though etched there by needles of fire.

It was obvious Lucy hadn't known. Flushing, she looked at him with surprise. She hadn't dreamed that this boyish Union private would be so singularly well informed.

"Then why was it left out of the final draft?"

"Because, mam," Jeff explained patiently, "two states disagreed. They were Georgia and South Carolina. All the other states, both North and South, agreed. But in order to preserve harmony, the expressions were omitted from the final draft. However, it showed what most of the country, even most of the South, thought about slavery. And that's why President Lincoln didn't want to see slavery started in the new territories."

Lucy abandoned her arguments concerning the American Constitution. She thrust the needle through the underside of the coat and, threading one of the brass Confederate buttons through it, began vigorously to stitch it to the material.

Passionately she said, "Slavery and preservation of the Union have very little to do with the Cherokee Indian Nation. Your country took our homes and our land away from us once, back in Georgia and Alabama. And now you're getting ready to do it again. Is it any wonder we don't like the United States and that we made a treaty with the Confederacy?"

Jeff remembered Joe Grayson, the Cherokee boy, telling how his mother had lost her home in Georgia.

"What do you mean, mam, that my country is getting ready to do it again? Jackson was a Democrat. My government is Republican."

She bit her lower lip. "That doesn't change anything. During the 1860 campaign, Seward, your leading Republican, wanted to seize our lands and fill them with white settlers. For years, the people of Kansas have wanted to get rid of their Indian tribes. Where do you think they'd send them, to Nebraska, or Missouri, or Colorado? They'd send them to our country and force us to give or sell to them cheaply our lands here. So why should we remain loyal to you? Besides, your government deserted us when the war started."

"It's true, mam," Jeff admitted, "that we had to take out our soldiers to keep them from being captured. We weren't prepared for war. We weren't planning a war. The South was.

They were organizing home militia and making treaties with the Indians."

Lucy lifted her chin proudly. "And it was the finest treaty we ever got. We can partition or sell our surplus lands. We can sell our personal property. We can move out intruders whenever we wish and the Confederate army will help us. No agent can be assigned to us without our consent. Funds that the United States owes us and won't pay us will be paid in full by the Confederacy. We have been given our own judicial district, just like any Confederate state. We are allowed our own delegate to the Confederate congress. All these things have been denied us by your United States government." She had almost finished stitching on the last button. Her fingers began to tremble.

Jeff's lips compressed. Now she had him going. What a stupid war it was. To him, the issues seemed all mixed up. Each state in the Union seemed to have a different reason for fighting. In Kansas, it was the Free State party versus the proslavery people. In Missouri, the Union faction living in the southern part of the state was fighting the rebels living to the north. In the Cherokee Indian Nation, it was the Stand Watie Cherokees fighting the John Ross Cherokees over the old removal bitterness, and slavery seemed very little involved. In fact, he had heard that John Ross, leader of the Northern Cherokees, owned a hundred Negro slaves and apparently was satisfied with the custom. And in all the states and territories, gangs of bushwhackers who didn't know what they were fighting for, roamed and pillaged the war-torn country, defying both the Union and rebel armies.

"Mam, I had no idea all this had happened. It does seem that my government has treated your country badly. But . . ."

Jeff saw that she had grown suddenly pale. Her lips parted as if to speak. She took a long, tremulous breath.

She said, "What do you mean, it seems so? You raid our country, rob us of our valuables, despoil our property. Your officers are insolent and make us cook for them. Your soldiers, like those this afternoon, insult us. If my father or my brother wants to see us, they have to slip across the river like thieves in the night and risk being captured or shot. . . ." Her low voice, vibrant with passion, failed. She began to sew faster than ever. Jeff didn't dare speak.

Tears welled into her eyes. Suddenly she flinched and gave a little gasp of pain. A tiny spot of blood appeared on her finger. She had accidentally stuck it with the needle. Throwing his coat upon the floor, she ran weeping from the room.

Shaken, Jeff stood, looking after her in wonder and pain. Finally he stooped and picked up his coat. Clumsily he broke the remaining thread off the second button, noticing it was sewn on strongly and neatly. He thrust Lucy's needle into the padded top of her sewing basket, where she could find it, and stood indecisively. Corn, he'd never seen such a peculiar, independent girl.

Always foamed up about the war. In any war, there were robbing and killing and despoiling by both sides. Surely she knew that. Sighing, he shook his head helplessly. He had wanted to comfort her, but his courage had failed him.

Resignedly he drew a long breath and looked resentfully around the room with its elegantly upholstered furniture and its large Bible bound in blue leather with the name "Levi Washbourne" engraved proudly on it in silver letters.

He felt miserable. He guessed he was head over heels in love with Lucy. But he might just as well be in love with some girl living on a star. The only thing they had in common was the war, and they were hopelessly crossed on that. Why had he been so foolish as to fall for a rebel girl?

He put on his coat and buttoned it. Lucy did know a lot about politics. He had learned more in the last five minutes about the Cherokee Indian Nation than he had ever dreamed existed. He hadn't realized the Cherokees had a small republic of their own within the United States.

He had picked up his cap and turned to go when Mrs.
Adair came into the room.

"Where's Lucy?" she asked, surprised.

Sheepishly Jeff shook his head. "We were arguing about
the war, mam, when she stuck her finger with the needle. She
began crying and ran from the room."

Mrs. Adair stared at him thoughtfully, her hands clenched
tightly in front of her. Jeff could tell she felt sorry for him. He
guessed she could tell by his face how smitten he was on
Lucy. But there was something else in her face, too. Something
that bordered on fear. Lucy's sister seemed to be hesitating,
as though weighing something carefully in her mind.

She said impulsively, "Mr. Bussey, even though you are in
the Union army, I feel that I can trust you and that some explanation of Lucy's conduct is due you. We're all worried
frantic about our brother Lee. We haven't told Mother yet,
but he's been missing two weeks after being out on scout.
Lucy, especially, has been prostrate with worry and fear. She
and her brother are very close. She has a horror of Lee or
Father being killed. That's why she can never talk rationally
about the war."

Jeff swallowed hard. No wonder Lucy hated the sight of a
blue uniform. He'd never be able to make her like him so long
as the war lasted, and it would probably last a long time.

He turned glumly toward the door, cap in hand. "Mam,
please tell her that I'm grateful to her for sewing on my buttons. I mean her buttons. I mean her father's buttons. And that
I'm sorry we have to fight against her brother and her father.
And I hope her brother gets back safely from his scout."

Mrs. Adair nodded. Tears came to her eyes, but her voice
was steady. "Thank you. I'll tell her."

As Jeff walked up the road, he wished he could help the
Washbournes find Lee. But how would you go about trying
to find an enemy missing on scout? The Union couldn't even
keep track of its own men missing on scout.

☆ 15

Fate of the Brandts

A week later Jeff was standing at dusk near the north gate of Fort Gibson when he heard wagon wheels rumbling and hundreds of slow hoofbeats.

His heart leaped hopefully. Maybe it was a food train. Forage and provisions were running low. With Watie raiding so widely, no corn had been raised in the Cherokee country. The fort was wholly dependent now upon the food freighted overland by mule train from far-off Kansas, and upon the small acquisitions of flour and meal ground at Hildebrand's mill on Flint Creek from corn and wheat secured by stealthy dashes into nearby Arkansas. Weeks had passed since a supply train had come from Fort Scott. Everybody was tired of the weevily meat and the quarter rations of salt horse.

Besides, ten thousand rebels stationed along the south bank of the Arkansas River from Webbers Falls to the north of the Grand were poised for an attack. The fort's plight had become desperate. Jeff kicked at a small rock embedded in the ground. Federal blunders and indifference had done it. Located hundreds of miles west of the main theater of war, the fort had been virtually abandoned by Union authorities at St. Louis.

A double column of dusty figures rode horseback through the fort's great wooden gate. Their black campaign hats and their blue shoulders bobbed over the top of the fort's sharply pointed, close-set log palisades. As they drew closer, Jeff saw they were cavalry. Their faces were raw and swollen from the stings of horseflies and the scratches of tree branches striking them as they traveled through the woods. They looked as though they had been choking in their own dust all the way from Kansas.

Disappointed, he walked out to meet them, hoping they were escorting at least part of a food train. But only their own baggage wagons followed, and when he saw how easily the tired mules pulled the wagons, he knew they were loaded only lightly. When he tried to question them about where they had come from and how the war was going in the east, they stared at him and never spoke. Unabashed, he walked with them as they rode past the new stone supply buildings covered with slate that Colonel Phillips had ordered constructed atop the bluff overlooking Grand River. Moving on to the lowlands, they halted near the site of the original fort, now two decaying blockhouses.

There they dismounted slowly and, once on the ground, staggered unsteadily and stomped their feet to restore the circulation. With their hands they beat clouds of dust off their pants and blouses. Some of them hawked deeply and noisily spat the dust from their throats. Others gave gruff commands to their horses and clomped about in their boots, their brass spurs jingling as they began to set up camp.

Despite their lack of hospitality, Jeff was impressed with the careful way they attended to their horses before they ate a bite of supper themselves. They removed the saddles, permitting the animals to roll on the ground. They shook out the brown saddle blankets and began to groom the horses briskly. Standing well away and leaning hard on the currycombs and brushes, they wiped the dry mud and the scurf from the horses' skin. Then they hand-rubbed the horses' legs and sponged out their nostrils and docks. Only after they had cared for their mounts and fed them hay and grain did the weary men unbuckle their saber belts and head gratefully for the mess halls at the top of the bluff.

"Jeff!"

One of the cavalrymen trudging up the rise left the column and ran awkwardly in his boots toward Jeff. Jeff didn't recognize the husky young fellow with orange freckles all over his face who grasped his hand in both of his. On the front of his soiled black felt hat was a brass insignia of swords crossed. He wore low, reddish sideburns, and his eyebrows were heavy and white as corn silk.

"Goshallmighty, Jeff, don't you know me? I'm David Gardner."

A glad grin spread over Jeff's face. "David!" he blurted. He couldn't get over how David had grown. "Where'd you come from?"

David spat a big chew of tobacco into one of his freckled hands and hurled it onto the ground behind him. He was grinning happily, too. "From Fort Scott."

"When's the next supply train coming out?"

David pointed back up the road. "It's only about two, three days behind us."

"Been home lately?"

David shook his head. "Not since that mornin' you caught Ma and me jawin' in th' yard." He looked thoughtfully at the ground. "I 'spect Ma's had a hard time th' last two years."

"You haven't heard word from any of my folks, have you?" Jeff asked hopefully.

David took off his hat. He whipped it across his knee, and the trail dust flew. "Naw. I met a conscript from Sugar Mound several months ago when I was on the ditch crew at Rolla. He told me they'd had plenty o' rain back home the last two years. Finally busted the drouth. No more desertin' for me, Jeff. I worked out my punishment. Now I'm reinstated. You and Ma was right."

David's voice was deeper, and there was an air of assurance and competency about him. He didn't look anything like the lonely, scrawny, homesick fellow Jeff had known back at Fort Leavenworth.

David's glance shifted back to the horses. His forehead wrinkled in surprise. "Hey, what's she doin' that for, Jeff?"

A thin-faced Indian girl carrying an empty pan glided up where the newly arrived horses were eating and began timidly to pick up from the ground the grains of corn dropping from the horses' mouths.

"She's hungry," Jeff explained. "She'll take the corn home and wash it. Then they'll parch it and eat it. We've got more than six thousand Indian refugees here, mostly women and children, lying under trees, most of them sick and half starved. They had to come to the fort for protection. The whole country's thick with rebels and bushwhackers robbing and killing people."

David began to fan himself thoughtfully with his hat. "I didn't know things was that bad. Le's go up to the fort, Jeff, and git some drinkin' water. I'm drier than a cork leg."

"How'd you get in the cavalry?" Jeff asked as they walked along.

"They're convertin' lots o' infantry into cavalry at Fort Scott now," David said. "We brought several cavalry instructors out with us. One of 'em is Lieutenant Foss. You otta see that feller ride, Jeff. He sets up there as easy as a hossfly on a mule's ear. They're gonna convert lots of your infantry here into cavalry, too. How would you like that, Jeff?"

"Corn, David, I'd like it." Jeff had always wanted to be in the cavalry. "Only I still don't have a horse."

David scoffed, "Goshallmighty, Jeff, that won't keep you out no more. We got hosses to burn now. The supply train escort is bringin' a thousand head down with them. It's men the cavalry needs now, not hosses. We hear they're gonna start trainin' you in a week."

Instead, they started in three days. Jeff enjoyed the look of

surprise on Noah's somber face when he told him about it at
breakfast a full day before it was announced at the fort.

Noah frowned, stirring his coffee. "I'd druther stay on the
ground. Ridin' a hoss makes my head spin an' my feet hurt.
But it's a wise move. Cavalry is more important out here in the
West than it is back East. Here the distances are greater, and
the rival armies smaller. If a blow needs to be struck here, it
might take the infantry several days to walk to where it's goin'
but cavalry could get there in a few hours. Wonder where they
gonna train us?"

The training began on the fort's drill ground located on the
open prairie to the west. Despite the unfamiliar routine of the
cavalry drills, Jeff liked the change. Back home, he had ridden
horses almost before he had learned to walk, so he had no
trouble managing the big, slow sorrel checked out to him.

He discovered that the animal, which had belonged to a
cavalryman who had died of dysentery, could teach him more
than any of the drillmasters, and without cursing him, too.
When the bugles blew "right about" and "left about," the
sorrel knew instinctively what to do and when to do it. He
was smarter than any sergeant on the premises.

But not even the horse could help him when they were introduced to the saber drills. Jeff didn't like the short, curved
cavalry sword known as the saber. In the first place, he couldn't
walk, wearing one, without its barking his legs or tripping him
up. On a horse, it was even worse. When he was commanded to
draw and brandish it while galloping, it became positively
dangerous. He did pretty well with the commands "right cut
against infantry" and "left cut against infantry" but when
ordered to execute the "rear moulinet" he quickly came to
grief.

At the first pass of the saber behind his back, Jeff slashed a
long gash in his new oilskin slicker rolled up on the rear of his
saddle. Later, he was reminded of it every time it rained, and

cold water rushed through the rent and down his back. And when the command was "front moulinet" he whipped his blade so near the sorrel's ear that the horse lurched in fright, and he was almost unseated.

"Do it like this!" bellowed Lieutenant Foss, a tall, leather-faced Coloradoan, bowlegged as a hoop. He was in charge of the drill and skillfully performed the various passes.

"Corn!" Jeff marveled to Stuart Mitchell, riding nearby. "He makes that old cheese knife spin like a circular saw!"

But the lieutenant was the only man in the outfit who could come even remotely close to doing the saber cuts correctly. Jeff decided that if he ever got into a cavalry battle, he would forget about the saber and try to get in all his licks with his one-shot Sharps carbine or his "pepperpot," as he called the big cap-and-ball pistol he was given to wear in his belt.

When he looked over his shoulder at Noah astride a hard-mouthed bay, Jeff straightway forgot his own troubles amid the hilarity of watching another's. Noah was obviously no Cossack. His face turned a chalk white when he first mounted the bay.

Panic in his face, he dropped his shiny saber in the green prairie grass and lost one of his bridle reins, too. His infantry cap, not much bigger than a postage stamp, had fallen forward over his eyes. His mount was trotting roughly and every time Noah's gaunt body came down, it bounced so high in the saddle that Jeff could see a foot of daylight under the seat of his pants.

"Circle yore leaders and keep up the drags!" a former cowboy in the company yelled, giving Noah's awkward effort the flavor of a cattle stampede.

Noah's big feet escaped the stirrups and his long legs, swinging comically far below the bay's belly, began to churn so violently up and down the sides of the horse that his blue trousers were pushed up high, exposing the legs of his long red underwear. Jeff rode out and caught the horse by the bridle until Noah, cursing beneath his breath, could recover his lost rein, pull down his pant legs and thrust his feet back into the stirrups.

The new cavalry was quickly pressed into service despite its greenness. The guerilla warfare, that summer of '63, was increasing in savagery every day. The position of Fort Gibson was critical. When Colonel Phillips sent eight hundred cavalry up the Texas road as an escort to the first Federal supply train that had come through in months, the rebels boldly crossed the Arkansas River and captured more than one thousand Union horses and mules. General Douglas Cooper's rebels were now camped so close that every night Jeff could see the rebel campfires across the river.

Groups of Watie's rebel Cherokee horsemen made raid after raid behind the Union lines in the vicinity of Spavinaw and Grand River, destroying the fields and gardens the Union refugee women and children had planted so laboriously on their small farms. It was Watie's intention to drive every Union refugee family he could find back upon the protection of Fort Gibson, compelling the fort to feed them from the limited stores hauled at such labor by mule and ox trains from far-off Kansas. And Watie did all in his power to keep those trains from getting through. Thus he hoped to force Phillips to evacuate the fort and return to Kansas, leaving all the Cherokee Nation to the Confederates. It was the duty of the new Union cavalry, of which Jeff was now a part, to prevent those depredations if it could.

Jeff's detail was patrolling an area north of Tahlequah late one hot June afternoon when they saw a cloud of gray and brown smoke rising above the distant oaks.

"Ho!" called Jim Pike, the sergeant, pulling his horse to a stop. Scowling, Pike peered hard ahead at the smoke, trying to assess its origin.

"Look's like a haystack burnin'," guessed Sam Sukemeyer, a private.

Pike touched spurs to his mount. "Maybe we better go see. Might be somepun else."

Riding toward the smoke, they found a small cornfield, and Jeff was dismayed to see a crude wooden drag had been pulled across the crop and the plants jerked out of the ground by the roots. Fresh horse tracks lay plain in the sandy soil.

Alarmed, they quickened their pace. Jeff had heard so many firsthand accounts of the rebel depredations that he dreaded what they might find.

They found it in the barn lot of a small farm. The troopers pulled up their horses and stared with horror.

A fine chestnut mare lay dead, her head in a pool of blood. Her two small colts stood tugging at their lifeless mother's teats. Jeff heard Stuart Mitchell begin to curse, slowly at first, then more loudly and with increasing bitterness. And then he heard something else, something that froze the marrow in his bones.

A woman was screaming hysterically somewhere in the smoke ahead. Rapidly they followed the noise. A two-room log dwelling blazed brightly in broad daylight, the red flames crackling fiercely as they consumed the thatched roof.

Beneath some cedar trees in the yard, two women and a small boy were huddled like frightened sheep around the body of a man. The older woman, obviously the grandmother, was trying vainly to comfort the mother, while the child crouched nearby, his boyish countenance stiff with shock.

The older woman heard them ride into the yard. Raising a white face etched with terror, she drew back as if expecting a blow, one wrinkled hand held over her open mouth. Then she saw their blue coats and realized they were Union.

Pike got down from his horse and questioned her. They learned the dead man was Frank Brandt, a mixed-blood soldier from the Union Indian brigade at Fort Gibson, who had been given a short furlough to help his family work the corn on their farm. The Watie party had ridden up suddenly, surrounded him, and shot him while his family stood begging for his life. Gently Noah led the wife to the smokehouse and persuaded her to sit on a log and stop her screaming.

"They came an hour ago," the grandmother told them, her voice broken with emotion, her eyes twin pools of horror. "First they kilt Frank. Then they tuck all we had to eat, a small midgen of sugar, half a ham, all our flour. They went through the house and tuck all our blankets, quilts, pillowcases, even the children's shoes. They ripped open our feather beds with their bayonets. They said they was searching for guns, but we knew they was after rings and jewelry to carry back to their families. They went to the barn with their cavalry ropes an' stole our cow. They couldn't take the mare on account of her two small colts born three, four day ago. So they shot her. They tuck every chicken and goose. Then they fired the house. I used to love to see the spring come, but now I hate it. I knew the bushwhacking would begin in dead earnest once the leaves came out agin." She stood indecisively, wringing her hands in her apron.

His heart in a turmoil, Jeff turned away. Suddenly there was a slight movement ahead, and he discovered a small boy cowering behind a cedar hedge. He held both hands over the stomach of his blouse and looked fearfully at the ground.

"What's the matter?" Jeff asked kindly.

Shrinking back into the hedge, the boy gripped his stomach so tightly that his hands grew white, but still he wouldn't speak.

"He's scared," piped a childish voice behind Jeff. "The rebel soldiers told him that when the bluecoats come, they'd rip his belly open with their swords." Aghast, Jeff looked around. The older boy had followed him from the yard.

"Pa's dead," the older boy bluntly told the younger. "The rebels bushwhacked him." The child stared woodenly, as though he hadn't heard.

A wave of pity surged over Jeff. He turned to the older boy.
"What's your name?"

"Johnny. Can I see yore gun?"

"And what's his name?"

"Jackie. Is yore gun a Springfield? Pa had a Springfield, but
when the rebels bushwhacked him, they tuck it with 'em."

"Johnny, tell your brother the rebels were lying. We won't
hurt him. Tell him to take his hands down."

Obediently Johnny walked over to where his little brother
was standing, frozen with fear. "Take yore hands down, Jackie.
They won't hurtcha."

Jackie shook his head. Eying Jeff's saber fearfully, he kept
his fingers crossed tightly across his stomach.

Johnny frowned impatiently. Stooping over until his face
was only inches from Jackie's, he said, "Aw, Jackie, they won't
rip yore belly open. See here. They didn't hurt mine." Pulling
up his blouse, he bared his own midriff.

That seemed to satisfy Jackie. The fear went out of his face.
His hands came down.

Jeff knelt, holding out his arms. "Come here, Jackie, and
I'll show you my horse." Jackie came, haltingly. Jeff picked
him up.

Johnny followed, still chattering brightly about the tragedy
that had befallen his family. "Mama screamed and Pa swore.
But they bushwhacked him anyways."

At dusk the fatherless family was loaded into a wagon and
they started back to the fort. Building a rough coffin out of
some planks they tore off the barn, the cavalry had buried
Frank Brandt beneath a lilac bush in the front yard. Jeff and
Noah erected a rude headstone of rocks near the grave.

The wagon jolted along over the rough ground, its hubs
squeaking.

"What about the two colts?" Noah asked, after they had
ridden a quarter of a mile. Pike looked uncomfortable. He
pulled back on his reins, stopping his horse. With his big hand,

he wiped a gnat off his neck. The wagon lumbered on, accompanied by part of the platoon.

"They's too young to travel or to graze. If we leave 'em, they'd only starve or the wolves ud get 'em," Pike said. He looked around hesitantly. They all saw he hated to give the order.

"Aw cripes, I'll do it," growled Seth Wilson, a farmer from Woodson County. "Gimme a couple extra cartridges, somebody."

Silently Mitchell dug in his cartridge box and handed him three. Jerking his carbine out of its leather sheath, Wilson turned his horse around and rode at a slow trot back toward the lonely barnyard, grumbling to himself.

Later the sound of the two shots caused the wolves back in the hills to set up an unhappy wailing that seemed the consummation of grief and loneliness.

When they drove through the fort's big gate six hours later, the western moon was sinking over a row of whitewashed blockhouses. Johnny and Jackie Brandt were sound asleep beside their mother. Wide awake, she sat like a post, staring wretchedly into the semidarkness, trying to plan a new life without a husband or a home.

Just before he dozed off in his tent, Jeff thought of Lucy and of her brother Lee. He wondered if Lee Washbourne had been with the Watie raiding party that had burned the Brandt home. He doubted it. Judging Lee by the Washbourne womenfolk and by their home, Jeff was sure he hadn't. He wondered whether Lee were high-spirited and proud, like Lucy, or whether he could control his emotions, like the other Washbourne women?

Pulling a light blanket over his shoulders, he thought of what Mrs. Adair had told him of Lucy's devotion to her brother. He wished he could help Lucy find him but he didn't quite know how to go about it. He resolved to talk to Noah about it in the morning.

☆ 16

The Name on the Watch

Jeff heard the sentries calling off all around the sleeping fort, their singsong voices bawling dutifully through the darkness, "Number one. 'Leven a'clock. Aw'swell."

It was three nights after Pike's patrol had brought in the Brandt family. Jeff, accompanied by Dixie, was walking sentry along the north shore of the Neosho River below the fort.

He stopped for a moment, listening to the "Aw's well's"—gruff voices, nasal voices, sleepy voices, bored voices—traveling slowly westward up the side of the bluff, passing out of hearing behind the distant palisades, then emerging faintly on the far side, and returning, station by station, to the original point of call. Girding the darkened fort with a ring of security.

It was stiflingly hot. Wearily Jeff slapped at a mosquito. His uniform, stiff with dirt and dust, chafed, and his body smelled of stale sweat. His musket was heavy. Switching it to the opposite shoulder, he wished he could have drawn the duty on top of the bluff, where there was a breeze. Although it was an hour before midnight, and everything was black as pitch, it seemed to him the night was very much alive.

He knew the rebels were very much alive on the south bank of the nearby Arkansas River that divided the two armies. When he had been on outpost duty there the day before he had heard the voices of their pickets as they met across the river, and seen the faint illumination of their pipes through the shadowy cottonwoods and willows that lined the opposite shore, and smelled the fresh beef broiling over their campfires. The rebels always had twice as much to eat as they did.

He thought of Lucy and her dark beauty, and an intolerable longing assailed him. If she could ever forget the war long enough, maybe he could make her like him.

A low growl came from Dixie. Crouching, she advanced on the bushes, ears flat, fur bristling. Startled, Jeff wheeled and raised his musket to the ready, remembering how Sparrow had been knifed in the back while on sentry.

"Jeff." The voice came in a half whisper.

"Who's there?"

A shadowy figure loomed out of the darkness. "It's me— David Gardner. I've got the duty two stations down. Say, Jeff. let's walk over to the other river and talk to the rebel pickets. Want to?"

"Corn, no!" said Jeff, recoiling. It was the craziest idea he'd ever heard. "I'm scared of 'em. Besides, we're not supposed to leave our posts. If the officers caught us, they'd court-martial us."

"Naw they wouldn't, Jeff," David argued. "Besides, the officers in both armies is all asleep. McCoy says he'll walk my beat and his, both. John says he'll watch yours. Our outpost pickets over at the other river always lets us go through if we give 'em some of the tobaccy we git from the rebs."

Jeff thought of Pete Millholland and the Brandt family. "You can't trust the rebels, Davey. I wouldn't trust one of Watie's men any farther than I can throw an ox by the tail. They'd slit your throat. They're treacherous."

"Naw, they're not, Jeff. Not when we meet 'em thisaway," David insisted with quiet stubbornness.

"How do you know?"

"Because we been meetin' 'em ever' night in the middle of the river an' swappin' knives an' talkin' to 'em."

Jeff stared at him incredulously, unable to believe his ears.

David went on, "Some of their pickets is mean, but I don't think they're Watie men. There won't be any Watie men there. When the mean ones is on sentry, our guys will holler over jist to devil 'em an' say, 'How much is Confederate money worth today?' an' the rebels will sass us right back by askin' us if the niggers we are fightin' for have improved the Yankee breed any yet, an' things like that. But mainly they're purty good fellers—fer rebels. Tonight the good ones is on duty. They promised to bring us some plew tobaccy. We're gonna swap 'em some of our coffee fer it."

Jeff thought it over. It still sounded hairbrained to him. "What do you talk to 'em about?"

"Oh—jist everthing—girls, rations, officers, the weather. How the common soljers on each side is the victims in the war. How we'd both stop the war tomorrey and hang all the politicians thet got us into it if we was runnin' th' show."

Jeff laughed in the dark. "Which we aren't."

"But mainly, we just talk about our mothers an' our fathers an' our sweethearts. Better come with us, Jeff. It's fun."

In the dark Jeff rubbed his thumb along the smooth stock of his musket. Maybe some of the rebels knew Lee Washbourne and would volunteer some news that Jeff could pass on to Lucy. He drew a long breath and decided to take the plunge.

"All right, Davey, I'll go. But I still think it's crazy."

Half an hour later, with three other Union pickets, they stole down to the north bank of the Arkansas, stacked their arms carefully on the bank and peeled out of their clothing. They left one sentry to guard the clothing and stay with Dixie, whom Jeff tied to a willow back away from the shore so she wouldn't bark. Then they walked a hundred yards through the warm sand to the water's edge.

David cupped his hands around his mouth and called cautiously toward the opposite shore.

"Hey, Pork and Molasses. You there?"

There was silence. A small sandbank caved with a slight

splash into the murmuring current. A bullfrog bellowed sleepily from a swale. Jeff listened and his breathing quickened as
a voice came softly, furtively, from the rebel side.

"We's heah."

One of the Union pickets with David and Jeff called jocularly, "When is Cooper gonna march into Gibson?"

"When you all git yore last mule an' dog et up."

"Got any tobaccy?"

"Yep. Got any coffee?"

"Yep. We'll meet ya halfway."

"Won't shoot?"

"Nope."

Still suspecting treachery, Jeff stepped gingerly into the
warm water. His skin felt goose-pimply. This was madness.
What had he been thinking about, agreeing to do a thing as
stupid as this? This was the enemy, the people they'd been
fighting against two long years.

They waded out a few yards, then stopped to listen. From
the darkness ahead came a faint splashing of men wading.
Half a dozen naked figures appeared from the opposite bank
like ghosts out of the gloom. They met at a shadowy sandbar
in the middle of the river and halted, the water dripping
noisily off their sleek bodies.

"Hello, Johnny. How are ya?" David said to the nearest one.

"Fine, Yank. How y'all?"

Jeff relaxed a little. It was lighter here in the open, away
from the dark trees.

Some of the rebels were carrying twists of tobacco, scarce
in the North. Some of the Union pickets bore small sacks of
coffee beans, dear in the South. After the swap was made,
they stacked the bartered goods on the sandbar and, to Jeff's
astonishment, went swimming together in midstream.

Jeff found himself with a small, wiry rebel who swam like
a bullfrog. Cautiously they began to talk, watching each other
like hawks.

"We's Armstrong's men. From Texas. What's yo' outfit?" the rebel asked.

"Clardy's Seventh Kansas Cavalry," Jeff replied. The rebels had captured six of his company, two weeks earlier, and sent them to a prison at Tyler, Texas, so he knew the information was no secret.

The rebel seemed interested. "Clardy? Seems like ah've heared o' him. Ah heared he's a rough 'un."

"You heard right." Jeff frowned in the darkness. "Say, you know a fellow named Lee Washbourne? He's with Watie." The rebel shook his bushy head in the half light.

"Ah don't know him. But wait a minute. Joe, ovah heah, is a Watie man. Maybe he knows him."

Jeff's heart began pounding furiously. David had told him there wouldn't be any Watie men.

Quietly the rebel summoned one of his comrades swimming a short distance away. "Joe, yo' know somebody named Lee Washbu'n? With Watie?"

As Joe bobbed his wet, black head up and down, Jeff thought he looked like an otter.

"Sure, I know him. But he never come back from a scout three weeks ago. Our officers is afraid the Yanks captured him. His father is captain of my company. Colonel Watie's bin tryin' to git Lee back on a prisoner exchange, but he can't get in touch with the Union commander." Jeff was disappointed. But at least he had some news for Lucy.

Soon it was time to go. The two parties bade each other good-by and parted, each wading back to its own shore. Jeff had swapped an old St. Louis newspaper for a twist of tobacco for Noah, Bill, and Stuart Mitchell. The swim had cooled him off. To his surprise he found he had enjoyed the unusual adventure. But as they dressed, he was curious about one thing.

"Davey, won't all this visiting and fraternizing make each side want to go easy on the other when they meet in battle?"

David snorted, "Naw. If we met in battle tomorrey, we'd still be tryin' to cut each other's hearts out. This was jest a recess."

There was a recess of a different kind on a quiet, moonlight night a week later. They were camped on the north bank of the Arkansas and the cavalrymen were bored. Lieutenant Foss had entertained them just before sundown with an exhibition of trick riding, hooking one toe around his saddlehorn and leaning low to snatch up a handkerchief from the ground while riding full tilt. But they were tired of the usual long jumping contests, the card games, and the tugs of war. Noah was slumped on his stomach by the campfire, reading a new novel by Dickens. Bill Earle had just finished shaving and was wiping the soap off the straight-edge he had borrowed from John Chadwick.

"Soldier, why don't you sing something?"

Clardy, the scar on his left cheek gleaming in the moonlight, had walked out of the shadows and confronted Bill. There was a smirk on the captain's face, as there always was when he tried to look pleasant and failed. He should have addressed Earle as "Trooper" but like all of them had difficulty adjusting his conversation to cavalry terms.

Bill put down the razor and saluted smartly. "Yes, sir. What song would you like to hear, sir?"

Clardy waved his hand as though leaving the choice to Bill. The troopers sat up with keen anticipation. Bill could sing, and the fact the captain had asked him to lent additional importance to the occasion. Jeff sat with his back braced against a cottonwood log. Dixie was at his feet. Everybody knew her now. She was the pet of the regiment.

The captain's sudden interest in singing didn't dovetail with an incident Jeff remembered from the long, hot march to Wilson's Creek. On that occasion, they had angered Clardy by singing a parody on the rebel tune, "Dixie," making up their own words as they marched.

"I wish I's back in Douglas County
Two years up and I had my bounty
Look away, look away, look away to Kansas land."

"Singin' soldiers won't fight," Clardy had snarled at them. Now Jeff eyed Clardy warily and wondered what lay back of the new-found enthusiasm for music.

Earle's tenor, clear and sweet, began the ever-popular "John Brown's Body" and on each chorus the troopers kept time by clapping their hands to the singing. At first Bill sang mostly what the soldiers asked for, such favorites as "Shoo Fly Shoo," "Gay and Happy Still," and "Wait for the Wagon." But when he began the hauntingly sweet notes of "Come Where My Love Lies Dreaming," everything became quiet, and the whole camp seemed to hang upon the song and drink in the emotional impact of the melancholy words. When the last sad strains were over, no one spoke.

A stick snapped in the shadow. It was Clardy.

"Soldier, can you sing 'Tramp, Tramp, Tramp'?" he asked Earle.

Bill sang the song, and at its conclusion, Clardy stared across the river, his body bent forward, listening.

"Listen!"

From the rebel side of the Arkansas, another voice was heard, a low, powerful baritone that carried strongly across the murmuring water. The rebel singer warmed up on "Johnny Fill up the Bowl" and then swung into "Pop Goes the Weasel" and "Lily Dale." He was accompanied by what sounded like a banjo.

In the bright moonlight Clardy's thin, nervous hands opened and closed spasmodically, and a sneering, triumphant expression crossed his face.

Suddenly the rebel singer lifted his smooth, vibrant voice in the old favorite, "Annie Laurie." And then a wonderful thing happened. On the chorus, Bill Earle joined in, singing the harmony. Two hundred yards apart, the rebel baritone and the Union tenor finished the old Scottish song together, their voices blending in the soft June night.

Then Bill began everybody's favorite, "Home, Sweet Home." Quickly the rebel singer joined him, and as the homesick men of both armies sang the chorus, Jeff, misty-eyed like the others, thought of his own home and family in far-off Linn County.

Later, after they returned to the fort, David stopped him at the water barrel. Looking carefully around, he whispered, "Hey, Jeff. I know who that rebel singer is. His name's Chasteen. He's a Texian lawyer from Goliad. The rebel pickets told us about him one night when we was swimmin' with 'em. He used to lead a church choir at Santone."

That night Jeff lay awake, wondering why Clardy, who ordinarily disliked music, had seemed so enthralled with the singing. Why had he asked Bill to sing in the first place? It seemed that Clardy had known what was going to happen.

An hour before dawn Jeff was awakened by a rough hand shaking his shoulder. It was the orderly sergeant growling, "Be dressed in fifteen minutes. Special duty."

Yawning, Jeff sat up and discovered that the weather had completely reversed itself. The morning was heavily overcast and wild with wind. As he pulled on his boots, he felt singularly depressed. He guessed it was because of the gloomy weather.

Special duty, the orderly sergeant had said. Jeff wondered what it was? The wind gushed so hard that he had to drop to his knees before he could stuff his blouse into his pants. Blown sand stung his cheek. The horses stood with their backs to the wind, their manes, tails, and forelocks tousled. As his company was ordered into infantry alignment and began to march, again he had the feeling of dread and foreboding, as though something unpleasant were about to happen.

Everything was sodden with moisture. It formed in tiny gray

beads on the walnut stock of Jeff's musket. Ahead, the men's feet left darkened trails in the wet grass as they marched to the drill field.

"What's up?" Bill whispered as they did a right oblique. "Where they takin' us?"

"Dunno," muttered Stuart, "but we'll soon find out."

Colonel Phillips was off on a scout and Clardy, next in rank, was in temporary command at the fort. What was it all about?

Finally, after they were formed into a rectangle at one end of the drill field, Noah had it figured.

"Must be an execution," he guessed, "or they wouldn't be puttin' us in hollow square. Probably some deserter Clardy figures on shootin' before Phillips gets back."

The wind howled like a demented giant. It flattened the prairie grass and turned the small oaks so topsy-turvy that they looked like capsized umbrellas. The air smelled of rain. Jeff shuddered. What a desolate morning to have to die.

Above the roar of the weather came the thin squeak of a fife, strangely flawed by the wind. It was accompanied by a drum. It was the saddest, dreariest music he had ever heard.

"That's the 'Dead March,'" growled a grizzled corporal nearby.

"There they come," quavered somebody else.

Jeff felt the back of his neck prickling. Marching slowly side by side came the fifer and the drummer, followed by a guard of twelve armed men. Then came four troopers carrying a new coffin of cheap, yellow pine. And behind them, the condemned man.

Bareheaded, he marched stoically, a heavily armed guard on each side of him, a chaplain at his elbow. And last of all trudged the ten-man firing squad whose faces revealed plainly their distaste for the job ahead, despite the fact that the musket of one was loaded with a blank charge, and none knew who carried the harmless gun.

The grim procession halted. The coffin was placed on the ground beside an open grave. The prisoner, dressed in shirt and trousers of butternut, looked first at the coffin and then at the grave. And when, for the first time, he paled a little beneath his tan and stared desperately about him as though hunting for the face of a friend, Jeff saw with astonishment that he was only a boy.

The sergeant of the guard directed the prisoner to be seated on the coffin. Shaking his black head, the doomed youth refused and stood facing the firing squad defiantly, his hands tied behind him.

Jeff marveled at the rebel's courage. His high cheekbones, brown skin and straight black hair showed he had Indian blood.

"He's a rebel spy," hissed somebody. "They caught the sneakin' bugger behind our lines with a tissue drawin' of the fort's new breastworks hid in the sole of his boot. When they tried to get him to talk, he jest laughed at 'em."

"He ain't laughin' now," somebody else added.

Shivering, Jeff breathed a silent prayer for the prisoner, praying that he would not lose his courage during the ordeal ahead.

When the provost marshal stepped up to blindfold him, the rebel brushed him away for a moment and turned his clenched, youthful face southward for one final, farewell look across the river to the land of his people and his home. Then the blindfold was tied around his eyes and he stood impassively, his black hair disheveled by the wind, while the official order of execution, signed by Clardy, was read by the provost marshal.

Suddenly Clardy swore fiercely and sprang forward.

One of the men in the firing squad had fainted, dropping his musket and tumbling on his face in the wet grass. Clardy stood over him, drawing back his boot as though to deal him a kick.

But he restrained himself, and while the surgeon came

forward and worked to restore the man to consciousness, Clardy wheeled and began stamping down the long line of troopers, his nervous eyes darting from side to side as he searched for a replacement. Every man in the company stood rooted in his tracks, afraid he would be the unlucky one.

The captain halted in front of Jeff. His wild, suspicious eyes burned with triumph.

"Bussey!"

Jeff felt the marrow freezing in his bones. "Yes, sir."

Clardy gestured toward the man who had fainted. "Take his place in the firing squad!"

A slow anger burned in Jeff. Sweat formed on the insides of his palms. He wanted no part of shooting down anybody who stood helpless with his hands tied behind him. Defiantly he squared his shoulders.

"Sir, I will not."

A murmur of surprise broke from the ranks. Clardy's face reddened with rage. Half drawing his saber, he fixed upon Jeff a look of hatred. At that moment the surgeon came hurrying up and saluted.

"Sir, the man who fainted has recovered. He's back in his place now with the firing squad." Clardy scoured him with a look that had murder in it. Suddenly his voice went woman-shrill.

"Don't think you're going to escape seeing the execution, Bussey. And soon as it's over, I'm arresting you for dis-obedience." Wheeling, the captain stamped back to his place by the firing squad. Glaring at the sergeant, he nodded curtly, his face hard and merciless.

The sergeant barked an order. The firing squad raised its muskets. The click of the hammers sounded above the wind. At the command "Fire!" Jeff felt a weakness in the pit of his stomach and his toes contracted in his wet shoes. Then the simultaneous discharge of the ten guns, muffled by the wind, brought a merciful end to the scene.

The body was placed in the open coffin, and the company was made to march past and view it.

While the line in front of him was filing slowly past the casket, Jeff saw Lafe Appleman, one of the guards, pile something in a small heap on top of the foot of the coffin.

"Them's the dead man's personal belongin's," somebody whispered in awe.

Suddenly the morning sun broke through the fast-scudding clouds, glinting brightly off something golden lying on top of the pile. Jeff saw it was a gold watch, the handsomest he had ever seen, lying on its glass face.

A name was engraved across the back. When he saw the name, his hands shook, and his face turned to ice. Trembling, he hoped he had read wrong.

He hadn't. The name was still there, plainer than ever. In small, neat script, it said "Lee Washbourne."

Jeff's hunt for Lucy's brother was over. . . .

A hot and bitter rage at Clardy flared in Jeff. He knew he had to think fast or Lee Washbourne would lie forever in a nameless grave. Quickly he turned to Noah. Pressing two shinplaster bank notes, all he had, in Noah's hands, he explained, talking fast.

"Noah, the boy Clardy just had shot is the son of that rebel family our officers boarded with a year ago at Tahlequah. We've got to get his body back to them. I'd go, but Clardy is going to arrest me. Go to Sergeant Pike and claim the body. Ask him for permission to go find old Belle, the old woman who lives in that run-down store at the crossing of the Illinois River. She knows the Washbournes in Tahlequah. Tell her what happened. Give her this money, and tell her to hire somebody to help her take the boy's body back to his folks in Tahlequah. It's only twenty miles from here."

Noah nodded gravely. "I'll do it, youngster."

"And be sure to have her explain to his folks that you, nor I, nor none of our enlisted men here had anything to do with this awful thing. Or even knew who the boy was, until just now when we saw his name on the watch."

The sergeant walked up and said briskly, "You're under arrest. Cappen's orders." Jeff hardly heard him. He knew Lucy would blame him for her brother's death. She always blamed him for everything connected with the war.

That night he sat glumly on a cot in the fort's small guard-house, surrounded by four whitewashed walls. He kept fretting about the terrible surprise in store for the Washbourne women when old Belle arrived with the body of the only son. He tried to estimate the old woman's arrival by the fort's various bugle calls.

At the dinner call, he told himself, "She's on her way now." At tattoo, he figured she was nearing the river crossing, close to Tahlequah. At taps, he knew she must be almost there. Still agitated, he went finally to sleep.

Next morning he awoke more depressed than ever. He ate very little breakfast. He knew that, barring an accident, old Belle had probably completed her sad errand of mercy, and that at last the Washbournes were alone with their dead.

As commander of the fort until Phillips returned, Clardy had supreme authority in fixing Jeff's punishment and he made the most of it. Jeff was required to forfeit a month's pay and carry two heavy saddles around and around the fort's palisades in the heat of the day. Whenever a horse died, it was his task to bury it. Clardy was clever at varying the punishment.

Once he had Jeff tied by the thumbs from a tree limb, per-mitting only his toes to touch the ground. However, the guard, who hated the captain, loosened the cords so that Jeff could drop down flat on his feet and rest, tightening them only when another guard warned him the captain was coming. Jeff bore all the punishment manfully. Finally, on July thirteenth, he was released and returned to duty.

On the same afternoon, General Blunt arrived at the fort

with reinforcements from Kansas. There were two companies of the Sixth Kansas Cavalry with him.

Mingling with them, Jeff learned that a Union force sent out by Blunt had successfully defended a big Union wagon train from an attack by Stand Watie's rebels and that the train was now only a mile from the fort. There was bigger news than that, too.

Before leaving Fort Scott, Blunt's command had been notified of the defeat of the rebel General Robert E. Lee at Gettysburg and of the surrender of the rebel port of Vicksburg to General Ulysses S. Grant. In nearby Arkansas, the Union General Prentiss had inflicted an overwhelming defeat upon Confederate troops led by Generals Holmes and Price. Everything looked much brighter for the Union cause.

That night Jeff went on sentry duty again. This time, his beat was in the timber southeast of the fort, where the newly arrived cavalry had camped. He had supposed that General Blunt would prefer to sleep in a bed in one of the commodious rooms in the officers' barracks, but to his surprise, he discovered the general's large brown Sibley tent, its edges raised from the ground for ventilation, pitched in the timber with his command.

After taps were blown, the general's tent was the only one in camp with a light. As Jeff, followed by his dog, walked back and forth past it, he could hear the scratching of the general's pen as Blunt worked busily into the night on his dispatches.

Shortly after the sentries had called one o'clock in the morning, Blunt emerged from the tent. Walking to the fire, he stooped, lifting a small kettle off it. He poured a steaming dark-colored liquid into a small metal cup. Adding sugar which he took from an envelope in his shirt pocket, he raised the cup to his bearded lips as though to drink from it.

Changing his mind, he set the cup on a rock, probably to let it cool. Sniffing, Jeff could not detect the odor of coffee. He figured the drink was hot tea.

The dog was watching the general too, her plumed tail waving slowly in the reflected firelight. Suddenly she trotted over to the rock, thrust her slender nose into the cup, and began to lap up the tea.

With a bellow of irritation, the general rushed to drive her away. At the same time a wild, savage barking came from inside the tent. Apparently Blunt owned a dog, too. But he kept it tied. Dixie, her ears flattened and her tail down, bolted from the scene.

Gaping, Jeff shrank back into the darkness. He hoped the general hadn't seen him. When he finally got to bed at two, he heard raindrops pattering timidly on his tent and then swelling into a steady deluge.

Next morning Blunt's orderly came to Jeff's company headquarters shortly after reveille. He conferred a moment with Clardy, who barked something at a sergeant. The sergeant sloshed down the muddy company street, bellowing, "Private Bussey!"

Jeff was busily digging trenches to divert the rainwater that flowed everywhere. He looked up, leaning on his shovel. "Here, sir."

"Report immediately to General Blunt."

"Yes, sir."

Jeff's face paled beneath its tan. He knew what that summons was for. The general had made inquiries about the dog that had drunk his tea. Everybody in the regiment knew Dixie and to whom she belonged.

Jeff followed the orderly, buttoning his jacket with fumbling fingers. As they marched up to Blunt's tent, Jeff wondered what his punishment would be this time. He didn't want any more of the ditch crew, or the road crew, or the horse-burying crew.

"Wait here," said the orderly. Pausing a moment to look about him, he whispered behind his hand to Jeff, "An' when

you go in, watch out for his bulldog that he keeps tied up.
He's mean. If you get in range of him, he'll bite a chunk out
of you so big it'll look like a bear chawed you."

Jeff thanked him and snorted to himself. He'd take his
chances with the bulldog. The general was what he feared
most. He took off his cap and tried to part his rumpled hair
with his fingers.

The orderly came out and held the tent flap open for him.
"General Blunt will see you now."

Jeff took a long breath and licked his lips nervously. "Yes,
sir," he said and ducked inside.

☆ 17

The Ride of Noah Babbitt

It was dark inside the tent, save for a candle that
flickered brightly from the far end, throwing moving shadows
on the brown canvas walls. The air was clean and damp, with
a slight, pleasant smell of tobacco and pomade. Despite the
night's rain, the bottom canvas had been raised six inches. A
bayonet stuck into the earthen floor held the candle on its
round, upthrust end.

In the weird half light cast by the candle there was a small
table covered with maps and papers. And behind the table sat
General Blunt. The general was wearing his blue dress coat,

but this time the brass buttons at the top were undone, and his white shirt front showed at his open throat. His strong, mustached face was thrown partially in shadow, accentuating its swarthiness. He raised his dark, quizzical eyes.

Jeff saluted. "Sir, the orderly said you wanted to see me."

Gesturing slowly with one hairy hand, Blunt indicated a campstool. Jeff sat down. This was it. He was on the general's black list. As fast as he worked off his punishment for one officer, he was back in hot water with another. This time he had outdone all his previous efforts. He had incurred the wrath of a general, the commander-in-chief of the entire Kansas department. He swallowed resignedly. Anything but the stump-digging detail or the horse-burying crew.

Something nudged his leg. A large tan and white bulldog, tied by a leather leash to a tentpole, was sniffing at his trousers. Forgetting the orderly's well-meant warning, Jeff reached down automatically, as he did with all dogs, and began to rub the bulldog's ears.

The general grunted, suddenly, "How would you like to be a scout?"

Jeff was so jarred by the unexpected question that he sat speechless. His first thought was of Lee Washbourne and the execution on the drill grounds. Sometimes scouts didn't get back alive.

"General, I don't know anything about it. I'm afraid I wouldn't be any good at it."

The general looked annoyed. He threw back his massive shoulders. "That's what your captain thinks, too. In fact, he went further and said some harsh things about you and about your attitude. Your record with him is very bad. But I saw you in action at Prairie Grove. I think you'd do all right. That's why I called you in to talk to you."

"Thank you, sir. But I'm afraid I hadn't better. I haven't had any training for that kind of work. I'd probably mess things up." Jeff could still hear the fife squeaking the "Death

March" and see the lonely, bitter look on Lee Washbourne's face as he stood by the cheap pine coffin just before they shot him.

Blunt scowled and took a long drink from a small tin cup on his table. His deep bass voice seemed to rumble from way down in his black boots.

"Colonel Phillips tells me that he has trouble getting information about the enemy over the river. He says he sends out spies, but they don't come back. I think all his scouts have sold out to the enemy. So I've decided to organize my own. I've got to have information about the enemy and I've got to have it quick."

Jeff stopped scratching the bulldog and squirmed on the stool. The general didn't seem to be paying any attention to his lack of enthusiasm. He guessed that a soldier should always do what his commander asked, regardless of the risk. Anyhow, this might be far better than the punishment he was expecting. Maybe he ought to look into it a little further.

"Sir. if I became a scout, how would I go about it? How would I get across the river? What would I be expected to do after I got across?"

"Can you swim? Can you ride a horse?"

"Yes. sir."

Blunt put his cup down and belched delicately. "We will escort your patrol across the river and post a guard there until you return. You will ride behind the enemy lines and try to capture some of his soldiers and bring them back with you. It is imperative that you do bring back enemy prisoners. Try to take at least two or three so we can question them separately and cross-check their stories. Also, keep your ears open for any other information regarding the enemy you might hear."

"Like what, sir?" Jeff couldn't help noticing that the general was now speaking in the present tense, as though he had already agreed to accept the dangerous mission.

"Like trying to find out if Cooper has any reinforcements coming up from Texas. I want an estimate of all Cooper's forces south of the river, how much artillery he has, the extent of his earthworks, anything you can find out about their supplies, morale, position, names of their most prominent officers. But the main thing is to bring me back some prisoners."

Jeff nodded uneasily. He'd be lucky if he got back across the river himself. Still, he had joined up to get the war over with quickly as possible. Maybe this would help speed things up.

"The river's up. Cooper has dug rifle pits and posted heavy picket stations at every ford. But we'll get you across some way."

"Yes, sir," said Jeff. His skin began to goose-pimple, half in excitement, half in fear. Then a disquieting thought struck him.

"General," he blurted. "Could I have a new horse? The plug I've got now is a good cavalry horse. But he's so poor his ribs look like bed slats. The rebels have got good horses. They outrun ours every day."

Blunt nodded, soberly. "That's because the grass has already risen in Texas. Their horses are further along than ours. But you'll get the very best stock we've got. Report at once to Lieutenant Orff. He's in charge."

The general stood. Jeff stood too, saluting. He turned and left the tent. He was now in the Union scouts.

Three hours later the Union patrol of forty men started. The sky was cloudy. At first they traveled in the timber so the rebels couldn't see them from the opposite shore. Despite his lack of horsemanship, Noah was in the patrol, too, his tall body bouncing up and down as he sat his mount awkwardly, one hand tightly gripping the saddle gullet.

After they had ridden for two hours, they turned southward through the trees, searching for the river. Jeff guessed they would avoid the fords, heavily guarded by the rebels, and try to cross at a deep spot. Soon he could hear the Arkansas gurgling noisily ahead and smell the earthy odor of its brown flood waters. They rode up to its north bank and stopped near a gigantic black walnut tree. The sun broke momentarily through the clouds, lighting up the tip of each dirty brown wave. Heavily swollen by the rains, the stream looked a quarter of a mile wide and was running bank-full. Jeff doubted if they'd ever get across.

Orff, a blond Missourian with a big Roman nose, left a dozen men in the tall grass on the Union side of the water, Noah among them. He sat down, pulled off his boots, and tied them on his saddle. Jeff did the same. Orff also took off his trousers and tied them by the legs around his neck. Then his sharp hazel eyes fell on something fastened to his saddle.

It was a rifle scabbard of soft tan leather, and Jeff could tell from the shape of it that there was a gun inside. For a moment the lieutenant hesitated, as though debating whether to risk wetting it in the river water. With a grunt, he disengaged the sheathed weapon from the saddle and handed it to the corporal of the detail staying behind on the shore.

"Don't lose it," Orff charged seriously. "Let me have your carbine."

Quickly the trooper made the exchange, unslinging his weapon from his shoulder. Orff looped it around his own neck. Shifting his pistol and ammunition as high as possible, he thrust his bare foot into the stirrup and swung into the saddle.

"Le's go," he said and urged his black horse into the flooded stream, the others following. They crossed the river without trouble.

Jeff liked the dun that had been issued to him. He was splendidly formed from the loins forward and his legs were flat and clean. He had endurance and he could move. He didn't like to walk, preferring to be ridden at a canter or a lope. Jeff

found he could guide him with the outer knee. Twice he felt
the cold water rising to his crotch but since he rode naked from
the waist down, he kept his clothing and his weapons dry.

On the rebel side of the stream, Orff planted another dozen
men in the willows. Then taking Jeff and fourteen others, he
spurred southward through the timber.

"They won't be lookin' fer us," Orff reasoned, his mouth full
of fresh chewing tobacco. "They probably figger th' river's
too high." With a striking motion of his chin, he spat an amber
stream at an alder bush and wiped off his mouth with the palm
of his hand.

Jeff hoped the lieutenant was right. But this was rebel territory and they might meet a rebel patrol at any time. Their
guide was an Indian lad from Drew's Union Indian brigade,
who had once lived in this area. Orff called him Frank. They
rode at a swinging trot, and as the sandy trail, bordered by
willow and tamaracks and Indian grass, opened ahead of
them, Orff sent out flankers on both sides.

Another hour and they came upon the Fort Smith road, a
wide, sandy, wagon-rutted thoroughfare over which Cooper, the
rebel Indian commander, kept in constant communication with
rebel forces in nearby Arkansas. It was bounded on both sides
by pine, hickory, and oak.

Orff raised his right fist and the column halted. There was
nothing in sight. All Jeff could hear were the mockingbirds
singing their heads off in the oaks. Orff looked shrewdly
around him at the thick underbrush, mostly dogwood, strawberry bush and papaw.

"Le's hide here an' see what comes along."

The lieutenant planted a guard half a mile up the road in
either direction and concealed his main force in the roadside
brush. Jeff, the guard on the west approach, guided the dun
behind a clump of alder where he had a clear view of the
road. As he adjusted the one-shot pistol in his waist, his nose
caught the resinous whiff of pine needles as the hot sun shone

on them. Big yellow-bodied grasshoppers arose from the grass clumps and cruised in the warm sunshine, snapping noisily while in flight. For two hours nothing happened.

Suddenly Jeff heard shots down the road, then men shouting and horses running. Apparently Orff's patrol had jumped a small party of rebels. Jeff grasped the dun's bridle reins and listened nervously. Sounded as if the chase was going away from him. He had just decided to follow when he heard hoof-beats coming up the road.

A single horseman, clad in Confederate gray, hove in sight, galloping easily, as though bound for a far-off destination. He was an older fellow, good-looking, with low black sideburns showing beneath his gray campaign hat. Instantly Jeff drew his pistol and, putting spurs to the dun, burst from the woods and rode straight across the rebel's path.

"Halt!" he cried. "You're my prisoner."

The rebel seemed to have a different opinion. His face white, he ducked behind his horse's neck, snatched a pistol from his belt, and threw a quick shot at Jeff. The bullet missed and the rebel horse reared, neighing shrilly. Cursing, the rebel dropped his pistol, got both hands on the reins, and turned his mount off the road into the trees.

Jeff followed closely, holding his unfired pistol shoulder high. Their orders were to take prisoners without shooting them, if possible. Both horses were galloping almost at full speed, but the dun, hunching himself low as he skimmed over the ground, quickly overhauled the rebel horse.

Abruptly, the rebel horse stumbled, spilling the rebel from his saddle. Riding past him, Jeff heard the heavy thump of his body as he fell in the sand.

Elated, Jeff sawed at the dun's reins. Finally he got the dun turned and retraced his steps. For five minutes he carefully combed the dark pine scrub and sumac, but there was no sign of the rebel. All he found was the rebel horse grazing quietly in the woods. She was a small black mare. On her back was a shallow Mexican saddle, a haversack lashed to its large, flat horn. Jeff switched the haversack to his own saddle and, leading the rebel mount, rode slowly back over his tracks, taking one final look. But the man had vanished.

"Corn!" Jeff growled, thoroughly chagrined.

He put the dun at a gallop, heading back to the river as Orff had ordered him to do if they became separated. He figured some of the rebels had probably escaped and would quickly bring back cavalry to intercept Orff's patrol. Better get home before it was too late.

When he struck the river, it was midafternoon. There was no sign of Orff, nor his patrol. The water had gone down and the stream looked easier to ford. Finally he saw the gigantic black walnut tree on the opposite bank. Gratefully he pulled rein.

"Bussey," somebody called in a low voice. The patrol was waiting for him in the brush. Orff rode out of a clump of cottonwoods. From collar to cuff, the lieutenant's blue uniform was soiled with mud. He frowned anxiously as he saw the extra horse, its saddle empty.

"What happened?"

Vexed at having to report his failure, Jeff told him. "Did you do any good, lieutenant?"

Orff gestured behind him at the riverbank, disgust and passion in his tired face. "We got one, but I don't think he's gonna live to tell the general nothin'. Joe had to shoot him off his horse to stop him. These brush rebels don't know what halt means. They'd rather get shot than captured. Even when you throw down on 'em, they break an' run like turkeys." He glanced nervously up and down the stream. "Le's get outa here. The ones that got away went after help. The woods is full of rebels right now lookin' fer us. We're a long ways from Gibson."

They plunged into the dirty water. Orff's prisoner, bleeding from the back, lay on his stomach across the saddle of his own horse, limp as a sack of oats. He looked like an Indian. His black eyes were open and he was moaning with every step his horse took, his arms dangling, his black hair fluttering in the breeze.

Orff rode alongside him in the water, one hand on the back of the rebel's saddle. When the horses swam, he steered his mount with his knees, using his hands to hold the rebel's face out of the water, so he wouldn't drown.

As they waded out on the north shore, Jeff saw the Union troopers rise cautiously out of the green river cane, only their black hats and white faces showing. They gawked curiously at the wounded prisoner.

"They got one."

"Looks like a Creek or a Choctaw."

"He shore looks bucked out."

"Dead as Santa Anna. Jest as well git a shovel an' cover him up."

Orff still didn't like the situation. He unslung the carbine he had borrowed and returned it to its owner, reclaiming his own beloved gun. He tied it securely to his saddle and barked an order. "Mount!"

While they ran to get their horses, he walked over and looked anxiously at the prisoner, examining his wound. Then he shook his head. The man was obviously dying.

They took him with them, anyhow, traveling at a gallop. One trooper rode double behind him, holding him on. As usual, Noah was having trouble staying in the small army saddle. It was a McClellan, just rawhide fitted over a hardwood tree. It had no horn. His red face screwed in pain, he sat straight up, one hand on the reins and the other clutching the saddle's gullet, his long legs clinched tightly against the horse's sides.

When they stopped at a small creek, the prisoner looked more dead than alive. The panting horses thrust their muzzles gratefully into the water, their wet sides heaving. The prisoner

was lifted off his horse and laid on the grass of the creek
bank.

Orff lifted his head, his empty canteen in one hand. He had
the other arm under the prisoner's neck. He looked around.

"Anybody got any likker?" Nobody answered.

"Lieutenant," Jeff said, "this water looks cool over here.
I'll get some in my canteen. Maybe we can get some down
him."

Leading the dun, Jeff headed for the shady spot.

It was there the rebel cavalry struck. Jeff was on one knee
emptying the stale water out of his canteen when suddenly he
heard the rebel yell—a long, low-pitched howl that swelled
into a couple of high-pitched yelps and a long, shrill scream, all
of it in one breath.

A long line of brown-clad figures, all mounted, bulged suddenly into the clearing, fanning out. They were a hundred yards
away but coming like the wind, pistols, carbines, and shotguns in their hands. There must have been seventy-five or
eighty of them.

A rebel ball clipped off a sunflower six inches from Jeff's
nose, as though somebody had severed it with a whip. As he
ran for his horse, he wondered with amazement where they had
come from? Gunfire laced the clearing, echoing hollowly off
the distant timber. Horses' hoofs drumming menacingly, the
rebels came on and on.

"Stand an' fire on 'em!" Orff roared.

Obediently Jeff unslung his carbine and crouched in the
brush by the lieutenant's side. Noah joined them, his carbine
in his hands. Orff reached for the leather sheath tied to his
saddle and yanked out a small, shiny, newish-looking gun.

Kneeling, the lieutenant pressed the gun's polished walnut
stock caressingly to his cheek. Aiming deliberately, he began
to pump bullet after bullet into the rebel advance. His muddy
face grim with purpose, he fired with unhurried confidence.
Spang! Spang! spoke the rifle, neatly and mortally.

Jeff was amazed. He saw Orff knock two rebels out of the saddle. While Jeff was reloading, the lieutenant emptied a third saddle and hit a fourth man in the arm. Each time he fired, he worked a lever behind the trigger, ejecting empty shells and pumping new ones into the breach.

After reloading laboriously, Jeff raised his carbine for a second shot, leveling down on a rebel who, charging at full gallop, was in the act of lifting his horse in a spectacular jump over the narrow creek. But before Jeff could get the man cleanly in his sights, Orff's rifle cracked at his elbow and the rebel, arms and legs flung wildly into the air, slid out of the saddle and hit the creek with a loud splash. Orff was firing so fast and with such deadly effect that the nearest rebels pulled up, their horses grunting and rearing, and retreated. Most of Orff's men were able to mount.

But the rebels wheeled, reformed, and charged again. The lieutenant bellowed, "Mount an' let's git out o' here!" Everybody able to travel hit the saddle, save Jeff and Noah.

They ran toward their horses. Jeff was in the saddle and had the dun turned around before Noah reached his horse. He shoved the bay's reins into Noah's hands. Noah dropped them on the ground and stooped to grope for them.

The bay began to lunge and back wildly through the brush. Noah, clutching the front and back of the saddle, got one foot in the stirrup. Hopping on the other foot, he pawed the air desperately as he tried to swing his long legs over the bay's back.

"Waw, you danged ole . . . Look at the gray devils swarm! What a fool Orff was to stop here. . . . I'm comin', youngster. . . . Waw, dang it! Dang the cavalry an' every hoss in it!"

Now the thicket blazed with fire. Jeff drew his pistol, praying that Noah would mount before they both got killed or captured. Noah had saved his life at Prairie Grove, and he wouldn't leave him now.

"Turn him loose, Noah, and jump up behind me! It's our only chance." At that instant, the rebels burst upon them.

"Surrender! Surrender!" they cried. The dun began to rear. Angrily Jeff jerked him down. He had no idea of surrendering. Surrender meant a long, weary walk to Texas, a terrible ordeal for a cavalryman, and mighty little to eat all along the way.

Just as Jeff reached down to give Noah a hand up, the bay leaped forward with the reins flying loose. Noah lay crossways on his stomach in the saddle, one hand clutching the horse's mane. Jeff thought he had been shot, but suddenly Noah wiggled one leg over the back of the saddle and sat up. He was still wearing his black campaign hat.

They galloped off side by side.

Noah was doing some wonderful riding, although not in the generally accepted fashion. Neither of his feet was in the stirrups. Everytime the bay made a jump, Noah came down on him in a different place—behind the saddle, in front of the saddle, onto the horse's neck, back on the horse's rump. He was riding the bay from his ears to his tail. But somehow he was riding him.

Suddenly Jeff paled. A fallen cottonwood log of gigantic proportions loomed on the ground ahead of them. Both horses leaped it as one, their bodies describing a graceful parabola. As Jeff squeezed the dun's body with both legs and looked back, with horror he saw Noah disappear entirely from sight.

Jeff gasped. Now Noah was gone for sure. His horse seemed to be racing without a rider, the reins flopping loosely in the breeze. Then Jeff saw something that made him yell with joy.

A hand was still enmeshed tightly in the bay's black mane. Another hand gripped the back projection of the saddle. Then a long leg appeared over the horse's undulating buttocks, groping blindly for a hold. Noah's black head followed. He had lost his hat, and his long hair was blowing in the breeze.

"Hang on, Noah! Stay with him!" Jeff yelled.

Slowly Noah wiggled his long body back on top of his horse.

Lying mostly on his stomach now, he grasped the bay around the neck with both arms, hanging on like grim death.

The clamor behind them grew fainter and fainter. With a parting volley, the rebels gave up the chase. Noah and Jeff rejoined their scattered squadron.

Back at Fort Gibson that night, an old woman rode into the fort. She had a sack of whortleberries to sell and had seen part of the skirmish. She came around where the cavalry was encamped, seeking to learn how the chase had terminated.

"They came mighty near capturing Lieutenant Foss, didn't they?" she said.

Orff, who had lost his dying prisoner to the pursuing rebels, was in a bad mood and turned away without answering. But another of his patrol spoke up.

"You must be mistaken, mam. Foss wasn't in the fight at all."

"Oh yes he was," she replied "I saw him. The rebels saw him, too. I heard them talking about it as they rode back. Their leader said that he had never seen such clever riding in all his life. He said Foss just played along in front of them, riding all over his horse, one leg dragging the ground. He said Foss was teasing them with his horsemanship, trying to trick them into an ambush, but they were too smart to fall into that kind of a trap."

Roars of laughter interrupted her.

Noah was rubbing down his horse. He looked around at them and spat sideways, slowly and deliberately. "G'wan, you fly-slicers! Have your fun. There's no danger any o' you bein' mistook for your betters."

The sun was setting red and clear when Orff and Jeff were ushered into the general's tent. A candle still sputtered in the end of the upturned bayonet.

Blunt heard Orff's account of their failure. It took Jeff only one minute to tell about losing his man.

The general was disgusted. He said, "Humph! I send out

forty men to capture a couple of prisoners. You're gone all day. You suffer casualties. And all you bring back is one rebel pony." He looked at them sourly.

"Sir, there was a haversack lashed to the saddle of the rebel I chased. I brought it along," said Jeff.

He thrust it toward the general. It was sealed, but Blunt broke the seal and drew out a letter. As he read it, excitement and pleasure came into his swarthy face.

"The man you chased was Cooper's courier. Now I think I can guess what Cooper's plans are."

Jeff shook his brown head. "Sir, I should have brought him in."

"I'd rather have this. It tells me more than the courier would have. This is a dispatch from Cooper to General Cabell, the enemy commander in Arkansas, asking Cabell to hurry over here with his army. Cooper knows I'm here. He must anticipate I'm going to attack him. He's right. Maybe I can hit him before Cabell joins him." Standing, the general began to bellow for his aides. . . .

After supper Jeff looked up Orff. He found the lieutenant enjoying a pipe in front of his tent, trying to forget his unhappy adventures of the afternoon. Jeff saluted.

"Sir, could I see that rifle you used in the battle today? The one you stopped the whole rebel army with?"

Orff's hazel eyes gleamed proudly. The rifle was his pride and joy. He ducked into his tent and produced the gun, pulling it out of his scabbard, and handed it to Jeff.

Jeff had heard about the new repeating rifles being manufactured in the North but this was the first time he had ever seen one. Curiously he passed his fingers over its smooth barrel of dark steel and its smooth walnut stock. He liked its lightness.

Orff took his pipe out of his mouth and gestured with it toward the gun. "She's a seven-shot Spencer. You load her through the aperture in the butt of the stock. You pump the empty shells out with the finger level there. Ammunition comes ready-made in brass cartridges and will always shoot, no matter how wet it gets. An' you can load her on a runnin' hoss."

Jeff shook his head incredulously. He looked down at his own muzzle-loading one-shot Springfield and thought of all the trappings he had to have to make it shoot once—powder, charger, cap box, ramrod, Minie ball. He had believed it the best gun in the world. Now it seemed as obsolete as the ancient muskets George Washington's infantry had used at Valley Forge. He was frankly envious. Seven shots without loading!

"Corn!" he gasped. "You could load her on Sunday and shoot her all the rest of the week."

"Prettiest little gun I ever owned," Orff said, "I gave thirty-five dollars for it, all the money I had in the world. She'll shoot straight, too. I went down the river with it last week an' killed eleven squirrels in thirteen shots. An' I cut the forefoot off the twelfth, but he got away."

Reluctantly Jeff gave the gun back to Orff. As he walked back to his tent in the darkness, he thought what a tremendous advantage an army would have if every soldier in it owned one of the new repeating rifles.

Next day was Sunday. Jeff's company, on scout, was camped on the Illinois River, four miles south of Tahlequah. He had the afternoon off so he decided to ride into Tahlequah and see Lucy.

He dreaded the trip, but he felt he should say how sorry he was about Lee. And tell them how courageous Lee had been. He wondered if Lee's body had reached them safely? They'd probably hate him because his company had witnessed the execution and provided the firing squad. Maybe they wouldn't even talk to him. Lucy would probably blame him. She always seemed to think the war was his fault. Also, he had to find out whether Lucy liked him even a little.

This might be his last chance to find out. Blunt was getting ready to jump off on another campaign. There would be a

battle and lots of shooting. Jeff cleaned the mud off his boots
with a cottonwood twig. That pistol shot Cooper's courier
had taken at him was close. So was the rebel ball that had
severed the sunflower six inches from his nose. He couldn't
hope to keep dodging rebel bullets forever. This might be the
last time he would ever see Lucy.

Obeying a whim, he took Dixie along. It was almost noon.
The day was hot and humid. He jogged the dun slowly so the
dog could stay up. It would be a good outing for her. With an
air of mingled discouragement and keen expectancy, he trotted
into the outskirts of the town.

☆ 18

Sunday

His heart swelling with excitement, Jeff rode up to the
Washbourne home, and his body stiffened. Both the big log
house and the premises around it looked deserted.

The lawn was unkept and full of thistles. The empty barn-
lot was hidden by tall weeds. The Washbourne women were
gone. Lucy was gone. Appalled, he slid his left hand down the
reins and leaned forward in the saddle, scanning the yard.

Then he saw that one of the flower beds was planted to
potatoes, onions, peas, and beans. And that a kitchen window
was open. On a clothes prop in the back yard, a petticoat
fluttered lazily in the hot southwest breeze. Swinging off the

dun, he tied the horse and the dog in the shade of one of the large sycamores in front of the gate.

Walking onto the front porch, he knocked. Inside the house, somebody's footsteps approached. His heart hammered madly against his blue hickory shirt. He squinted anxiously at the brown oaken door, the same door Lucy had opened that hot July morning a year ago. Would she slam it in his face now? Trembling, he swept off his hat.

Slowly the heavy door swung back, revealing a small, aged Negress. As she surveyed Jeff's faded blue shirt, his shaggy blue trousers with the yellow stripes of the Union cavalry down the sides, and his broken but neatly polished brogans, her thin, heavily veined hands began to shake.

Jeff asked, "Is Miss Lucy home?"

The Negro woman's eyes grew wider and wider, as though surprised that any Yankee soldier knew her young mistress. She shook her head vigorously. The whites of her eyes shone like glass. "Naw suh! She's gone down to Mary's to rub her mothah's back." She started to close the door.

Frustrated, Jeff said, "When is she expected home?"

Before the woman could answer, Lucy's mother came to the door. She walked slowly and heavily. One look at the grief and sorrow apparent in her face, and Jeff knew Lee Washbourne's body had reached home safely. She recognized him instantly.

She stepped back, opening the door wider. "Won't you come in, Mr. Bussey?"

She spoke and moved with a well-bred restraint. Her low, deep voice sounded courteous. "Lucy has gone to my sister's home. My sister has been ill, and Lucy's visits seem to cheer her. She will be back soon. I know she'll be glad to see you."

"Thank you, mam," said Jeff. He knew the odds were about ten to one against Lucy being glad to see him. But he stepped inside.

Moving slowly, Mrs. Washbourne shut the door behind him. "Mr. Bussey, first of all, I want to thank you sincerely for your thoughtfulness in connection with my son Lee's death. It has been a sad time for all of us. Belle Lisenbee and Mr. Hicks got here about midnight with Lee's body. They had to awaken us. Of course, nobody slept any more that night. They stayed until the next morning, and Mr. Hicks dug the grave. We buried Lee on the same hillside where he and Lucy used to play with their sleds when they were children. It was God's will, I suppose, that my son died so young, but it has been very hard for me to bear."

She led Jeff into the parlor. It was dark and cool there. He looked around and saw the same armchairs and divan, upholstered in blue. The spinning wheel stood neatly in a corner. The large family Bible lay on the same table.

Mrs. Washbourne turned around, her eyes wet. "I last saw Lee one night four months ago. He had ridden alone across the river, risking his life to see us. I heard him laugh at the back door and call, half in caution, half in fun, 'Hello, Mama. Anybody here I don't want to see?' And then came that awful night when Belle Lisenbee and old Mr. Hicks knocked on the front door you just knocked on. As long as I live, when I hear someone knocking on that door, I shall be reminded of my son's death. It has been sultry today, hasn't it? Won't you sit down?"

"Thank you, mam."

The back door slammed. "Excuse me. That must be Lucy now." She left the room.

Jeff stood, breathless, twisting his hat in his hands, a look of shy longing in his pleasant, boyish face. His heart was thumping wildly again. He heard Lucy's skirts swishing and her quick step approaching through the back of the house. He knew it was she. When she entered and saw him, her small, round mouth parted with surprise.

Hungrily, Jeff stared at her. There were faint shadows beneath her eyes. She looked more subdued than he had ever seen her.

To his astonishment, she came right up to him and gave him both her cool little hands.

"Mr. Bussey," she said, with a welcoming smile. "What a nice surprise." She sounded as if she really meant it.

Flabbergasted, he took her hands and stammered, "Good afternoon, mam." He released her hands, shyly, and stooped to pick up the hat he had dropped in his confusion.

She was brown as saddle leather. There were a few freckles on her nose, and Jeff thought he knew who had been tending the vegetables he had seen in the flower bed. The long blue cotton dress she was wearing emphasized her slim young figure.

"Mam, my patrol camped last night on the Illinois River, near here, and I thought I'd ride over and see you . . ."

He halted, awkwardly, rephrasing it. "I mean—see how you and your family were getting along." Corn! There he went, messing things up again. He had a lot of nerve, announcing he had come to call on her when she wouldn't even wipe her feet on him.

But Lucy didn't seem to mind. She looked around for the Negro woman.

"Perce," she called, "please bring Mr. Bussey a cool drink from the well. He's been riding in the sun." She turned again to Jeff. "May I take your hat?"

Jeff looked at it. It was battered almost beyond recognition, but he couldn't help it. It had been months since the ordnance department had received replacement clothing from Fort Scott. Ashamed, he thrust it toward her. She took it, watching him, a little smile of pleasure on her face. Then her face grew suddenly grave. She sat down facing him, still holding his hat in her hands.

"Mr. Bussey, I can't begin to thank you enough—for—your kindness—regarding my brother. . . ." She was unable to go on.

Tears came into her eyes. She raised her oval chin and went on bravely, "Our whole family is sincerely grateful to you for going out of your way to do what you did—for sending Lee's body to us so we could bury him decently in our own family cemetery—and for paying Mr. Hicks to come with Belle and dig the grave . . ."

Jeff thought she was more beautiful than ever.

"Mam, I'm sorry there was so little I could do under the circumstances. Every soldier in our company was made to view the whole thing. None of us liked it. None of us even knew it was your brother until later. Your brother behaved very bravely. I'm heartily ashamed of my commander for ordering it, mam."

She looked up at him, her wet eyes shining.

"Belle told us how you refused your captain's order to serve on the firing squad and how you were punished severely for it."

Jeff dropped his eyes uncomfortably. That blasted Noah had done too much talking. Abashed, he shook his head. He didn't want credit for something he hadn't done.

"Yes, but mam—I didn't know at the time I refused—that it was your brother."

He saw that he should change the painful subject. "As I rode up just now, mam, I could see that you haven't had a cow for some time. What happened to her?"

A shadow passed across Lucy's face. "The Yankees stole her and butchered her calf for veal. They came one morning at breakfast. They took the cow and the calf and all our food, too."

Jeff moistened his lips, angry at the depredations of his own army. There were laws against looting.

Seeing the remorse in his face, Lucy added, practically, "There's no need for you to feel badly about it, Mr. Bussey. You've already shown us how you felt about the cow. Besides, these weren't infantry. They were cavalry."

Jeff felt a slow crawl of shame. "I've changed services, mam, since I saw you last. I'm in the cavalry now." He looked forlornly out the window where he had tied his horse in the yard, trying to think of something else to say. "That's my horse out there, mam. Would you like to see him?"

They went outside. Jeff untied the dun and got into the saddle. He turned him around a couple of times so Lucy could see how he handled.

Lucy stooped to pat the dog and bury her fingers in the thick hair behind Dixie's neck. "She's a beauty, Mr. Bussey. But why do you tie her?"

Jeff felt his ears reddening. "So she won't fight with your cat, mam."

The corners of Lucy's mouth turned upward and this time she didn't try to suppress her smile.

"Then you can untie her, if you like, Mr. Bussey. Our cat is gone too. She left the same night the soldiers left."

Jeff fell silent. Dad gum! Stealing the family cat while the family was still on the premises. How low could cavalry stoop? Lucy sat down on the wooden stile and rubbed the fur on Dixie's back.

He told her about Dixie drinking General Blunt's tea, and she laughed merrily. He wished he could make her laugh more.

"Mam, I'm a scout now," he said proudly. Her laughter ceased. When he told her about Noah Babbitt's ride, she listened very quietly, and he saw the fear come back into her face. He guessed he was reminding her too much of Lee, so he switched to other things.

"Mam, has your family had enough to eat?"

"We haven't had much lately," Lucy admitted, smoothing her skirt over her knees. "It's almost impossible to buy food here now. Since we lost the cow, we have no milk nor butter. And we have no wheat for bread. Father wants us to live in Texas but Mother hates to leave our home and our furniture. Occasionally, Father sends us a quarter of beef or some side meat. We have our vegetable garden. When the Union cavalry took all our meat, Mother sent word to Father not to send us any more. She says it's too risky. She's afraid he will try to bring the food himself, so he can visit us. The Union army is all around us now." She looked at him honestly. Jeff liked her for it.

"But that doesn't mean we are starving," Lucy added, smiling. "We'll be honored if you'll have dinner with us. It will be mostly vegetables, both cooked and raw."

Jeff said, "Thank you, mam. I'll be happy to." He stood and, reaching into the saddlebag on the dun's back, produced a gallon sack filled with shelled corn.

"If you've a small grinder, mam, we can have fresh corn bread." He had swapped a pair of spurs for the corn. Stuart Mitchell had given him the spurs. He had taken them off a dead rebel cavalryman he had shot at Cabin Creek, but Jeff didn't tell Lucy that.

As he went with Lucy to the smokehouse to grind the corn, Jeff felt hungry. He guessed you were always hungry in a war. Although the dinner was plain, he was impressed with the heavy silver tableware, the brown plates of stone china, the yellow linen tablecloth, and the brown linen napkins. Perce, the Negress, was openly nervous every time she waited on Jeff and was always careful to walk far around him when she passed.

After dinner, while Lucy helped Perce wash the dishes, Jeff walked outside. He saw that the windlass over the well was broken and he repaired it. He found hammer, nails, and saw and substituted a new board for a broken one in the small plank walk leading to the smokehouse. He found a sickle and leveled the weeds growing rank around the stone boundary fence. He tied up the tomato vines in the flower gardens. And all the time he worked, he marveled at Lucy's changed attitude toward him. He had never been so happy in his life.

Later, when they sat alone in the parlor, Lucy sewed a button on his shirt and skillfully mended a torn place. As she stitched fast and deftly, she said wistfully, "The thing we miss the most on Sundays is never hearing a church bell. My people are Methodists. But most of the churches have been destroyed and the ministers scattered. Riley's chapel, two miles south of town, has been torn down. The big church at Park Hill burned two years ago. As long as our army occupied the country, we usually had preaching of some kind. Colonel Watie used to send Mr. Slover, his chaplain, across the river, horseback, to preach to us in private homes on Sunday nights. But now it's too dangerous."

Jeff told her about the rock mission house at Sugar Mound, back in Linn County, and how it was nearly a two-hour drive in the buckboard to the mission from the Bussey homestead. And about his family and about the Missouri bushwhackers stealing the family horses from Bess and Mary, and trying to kill his father. And of his ambition some day to attend the new state university that would be built in Kansas when the war was over.

Lucy took up her knitting and described the seminary at Cane Hill, what she studied, what the school was like. She seemed lonely and anxious to talk. For the first time he felt he was really beginning to know her.

Across the room Lucy's knitting needles clicked busily, her eyes on the brown worsted stocking her fingers were fashioning. "At the Cherokee Female Seminary where my sisters went to school, the students worshiped at the Sehon Chapel, a half mile east of the seminary."

Curious, Jeff said, "What happened to it?"

With a graceful movement Lucy spread her hands resignedly.

"It's deserted now. We heard that some guerillas stayed there early in the war." Her eyes lighted up. "Would you like to see it? It's just over the hill. I haven't been there for two years."

Her eyes glistened with anticipation. She looked like a girl who liked to go places and do things, probably with scores of rebel beaux following her, Jeff thought.

She looked at him challengingly and said, "Maybe Perce will let us borrow her rig."

The Negress' vehicle, drawn by an old, blind mule, was an ancient cart with one buggy wheel and one plow wheel, and a quilt-covered box for a seat. Laughing at the novel transportation, Jeff and Lucy sat together on the box. It was great fun.

Jeff drove. Dixie explored the brush on each side of the narrow, rocky road that zigzagged through the hills. Overgrown with bluestem and protruding dogwood, the road obviously had not been used for some time. The old cart rattled and creaked as it rolled down gullies and over washed-out sections, listing frightfully as they passed over a root or stump. Finally the boney mule pulled the squeaking cart into a small clearing and halted.

On top of a green knoll nearby, Jeff saw the old chapel, standing in lonely solitude. It was a small church built of red brick. Most of its stained blue window glass had been broken out. Jeff decided that while it would have looked well in any spot, here it was beautiful. A small grove of black locusts grew around it. From the ruins of an outdoor arbor nearby, the intoxicating smell of wild pink azalea was on the air.

Jeff helped Lucy from the cart and tried to imagine what the chapel had looked like before the war had scattered its communicants and hastened its ruin.

"There's a gallery inside where the colored people worshiped. Most of them were slaves of the congregation," Lucy explained.

She glanced upward at the belfry where the bronze-surfaced bell was still visible. "They rang it to summon the seminary students. Many Tahlequah people attended services here. Lee and I used to come often together." Her low voice had grown quiet, almost hushed.

Finally they turned back toward the cart.

And so the day they had spent so pleasantly together flashed by like a meteor and like a meteor would be gone forever—the simple dinner, the talk, the ride in the old cart. With a war going on, he had so little time. It wasn't right. A fellow who might get shot tomorrow shouldn't have to wait a whole year to call a girl by her first name or tell her that he loved her.

Silently he helped her into the rickety cart and turned the old mule homeward. Lucy was very quiet. They started back to Tahlequah, the wheels turning silently as they passed over sandy spots. The sun sank low, throwing long black shadows across the road. Jeff was busy piloting the mule around the rough spots. As he drove, he was thinking.

Thinking that he wouldn't see Lucy Washbourne again for a long, long time. Might not ever see her again, if the rebels began shooting straighter. He figured he had stretched his luck about as thin as it would go. He knew Blunt's carpenters had almost finished the log rafts they were building to ferry the infantry and the artillery across the river. The new campaign against Cooper would probably start tomorrow.

It was almost dusk. When he saw the lighted windows of the Washbourne home, his heart fell. He wished it was a thousand miles away so he could prolong his ride with Lucy. He looked at Dixie trotting alongside the cart, her nose sniffing out the grass ahead.

He said, "Mam, I've a favor to ask. Now that I'm in the cavalry, it's hard for me to keep my dog. Would you want to keep her for me until I get back? You'd find her an excellent guard around the house."

Lucy said quietly, "I'd like to keep her."

"Thank you, mam."

As they approached the house, the dun heard the old cart's axles creaking. Raising his head, he looked at them and nickered softly.

Jeff stopped the cart by the gate and, climbing out, walked

around behind it to help Lucy out. He didn't want to go back to the camp on the Illinois or anywhere else. He didn't want to go back to war.

Lucy stood and put her hands on Jeff's shoulders. As he lifted her lightly to the ground, she looked at him. Her eyes softened as she read the dejection in his face. Passing her left arm around Jeff's neck and rising on her toes, she kissed him gently on the mouth.

Looking up at him with quiet amusement, she said in her low, drawling speech, "I like you, Jeff Bussey. But I warn you: I haven't changed my mind about the war. I'm still a rebel— to the backbone." But she smiled when she dropped her arms.

Jeff was thunderstruck. You could have knocked him over with a feather. Lucy Washbourne had kissed him! Shaken clear to his toes, he could still feel the pressure of her cool lips on his. He knew he would never forget it, as long as he lived.

Later, when Jeff untied and mounted the dun, Lucy sat on the wooden stile in the twilight, her arm around Dixie's neck. Behind them, the Washbourne home was etched blackly against the red sunset. Dixie started to get up and follow Jeff.

"No, no. You stay here," Jeff told the dog gently. Puzzled, she sank back obediently on her haunches.

Both the girl and the dog watched him until he rode out of sight. . . .

Next morning, Jeff awoke early. The morning gun crashed noisily, echoing against the neighboring hills and rumbling and reverberating across the distant flats, but Jeff didn't hear it. The starry new flag Blunt had brought from Fort Scott was run to the top of the mast and, unfurling slowly and gracefully in the morning breeze, caught the rays of the rising sun. But Jeff didn't see it. His mind was too busy reliving his day with Lucy.

Lucy was all he could think about until he ran into David Gardner on the picket line. An expression of urgency on his florid face, David led him off to one side, out of earshot.

"Jeff, are you goin' out agin today with the scouts?"

"I don't know. They haven't told us yet."

The big orange freckles on David's face and neck seemed to pale. "Goshallmighty, Jeff, don't you dare ride anywhere nears the Watie outfit."

"Why?"

David's eyes blinked with fear. "We went swimmin' agin last night with the rebel pickets. They know all about Clardy havin' Lee Washbourne shot. The whole rebel army is sore about it. Their pickets said the Watie men have sworn that the first Clardy man they capture behind their lines will go before a firin' squad before he can say God with his mouth open."

Jeff felt that cold, flat statement clear down to the toes of his boots. He was the only Clardy man in Blunt's scouts, now that Noah had been put back in the cavalry to improve his horsemanship.

David cocked his head in a listening attitude. "Hear them hammers goin'? Blunt's flatboats is nearly done. We hear there'll probably be a big battle tomorrey or next day. Maybe they won't need to send out the scouts."

Jeff swallowed uneasily. He had never heard of an attacking army that didn't send out scouts. After watering and feeding the dun, he returned to his quarters.

"Bussey."

Jeff froze. Just as he feared, it was the orderly sergeant summoning him to an emergency meeting with Orff and the scout patrol. First, the sergeant took them to the ordnance department, where they exchanged their blue uniforms for ragged butternut attire, careful to divest themselves of any article that might identify them with the Union cause. Then Orff led them to a vacant room in the fort, where they wouldn't be overheard.

His pipe in one hand and a sulphur match in the other, Orff explained their mission. "The general wants to know if the rebel General Steele is bringin' reinforcements up from Texas to join Cooper. Soon as it gets dark, we're to cross the river, ride in behind the reb lines and, mixin' with the reb civilians, teamsters, anybody we run into there, try to find out when Steele is expected and how many men he's got."

Jeff squirmed nervously. It didn't sound a bit good to him. Orff dragged the red-tip of the match across the seat of his corduroy pants and, holding the tiny flame in midair, gave them a level look.

"I don't have to tell you that this patrol is on probation. We didn't do so good two days ago. If it hadn't been for that haversack Bussey got, we'da been blanked. The general's watchin' us close this time. Le's don't bumble it." Frowning, he touched the flame to the bowl of his pipe.

Throwing his match away, he blew a puff of gray tobacco smoke toward the ceiling. "We're to split up in pairs. This is Monday. If ever'thing goes well, the general says he will start movin' down the Texas Road Tuesday. He says soon as we git the information he wants, we are to hit for the Texas Road and identify ourselves to the Union pickets, who will be told in advance to expect us. They'll take us back to Blunt."

They started at midnight. There was a full moon. This time they went west instead of east. Avoiding the fords again, they swam the Arkansas six miles west of the fort. Although the river was falling, Jeff gasped once as the water rose to his knees and spilled into his boots when the dun stepped into a deep hole and had to swim. But they got across safely. On the rebel side, Orff divided the patrol into pairs. With a brief handshake, they separated, riding in different directions.

Jeff's companion was Jim Bostwick, a big, easy-going Missourian who drank black coffee by the quart, and now that he was to be absent for two or three days, filled his canteen with it to the brim. Bostwick had been a Union scout for General Curtis ahead of the Battle of Pea Ridge.

"Better let Bostwick do the talkin' if you get in a jam," Orff suggested. That was all right with Jeff.

As Bostwick and Jeff rode through the moonlit countryside they were careful to skirt roads where rebel sentries might challenge them. They wanted to avoid all contact with enemy military forces, if they could. But that was not to be.

Two hours before daybreak they splashed across a small creek and, wading out upon the opposite bank, ran squarely into several dark figures.

"Halt or we'll fire!" a thin, high-pitched voice snarled.

Jeff felt a strong hand grab the dun's reins. A pistol was thrust into his face. A hammer clicked.

"Who are y'all? Wheah you goin'?" the same voice demanded, coldly and menacingly. Drawing a long breath, Jeff fought to get control of himself.

Bostwick said boldly, "Hold yo' fire. We jest wanta get through to Honey Springs." He spoke easily and with a tolerant good humor natural to him.

In the moonlight Jeff saw they were now surrounded by rebel sentries. Forty or fifty hobbled horses were night-grazing close by. Near them, using their saddles for pillows, the ground was black with men sleeping. Jeff could hear their snores.

"Lotsa people in that fix. Why y'all wanta go to Honey Springs?"

"We're on our way there to join Watie's outfit," Bostwick lied glibly.

Jeff felt his breathing quicken. Bostwick was certainly laying it on thick. Jeff hoped the explanation was satisfactory because there was no hope of escaping now. Apparently they had blundered onto a large detachment of rebel cavalry.

"If that's all ya want, then you can climb down off yo' hosses. Cunnel Watie an' his outfit is camped right heah."

☆ 19

Wrong Side of the River

Watie men! Jeff's heart leaped so violently it almost jumped out of his shirt.

Cold sweat beaded on his forehead. Bostwick wasn't a Clardy man, but Jeff was. Already he could feel the execution blindfold tightening around his eyes.

There was nothing to do but dismount and unsaddle. Surly Voice gave them each a short stake rope and they tethered their horses to small saplings nearby.

"Yuh can sleep here till mawnin'," he rasped commandingly. "Then maybe the cunnel or the recruitin' officah will talk to yuh. Or maybe they won't."

With a gesture of mingled hostility and contempt, his arm indicated an unoccupied grassy spot.

Pillowing their heads on their saddles, they lay down in their clothes. The grass was wet with dew but Jeff was too worried to notice or care. It felt good to lie still and relax. He was dog-tired.

But he couldn't sleep. Surly Voice lay between him and Bostwick. Even if he devised a plan of escape, there would be no way to tell Bostwick. And if he got away and Bostwick didn't, things might go hard with the Missourian. Maybe they'd learn more, pretending to join the Watie cavalry, than they would consorting with rebel civilians in the rear.

Why not play along until they found out what Blunt wanted

to know? The main risk was talking their way past Watie or his recruiting officer in the morning, but that seemed a much better gamble than trying to shoot their way out of an armed camp tonight. The more Jeff thought about it, the better he liked it. Turning on his side, he closed his eyes and fell asleep almost instantly.

He was awakened just after daybreak by somebody stamping the ground near his head. The stamping was accompanied by an odd, jingling noise. Opening his eyes, he saw somebody's boots. On the heel of each boot was a large rusty spur with a drag rowel. Jeff dodged back and recoiled in fright.

Over him hovered an old man, ugly as a gargoyle. He was heavily built and bareheaded. In the early morning light, the man's head was almost twice as large as that of a normal human being. His huge, misshapen nose was pock-marked. His little, round ears were cauliflowered and looked as though they had been screwed forcibly into his head. His eyes were unsightly little slits that peeped out cunningly from beneath the most beetling brows Jeff had ever seen.

When the man saw Jeff looking at him, his face broke into such a hideous grin that Jeff thought quickly about the pistol in his belt. But the man seemed to want to be friendly.

"Wake up, boys, day's abreakin', beans in the pot, sour-doughs abakin'," he mumbled in a weird, tuneless key. His voice was broken and had a low, whining quality. He sounded as if he were about to break into tears. The man walked off, awakening others with his novel method of stamping almost in their faces.

Jeff sat up. A lemon flush of daylight lay across the eastern horizon. The robins had just awakened. In the pale hush of dawn, he smelled smoke and heard something bubbling in a pot. It was light enough to distinguish objects. Scores of baggage wagons were parked ghostlike with their tongues up and hundreds of horses grazed near them. Gasping with surprise, he realized this was no rebel patrol. This was the main body of the enemy force. Something big, some major enemy movement, was in the air.

Other figures were sitting up, yawning and stretching, throwing off brown and gray horse blankets. Jeff looked for Surly Voice. He was gone.

He toed Bostwick into wakefulness.

"What are we going to tell them when they ask us where we're from?" he whispered.

"Y'all can eat with ouah mess heah," growled Surly Voice, coming up suddenly behind them. Startled, they spun round, staring guiltily.

He was a thin, red-haired, consumptive-looking fellow with hard blue eyes. Jeff estimated him to be about twenty-five years old. He wore a medium-brimmed slouch hat. On the sleeve of his faded gray uniform shirt were the yellow stripes of a sergeant. He glared at them with open suspicion and gestured arrogantly toward the fire. It was plain he considered them prisoners until they established their identity.

At the fire, the repulsive-looking old man, who apparently was the cook, was broiling pieces of beef on a hickory spit and baking sweet potatoes in the coals. The bubbling noise came from a large fire-blackened can of coffee.

While they helped themselves, with their fingers, to chunks of the delicious hot beef, Jeff had his first look at the Watie men. They were the roughest, raggedest troops he had ever seen. Most of them were dressed in tattered homespun gray or dingy, yellowish-brown butternut. But they had tough, shrewd faces and looked as though they could obey an order or fight intelligently without one, if they had to. Despite their Cherokee blood, most of them looked more white than Indian. Jeff stared with nervous fascination at their weapons.

There wasn't a saber in the whole outfit. Instead, each man wore a broad, straight, double-edged Bowie knife in his belt. Their rude bayonets seemed to have been made by local blacksmiths from saws, butcher knives, and files. Surly Voice, whom the others called familiarly "Sam" or "Fields," had serrated the edges of his knife so it could tear Yankee flesh. They sat around on their heels, drinking tin cups of hot coffee and smoking shuck cigarettes. Jeff could tell from their conversation that they were getting ready to go into battle.

As the men wolfed down the beef and the sweet potatoes, they called the cook "Heifer" and openly insulted him about everything from his food to his deformed face. The old man took the rough banter good-naturedly. Jeff saw that the nickname "Heifer" was appropriate: the shape of the cook's head was not greatly unlike that of a full-grown female calf.

But his food was clean and tasty, and Jeff bit hungrily into his third chunk of hot beef.

"How d'yuh expect me to fight after eatin' this tripe?"

"Heifer, yore gonna have to cut down on the sody in these biscuits. I'm gettin' plumb yaller," a gaunt, blond fellow growled amiably. The remark drew a general laugh. Obviously there were no biscuits.

"Yuh always was yaller. Don't blame the biscuits," Heifer retorted in his sobbing, hysterical speech, and everybody roared and slapped the blond fellow sympathetically on the back.

"Got ye that time, Ben," somebody said, and they all laughed again. Jeff thought they were the gayest, most light-hearted troops he had ever seen.

They didn't act like men going into battle. They seemed more like cattle herders getting ready to do a long day's work on the range. Still dreading his ordeal before Watic, Jeff wondered where the rebel cavalry leader was and what he looked like. Where he had seen only fifty men last night, there were hundreds this morning, all of them eating their breakfasts over small campfires and saddling their mounts.

The cook saw Jeff had no cup. Grinning, he handed him half a canteen that looked as if it had been blown in two with powder. Jeff saw with surprise that it was a Union canteen.

The Watie men had few canteens. Instead, they carried clay jugs, straw-colored bottles or just plain tin cups.

He dipped the crude vessel full of coffee from the big can on the fire.

Jeff nearly gagged on his first swallow of the foul-tasting concoction. It was all he could do to keep from spitting it out upon the grass in front of everybody. This was his first introduction to rebel "coffee," made by pouring corn meal in a skillet, stirring it until it parched brownly and evenly, then spooning it in a pot and pouring boiling water over it.

Jeff looked at Bostwick across the fire from him and froze with alarm. Chatting in friendly fashion with the rebels around him, the Missourian was boldly drinking the cold Fort Gibson coffee he had brought along in his canteen. Nobody in the south had coffee like that. If the rebels caught a whiff of that authentic northern beverage, they would know certainly that both Jeff and Bostwick were spies.

Well, they'd know it soon enough anyhow. Any minute now, they would have to face Watie. And they still didn't have a story made up.

Fields, the hostile sergeant, bulged in Jeff's path, glaring sourly down at him. "Let's go and see the cunnel."

Silently Jeff and Bostwick followed him. He led them to a wagon in the middle of the camp and up to a handsome man who wore his long, sweeping black hair down the back of his neck. It stuck out underneath his slouch hat. Clad in open shirt and butternut pants, he was busily stuffing some papers into a haversack. Behind him, draped over a wagon wheel, was a gray uniform coat with a major's insignia upon the collar.

"Mawnin', Will. Wheah's the cunnel?" Fields greeted without saluting. With pounding pulse, Jeff realized this wasn't Watie.

"Left an hour ago fo' a staff meetin' with Cooper. Whatcha got there, Sam? Couple deserters?" The major's resonant, far-carrying voice sounded more jolly than threatening.

"Naw. Couple fighters. At least, that's what they claim. Came in about three this mawnin'. Said they wanted to join Watie." He looked scornfully at Jeff and Bostwick and scowled at the major, as though reminding him that he expected him to do his duty.

The long-haired major turned his intelligent brown eyes fully upon them, and Jeff could tell from the color of his skin that he was part Cherokee, too. He was obviously in a hurry.

"How come y'all want to join us?" he asked seriously, look- ing keenly from one to the other.

Remembering Orff's instructions, Jeff decided to let Bost- wick do the talking. But the major wasn't looking at Bostwick. He was looking directly at Jeff. Jeff's mind worked fast. For the first time in months, his stomach felt satisfyingly full.

He grinned. "Sir, we like the grub better here."

"Better here than where?"

Frightened stiff, Jeff turned his grin on wider. "Better here than anywhere, sir."

The rebel major scrutinized Jeff from the top of his tousled brown hair to the soles of his dusty boots. He saw nothing but a boy, a pleasant-faced, clean-cut boy who looked a little scared.

His face softening, he took his coat off the wagon wheel and put it on, and suddenly Jeff had the feeling that everything was going to be all right. The early morning sun peeked sud- denly over the oak-covered eastern ridge, stabbing the scene with long streamers of golden light. Now the parked baggage wagons didn't look quite so spectral. Jeff saw the initials CSA stenciled in white on their sides.

"What's your name?" the major asked.

"Jefferson Davis Bussey, sir," answered Jeff. Then he caught his breath. He had given his right name. It had never occurred to him that he might need another in enemy country.

A surprised expression came into the major's eyes. Despite his rank, he wasn't accustomed to being addressed as "sir." He liked the boy's politeness. He began hurriedly to button his uniform coat and turned apologetically to Fields.

"Oh, bosh, Sam. With a name like that he must be all right. You swear 'em in. I was supposed to meet the colonel at brigade headquarters five minutes ago." Snatching a high-pommeled saddle off the ground, he carried it, stirrups dragging and cinch rings and spurs tinkling musically, to his black horse staked nearby.

The hostile sergeant had no choice but to swear them into Company H of the Cherokee Mounted Rifles. Slowly and laboriously he wrote their names on the company roll. With his quill he pointed at Bostwick, who had also given his correct name.

"What's your full monicker? Robert E. Lee Bostwick?" he growled insolently.

Later Jeff learned that the major was William P. Adair, a lawyer who lived on Grand River and was one of Watie's most highly trusted officers and personal friends.

Quickly the irritable sergeant lined everybody up and called the roll. Jeff was amused at some of the Indian names in his unit—Beamer, Dreadfulwater, Duck, Doghead, Hogtoter. The sergeant rattled them off glibly, ending up with the three oddest names of all, Kickup, Turnover and Roundabout. Jeff also noticed that every man on the roll was present and accounted for. It was the stamp of a good outfit. Apparently the Watie forces had lost nobody because of desertion.

Later a lieutenant began dispatching guard patrols in all directions. As Jeff rode out with his, he asked the man next to him about the cook.

"Who, Heifer? He's a loner. Sleeps outdoors on the ground, even in winter. Says sleepin' inside smothers him. Everybody likes him but nobody wants to be close pals with him. It's the way he talks and the way he looks, I guess. Heifer's so ugly that the flies won't light on him. They say he had a son of his own, once, a handsome-looking boy. Heifer worked hard to get money to send the boy back East to school. But the boy was ashamed of his pa's ugliness and never came back home or had anything to do with Heifer afterward. Heifer hails from Texas. Used to cook for some big cattle spreads there."

The patrol dropped Jeff off near a weather-beaten church. Alongside it was a small graveyard, whose wooden monuments, gray with age, leaned crazily this way and that. All around, like somber guards, stood several old oaks. It was quiet and peaceful.

After staking out the dun, he lay on his back in the graveyard grass, worrying about the battle to be fought the next day. Would he be ordered to fire upon his own troops while riding with the forces of the South? He resolved not to fire directly at his comrades.

Above him in one of the big oaks, a mockingbird was splitting his throat. As he sang, he threw himself angrily into the blue sky, wings fluttering, then stood suddenly on his head in the air and flew back down to the same branch, scolding and fussing. Jeff wondered idly what the bird was upset about.

It was hot. For want of anything better to do, he read the inscription carved on the wooden face of the monument nearest him.

It said "Sarah McDivitt. Born June 2, 1788. Died Nov. 6, 1854." There was a verse under it too, a wistful little verse that seemed to express all humanity's sad yearning not to be forgotten completely after death. Jeff got up on his knees so he could read it better. It said,

> "As you are, so once was I.
> As I am you soon will be.
> When these words you see,
> Remember me."

Jeff wondered who Sarah McDivitt was and how old she had been when she chose the pensive lines for her gravestone. The church reminded him of the deserted chapel he and

Lucy had visited two days before. With a stab of longing, he thought of her, and then of her abrupt, "I like you, Jeff Bussey. But I warn you: I'm still a rebel—to the backbone." He wished the war would be over tomorrow.

Several hours passed. He was so sleepy that he almost dozed off. Finally he heard something coming down the road.

It was a husky young Negro driving a small herd of red cows ahead of him. They moved very slowly, the cows grazing as they walked.

"Howdy," Jeff said as they passed in front of him.

Startled, the Negro boy jumped. Then he saw Jeff and looked with wonder at his horse, and at the pistol in his belt.

"You a soljuh?"

Jeff nodded. "Why do they always build their graveyards next to the churches in this country?" he asked.

The Negro boy looked solemn. He was wearing a gray home-spun shirt, striped trousers, and had a sweat rag tied around his bare head. He was barefoot. Jeff wondered how he could stand walking on the sharp rocks.

"So the dead folks can heah the organ music an' the singin' on Sundays, I reckon," he said simply.

Jeff stood and pointed to the church. "What's the name of it?"

"Hancock Mission," replied the Negro, slowly and proudly. "They built it fifteen years befo' I was borned. They sho' did do somethin' when they built it. It stands theah in the woods apointin' its spire up towards heaven. Evah time I passes it, I feels kinda reverent-like. I always sings somethin' religious when I drives the cows by."

"Have you ever been in it?"

"Naw suh. It's jes' for white folks an' Indians."

They fell silent. A warm wind gently stirred the long grave-yard grass. A flock of green parakeets circled a nearby field with shrill cries, searching for cockleburrs. The old church dozed peacefully in the warm sunlight.

"You're a big, strong-looking fellow. Why aren't you in the Southern army?" Jeff asked.

The Negro boy looked at him strangely. "The South don' want slaves in theah armies," he said. He added, proudly, "We's too valuable. We's property."

Jeff's mouth fell open. He hadn't realized that.

"Are you a slave?"

The Negro nodded soberly. He looked at Jeff with narrowing eyes. "How come you nevah knowed slaves can't get in the army? Wheah you from?"

"Kansas," said Jeff boldly. He decided that if the rebels ever did question him at length, he would be safer giving his own name and home than trying to fabricate false ones.

"Isn't that wheah Mistah Aberham Linkum lives?"

"No. He was born in Illinois. But now that he's President, he lives in Washington. Why? What do you know about Lincoln?"

The Negro boy smiled, and a rapturous look came into his dark eyes. "I know mo' bout him than anybody. All the slaves talks about him all the time. We loves ouah mastahs but we all want to be free some day."

He spoke so guilelessly that Jeff was impressed. It was an odd speech for anybody to make in rebel-held country. He supposed the community was so isolated that no military force had ever passed through it before.

Jeff picked up a small rock and tossed it at a nearby gravestone. "If you were at Fort Gibson, you'd be free right now. In the Northern army there's a battalion of Negro soldiers from Kansas. They're all free. They wear blue uniforms, just like the white soldiers. And they're good fighters, too."

An eager light came into the young Negro's eyes. "I been to Fote Gibson. I knows a short way to get theah without goin' up the Texas Road. Two years ago I helped drive a herd of cows to Fote Gibson fo' my mastah. While we was theah I saw one of them big cannon guns. How fah will one o' them things shoot?"

"Oh, if it's big enough, about two miles, I guess."

The Negro rolled his eyes in awe. "Um! Um! A man could run all day an' still get killed."

Laughing, Jeff brushed the grass off his pants. "What's your name?"

"Leemon Jones. I b'longs to Mastah Saul Hibbs, a Chicka-saw Injun farmer. I lives half a mile down the road theah."

Jeff looked at the sun. It was about time for him to be relieved. He mounted the dun and, lifting his hand in farewell to the Negro, jogged off down the road.

As he swung along, he thought that if he ever got in trouble, real bad trouble, he might find an ally in Leemon Jones. He bet he could have made Leemon's eyes stick out like marbles if he had told him he had once heard Abraham Lincoln make a speech.

At daybreak next morning, Jeff saddled, mounted and, join-ing hundreds of hard-faced Watie riders, rode twenty miles north to Elk Creek, where Cooper's rebel battleline was being formed on both sides of the Texas Road. In the timber north of the creek, they dismounted and, building log barricades, awaited the onslaught of Blunt's Union army.

Jeff could hear cannon fire north of him and he knew that the Union artillery commanded by Hopkins and Smith had gone to work on the rebel artillery. He couldn't help feeling excited and uneasy. He had never gone to battle under such strange circumstances. Horrified at the possibility of fighting his friends, he had to stay and try to get the information Blunt wanted. Besides, if he left now it would draw suspicion on Bostwick. Keeping his eyes open, he had a good view of the rebel preparations for the battle.

Cooper's army consisted mainly of Texans and Indians. Jeff saw the Texas cavalry riding their little mustangs into position in the rebel center. They were mostly blond men, who controlled their mounts with chain bits and thrust their booted feet into big, wooden ox-yoke stirrups. Cooper posted on his left two Creek regiments commanded by Colonel D. N. McIntosh. His right wing was composed of Watie's First and Second Cherokee regiments of which Jeff was now a part.

Jeff was most surprised of all when he saw Cooper's reserve, a regiment of Choctaws and Chickasaws. Before he saw them, he could hear the jingling of the little bells and rattles they wore on their arms and in their horses' bridles.

Then they appeared through the trees, mounted on their small ponies. Their faces were painted orange and green. Although they looked active and sinewy in their buckskin hunting shirts and leggings, Jeff was amazed to see that their weapons consisted only of obsolete Indian rifles, knives and tomahawks. They were whooping and yelling shrilly as though to keep up their courage in spite of their incredible lack of fire power.

A crackle of musket fire broke out ahead, and the Watie men began to unsling their weapons, mostly shotguns and one-shot Southern Enfields with brass mountings.

In plain hearing of nearly everybody in the detail, Fields, the bossy rebel sergeant, ordered Jeff to the rear. "Yore too young for the front line," he said, curtly. "We fight dismounted with every fo'th man holdin' fo' hosses in the rear. Today you'll stay in the rear and be a hoss-holder." He thrust his reins into Jeff's hand.

"Yes, sir," said Jeff, saluting.

He took the reins, secretly pleased that he wouldn't have to oppose his own side in battle. Bostwick wasn't so lucky.

The Missourian was drafted for duty on the firing line but he seemed to be taking it well. As he trudged off to the front, his boots clumping awkwardly in the underbrush, he winked at Jeff and reaching behind him, patted his canteen, still one-half full of cold Union coffee.

A shower of rain fell about an hour before the battle began, rendering the rebel powder, obtained from Mexico, useless. In the damp weather it became pastelike and would not ignite. Jeff heard some Creek soldiers complaining because even when they built fires, they could not dry out their wet musket caps.

When the Northern bombshells, screeching through the trees overhead, began exploding with a roar, setting the grass and brush afire, it took all of Jeff's strength to hold the four saddled horses he had been entrusted with. Soon, rebel after rebel began to pass him, running from the front.

Jeff kept his own eyes and ears open, making cautious inquiries about both Steele's and Cabell's troops. All he could learn was that while both were on their way to the battle, neither had arrived. Blunt's timing had been superb.

The firing ahead of him redoubled and seemed to be coming closer. The two Watie regiments were being driven back. Now he could smell the smoke from the black powder. He wrapped the four sets of bridle reins more tightly about one hand. Soon the rebel Cherokees began to appear, grabbing their reins from the horse-holders, mounting and spurring southward, away from the battle. Two of them claimed their horses from Jeff.

"Their bombshells shoot twice—over there and over here," one gasped in protest.

"Where's Fields?" Jeff shouted, as they swung into the saddle.

"He's comin' yonder," they yelled and rode off, whipping their mounts with a frenzy.

Watching them, Jeff laughed bitterly. Although he was just a horse-holder, he aimed to be the best dad-gummed horse-holder in the rebel cavalry. He didn't like the sassy sergeant's crack about his youth. Vaulting onto the dun's back, he waited.

The figure of a man burst from the trees, crashing through the underbrush and sweetbrier. His shoulder was bleeding, and one arm hung limp. His hat was gone, exposing his red hair.

It was Fields. Jeff knew the Federal troops must be close behind him.

Leaning down, Jeff handed him his reins. But the horse was
plunging excitedly and, with one arm paralyzed, Fields had
trouble mounting. Jeff saw he wasn't going to make it. Federal
bullets were bouncing along the ground, like tiny frogs around
a millpond.

Jeff got off the dun to help, but Fields' horse jerked loose
and galloped wildly into the woods. Cursing, the rebel sergeant
ran a few stumbling steps in pursuit, then gave up.

"Here, Sergeant!" Jeff led the dun up to him. "He'll ride
double. I'll boost you into the saddle, then I'll crawl on behind."

Panting hoarsely, Fields stared at Jeff with fierce, pain-
glazed eyes, and for a moment Jeff thought he meant to refuse.
Then he put one foot in the stirrup and grasped the pommel
of the saddle with one hand. Jeff put his shoulder under Field's
rump and shoved him upward. Then he leaped on behind.

"Here, Sergeant, you take the reins. I'll need both hands to
hang on." After standing around all morning, the dun wanted
to run, even with a double load.

It was a wild ride. Legs flopping crazily, Jeff clung with
both hands to the cantle of the saddle. With every stride, the
sergeant's shoulder wound was irritated, and he alternately
cursed and groaned.

After they encountered the Texas Road, their progress was
easier. They began to overtake and pass other Watie men.
Soon a horse with an empty saddle was commandeered and
Fields put upon it. They kept going.

The skies were still cloudy and the air sticky and close. Inside his shirt Jeff could feel sweat running down his stomach
and ribs. His shirt was torn and the bare skin low on his
right side smarted where the bull briers had clawed him. The
Watie men rode silently, shame and discouragement in their
faces.

Once they stopped at a well to hold a gourd dipper of water to Fields' hot lips and to smear post-oak bark ooze on his wound.

"How do yuh feel, Sam?" somebody asked.

Fields snarled savagely, "What do yo' care how I feel? Yore no doctor. Yo' wouldn't know what to do if I did tell you how I feel."

Doggedly they resumed their flight. Others had been wounded, too, but there were no doctors to minister to them, either. They just bore the pain and kept riding.

They came to a low, sandy spot in the big road. Jeff could see the tall swamp grass and smell the stagnant water.

Up ahead somebody began to curse.

"Gallinippers!" he yelled, pulling up his coat collar. Jeff soon found out what gallinippers were.

The salt grass abounded in mosquitoes. When the horses' feet stirred the grass, the insects swarmed on the cavalry, humming ominously. Soft as lace, they alighted on the exposed parts of his body. The men whipped up their horses, ducking their heads and brushing the insects off their faces and necks with their shirt sleeves.

All afternoon long they retreated down the Texas Road.

The rebel farms they passed were untouched by raiders. The cotton had been hoed neatly and looked abundant. And while it would be two weeks yet before the corn would be fair for bread, it was tasseling clean. Grimly Jeff thought of the violence and terrible destruction the Watie men had wrought on the Union farms farther north. He felt very little compassion for the men with whom he was riding. But he stayed with them because he had a job to do.

At midafternoon, just below the junction to North Fork Town, they met Cabell's advance. While a halt was called so the generals could parlay, Jeff was careful to count Cabell's forces—more than two thousand Arkansas cavalry and four

pieces of artillery. Jeff was surprised to see that so many of
the Arkansawyers were gray-headed men and young boys.
Mingling with them, he soon learned that desertion from
Cabell's brigade, many of them conscripts of Union sympathy,
had been so widespread that the officers had very little control
over the situation. Quickly Cabell joined Cooper in the headlong flight southward.

Just before dark a slow, chilling rain set in. Owning very
few slickers, the Watie men had to take it like the cattle in
the nearby fields. The road had now become so slippery that
they slowed their pace to a walk. Wet to the skin, Jeff was so
exhausted that he dozed in the saddle. He discovered that by
balancing himself squarely over the horse and kneeling slightly
forward, he could sleep while the dun was walking.

Once when they were crossing a creek, Hooley Pogue, a
wiry, rollicking little Cherokee mixed-blood who was sound
asleep in the saddle, tumbled off his horse into the water with
a loud splash.

"What happened?" Fields asked irritably.

Gasping and thoroughly awake now, Pogue scrambled to
his feet in the knee-deep water.

"Excuse me, Sam," he sputtered. "I thought you said dismount."

A roar of amused laughter arose above the noise of the
downpour. It was the first laugh Jeff had heard since the battle.
Again, he marveled at privates and sergeants conversing as
equals, addressing each other by their first names.

The gray rain sluiced down in long, wind-slanted lines. Jeff
could feel it pelting his shoulders and spattering noisily off his
hat brim.

"Whew!" somebody called. "It's sho comin' down. Sounds
like pourin' peas on a rawhide."

They had ridden two hours in the rainy darkness when
they were hailed to a stop between North Fork Town and

Perryville by a man standing in the road waving a torch. He wore an old carpet strip for a raincoat. It had a hole in the top for his head.

"Camp's over here," he told them, pointing his torch to the right. The torch flickered feebly, threatening to go out.

As Jeff obediently followed the others, he felt a sudden chill and wished for a warm coat. Then he saw the round bulge of a commissary wagon wheel and heard the peculiar sobbing voice of Heifer Hobbs directing the weary men to their tents. They were back at their original camp.

The cook had made a rude lamp from a bowl full of sand, thrusting a nail through a rag and then deep into the sand, with the rag emerging at the top. Using oil he had rendered from a fat possum he had killed that afternoon, he poured the possum oil in the sand and onto the rag, then lit the rag and set the lamp on the shelf at the rear of the commissary wagon, out of the rain and the wind. The homemade device smelled a little but Jeff was surprised at its good light.

Feeling his way in the blackness, he staked out the dun and gave him a ration of corn from the commissary wagon. He felt ravenously hungry but figured he would either have to eat cold food or go without. Nobody could cook in this downpour. But again he reckoned without the resourcefulness of Heifer.

For weeks the cook had saved all his bacon rinds and axle-grease boxes for fires. He also had a few dry tree branches hidden away in his commissary wagon. While Jeff held a blanket over the fire, keeping it alive, Heifer went to work.

Quickly he mixed a great dishpan of corn-bread dough, plastering some of it on small boards, which he leaned near the fire. He wrapped the remainder in corn shucks and buried them in the hot ashes. Soon he was able to offer the wet, exhausted men hot corn bread and steaming plates of a Southern dish Jeff had never tasted before, Irish potatoes and green apples boiled together, mashed and seasoned with salt, pepper and onions. And there was plenty of hot "coffee" to wash it down.

Nobody joshed or teased the cook tonight. Gratefully the tired men in Fields' mess scooped up the food with their fingers or their bowie knives as they discussed in hushed tones the battle they had just lost and the comrades who had been killed or wounded.

Afterward Jeff threw the blanket around his shoulders and wondered where Bostwick was. A doctor had ridden up from the rebel hospital at Boggy Depot to treat the wounded. Tents were going up all around, hog-fat lamps were lit, and soon the place began to look and sound more like a military camp.

Jeff had pitched in and was helping Heifer clean up when he heard feet sloshing toward them in the dark. The slim figure of the sergeant appeared, his wounded arm in a sling and an oilcloth thrown carelessly over his shoulders, in the fashion of a cape. The rain had slackened somewhat but now the wind had arisen and the cold seemed to blow right through Jeff's sodden clothing.

Fields stood looking accusingly down at Jeff.

"Yore pal, Bostwick—he ain't comin' back. Shell got him," he reported, his voice low with passion.

Shocked by the bad news, Jeff eyed Fields bleakly in the flickering light that came from Heifer's "possum" lamp. Bostwick dead! Jeff breathed a silent prayer for the Missourian's soul and waited. There was something sinister in the sergeant's manner.

Fields went on, "He fell close to me. All day long I watched him drink from that canteen of his. I figured it was whisky. After I got hit, I needed a shot of whisky. So I took the canteen off his dead body and upped it. You know what I found? Coffee! Yankee coffee! He was a blue belly. And so are you!"

Jeff felt a premonition of disaster. He stood facing Fields, grateful for the partial darkness that blotted out the guilty expression he was certain must be on his face. He thought fast. He was on the wrong side of the river. His life might depend upon what he said next.

Heifer said it for him. The cook straightened over his pots and pans, the firelight playing fitfully over his terribly deformed face. Suddenly, he blew his nose into the fire, using his finger and clearing one nostril, then the other, with nasal blasts that rang like a horse snorting.

"Sam, yore addled," he blurted. "What else does the boy have to do today to prove himself to ya—tote cha on his back all the way from Honey Springs to Red Rivah?"

Fields snarled something unintelligible.

Heifer kept talking. "You otta git down on yore knees and beg his pardon. Where'd yuh be today if it wasn't for him? I'll tell yuh where. Walkin' to a prison camp someplace in Kansas. If this boy's what yuh say he is, he coulda left you on the battlefield an' gone on ovah to Blunt. Or he coulda taken yuh with him to Blunt. You was helpless."

"Sam!" somebody called from the darkness, "Sam Fields! Major Adair wants to see you."

Turning on his heel, Fields stamped off through the mud. He didn't seem convinced. Relief flooded over Jeff like warm sunshine. Gratefully he thanked the cook.

Heifer snorted. "Don't pay no attention to him," he advised, turning toward the fire. "When he gits this away, he don't know skunks from house cats. He's a good officer but he's been all tore up inside evah since the Feds shot his best friend, boy name of Lee Washbu'n, befo' a firing squad. That made Fields crazy suspicious of evahbody. Now he can't wait to catch some Fed scout behind ouah lines. An' if he evah does, God help 'em. He'd cut 'em to pieces with his bowie."

Jeff remembered the jagged edges of Fields' knife. So Fields knew Lee Washbourne. No wonder Fields was suspicious of anybody who drank Yankee coffee.

Wet, cold and miserable, Jeff looked around for a place to

sleep. He didn't even have a quilt. Soaked to the skin, he felt weak and flushed and feverish. He looked longingly at the tents close by, revealed by the lightning flashes. Nobody had asked him to share one. And he hadn't slept much the last two nights. He was so tired he didn't think he could take another step.

"Yuh can bunk with me under the wagon, if you wanta," Heifer offered suddenly. "It ain't fancy. But it's dry. I got my bed laid on some bee-gum logs an' I gotta canvas fly to keep the rain out." Thankfully Jeff accepted.

Even if Heifer did have a face that would stop a clock, Jeff was too tired to care. The cook splashed off into the darkness and returned holding something in his hands under his uniform coat, away from the cold drizzle. He thrust dry clothing toward Jeff.

"Heah, kid," he said kindly. "Pull off those wet duds and put these on. Theah full o' holes but theah dry. Gimme yore shoes an' wet clothes an' I'll dry 'em out fo' yuh by the fire soon as it quits rainin'." Gently he helped Jeff pull off his boots and his sodden trousers.

"Heah," he said, holding back the tarp that dangled down the side of the commissary wagon, "hop in theah an' crawl 'tween the covahs. You'll be snorin' in five minutes."

Jeff beat even that. He was sound asleep in three. . . .

Next morning he and the cook were up with the birds. The sun came out warm and hot. Feeling better, Jeff helped Heifer with the breakfast. He rustled the firewood, carried water, and did a score of other odd jobs besides. He was clearly the cook's favorite now.

The Watie men stayed in camp all day, drying out their wet clothing and their powder caps, doctoring one another's minor wounds, and cleaning and overhauling their weapons. Still listening keenly for news of Steele and his Texas reinforcements, Jeff strolled into the shade of a nearby baggage wagon and came upon Hooley Pogue.

Hooley was clumsily sewing a white "flag of truce" into the seat of his worn trousers. Except for his big hat and his boots, he was naked. His wet cotton shirt was draped over a nearby wagon wheel, drying in the sunshine. He had taken off his pants to repair them and was sitting bare-shanked on his saddle.

Hooley waved his needle in greeting and smiled, his white teeth flashing in his brown face.

"Howdy. In this army, one patch on the seat of yore britches means a captain; two patches, a lieutenant; three, a buck-tailed private. That's me." Gaily he held up the tattered butter-nut so Jeff could inspect the repairs he had made. Sure enough, there were three big patches.

Jeff was greeted with respect by the bearded rebel horse-men. They had heard how he had rescued Fields. They seemed so friendly that he almost hated to leave. But all that was keeping him now was news of Steele. He had all the informa-tion he needed on Cabell. He knew Blunt had nothing to fear from the Arkansawyers.

He decided to stay close to Heifer's commissary wagon. It was the social center of Company H, Cherokee Mounted Rifles, and a good place to get information. Everybody knew the cook and came by to banter him. All day Jeff listened carefully. Finally, about midafternoon, he got what he was after.

At the water barrel, he overheard one rebel lieutenant tell another that Steele and his fifteen hundred Texans had just arrived, and with Steele in command, all the rebels would soon move northward to Prairie Springs, fifteen miles east of Fort Gibson, to await the arrival from Red River of a brigade of Texas cavalry under General Smith R. Bankhead. Then they would all move together against the fort.

Eager now to take the news to Blunt, Jeff made his plans. He saddled the dun. During supper he hid two large chunks of cooked beef in his haversack and several large sweet potatoes.

He felt mean about deceiving Heifer. Heifer had been good to him. When the rebels discovered him gone, it might go hard with Heifer. But this was war and Jeff had a job to do. The dun was fresh. When darkness came, he would just ride off, heading northward up the Texas Road.

The violent stomach pains struck him as he was filling his canteen from the water barrel. Nauseated, he reeled blindly against a wagon wheel. He didn't know what ailed him. He had never felt like this in his life before. Surely it was just a sudden cramp that would pass.

But the stomach pains kept coming, hard and relentlessly. He felt suddenly cold, then hot. Heifer found him crouched against the wagon, so dizzy he could hardly walk.

The big cook picked Jeff up and carried him bodily to his bunk. Quivering with cold, Jeff pulled a blanket over himself and lay still, his mind in turmoil. He had to get through to Blunt right away. Any delay would be ruinous, jeopardizing Fort Gibson and the lives of thousands.

Unable to find any quinine, Heifer came back and dosed Jeff with a foul-tasting tea he brewed from dogwood bark. Jeff began to sweat and threw off his blanket. He was burning up. Panting, he felt as though he could drink gallons of cold water.

Like a distraught father, Heifer hovered constantly over him. Finally he left again to hunt for the ingredients for what he called his "iron medicine," made by dropping several rusty nails into a bottle of water. "If you drink it, you'll have plenty o' iron in your blood," he told Jeff.

Jeff watched him go and, feeling his chills subsiding slightly, crawled to his feet and staggered over to the dun. It took nearly all his remaining strength to gain the saddle. A sentry stopped him, saw he was sick and let him pass.

The dun's galloping jarred him so much that he slowed the
horse to a walk. He felt so weak that twice he almost fell off.
He would never make it to Fort Gibson. He would be lucky
if he made it back to camp. How was he going to warn Blunt?

He saw a church in the distance, the church where he had
met Leemon Jones. Hancock Mission, Leemon had called it.
He remembered Leemon "lived half a mile down the road
theah." Groggy, Jeff walked the dun until he came to a big,
well-kept farm set back against the woods. It was growing dark.
Several slave cabins stood in the open clearing. He saw Leemon
Jones in a corral milking a cow.

Desperate, he decided to be thoroughly honest. He knew it
was risky, but it was a chance he had to take. Orff had told
him once that all scouts had to take lots of chances. Jeff laid
it on the line.

"Leemon, I'm not a rebel. I'm a Union scout from Fort
Gibson. I've got an important message for General Blunt at
the fort. I'm too sick to deliver it myself. I want you to take
my horse and gun and go in my place. I've got food packed
in my haversack here. You said you knew a shortcut. Will
you go?"

The young Negro's eyes gleamed proudly. "I sho will. I
can be back in two days if they give me a fresh hoss at the
fote. Or maybe I'll stay theah an' jine that colored regiment
you told me about." His face fell momentarily. "But I sho hates
to leave mah ole mammy an' mah dog." Jeff waited for him
while he hurried inside to tell his mother good-by.

Soon Leemon came gliding back. "Yessuh. Now what's de
message?"

Jeff decided to have him memorize it, then if he was captured, they wouldn't find any dispatch. Keeping the information brief, Jeff told Leemon twice and had Leemon repeat it
back to him each time. The Negro leaped up behind him and,
reaching both arms around Jeff, steered the dun and held Jeff
on at the same time.

Using a short cut to avoid the rebel sentries, he returned Jeff close to the rebel camp. Dismounting, Leemon lifted Jeff out of the saddle.

"Good luck," breathed Jeff and felt the cold chills coming back. He wished with all his heart he was going too. Leemon's white teeth gleamed in the dusk.

"Ah'll make it," he said. He swung easily, lithely into the saddle.

Puzzled, the dun curved his graceful neck around to look at Jeff. He nickered softly as if asking, "What's going on here?" Jeff reached out feebly, grasping the animal's black mane with one hand and giving him a couple of pats.

"Tell them at the fort I said to take good care of my horse until I get back. Tell them to salt and water him often," he charged.

The Negro nodded and dug his bare heels into the horse's flanks. A minute later the dusk swallowed them.

☆ 20

The Jackmans

The big four-poster bed was soft and comfortable. Jeff's head still felt heavy on the pillow, but his fever was gone, and for the first time in days he could think clearly. He opened his eyes wider and saw it was late afternoon and that he was lying in bed in somebody's house.

Looking down at his legs, he could scarcely believe they

were his. They looked thin and emaciated instead of hard and wiry. And he could see his ribs showing above the pair of clean, white drawers somebody had drawn on him.

A Negro woman, huge and billowy, her shining, blue-black hair bound in a red handkerchief, waddled into the room, wheezing heavily at every step. Weakly Jeff jerked the sheet up over his bare legs and midriff.

"Hey, now," she cackled in a strong, lusty contralto that rang through the hall like a man's, "you got yo' eyes open fo de fust time since you got heah!" When she opened her vast mouth to grin at him, her teeth reminded Jeff of a row of white piano keys. Her friendliness made him feel good all over.

He opened his eyes wider and saw he was in a large room with a highly arched ceiling. In all his life he had never seen a bedroom as nice as this. The walls were stained blue and there were pictures on them. There was a rag rug of red and blue upon the polished brown floor.

But the floor seemed farther away than it should be. At first Jeff thought it was his head swimming again, until he slid his chin over the side and saw that the bed was elevated. There was a dresser in the corner and nearby stood two handmade chairs with half-spindle backs. The room even had a fireplace. From the open window, yellow curtains ballooned toward him, propelled by the slow breeze. Everything was clean as a pin.

"How long have I been here, mam?" Jeff breathed and was surprised at the physical effort it cost him to speak.

"Oh, erbout two weeks."

"What's the matter with me?"

Rolling her eyes in fear, she wrapped her heavy black arms nervously in her blue apron.

"Honey, when dey fust brought you heah, you looked all flaxed out an' dead on de vine. You had de flesh creeps an' de shivery-shakes. Den it went into de wee-waws. Den you got de heaves; evah time we fed you, you'd unswallow yo' food." Jeff stirred restlessly on the pillow. He had never heard of any of those diseases. He wished she wouldn't talk so loudly. She made his head ache.

She went on, excitedly, "You even took spells wheah you'd get unnoodled an' queah in de head. When we bathed you, you'd call me Mama an' Bessie an' Mary an' Lucy. An' Honey, when you'd call me Lucy, you'd say de sweetest things." Again she broke into a wild cackle of laughter. In spite of his pallor, Jeff blushed.

If, in his delirium, he had talked freely about his family and about Lucy, what had he said about himself? Had he also divulged that he was a Union scout? There was no sign of it in her beaming countenance.

From the buxom Negro, whose name was Hannah, and who told him she had come from Louisiana on a steamboat, Jeff learned he was staying at the home of the Jackmans, a wealthy rebel family living north of the Canadian River, near Briartown. Heifer had brought him here in a commissary wagon and Colonel Watie had personally sent a message to Mrs. Jackman, whom he called Aunt Maggie, asking her to take Jeff in until he recovered. With no hospital available, it was the custom to billet sick soldiers with friendly civilian families.

With one hand Jeff pushed his scraggly hair out of his eyes and felt a little ashamed. He found it hard to identify Watie the raider with the Watie who had found him a princely refuge like this.

Laboriously he turned from his left side to his right in the big bed. He didn't understand it. He wondered if Leemon Jones had made it through to Fort Gibson with his messages for Blunt.

Hannah left and came back presently with Mrs. Jackman, mistress of the home. She was small and prematurely gray, with a high forehead and a determined little twist of mouth. Her gray eyes were so wise and knowing that Jeff felt a twinge of panic, wondering if she were on to his masquerade. But she smiled cordially, saying, "Welcome to our home, sir. How are you feeling?"

Jeff managed a wan smile. "Kinda peeked, mam. And kind of embarrassed, too. I've never been sick a day in my life before. I don't know how to thank you, mam, for taking me in like this. I know I've been lots of trouble to everybody."

She placed a cool hand on his forehead. "Nonsense, Mr. Bussey. You've been no trouble at all. We've enjoyed having you. I've never seen a worse case of malaria, but your fever seems to have subsided. Before long, I hope, we'll be able to send you back to Stand, well and strong."

Smiling shyly, the rest of the family came into the room and were introduced. There were five of them, all girls. Like Lucy Washbourne, each had the same brownish cast of skin that denoted their Cherokee blood. They were black-haired, with high foreheads and small mouths and shrewd, intelligent eyes like their mother's.

When one laughed, they all laughed, and with the same soprano inflection. Marjorie and Sophie, the oldest, were married and had husbands in the rebel army and infants at home. Then there was Jill, eighteen, Janice, sixteen, and Patricia, thirteen, who wore boots and a riding habit. She looked like the tomboy of the family.

The following day was Sunday, and Jeff was awakened very early by a feminine voice calling insistently from outside his window, "Mr. Davis. Mr. Davis." Whoever was calling was trying to do it quietly but wasn't succeeding very well. And she was "mistering" him by his second name, not his last one.

Jeff winked his eyes sleepily open and looked out into the cool flush of early morning. The east was oranged over with daybreak. A cowbell jangled down in the barn lot and he knew the cattle were getting up and stretching themselves. The insect drone had died to a small, tremulous murmur. It seemed that the whole world was just waking up and throwing off the covers.

"Mr. Davis. Mr. Davis."

Standing bareheaded in the wet grass, an excited smile on her face, was Patricia. Her brown hair fell in a long braid down her back. Her boots were wet and had strands of wet green grass plastered to them. She was holding by the bridle reins a beautiful black colt with a red quilt strapped to his back. Young and irresponsible as his mistress, the colt was hungrily nibbling Marjorie's beloved hyacinths from the flower bed beneath the window.

"This is my horse, Barney," the girl told Jeff. "Watch him go."

She led him over to a wooden horse block and mounted from a flying leap. The instant she hit the red quilt, Barney broke fast, like an arrow from a bow. In a dozen quick strides he was galloping full tilt across the dewey Cherokee countryside. The girl rode as if she were glued to him, her brown pigtail floating horizontally behind.

After had ridden a hundred yards, she turned him and cantered back to Jeff's window, her face beaming blissfully. The colt was panting gently.

Jeff put both his arms on the window sill. "Where's your saddle?" he asked her, trying to keep his voice low so he wouldn't awaken the household.

"I'd rather ride him this way," Miss Patricia confided, with a frank grin. "That's why I get up early and ride. Mama doesn't like for me to ride without a saddle. So just before she wakes up, I go saddle him."

Half an hour later she tied her horse, saddled this time, to one of the white front porch columns. With the dewy grass still plastered to her black boots, she strode into the parlor and began pounding on the grand piano to awaken the family for breakfast, which the slaves, moving everywhere on tiptoe, were leisurely preparing.

Jeff knew the Jackmans lived in a two-story house, because for days he had heard people walking around upstairs in the room over his head. Apparently they lived on a plantation; looking out the window he saw acres and acres of green corn stretching back to the woods.

His gaze traveling curiously about the room, he saw that somebody had brought him books to read, leaving them on the heavy walnut dresser, within easy reach of his hand. Jeff leaned across the bed, reading their titles. There was G. P. R. James' *History of Chivalry*, two novels by Sir Walter Scott, two border novels, *Guy Rivers* and *The Yemassee* by William Gilmore Simms and an old copy of *Harper's Weekly*.

He heard kitchen utensils rattling and smelled food cooking. Later, Hannah brought him a fine breakfast, complete with a napkin on a tray, but he ate very little of it. He had completely lost his appetite.

With nothing better to do, Jeff listened to the conversation of the family at breakfast across the hall. All Miss Jill and Miss Janice talked about were their beaux in the Watie branch of the Confederate service. To his surprise, they seemed proud of it, as though it were the cavalier branch of the whole rebel army in the Indian country and being privileged to belong to it was some special honor. He remembered that the Washbourne family's menfolk had also gone into one of the Watie regiments and that the Washbourne women had seemed proud of it, too.

He was puzzled. The Jackmans, like the Washbournes, appeared to be intelligent, respectable, Christian people with a high reputation in the country. He couldn't understand why they wanted their husbands, sons and brothers to serve under a leader whose followers raided as barbarously as did the Watie men.

He was surprised two days later to see Miss Janice and Miss Pat walking about the house wearing hoop skirts and carrying books on their heads. And when the books on Miss Pat's head fell with a heavy crash to the hall floor, Hannah, who was cleaning Jeff's room, threw up her black arms in resignation.

"Dat Miss Pat done it agin," the big Negress moaned. "She nevah gonna leahn to walk graceful, lak a lady."

Jeff soon learned that in the Jackman home everything possible was done to teach the girls good breeding. They had to learn to sing, dance, play the piano, ride horseback, read the classics and flirt with boys without seeming forward or immodest. They were taught how to be good hostesses and how to manage a home. But they rarely did any actual cooking or sewing or cleaning. Apparently that was reserved for the slaves. Jeff wondered what kind of social training would have been imposed upon sons, had the Jackman family had any.

One morning a rebel courier trotted up to the front porch and talked for a few minutes with Mrs. Jackman. Then he rode off at a gallop, refusing her invitation to dine with them. A somber change came over the entire family. There were long conversations in the parlor, and a worried look appeared on Mrs. Jackman's face.

Jeff soon found out from Hannah, the news-bringer, what it was. They were going to leave the big house and go south to live for the duration of the war. With Blunt's Union army prowling about so closely, it was the safest thing to do.

"An' we ain't goin' as refugees, eithah," she said proudly.

She explained that Mr. Jackman, an adjutant in one of the Watie regiments, had rented a plantation near Bonham, Texas, just south of Red River, and was sending the family, their slaves, and his herd of cattle there in style.

For days the Jackman women and the slaves packed supplies and personal belongings in several big tar-hubbed wagons for the long trip south. They were even taking Marjorie's grand piano. Already it was lying on its side in one of the wagons, heavily buttressed by hams from the smokehouses to keep it from becoming scratched.

"Yo's goin' wid us too, honey," the old colored woman told

Jeff. "Dey's fixed you a pallet in de back ob one ob de wagons."

Not if I can help it, thought Jeff, twisting impatiently on the bed. The sooner he could return to the fort and be out of this hospitable rebel family's debt, the easier he would feel. He disliked this sailing under false colors.

Two nights before the Jackmans were due to start south, he decided to make the effort. Fort Gibson couldn't be much more than thirty miles north, and he had been feeling better lately.

He waited until everybody had gone to bed and the big house became quiet. Outside he could hear the whippoorwills whistling in the woods. Bracing himself, he sat up, sliding his legs over the side of the bed. He looked out the window toward the barn. He even had his getaway horse picked out, an old Roman-nose gray that had long since been turned out to pasture because of his age. Jeff knew he would carry him to the fort, riding bareback.

He took a couple of steps toward his clothes, hanging from a peg on the wall. Instantly he became so weak and dizzy that he toppled back onto the bed. For nearly five minutes he lay there, fuming at his accursed feebleness and gathering strength for another try.

It ended even more ingloriously. In the darkness he lost his balance on the stair leading to his bed and fell flat on his face. Shaken and downcast, he lay on the floor, panting.

At this rate he would never get back to the fort. Railing at himself for not having exercised more, he finally crept back to the bed. Looks like I'm going on a long trip to Texas, he told himself.

The Jackmans' final night in their beloved home came all too soon. Everything had been put in readiness for the leave-taking on the morrow. The wagons were loaded, the cattle herded into the family stockade, the small children bathed and put to bed early. Mrs. Jackman and the girls took one last farewell walk about the premises, pausing at the family

well to bury their china in the yard. Joel, the aged Negro
body servant, dug the hole with a spade, carefully placed the
dishes in it, then gently covered them up.

Mrs. Jackman was taking with her half a trunkful of the
new Confederate paper money. A stanch rebel patriot, she
had earlier gone to Little Rock, Arkansas, and exchanged
all her gold and $75,000 worth of State of Georgia bonds for
the new Confederate paper specie. It was all the money she
had in the world. Hers was no halfway loyalty. Resigned to the
trip, Jeff pulled up his sheet for the last time in the big southwest bedroom and closed his eyes.

When he awoke next morning, the sun was two hours high.
Blinking uneasily, he realized he had overslept. Everything
about the plantation was ominously quiet. He knew Mrs. Jackman had planned to start at daybreak so they could reach the
Texas Road by nightfall of the second day.

Alarmed, he sat bolt upright in bed. Swiftly, he looked out
the window into the yard and caught his breath with relief.
There sat the six tar-hubbed wagons, each packed and ready
to go. But there were no teams being hooked into the traces,
no jingle of harness from the barn, no bawling of cattle from
the stockade. House, barn, corral, stockade—everything was
terrifyingly still.

From somewhere within the vast silence of the big house,
he heard the faint sound of feminine weeping. Now he knew
there was trouble of some kind.

"Hannah. Hannah." His voice echoed through the silent
halls. Soon he heard heavy footsteps approaching. Hannah
ambled into the room, despair in her face, a white dish towel
clutched in one hand. Her eyes were wet. Sniffing noisily, she
kept dabbing at them with the dishcloth.

"The Pins come last night," she moaned. "Ouah slaves has
all left us. Evahthing on de place has been stole. Yankee ahmy
sho gonna git us now."

The Pin Indians were Cherokee full-bloods sympathetic

to the Union, who got their name from the fact they wore crossed pins on their coats or hunting shirts as a badge of their order. They had encouraged the Jackman slaves to steal all the stock and run it off toward Fort Scott, Kansas. The stables had been swept clean. Gone were the mule teams that were to pull the heavy wagons to Texas. Gone from the stockade were the cattle. The thieves had even stolen the pet saddle horses the girls were planning to ride to Texas. There sat the six loaded wagons all ready to roll, and not a hoof on the place to turn a wheel. And all the men were off at war!

Dry-eyed, Mrs. Jackman wasn't giving up.

"There's no use of our fretting about it, Mr. Bussey," she said practically. "The milk is on the floor. But I've got to think of some way to get our wagons and our family to Texas." She looked at him expectantly.

Behind her stood Miss Pat, red-eyed and inconsolable. The thieves had taken Barney. She had raised him from a colt. No other hand besides hers had ever fed him.

"Mam, haven't you got some old worn-out stock somewhere on the place that you could use to pull the wagons?" Forgetting the war, Jeff wanted desperately to help them. "If you went slowly, you might get through. With so much stealing going on, the families with the sorriest teams might have the best chance to make it. Nobody would want to steal any broken-down stock."

Mrs. Jackman decided to try it. She and Miss Pat walked out on the range and found several old horses, two sick oxen, and a lame mule the deserting slaves had considered too worthless to steal. Old Joel helped Jeff put on his clothing and assisted him to the rear wagon. He felt faint after all the exercise and lay down on a pallet that had been fixed for him, his head aching dully. At this rate he would never get to Fort Gibson. It was hot in the wagon despite its canvas top, much hotter than in the house.

With a final look at her beloved home, Mrs. Jackman, in

the front wagon, shook out her lines and clucked to her team.
The caravan began slowly to move.

The long trip was pure torture to Jeff. Mile after mile he
lay helpless, eating the thick dust and listening to the creak
and groan of the wheels. The wheels lurched, jostling him
cruelly. When Mrs. Jackman bought some oxen from a settler
living along the trail, replacing their worn-out stock, their
progress became faster.

Swinging around the San Bois Mountains, they came out
on the Texas Road. The big thoroughfare was crowded that
summer with wagons of Cherokee families going south to Red
River to live near their menfolk for the war's duration. Jeff's
malaria returned. His weight shrank. The Jackmans dosed him
with everything, from a tonic they made of wild cherry and
dogwood bark to a vial of quinine they secured from the
apothecary at Boggy Depot. When the long trip finally stopped
deep in the Choctaw country, he felt he never wanted to ride
in a wagon again.

The journey ended unexpectedly one night at a deserted
log house a quarter mile off the road, where they stopped to
rest. They found a large garden, neatly weeded, and an
orchard heavily laden with late peaches and early apples.
There were a barn and several outbuildings, even a cool spring
and a cellar close by.

"Why don't you move in?" a neighbor family advised.
"You'll like it here. The Choctaws and Texas people are wonderful. They opened their corn cribs to us and helped us with
our crops. The winters here aren't severe. Spring comes much
earlier than at home. And it's safe. General Cooper's army
usually winters at Fort Washita, close by."

Despite her husband's earlier arrangements for them to
live in Texas, Mrs. Jackman sent word to him they had decided
to stay here for the present. With all their slaves and cattle
gone, they wouldn't need a large place anyhow. With the help
of their neighbors, the wagons were unloaded and the family

moved in. Jeff was installed in a small shed room south of the house, overlooking the Texas Road.

It was a much different life from the one they had led in their luxurious two-story manor back near Briartown. Still too weak to help with the farm work, Jeff could only give directions. The women borrowed a small walking plow and, hitching one of the oxen to it, planted late corn and black-eyed peas. They worked all day in the field. The cinch bugs devoured nearly everybody else's corn, but not the Jackmans'.

"Everybody says our rows are so crooked, the bugs can't find our corn," Jill laughed one night when she brought Jeff his supper.

Talk was always about the war. Stand Watie's name was on everybody's lips. The whole rebel country seemed to lean on him. Jeff was surprised to learn that he had been elected principal chief of the southern segment of the Cherokees and it was his responsibility to feed the destitute refugee families camped in the Choctaw country. Under his direction, the Confederate government furnished the refugees corn, wheat, molasses, and sugar when they were available from the rebel supply center at Boggy Depot. The Jackman women went there quite often for their supplies.

Hour after hour, Jeff lay on his stomach watching the traffic go by on the Texas Road. It increased so greatly in August of '63 that he knew another battle was looming. Company after company of marching rebel infantry and dusty rebel cavalry, accompanied by supply trains, ammunition wagons and large droves of sheep and longhorn cattle and small Mexican mules, came up from Texas, bound for the north. The Southern refugee women living all along the road saw the grim preparations, too, and with mounting dread thought of their fathers, brothers, and sweethearts.

When news came in late August of the defeat of the rebel General Steele at Perryville, fifty miles north of Boggy Depot, the women waited in fear for the mounted runner Watie always sent south with the casualty reports. When Jeff heard the battle tidings, he found his emotions queerly divided. He was secretly elated at the Union success and yet he didn't want the Jackmans hurt by it.

He was the one who first saw the rebel cavalryman turn into the Jackman driveway four days after the battle. It was an hour before dusk. The lone rider came trotting in from the north. He was gaunt and dirty; the buckskin horse he rode looked sweaty and hot.

The Jackman women had just come in from working in the garden. Janice saw the rider as she was bathing her face at the spring.

"Look, Mama," she gasped and covered her mouth with her hand. They stood in a little cluster at the well, watching him ride up, a strange fascination in their faces, an odd paralysis in their legs. His horse shied nervously at the chickens, and, growling something unintelligible, the rider pulled rein about twenty feet away.

"Is this the Jackman home?" His brown, whiskery face looked like a weed-grown field.

Mutely the women nodded.

"Does a Mrs. Sophie Chavis live here?"

With a little cry of anguish, Sophie shrank back against the clapboard shed. Mrs. Jackman and Marjorie moved quickly to her side.

"I've bad news, mam. Your husband, Thomas Chavis, was killed in the Battle of Perryville. We didn't recover his body, mam. We was retreatin' too fast. The Feds will probably bury it, mam."

Thus did the war serve the women on both sides.

There were happier times, too. One afternoon in early September, Mr. Jackman rode into the yard for his first visit since the family had arrived in the Choctaw country. Deliriously happy, his daughters hurled themselves upon him, hugging him joyfully.

"Stir around, Hannah, and help get something to eat, but only the Lord knows what it will be," Mrs. Jackman called to black Hannah. Then turning to her husband, she embraced him, saying, "Why didn't you ring a bell, or blow a horn and let us know you were coming?"

After dinner was over and the girls had related all the exciting details of their flight by wagon from Briartown to the Choctaw country, they brought their father to see Jeff. He was a small, ragged, black-haired man with a drooping mustache. Soberly he told of the Confederate defeats at Vicksburg and Gettysburg in the East and at Perryville and Fort Smith in their own theater of the war, about the terrific rate of desertion among Cabell's Arkansas troops and of the rebels' appalling lack of arms, clothing, medicine, and shoes. With the Mississippi River patrolled by Union gunboats, the hard-pressed Confederate government at Richmond could not supply their westernmost forces in the Indian country.

And then he told them something that made Jeff's heart jump like a quail exploding from a grass clump.

"I think we'll do much better in the spring," Jackman added hopefully. "We've been getting a few new repeating rifles smuggled in from the North. Stand thinks he has worked out a way to get hundreds more. This rifle shoots seven times without reloading. It's lighter and more than a foot shorter than our muzzle-loaders. After you shoot, you crank a lever under the trigger. It opens the breach, kicks out the empty cartridge, pumps in a new cartridge, and you're ready to shoot again, all in the flash of a second."

A panic came over Jeff as he heard Orff's new Spencer repeater described in such exact detail. Any rebel cavalry force equipped with a rifle like that would have a tremendous advantage, might lengthen the war five years or even bring the Union to its knees in this far-off Western sphere.

He knew he must stay longer in the rebel country. If the rebels were getting repeating rifles from some place in the

North, it was his job to find out where they were coming from and stop it, if he could. But how was he going to, lying flat on his back in the Choctaw country, nearly a hundred miles below Fort Gibson?

In late September he got his appetite back suddenly. One afternoon Miss Pat brought him a piece of hot dried-fruit pie, made from the apples the women had sun-dried. As she held it out, tempting him, Jeff could smell the spicy odor of the nutmeg and the hot, brown juice. To his surprise, the smell did not sicken him. He gulped the pie down so hungrily that the girl ran excitedly to the house to tell the others.

That night Aunt Hettie Sloan came to sit up with Jeff, much to his disgust. Tall and stern, she was famous as a local humanitarian. She lived on Yarberry Creek, a mile and a half west of the Jackmans. She wore her gray hair roached upward in a strange-looking topknot into which she had thrust a tiny, jeweled comb.

Tiptoeing in, she seated herself decorously by his bed. Adjusting a faded green shawl about her thin shoulders, she leaned forward, staring long and soulfully at him. Then she wrinkled her long, high-bridged nose at Mrs. Jackman and shook her head.

"He looks bad, Maggie," Aunt Hettie whined. "I don't like his color a'tall. It's chalky. He looks jest like my Uncle Jeremiah did before he jined the great majority two years ago."

Startled by her ghastly diagnosis, Jeff blinked. "Mam, honestly, I feel better today than I've felt in weeks."

Aunt Hettie paid no attention. Shaking her gray head sorrowfully, she sighed, "Uncle Jeremiah rallied like that, too. It's what we used to call the False Recovery. Ever'body thought he was bucking up. Three hours later he commenced pickin' at the covers. We buried him up on Cowskin Prairie."

When they had gone Jeff broke out in a cold sweat of fear. Having no desire to emulate Aunt Hettie's Uncle Jeremiah and "jine the great majority," he sat up on the side of the bed.

His head felt almost normal. The hot fruit pie he had eaten seemed to have given him strength. With growing excitement, he stood and, leaning against the wall in the darkness, took half a dozen slow, halting steps to the door. He felt no dizziness, no headaches. Elated, he wanted to shout with joy.

Three weeks later he was able to help Mrs. Jackman and Jill sow wheat in the field. He knew he would be expected to rejoin the rebel outfit. Then Adair, who was now a colonel, sent word he need not report back until spring, since Watie had furloughed most of his men and sent them home to assist their families with the crops. So Jeff stayed that winter with the Jackmans, helping with the farm work and slowly recovering his strength.

He was eager to find out more about the new rifles and hoped that Mr. Jackman, on one of his visits home, might reveal more information. In this he was doomed to disappointment; Watie's adjutant never mentioned the subject again. Even so, Jeff was glad to be at the Jackmans' instead of at Watie's winter quarters at "Camp Starvation." There the heavy fall rains had left the roads so impassible that the men were subsisting upon small rations of parched corn and poorly dried beef and feeding their horses mulberry brush and tree bark.

Early in March Jeff walked to the door of his shed room and looked out into the darkness on the Texas Road. The cool air was invigorating. A small, bobbing light glimmered far to the south and Jeff could hear the faint clatter of a string of empty freight wagons, hitched together and drawn by mules.

He took a long pull of the night air and his nostrils caught the wild, sweet whiff of plum-tree blossoms. He knew that spring was coming fast to the Choctaw country, much faster than back home in his native Kansas. Already the burr oaks were wearing light green tassels and the redbuds' purplish

blooms brightened the hillsides and valleys. The robins had
stayed around all winter.

Jeff felt a surge of renewed hope. It would soon be time to
plow.

☆ 21

Boggy Depot

Jeff sat in the afternoon sunshine, his back against the
wheel of the commissary wagon, watching Heifer make sourdough biscuits.

It was the second day after he had rejoined the Watie brigade. He had tried to help Heifer unload and rustle the firewood, but the cook wouldn't let him lift a finger until he got
stronger.

Now Heifer was pinching off pieces of the white dough.
Rolling them into balls between his palms, he placed them in
the Dutch oven, turning them in the hot grease so that all
sides received a coating and they wouldn't stick together. As
he worked he hummed snatches of songs to himself. When
Heifer hummed, his sobbing, quavering voice sounded like one
of Cooper's squeaky baggage wagons making a sharp turn in
the road on an early frosty morning.

And yet Jeff had no difficulty recognizing the tune. Today
it was Heifer's favorite, the religious hymn "Amazing Grace."
Watching him, Jeff was ashamed.

Everybody in the rebel country had been nice to him. Heifer watched over him like a fussy old hen over a single chick. The Jackmans had taken wonderful care of him. The rebel riders had been good to him since he got back. Disturbed by all their kindness, Jeff felt mean about being against them in the war.

With a sweet gush of sorrow he remembered leaving the Jackmans yesterday. Heifer had come for him in the commissary wagon, a small gray mare trotting behind. All the Jackmans had gathered in the front yard to kiss Jeff good-by. He thanked them as humbly and gratefully as he knew how for all they had done for him. They seemed genuinely sorry to see him go. Miss Sophie even cried.

Heifer's cowhorn mustache looked a little shaggier and grayer, but otherwise he seemed the same. Mrs. Jackman had heard of him through her husband. She urged him to stay for supper.

"Can't, Madam," Heifer replied in his broken speech. "Gotta be gittin' back and fixin' my own supper fer the boys. But here's somethin' anyhow fer yore supper." And groping in the back of the wagon, he pulled out a middling of bacon and half a sack of wheat flour.

"The hoss is fer you, kid. Got her from our fo'age camp, down in Texas. Name's Flea Bite."

Jeff looked for the first time at the small mare daintily cropping the Bermuda greening along the Jackman driveway. She was more cream-colored than gray, with small brown freckles all over her trim, young body. Enchanted, Jeff felt the thrill of ownership. He liked her looks. She was sleek and lean. There was a saddle on her back, a small, tan Frazier with narrow stirrups bound in shiny brass.

Jeff gulped, "Corn, Mr. Hobbs, thank you for finding her for me." Heifer beamed happily. His distorted face seemed more frightening than ever when it was registering joy or pleasure.

Jeff saw Miss Pat big-eyeing the mare longingly. He felt

sorry for her. He knew she hadn't straddled a horse since her
beloved Barney had been stolen by the Pins. Since then, the
girl's only contact with stock had been driving an ox to the
walking plow they sometimes borrowed from a Choctaw neighbor.

Jeff walked to the back of the commissary wagon, untied
the bridle reins, and held them out to her.

"Here," he said, "why don't you take a gallop on her while
I go pack my things?"

He liked the way her eyes suddenly grew big and round and
starry.

"Oh, thank you!" she breathed. Quickly she tied the reins
to the wagon wheel. Squealing with delight, she raced to the
house to find her riding habit.

Later, when it was time to go, Jeff couldn't wait himself to
ride the mare. Putting his foot in the stirrup, he went up on
one side of her and came down on the other in a heap, Heifer
catching him with one arm just in time. He still wasn't entirely
over his dizziness. He felt silly, folding up like that in front of
everybody. He rode off seated in the back of the commissary
wagon, where he could lead the mare and look at her. . . .

Now Heifer was lifting the lids of other Dutch ovens and
turning the beefsteaks in them. The ovens were deep, iron
skillets with three small legs and a heavy lid with an upturned
lip so the hot lid could be picked up with a gouch hook. There
were red coals of fire on top of each lid as well as underneath
the oven.

The rebel cook certainly knew how to revive a balky appetite. Yesterday he had taken his shotgun and, riding out into
the brush, killed two fat quail, frying them for Jeff in the Dutch
oven. From the sack of dried apples the Jackmans had given
them, he had made a pie, rolling out the dough with a whisky
bottle and cutting the initials CMR, for Cherokee Mounted
Rifles in the top crust with his bowie knife.

The brigade had seemed glad to see Jeff back, too. One

shaggy fellow brought him four hen's eggs. Even Fields welcomed him with a stiff handshake. The sergeant wore his campaign coat buttoned neatly in front. His shoulder seemed entirely healed.

"Heared yuh been layin' sick. Too bad. Glad yore back."

Again Jeff felt the prickings of his stubborn conscience. He almost wished they weren't so good to him.

A week later the whole outfit moved north fifteen miles toward Boggy Depot. Gorging himself on Heifer's cooking, Jeff was feeling fine.

He rode Flea Bite alongside the commissary wagon. They splashed across a creek with clay-colored water and white haw blossoms blooming along its banks. He heard the redbirds whistling and they reminded him of home. The sun penetrated warmly through his old coat. Spring was on the way.

When they first saw Boggy Depot, it was late afternoon. In the sun's flat rays the rebel war capital looked like a handful of clods on a muddy creek bank. But as they rode closer, Jeff saw with surprise that the town sprawled all over the woodsy flat. It had been built in the edge of the woods. Stumps of trees protruded in the streets and patches of native live oak and hickory remained undisturbed in the very heart of the town.

It was an hour before sundown when they jogged into its outskirts. After helping Heifer set up in the military zone at the town's south edge, Jeff and Hooley Pogue rode down the middle of Main Street.

They drew rein at the public well and at the top of a crude flagpole Jeff saw something that startled him, something he had never seen before.

It was a ragged rectangle of gray and blue bunting. Two red bars crossed each other in the middle with a few white stars sewn crudely between them. He realized it was a homemade rebel flag.

He felt vaguely displeased. Compared to his own beloved

Stars and Stripes, it seemed cheap and bold and arrogant. And yet it made him feel a little alarmed. If the rebellion against his country had reached the point where the enemy now had a flag as well as a president, a congress and an army, no wonder the war had lasted three years. These people were fighting for something they believed in. They might be hard to subdue.

Suddenly a cannon boomed loudly from behind them. Flea Bite jumped nervously.

A troop of ragged Indian cavalry raced down the street on their small ponies, war-whooping shrilly and brandishing their stone tomahawks. They galloped round and round the flag-pole, singing loudly and fiercely something that sounded like, "Yakeh walih, he kanah he!"

Mystified, Jeff turned to Hooley. "Who are they?"

Hooley's lip curled scornfully. "Choctaws an' Chickasaws singin' the Choctaw war song. They always sing it when the sunset gun goes off. If they could fight as good as they can sing . . ."

Jeff remembered these same Indian troops riding blithely into the Battle of Honey Springs armed only with archaic weapons. He didn't think Hooley was being entirely fair to the Choctaws. They didn't have much to fight with. Maybe if they had been armed decently, and trained intelligently, they could have fought as well as anybody.

When Jeff and Hooley returned to camp, hundreds of Indian soldiers were hobbling their horses and cooking their suppers over campfires. Hooley led Jeff on a tour and he saw from close range how the Watie men lived during their spare time.

Cheers and shouts came from one of the few cleared spots, where the long grass had been trampled down. Men armed with hickory switches were flailing each other about the legs and hips with howls of mingled pain and laughter. Hooley said the game was called "Hot Jackets."

They wandered here and there, encountering teamsters repairing sets of heavy harness and greasing them with tallow and neat's-foot oil. Troopers were sharpening their long, fierce-looking knives on blue whetstones, or cleaning shotguns and horse pistols, or erecting torn dog tents amid the trees. Many were writing letters, using pokeberries for ink and sharpened corn stalks for pens.

Moving on, they heard the distant sound of banjo music and of feet stamping the grassy ground in rhythm. They hurried closer and saw, seated on a bois d'arc stump, a gangling, long-armed rebel banjo player. Dirty hands flying, he was strumming the merriest, rowdiest music Jeff had ever heard.

Listening to it, his feet itched, and he almost felt compelled to join the other Watie men who were grasping each other round the waist and, with shrill cries and yells, stomping about the leaf-strewn ground, hoedown style. Hooley told Jeff the name of the lively tune was "Billy in the Low Grounds." Like everything else in the rebel country, the banjo was home-made, with a drumhead nailed tightly over half a whisky keg and its five long strings fastened with small staples.

"Whar's Shoat?" somebody yelled.

A roar went up, and Jeff saw Adair, the long-haired colonel who had questioned him and Bostwick, standing in the crowd, a smile on his handsome face.

Then the crowd pushed "Shoat" out into the open space. A bashful, ragged little man, he held back and shook his head in refusal until somebody held out a green bottle toward him, whereupon he seemed suddenly to lose all his reluctance. Reaching, he swallowed deeply and, so enlivened, jumped beside the banjoist who, throttling down the volume of his instrument, began softly picking a warm, racy tune called "Blind Coon Dog."

"Shoat" began to pat his foot, snap his fingers and sway rhythmically from side to side. Suddenly he grasped his chin with one hand and began to make with his teeth sharp, clicking noises that sounded like bones rattling, keeping perfect time to the lively music. His performance was received with deafening applause. Several of the listeners were so delighted they rolled on the ground with laughter.

An hour after dark a small troop of heavily armed Cherokee cavalry rode into camp from the Fort Towson Road. Jeff was on night sentry duty. Fields strolled out to meet them.

"Bussey," he ordered, "take Major Boudinot to headquarters. He wants to see Cunnel Watie."

"Yes, sir," said Jeff, saluting. With a tiny shiver of excitement, he thought that he, too, would like to see the infamous rebel cavalry leader.

Boudinot, the man Jeff was escorting, was an important-looking fellow with high cheekbones and long black hair that was visible beneath his black, flat-crowned hat. He carried two bulging saddlebags.

Jeff led him to a brown Sibley tent pitched beneath a grove of locusts. Fields had told him it was headquarters. But the tent was dark, and all Jeff found was an old man asleep on a quilt spread outside on the ground. A small campfire glowed nearby.

Either Watie was absent or Jeff had the wrong tent. Reaching down, he shook the old man by the shoulder.

"Excuse me, sir," Jeff said, "but can you tell me where we can find Colonel Watie?"

The man sat up instantly, his grayish, long-cropped hair tumbling to his collar.

"I'm Colonel Watie. What do you want?" His low-pitched voice was quiet, courteous, dignified. He wore a knife and pistol in his belt.

Jeff's jaw flopped open. The man had no bodyguard of any kind.

Recovering fast, he clicked both heels together and saluted. "Sir, a gentleman is here to see you." With his musket, Jeff indicated Boudinot.

Watie rolled to his feet with a lithe, catlike motion that would have done credit to a far younger man. Now that the firelight glimmered squarely on him, Jeff saw that he was a little, dark-skinned Indian with a square face and a flat nose. He looked more like a full-blood than a mixed-blood. Jeff was never so disappointed in his life. He had always imagined Watie to be a big, sinister fellow. Instead, he looked like some gentle old Indian farmer taking a noonday nap under a tree.

Recognizing his guest, Watie exclaimed cordially, "Cornelius!" and, extending both hands, stepped forward to greet the visitor.

"Uncle!" Boudinot's voice was equally cordial. His pearly white teeth flashing in the firelight, Boudinot smiled again, and Watie went inside the tent. Jeff heard the scratch of a match and smelled the acrid sulphur burning. Limping slightly beneath the weight of his saddlebags, Boudinot followed.

Jeff stood rooted to the spot, staring after them. Boudinot's high, melodious voice carried outside the tent. He spoke with obvious pride.

"Uncle, I got the Nation an appropriation of one hundred thousand dollars. I brought forty-five thousand dollars of it back with me. Scott, the Confederate commissioner, is bringing the rest out in July."

Jeff heard Watie grunt with satisfaction. "Did you bring the gold?"

Boudinot was faintly apologetic. "Only twelve thousand dollars of it, Uncle. Richmond could give me only four thousand. I've been weeks scraping up the rest from our people living up and down Red River. Why do you need gold?"

Deciding he'd better get back on duty, Jeff shouldered his musket and started to move off.

"To buy rifles with. New repeating rifles. A Fed officer at Fort Gibson is smuggling them to us from St. Louis. They're seven-shot Spencers and if we had enough of 'em we could shorten the war fast out here. But they're expensive. I have to pay fifty dollars in gold for each gun and thirty dollars a thousand for fifty-two-caliber copper cartridges. The Fed officer won't take nothin' but gold." Jeff froze in his tracks.

"Who is he?" Boudinot asked the question inside the tent just as Jeff himself wanted to ask it, standing breathless in the dusk outside.

Watie's grunt sounded half sarcastic, half amused. "He's no fool, nephew. He's not going to tell us his name. When we pay him off, he always stands in the dark so we can't see his face. He's got a gang of Fed soldiers workin' for him. When the guns arrive at Gibson, he lets us know. He sold us a dozen that way last July. He said he'd have five hundred more this summer. Only I can't buy five hundred. With only twelve thousand dollars in gold, I can buy only two hundred with cartridges."

Outside, Jeff drew a long breath into his lungs. Who could the Union officer be? First he thought of Orff, who already had one of the guns. Then his mind went thrusting back to Clardy. However, Clardy had such a violent dislike for everything Confederate that he'd never approach a rebel without shooting first. He'd surely never do business with one. Jeff swallowed. It was probably somebody he didn't even know. There were hundreds of officers at Fort Gibson.

Boudinot's voice grew soft with cunning, "Uncle, why buy the guns at all? Why don't you just take them?"

"Because we need a thousand rifles, not two hundred. With a thousand repeating rifles, I could crucify their supply trains by land or water, starve 'em out of Fort Gibson and win back all our old country north of the Arkansas so our people could return to their homes in peace. If I take these two hundred rifles without payin', that's all we'd get. He wouldn't bring us any more."

Jeff was astounded at what he had heard. If he knew the name of the Federal officer who was peddling the contraband rifles, he could leave for Fort Gibson tonight. Once Fort Gibson knew the betrayer's name, he could be watched, trapped, and taken. Otherwise it would be hard to trace him. Cautiously he began backing through the brush.

The talking ceased abruptly. One of the shadows inside the tent moved with monstrous unnaturalness. Watie appeared at the door, staring suspiciously into the darkness. Jeff made himself so small and flat along the ground that a cabbage leaf would almost have covered him. Watie looked and listened and sniffed the night air carefully. Then he went back inside.

Soon Jeff heard the sharp, clear notes of a flute, blown by Boudinot, coming from the tent, and his nose caught the odor of tobacco smoke from Watie's pipe.

He was still scared an hour later when he ran into Hooley back at the sentry post. He learned from Hooley that Boudinot, a nephew of Watie's, had gone to college in the East and was now the Cherokee delegate to the Confederate Congress in Richmond, Virginia. He wondered what Watie would do with the forty-five thousand dollars in rebel bank notes Boudinot had brought from Richmond?

He found out next afternoon. At four o'clock they were mustered for pay. It was the first pay muster in two years, Hooley said. After a review and inspection, Boudinot himself acted as paymaster. Most of the money he had brought, Watie ordered spent to relieve the needs of the destitute rebel refugee families. But each trooper received a month's salary, too. Jeff looked curiously at the crisp, new green bank notes, two fives and five ones.

"Know what I'm going to buy first?" Jeff said to Hooley, later. "There's a man selling ginger cakes up on the street. I'm going to buy me a whole dollar's worth. Come on, Hooley, I'll buy you a chunk, too."

Promptly they found the vendor. He was a big, bare-headed fellow, who had built himself an oven in the hillside next to the town blacksmith. He was standing behind a three-foot square of freshly baked brown gingerbread, fanning the flies off it with one hand. The hot, sweet smell was overpowering. Jeff slid off Flea Bite.

"Give us a dollar's worth of that," Jeff said, waving his one-dollar bill proudly.

The vendor extended his dirty hand, plucked the bank note away, laid it on the square of gingerbread and, cutting around it neatly with his bowie knife, hewed off a piece exactly the size of the bank note and handed it to the surprised Jeff. Then he pocketed the bill. Thus Jeff learned for the first time of the weak buying power of Confederate paper money.

Hooley laughed uproariously as Jeff broke off half his small piece and handed it to him. Jeff grinned ruefully. "I guess that's what Pa meant when he told me once that money is the measure of value."

It was April of 1864 and the war, which had one more year to run, was raging with the convulsive fury of a final struggle. On the day before the Watie brigade left on its spring campaign, Jeff was still trying to learn the name of the Federal betrayer.

For a whole month he sought vainly to get a personal description of the Federal officer who had smuggled in the dozen rifles. But he couldn't find anybody who had seen him. Pretending that firearms were his hobby, he talked about them with almost everybody he met, starting the conversation on pistols and revolvers and then diverting it to the new repeating rifles. After weeks of the most persistent effort, he was able to locate five of the dozen repeating rifles Watie had bought. They were Spencers, like Orff's. But when he questioned the men who possessed them, each a crack sharpshooter, they could tell him nothing more.

There were other reasons, too, for delaying his return to Fort Gibson, reasons that were growing on him despite his Union background. When Jeff thought of them, he felt uneasy. And yet he couldn't help thinking about them. Just as he liked

the Washbournes and the Jackmans, he found himself liking
the Watie outfit more and more each day.

The Watie men weren't fighting a war over slavery. Both
the Union and rebel Cherokees owned slaves. Nor were they
fighting to break up the Union. Neither Cherokee faction belonged to the United States, consequently they had little interest in dividing it or keeping it intact. Among the Cherokees,
the Civil War was mostly a political fight. The Watie bunch
was fighting to keep the rival Ross party from planting its foot
on their necks.

Jeff had never seen men who got so much fun out of doing their hard, rough jobs. He liked the informal way they
waged a war. There weren't any Clardys among their officers.
*If I wasn't fighting to hold the Union together and clean up the
border trouble in Kansas, I could change sides mighty quick
in this war,* he thought. The Watie men fought well.

They ate well, too. The Union salt horse and hardtack was
a poor substitute for Heifer's Dutch oven T-bones and roasted
sweet potatoes. Besides, the lonely rebel cook lavished delica-
cies upon Jeff that the other rebels never saw—hot sourdoughs
six inches high when the wheat flour came up from Texas, or
wild grape cobbler, or a mess of fried eggs when he could get
them from some Choctaw farm wife. He'd miss Heifer's cooking when he made the break for Fort Gibson.

And he'd miss Heifer, too. Hardly a day passed but that
Heifer tried to make Jeff a better soldier. "Let me learn yo
some o' my experience," the rebel cook said. He taught Jeff
how to squeeze the trigger of a shotgun with both eyes open
and the gun swinging on the moving target. He taught him
how to ride a horse, steering with his legs, knees, and the
balance of his body without putting pressure on the horse's
mouth. He even took time to give Jeff advice on how to get
along with everybody.

"Treat evahbody like a gennelman, but let the ivory handle
of your revolver allus be in sight," Heifer counseled.

Jeff dreaded accompanying the Watie men on their savage raiding expeditions, but when he questioned Hooley cautiously about it, Hooley threw back his black head and laughed soundlessly.

"What would we raid now? Watie's already stripped the whole country clean as a gut. There's nothing left to raid."

Jeff was amazed at the endless variety of the Watie cavalry dashes. On their first scout in 1864, they penetrated seventy miles behind the Union lines almost to the state of Missouri to bring out in baggage wagons several Cherokee rebel families —old men, women, and children—who had been robbed and plundered by the Pins. And they never saw a single Union soldier.

Watie's men harassed the Federals with their bold cavalry forays along the western border of Arkansas, vanishing into the timber or melting into the river mists before a large force could be sent to intercept them. Fields still used Jeff as a horse-holder, so he was never put to the ordeal of having to fire on his own troops.

But he saw it all, anyhow. He was with the Watie outfit in April when as a part of General S. B. Maxey's force they took a Federal wagon train at Poison Springs near Camden. He was with them again when they chased a small Federal force off the Massard Prairie into the protection of Fort Smith, falling back across the Poteau River with the Union horses, mules and camp equipage they had captured. He rode and ate and slept with the Watie outfit, sharing the hardships and dangers that bind fighting men inexorably together.

Each day he became more and more impressed with the fierce loyalty of the Cherokee rebels to their cause. At Limestone Prairie in June, their enlistment period terminating, the entire Watie force re-enlisted for the duration of the war "be it long or short." Jeff had to walk right up with Heifer and Hooley and sign the re-enlistment papers too.

A month earlier he had seen the First and Second Cherokee

Regiments, forming with fife and drum, march around and around Watie's tent, whooping and cheering until their throats became raw, when Watie's commission as a brigadier-general, signed personally by President Jefferson Davis, arrived by courier.

Later he was with them at Camp Brassie when Watie, addressing the rebel Cherokees in national council, declared that the war should be prosecuted with the greatest vigor and recommended conscription of all physically fit Cherokees between the ages of eighteen and forty-five. Not only did the rebel council give him what he wanted, they went even further. When they passed the act, they set the age limits at seventeen and fifty. Jeff thought, *These people are in this war for keeps. And if they get those thousand repeating rifles, they might win back the whole of the Indian country in three short months.*

Early in June the spring rains set in and the Arkansas River began to rise. Three days later the cavalry was issued five days' rations and told to be ready to ride on an hour's notice. Swollen by heavy rains, the river had become navigable for steamers of light draft. The rebels learned that a Union steamer carrying a $120,000 cargo from Fort Smith to Fort Gibson for the Union soldiers and refugees there, was on its way.

Watie and his command rode secretly from Johnson's Station on the Fort Smith road to Pheasant Bluff, a high timbered spot overlooking the river channel where the steamer would have to approach. Next morning, Watie concealed his cavalry beneath the trees and posted three pieces of artillery halfway up the bluff.

Jeff, mounted on Flea Bite, lay hidden with the Watie horsemen in the cane along the river's south shore. Although the heavy brush and trees masked them, they could see the river plainly.

Soon Jeff heard a sound he had never heard before, the steady slap-slap-slap of a large paddle wheel. Suddenly a boat nosed around the river bend, a large boat with two tall chim-

neys bellowing black smoke and a Union flag whipping gallantly from the jackstaff. Disturbed, Jeff thought that if he ever
decided to stay permanently with the rebels, he'd have to get
used to riding against that flag.

The Federal steamboat came on. Heavily laden with the
cargo Watie wanted, it rode low in the muddy water, the white
foam from its paddle wheel flashing in the morning sunshine.
It was a long boat with a fancy pilothouse and a white cabin.
In evenly spaced letters of bright blue, Jeff could see the name
J. R. Williams printed across the front of the small cupola
atop the craft.

And then he saw something else, something that sent a chill
coursing down his spine. Blue-clad Union soldiers with muskets in their hands swarmed behind barricades of cotton bales
on the deck. Apparently this boat expected trouble and didn't
intend to take it lying down.

☆ 22

Pheasant Bluff

Jeff tightened his grip on Flea Bite's reins. The cannon
would start firing at any moment and when they did, every
horse in the rebel outfit would try to climb the bluff or jump
into the flooded river. It would be no picnic trying to board
an armed boat from a swimming horse. He knew the Union
escort, protected by the cotton bales, could pick them off neatly
or thrust them through with their sharp bayonets.

What an odd way to die, killed by your own countrymen as Bostwick had been at Honey Springs.

A drop of sweat ran down the bridge of his nose. Nervously he wiped it off with his sleeve and looked at the man on his right. His mouth fell open.

The man on his right was Heifer Hobbs. Astraddle his roan, the rebel cook had deserted his pots and ovens and was standing in his stirrups, squinting through the willow leaves at the approaching boat. In crude leather holsters in his belt he carried both his fighting knife, a bowie, and his eating knife, an old case blade of lead. His muzzle-loading double-barreled shotgun, souvenir of the Comanche wars, was clenched tightly in his hands. He looked at Jeff, and his ugly face broke into a hideous grin of affection.

Touched, Jeff knew now why Heifer had left his commissary wagon to fight at his side in what was to be Jeff's first battle with the Watie men in a role other than a horse-holder. Heifer's feeling for him was like that of a doting father. Heifer had poured out upon him all the fond attention he would have lavished upon his own son, had not the lad he sent East to school disavowed him because of his deformities. Moved by the rebel cook's devotion, Jeff squirmed in torment.

Here was a friend who would die for him, one he would wound deeply if he ever ran off to Fort Gibson. And yet, Jeff knew the time was coming when he would have to run, or stay.

"Blam!"

The middle gun on the bluff roared so closely that it deafened him. Flea Bite reared, neighing in terror, and the tree branches scraped off Jeff's hat. He muscled her down.

A small geyser of water rose brightly ten feet off the boat's bow and hung suspended in the morning air. An instant later, there came the kerplunk of the ball plowing into the muddy river and a loud, prolonged splash.

"Blam! Blam!" thundered the other two guns, higher on the densely wooded slope. One of the steamer's tall stacks had been shot away and black smoke was pouring into the windows of the pilothouse. The fourth shot scored a direct hit, puncturing the boiler and causing the boat to list out of control, toward the opposite bank.

The thin, clear notes of a bugle floated down from high along the bluff, sounding a charge.

With a mighty shout the long line of rebel cavalry burst from hiding and rode pell-mell into the muddy shallows of the Arkansas, spattering water six feet high. Finding that it relieved his nervousness, Jeff yelled as shrilly as the rest. Flea Bite was in the vanguard and as she encountered a deep spot, he felt the cool water rise to his armpits.

She began to swim, striking out strongly. The heads of hundreds of horses and men bobbed on the surface, their bodies entirely beneath the water. Heifer stuck close by. Brandishing his shotgun, he gobbled encouragement to his mount. Every rebel in the river was steering his swimming horse toward the boat.

The Union pilot swung on the whistle cord, hoping to attract help from any Union cavalry patrol north of the river. The whistle started on a single note, then slid into a deep, hoarse, three-toned blast that made Jeff's ear drums throb and echoed off the nearby bluff. But it didn't stop the Watie men.

The pilot ran the crippled boat aground on a sand bar. Leaping over the side, the Union soldiers hurried to the north bank of the stream and scattered into the woods.

The Watie men waded their ponies alongside the stranded steamer. Clambering over the side, they bored into the stricken boat like hungry squirrels into a hickory nut. With shouts of barbaric enjoyment, they began to plunder the cargo. Ignoring the barrels of flour and sides of bacon, they pounced upon the Union issue clothing and boots they needed so desperately.

A loud hissing came from the escaping steam. On the deck, two Union soldiers lay dead as mackerels, one with most of his head blown off.

In the captain's cabin they found whisky, rock candy and cigars. Jeff pocketed a handful of the cigars for Heifer.

Fields was scooping handfuls of Federal greenbacks out of a small iron safe. Apparently the boat had been carrying the Fort Gibson payroll, as well as cargo. Every rebel in the cabin had both hands full of money.

Yancey Pearl, a tall, raw-boned Arkansawyer, shoved some into Jeff's hands. Gaping, Jeff saw that they were twenty-dollar bills.

"Heah y'ar, kid!" Pearl guffawed, a lighted cigar from the captain's locker between his stained, jagged teeth. "Washington wallpaper! Hits yore's to play with. Hit ain't gonna buy nothin' now. We's gonna win the war. Jest as well throw it away."

Pearl twisted the wad of Federal bank notes in his horny hands, tearing them down the middle. He pitched them out the broken cabin window into the river.

One by one, the other rebels tore their greenbacks in fragments, or ignited them with their cigars and tossed them over the boat's side.

Pearl towered impatiently over Jeff. "Come on, kid! What cha waitin' on? Rip 'em in two and heave 'em into the drink! They're no good."

Jeff swallowed indecisively. They had a lot of nerve running down good Union money when their own cheap specie wouldn't buy a couple of bites of hot gingerbread. Three or four hundred dollars' worth of perfectly good Federal greenbacks in his hands was enough to buy a farm or pay his way through college.

Jeff saw Fields staring at him, his hard blue eyes ablaze with new suspicion. With reluctance, he hurled all his bank notes overboard. They floated for a moment upon the tan eddy, then slowly sank from sight.

The rebels moved the steamboat to the south shore and began to unload her cargo on the sand. A doctor was examining the handful of rebel wounded lying on the grassy bank beneath a cottonwood tree.

Among them was Hooley. He had caught a Federal Minie ball low in the stomach and the surgeon attending him looked grim.

Distressed, Jeff dropped the armload of booty he had acquired for the Jackmans—blankets, shawls, sugar, and Union coffee—and hurried to Hooley's side.

Hooley's brown, inscrutable Indian face was clenched in pain. He was half sitting, his arms braced behind him and his short legs stuck out helplessly, revealing the ragged soles of his broken boots. The muddy water dripped off him onto the sand. He had lost his hat; his long black hair was waving in the morning breeze.

He glanced up at Jeff. Perspiration was beading on his forehead. He was breathing fast.

"Jefferson," he mumbled, "gimme a drink outa yore canteen. I wanta see if I got any leaks."

Jeff carefully held his canteen to Hooley's lips. It never occurred to him that Hooley was a rebel and therefore his enemy. For three months they had knocked around together. Watie's surgeon stopped most of the bleeding but he had to do better than that. Everybody knew there would soon be hundreds of Federals after them.

Scowling, the surgeon stood, wiping his bloody hands on his shirt. He looked pityingly at Hooley. "It's a hundert miles to the hospital back at Boggy. You'd have to ride horseback. Think you can make it?"

Hooley was suffering now, panting faster and grunting every time the pain hit him. Angrily he glared up at the doctor.

"Hell, no!"

They moved him out into the sun, where the light was better. The surgeon gave him a drink of whisky, then handed him a lead bullet to bite. With men holding him forcibly on both sides, the surgeon quickly produced a scalpel, sterilized it with whisky and extracted the bullet which was lodged against his abdominal wall.

Jeff couldn't watch it. He walked off to one side, leaning against the trunk of a big walnut tree, listening to Hooley groan and curse while the surgeon worked. Twice Hooley yelled out and struggled helplessly, and each time Jeff felt so sorry for him he wanted to bawl.

In three or four minutes it was all over, and the crowd began to clear. The wound was swabbed with whisky, and Jeff gave most of his shirttail for a bandage that the doctor first sterilized by holding close to a fire. Then they put Hooley on his horse.

He rode half a mile in the heat and fainted, whereupon Jeff mounted behind him and held him on with both hands, while Heifer and Pearl, riding ahead, took turns leading Jeff's horse. They camped that night near Limestone Prairie.

Most of the Indian troops, their ponies heavily burdened with spoils from the steamboat, broke camp and headed for the homes of their destitute families in the refugee camps along the Red River. Jeff was puzzled. Watie seemed to know or care very little about military discipline, and his men reflected his attitude. What held them together and kept them going, Jeff asked Heifer?

"Depends on whatcha mean by discipline." Heifer blew his nose loudly. "We ain't got no West Point discipline. Watie's a Indian. He's educated, Christian, an' well-to-do. But he's still a Indian. He uses Indian discipline. Indians b'lieve in takin' booty. Makes 'em fight bettah. Watie fights bettah when he fights his own way. He took the steamboat, didn't he?"

The steamboat wasn't the only thing Watie took. September came and the scarlet sumac began to stain the sides of the ridges; cicadas led the heat chant from the trees. Steve Hildebrand, Watie's chief of scouts, learned while ranging in Federal territory north of Fort Gibson that a big Federal wagon train was coming by land from Fort Scott, Kansas.

He sent one of his men speeding horseback to Watie with the news. Watie notified General Richard M. Gano, an able Texas cavalry officer. With a combined force of two thousand men, Gano and Watie struck the Union train and its 670-man escort at Cabin Creek, capturing the train and its mule-drawn cargo valued at $1,500,000. It was the greatest disaster of the war to Union arms in the Indian country. Most of the captured stores were distributed among the needy refugee families along Red River.

The rebel morale soared sky high. The Confederate General Sterling Price had started his diversionary raid toward St. Louis and there was serious talk of a Watie raid upon Kansas in the spring. That sobered Jeff as though somebody had hurled a dipper of cold spring water in his face.

His family lived in Kansas and would be squarely in the path of the proposed raid. He worried about that all the way back from Cabin Creek. He didn't want a Watie raid hitting his father's farm. He drove back one of the captured Federal wagons, bringing with him blankets, shawls, sugar, and Union coffee for the Jackmans and a little bit of everything for Hooley, who had survived the long horseback ride from Pheasant Bluff and was recovering in the hospital at Boggy Depot. Arriving at Boggy Depot shortly before noon, he unhitched the big, black Union mules, watered them, unharnessed them, and staked them out to graze. Walking to a nearby creek, he stripped off his dirty clothing, took a bath and felt refreshed.

The things he had brought back for the Jackmans in a wooden barrel were left at the supply depot where Heifer had arranged for a teamster friend to drop them off at the Jackmans' home on his return trip down the Texas Road to Bonham. The town was filling with rebel soldiers and excited civilians dancing jigs of joy in the street. All they talked about was Watie's victories at Pheasant Bluff and Cabin Creek.

Jeff went to his bunk and pulled it into the shade. Lying down upon it, he buried his face in his arms.

He was awakened by somebody kicking the soles of his boots. It was the orderly sergeant.

"Fields say repote to him in half 'n hour, mounted and armed."

Jeff stretched and sat up. He looked at the sun and at the slant of the dark tree shadows. It was early afternoon. Resignedly he got to his feet and, walking to the commissary wagon, took a long drink from Heifer's gourd dipper. Then he splashed his face with cool water.

He put on his hat, cleaned and loaded his pistol, and saddled Flea Bite. Mounting, he rode to Fields' tent, ducking from side to side to escape the tree branches. Other troopers joined him.

Fields was lacing on a Federal boot taken from the captured Union supply train. He looked up sourly.

"Special duty," he snarled in his petulant, high-pitched voice. "Le's go!"

When they formed in column, Jeff found himself part of a twenty-man rebel escort. Accompanied by a single, empty, mule-drawn wagon, they started northwest on the little-used Wapanucka Road.

Fields rode ahead with Colonel Thompson, commander of the Second Cherokee regiment, and acting treasurer of the Southern Cherokee Nation. They traveled at a swinging trot, mostly in silence. The gravelly trail meandered in and out of clumps of roadside timber. Both men and horses began to perspire. From every tree cicadas sang shrilly and maddeningly, the piercing chant of one approaching before the stridulations of another had fallen behind. Yellow flowering weeds covered the dusty, heat-locked countryside.

An hour before sundown they halted on the bank of Clear Boggy Creek. There, beneath a towering cottonwood, stood a heavy green Conestoga wagon and a team of big gray mules. Half a dozen men, each well mounted, heavily armed and wearing blue uniforms of the Union cavalry, clustered watchfully around the wagon, obviously guarding its contents. Jeff attached no significance to the color of their uniforms. Half the men in Watie's command had abandoned their own shaggy garments for blue uniforms taken at Cabin Creek.

One of the strangers, apparently the leader, swaggered forward, confronting Colonel Thompson.

"General Watie?"

When Jeff heard the querulous voice he stopped breathing, every instinct sharp and alert. Instantly he knew the tall, stooping figure with the low, graying sideburns, the scar on his cheek, and the wild, suspicious eyes. Clardy!

"I'm Colonel Thompson, treasurer of the Cherokee Nation. General Watie has empowered me to act for him and for the nation. I have come prepared. Are you ready to deal with us?"

The reply didn't satisfy Clardy. Angrily he stepped back and his hand dropped to the butt of the pistol holstered in his belt. He flicked his nervous green eyes distrustfully over Thompson and then over the rebel patrol, as though suspecting treachery.

"I'll deal with nobody but Watie." He looked at the sun, low in the west, and scowled. "I said noon. Where is he?"

Thompson replied politely, "General Watie is out on scout but we expect him back tonight."

Jeff's heart was pounding in panic. He ducked so that his hat brim would hide his face.

He knew now that his long wait to learn the identity of the Federal officer selling the contraband repeating rifles was over.

Clardy glared at Thompson. He seemed to be making an effort to conceal his temper. Reluctantly he growled, "I guess we can deal. You got the gold?"

Thompson nodded and started to say something, but Clardy cut him short. "Order your men to stand back farther. They're lookin' down our throats."

Thompson looked at him queerly but gave the order. This was fortunate for Jeff. He turned Flea Bite around and walked her back with the others. All except Fields. Hands on his hips, Fields stayed where he was, looking coolly into Clardy's Conestoga wagon.

Clardy gestured toward the sergeant. "Him, too."

Fields grinned savagely and shook his head. Clardy's henchmen moved ominously forward. Jeff saw that each of them carried a Spencer rifle.

Fields fingered his pistol and stood his ground.

"That's Sergeant Fields, our gunsmith. I want him to examine the rifles before I pay you for them," Thompson said, civilly. Apparently satisfied, Clardy turned, barking an order to his followers.

Four of them climbed off their horses and, reaching into the back of the Conestoga wagon beneath a canvas tarp, hauled out several long boxes. The other two held the reins and kept a sharp watch on the rebel patrol. They all looked like thugs. Jeff didn't recognize any of them.

Using the butts of their carbines, Clardy's men broke open the boxes and Jeff saw row upon row of shiny, new repeating rifles, packed flat in sawdust.

While Fields came forward and personally examined each weapon, working the finger levers and inspecting the apertures built into the butts of the walnut stocks, Thompson spread a blanket on the grass. He walked over to his claybank and returned with two heavy saddlebags. They were the same ones Boudinot had carried into Watie's tent.

Pop-eyed, Jeff saw the gold coins gleam brightly in the sunshine and heard their metallic chink as Clardy and Thompson counted them on the blanket. Then Clardy scooped the gold into his saddlebag and stood. Fields barked an order and several rebels came forward to help place the Spencers back in the boxes and load them into the empty wagon they had brought from Boggy Depot.

Thompson turned inquiringly to Fields. "How many, Sam?"

Fields' face shone triumphantly. "Two hunnert even, Cunnel. Cartridges come out even, too. It's all heah. Purtiest sight ah evah seed."

"When can you let us have the eight hundred additional rifles General Watie sent word to you we would buy?" Thompson asked Clardy.

Clardy swore violently. "In two months, if he'll lay off our wagon trains so we can get 'em through. But the price is gonna be higher next time."

There was a moment of deadly silence in the clearing. For the first time Thompson's voice was edged with hostility. "How much higher?"

As he hefted the heavy saddlebags of gold into the back of the Conestoga wagon, Clardy looked shrewdly at Thompson.

"That's between me and Watie. That's why I want to talk to him privately. I want you to bring Watie here to me."

Thompson stared at him, saying nothing. Bold, insolent, and unafraid, Clardy stared back, a sneer on his thin lips. He knew that he and his twelve thousand dollars in gold were safe as a church. The rebels needed those other eight hundred rifles too badly. And he alone could get them for them.

"Why don't you come into Boggy with us and wait for General Watie yourself?" Thompson bargained. "You could wait at my tent. It's next to the general's. It will be dark, and you'll be safe. Nobody there will know you. Half our men are wearing Union uniforms. You could start back north later tonight."

It seemed to make sense to Clardy. He gave a surly nod.

Ignoring his followers, he reached beneath the canvas tarp and pulled out the bulging saddlebags. Staggering a little under their weight, he walked over to his bay horse and buckled the saddlebags on it. He swung into the saddle and, picking up the reins, joined Thompson at the front of the rebel column.

Fields mounted his horse and sat grinning sardonically down at Clardy's followers, doomed to a long wait.

He snorted with grim amusement. "I see he's takin' the loot with him. Don't trust yuh, does he? Wal, I don't blame him.

So long, you bloody-minded shikepokes. See you again some day." And turning his horse deliberately, he joined the patrol.

The darker it grew, the safer Jeff felt from discovery. He was alternately elated and depressed. Now the trap was ready to spring. All he had to do was slip through the rebel pickets and ride back to Fort Gibson and tell the Union commander what he had seen and heard. They would catch Clardy red-handed. It was odd how his Union friends back at Fort Gibson seemed almost like strangers.

All the way back to Boggy Depot, he rode tight-jawed and silent, fighting it out in his mind for the hundredth time. He was thinking hard and sweating hard. His hands were shaking as they held the reins. Half a mile from Boggy Depot he relaxed suddenly and let his breath out slowly in one long, weary exhalation. He had finally made up his mind. It was time to leave Stand Watie. He didn't want to, and he knew it.

At headquarters Fields dismissed them. Jeff walked to the commissary wagon. Heifer was gone. He unsaddled Flea Bite, led her to the creek for water, then tied her loosely to a wheel of the commissary wagon, where she would have plenty of room to graze. Heifer would find her there.

Reluctantly he fondled the little mare's soft ears, his throat suddenly tight. He knew he would never see her again. He hated to leave her but he couldn't run off to Fort Gibson on the horse Heifer had given him.

He couldn't take the saddle, either. Sighing, he lifted it into the back of the commissary wagon, passing his hand fondly over its smooth leather seat. He would take a horse and saddle from the inexhaustible rebel remuda at the camp's south border and leave two hours after sundown. He would be a long way up the Texas Road before daybreak. He felt like a thief. But he couldn't explain it to Heifer. Heifer was a rebel.

With time on his hands, Jeff took one last walk uptown. In spite of the dull misery in his heart, he felt calm and relieved at last. He was glad to have the struggle over with.

Boots clopping on the flagstone sidewalk, he neared the hotel. He heard the squeak of a fiddle and the tinkle of gay feminine laughter. Sounded like one of the "starvation" dances the rebels sometimes held. He walked onto the hotel's plank front porch and looked curiously into the open front door, a rectangle of yellow light. The place was crowded. The dance seemed some sort of celebration of the rebel victory at Cabin Creek.

In the lobby were rebel officers in worn, frazzled uniforms waltzing with girls in patched-up, made-over hoop skirts. The officers wore spurs, and when they danced, the spurs jingled rhythmically with the fiddle music. Everybody seemed to be having a gay time.

"Excuse us, sir."

Jeff spun around. Behind him, a girl stood smiling. She was a pretty girl. A band of black velvet encircled her brown throat, a brooch swung at her neck. Clad in a hoop skirt with pink crosswise ruffles, she was necessarily taking up lots of room on the porch.

A tall, blond rebel lieutenant stood stiffly at her side. Obviously they wished to enter.

Moving back, Jeff's eyes followed her in the half-light. At the same time she looked full at him and her small round mouth parted with astonishment. She gave a low cry of pleasure.

"Jeff!"

Jeff was so wonder-stricken he nearly fell off the porch.

The girl standing before him was Lucy Washbourne.

☆ 23

The Redbud Tree

"Lucy!"

Jeff breathed her name with a whistling gasp of surprise. She took both his hands tightly in hers.

Then her eyes dropped to Jeff's clothing. He was wearing what was unmistakably a pair of rebel gray cavalry pants. Moreover, he was roaming free and unmolested in the heart of the Southern Indian military headquarters. To Lucy, that could mean but one thing. She gave a low cry of ecstasy.

Insensible to all else, Jeff could only stand there on the hotel porch and stare at her, his nerves thrumming like a guitar string. Lucy was the first to recover from the shock of their meeting.

Skirts swishing, she spun around lightly, facing her escort. "Lieutenant Chavis, Mr. Bussey."

For once, Jeff forgot to salute. He only nodded mechanically, caring not a whit for the rebel lieutenant, his rank, nor his presence.

"Lieutenant, could you possibly excuse me for a moment?" Lucy said sweetly. "I will join you later on the floor."

The rebel lieutenant frowned. Plainly he didn't like it. But he bowed, mumbled something, and stepped back.

Still holding Jeff's hand, she led him off the porch and around the side of the building. There the heart-shaped leaves of a small redbud tree screened them from sight.

To his astonishment, she came lightly, eagerly, into his arms and, standing on tiptoe, put up her lovely mouth.

As their lips met and his arms went around her waist, he felt a blissful melting within him, an overpowering rapture that he had never known nor dreamed existed. For a moment there was no sound save that of their quick breathing and the leaves of the redbud tree soughing gently as the warm south wind stirred them. He could feel Lucy's warm, pliant body trembling.

"Lucy," he murmured, "I've been wild to see you. I've thought about you every single day."

Her soft arms were around his neck and her eyes were shut. He forgot all about the war. He forgot all about Clardy, the repeating rifles, or returning to the Union lines.

"Oh, Jeff," she whispered, "I've been so worried about you. It's been fourteen months since I saw you last."

As he held her close, Jeff's lips caressed her eyebrow, her cheek, her ear. He could feel her heart pounding beneath her bodice. This was something he never wanted to forget, a sweet miracle that couldn't happen again in ten thousand years. How wrong he had been to think Lucy didn't like him! Although she had her pick of all the swains and gallants in Watie's brigade, she was giving her heart to him. And making a rebel lieutenant wait inside while she did it.

Her eyes, soft and brown as pansies, were bright with emotion. A year and a half ago he would not have dared hope she would even speak to him. And now here she was, in his arms.

Her hands slipped down to his collar, absently tracing the button on his shirt.

"I've been worried to distraction about you," she said, feelingly. "I asked Belle Lisenbee to try to find out from Fort Gibson where you were all this time, but all she could learn was that you had gone on scout and were several months overdue." Her low, melodious voice, resonant as a deep-toned church bell, was vibrant with concern.

Sighing, she leaned back and looked up at him. "How tall you've grown, Jeff. I even asked Father to try to find you at the prisoner camp at Tyler when he went south to Texas several months ago. Then we left Tahlequah and refugeed south ourselves and I lost all trace of you—until now." Tears were on her cheek.

"Jeff—to find you here in the army of the South is a pleasure I never hoped to see! Tell me—what made you decide to join us?"

A cold, chilling breeze blew through him. He looked at her and felt the blood surging to the roots of his hair. What a fool he had been. Lucy believed he had switched to the rebel side. No wonder her greeting had been so ardent.

He released her, his pulses pounding dully with despair. Tired of the subterfuge he had been living, he decided to tell her everything and get it over with.

"Lucy, I hate hurting you—but now I've got to. I'm not in the Southern army the way you think I am. I'm a Union scout—out of uniform—behind the lines."

She stiffened and, in the yellow half-light of the window, regarded him with dazed wonder.

He told her how Bostwick's spur-of-the-moment remark had unwittingly enrolled both of them in the Watie cavalry, and how Bostwick had been killed at Honey Springs. He told her how, despite his illness, he had warned Blunt that Steele and Bankhead were moving on Fort Gibson.

Plunging resolutely on, he spoke of his own illness, and the Jackmans, and about Clardy's clandestine sale of the smuggled rifles. He described his enforced service with the rebel Cherokee cavalry, what fine comrades they were, and how much he had grown to like them. And when he told her of his fierce inner struggle, whether to go back to the fort or cast his lot whole-heartedly with Hooley, Heifer, and all his new friends, the color came back a little into her face and her dark eyes kindled with hope.

Earnestly she put her hand on his arm. "Then join us, Jeff," she implored. "We're going to win, Jeff. I feel sure of it. We have been winning lately, you know."

There it was, as plain as though this strong, intense rebel girl had written it herself on a blackboard. If he stayed with the South, he would have Lucy. If he returned to Fort Gibson, he would probably never see her again.

Now he had his decision to make all over again. And this time it was more agonizing than ever. He had to decide for all time between having Lucy or staying with his country. And he had to decide quickly. The thoughts tumbled wildly through his mind. His chest felt heavy. He saw that she was waiting, her face white.

"Lucy, I'm going back to the fort. I know my country has been wrong about a lot of things and that your people are fighting for their national existence. But Lucy, I'm just like you. I can't go back on my country or my state. In Kansas we're fighting for our existence, too. We're fighting to clean up the murders and bushwhacking over slavery and for the right to decide the kind of a state we want without the ballots being rigged by thousands of Missourians crossing the line to vote, or steal from us, or shoot us down. It's a nation-wide fight now and I think the only way it can ever be settled is for the North to subdue the South." He guessed it sounded oratorical but he had said it the best he could.

He looked miserably down at her. His voice grew soft with longing. "I'm crazy about you, Lucy—you know that. I wanted us to be married some day and live together always. I know this means I've probably lost you forever. But it's the thing I've got to do."

Lucy's small, oval chin lifted proudly. She stepped to one side, so he could pass.

Stricken, Jeff looked once at her, then walked quickly away.

"Jeff!"

She ran lightly to him. Crying softly, she came again into his arms, hiding her head against his breast. When her emotion had subsided and she raised her face, Jeff saw she had surrendered completely. All her fierce pride and violent patriotism was gone. For the first time in her life, she forgot the war and all its issues. She loved him, and that was all that mattered.

Swiftly she kissed him. Her eyes were large with fright.

"Good-by, Jeff. I hope you get away. Please be careful. I'll think about you every day until I see you again."

"I'll come back and get you after the war, Lucy. Will you wait for me?"

"I'll wait," she promised.

"It may be kind of a long wait. In the morning they may figure out why I left. If they do, they'll be after me. If they catch me, they'll hang me so high I could look down on the moon."

He looked at her fondly. "Good-by, Lucy," he said, kissing her cheek.

For a moment she clung to him. Then she let him go, watching his straight young body disappear from sight in the darkness. Even when she couldn't see him any more, she waited until his quick footsteps died away completely on the flagstone sidewalk. Then she turned and walked slowly back into the hotel.

Jeff decided to go first to his tent on the camp's outskirts and put food in his saddlebags. Hurrying, he saw ahead the headquarters tent with its fire blazing and its Betty lamps flickering brightly outside it. He would have to pass that way, but there was no risk because the sentries knew him.

Nobody knew he was leaving. And when they missed him in the morning, they still probably wouldn't know why he had left or where he had gone. He clenched his fists with satisfaction. If he stayed on the Texas Road and kept his eyes open, he shouldn't have any problems. He should be north of Limestone Gap by daybreak. Then he could cut straight across, riding into the fort by nightfall of the second day.

He didn't see the lone, fretful figure pacing the darkness outside Thompson's tent until he almost collided with it. Startled, the man gasped and cursed.

"Excuse me, sir," Jeff stammered, the light full on his face.

"Bussey!"

Jeff recoiled and felt the blood draining from his cheeks. It was Clardy. His mind busy with plans for his flight, and with sweet thoughts of Lucy, he had forgotten all about the Union captain.

Instantly he knew all his plans had collapsed and his life was in danger. Clardy would tell Thompson that he was a Union spy. Thompson would check with Fields. Fields would remember that Jeff had been with the patrol that saw Clardy unload the rifles. In a few short moments the rebels would be after him like forty hen hawks after a setting quail. They had to take him before he reached Fort Gibson or they'd never get their eight hundred rifles.

Desperate, Jeff put his hand on his pistol. He had a lightning impulse to kill Clardy on the spot. Instead, he ducked into the hazel brush and began running toward the horse lot, two hundred yards away. Behind him, he could hear Clardy shouting for the sentries.

From the rack outside the horse lot, Jeff grabbed up a saddle, a bridle, and a blanket. Aware of his deadly peril, he tried desperately to salvage what he could from the disastrous situation. Carrying the saddle, he ran awkwardly and felt his riding boots chafe his feet. Now the whole camp was in an uproar. Jeff heard Fields bawling orders. Weighed down with the heavy saddle, Jeff tried to run faster.

Suddenly he heard hoofbeats approaching at a gallop. Somebody—probably Fields—was thinking lightning fast in the crisis. Digging his boot heels into the ground, Jeff slid to a stop. They had cut him off from the horses.

Frustrated and panting, he looked wildly around him in the dark. Of all the rotten luck! Now he was on foot with the whole rebel camp alarmed and looking for him. And Fort Gibson was 125 miles away.

Fighting down his panic, he dropped the saddle and the blanket but kept the bridle. Maybe he could find or take a horse on the way. If not, he would have to walk, and his riding boots would be useless. He spun around and, sprinting back to his tent, grabbed up a pair of old infantry shoes.

He scooped up two handfuls of shelled corn and filled his pockets. There wasn't time to take anything else. Hearing voices and the sentries' running footsteps approaching, he ran from the tent into the timber, thankful for the darkness that would hide him until dawn.

☆ 24

Flight

Tying his shoes around his neck, Jeff hurried toward the thickest part of the woods. He knew there would be fewer pickets there. His eyes quickly became adjusted to the darkness. Staying in the heavy timber, he soon put the noise of the aroused camp behind him.

He tried to calculate where his pursuers would look for him first. Probably the last direction they would expect him to go would be south, toward Texas.

So he headed south, walking fast. After he had gone a mile

or two, he planned to cut straight east ten or twelve miles, toward Arkansas, then head northeast across the Gaines Creek Mountains and the Limestone Mountains to the fort. They would be after him at sunup from all directions. Without a horse the odds were heavily against him. He had to have a horse.

His feet began to hurt and he stopped and changed to his shoes. All he could hear was the whippoorwills cooing softly from the trees. Circling to the east, he came into a clearing and saw the red glow of the moon rising through the dark timber. It reminded him of the prairie fires he used to watch in Kansas at night. Now he could see everything more plainly. He was carrying his boots and the bridle. In his belt he wore the hunting knife and double-barreled pistol Heifer had given him.

After he had walked south a couple of miles, he bore straight east toward the rising moon, which had now cleared the tree-tops. He knew he had passed the last of the rebel pickets and had nothing to fear the rest of the night.

It was daylight he dreaded. Then the pick of Watie's men would be on his trail, men who could ride and track and knew the country and the people living in it. Jeff wondered where the Fort McCulloch Road was? If he was calculating correctly, he should cross it at any time.

Fifteen minutes later he saw its ruts gleaming darkly in the moonlight. Praise God, it looked empty. He listened carefully. From the grass clumps the katydids were singing their sad, bittersweet songs, as though lamenting the passing of summer. A coyote wailed lonesomely from the hills. But that was all.

Jeff felt a yearning and a discouragement that was almost intolerable. His thoughts kept straying back with pleasant melancholy to Lucy. At best he wouldn't see her again for several long months. And if the rebels ever caught him, his courting days would be over forever.

He felt for his pistol. Clardy, who sat in on all of Blunt's staff meetings, would know about the message Leemon Jones had carried to Fort Gibson. He would quickly acquaint Watie with the details. The rebels had more than one score to settle with Jeff.

He crossed the road and plunged into the timber on the other side. Tired of carrying the bridle, he tied it around his shoulders and under his arms. When he ran, he could feel the bridle's steel bit spanking him in the small of the back but he didn't care. He wanted to get back to the fort. He was unencumbered by baggage, and fear lent wings to his feet.

When the whippoorwills ceased marking the time and the owls took it up, Jeff struck a large creek which he judged to be Clear Boggy. The air was cool along the creek bottom. Taking off his shoes, he stayed in the water for three or four miles, splashing southeastward through the shallows or wading down the middle through the deep, cool mud. He knew there would probably be dogs on his trail in the morning. He aimed to make their work as difficult as possible.

When the moon began to drop behind him, Jeff left the creek, put on his dry shoes and stockings and began to walk northeastward again. He was growing tired but doggedly he kept going. He had to keep moving until he found a horse.

In the eastern sky the moonlight revealed a few white, fleecy clouds floating motionless like long films of cobwebs. When finally they began to turn darker and the stars around them to burn more sharply, he knew it was time to hole up. He figured the best way to avoid being seen was to travel at night and sleep in the woods in the daytime.

Half an hour before sunrise, he crawled into a plum thicket. Taking his knife and pistol out of his belt and placing them on the ground beside him, he lay down with his hat over his eyes.

Dozing off, he slept fitfully. He dreamed he was hidden in a tall tree overlooking the commissary wagon in the rebel camp back at Boggy. Heifer was serving huge plates of ham and fried potatoes to Fields, Watie, Thompson and Clardy. Perishing from hunger, Jeff was about to crawl down out of the tree and give himself up, begging for one good meal before they called the firing squad, when oddly, somebody began to throw cold water in his face.

Awakened by a growl of thunder, he opened his eyes to find the sky was overcast and big raindrops were hitting him in the face. They plunked softly through the plum leaves above him. A big black cloud was rolling out of the west, darkening everything. The wind was blowing fresh and cool from the north and smelled of rain. Sweeping up his knife, pistol and boots, he dove under a tree for shelter. Then the storm broke.

He thrust his loaded pistol into one of his boots to keep the two loads dry; they were all the ammunition he had.

All afternoon long, he sat drearily in the downpour, listening to the raindrops monotonously peppering his hat brim. The water ran off his hat onto his arms and shoulders, chilling him. The wind came up, plastering the wet grass to the muddy ground.

Hungry, he chewed some of the shelled corn in his pocket. As soon as it grew dark, he began walking again. It rained nearly all night. It was slower going now. He was tired. Clouds hid the moon. The ground was slick, and the mud balled up beneath his shoes. Dawn caught him halfway through a big patch of hazel brush.

He was just falling asleep in it when he heard the sound of a horse's hoofs striking the stony ground. Thinking it might be a loose horse, he reached for the bridle he had brought along. Then squinting through the brush, he felt his blood freeze in his veins. He didn't need any bridle. He wasn't going any place except maybe back to Boggy Depot.

Several mounted men, all heavily armed, rode toward him. They were rebels. Two black dogs that looked like Newfoundlands walked ahead, sniffing the earth.

Jeff wondered how they had traced him so fast. Probably

by his tracks in the mud. He gulped in despair. This was it.
They had him.

He flattened himself on the ground and began to pray hard.
A hundred yards away, the dogs entered the brush and came
toward him. The men followed. They came closer and closer.

Suddenly a man laughed. "Ah, thar y'are, Bussey! I see ya.
Come on outa thar er I'll shoot yuh full of buckshot." Jeff
heard him cock the trigger.

His heart hammering with fear, Jeff lay too frightened to
move. His pistol was in his hand. Carefully weighing his
chances, he wondered if he could catch the horse after he shot
the nearest man off it.

Before he could decide anything, the rebel rode off. "Dogs
don't trail worth a hoot. He's gotta be in h'yar somewhars," he
muttered.

"We'll hev the right kind of a dog in two, t'ree days," another voice answered. "Fields went to Preston fer Sully, Snoop
Sanders' best bloodhound. He's the one thet trailed thet mur-
derer clear 'crost northern Texas last spring. Got 'im, too.
No trail gits too cold fer thet Sully ta foller."

The two men rode to the head of the thicket. Jeff knew they
would beat it out foot by foot until they found him. He
crawled on his hands and knees.

Rolling into a gulley, he ran, bent low, until he came to a
small creek. Hoping to throw them off the scent, he waded
into the water with his shoes on. It was then he discovered he
had left his bridle and his boots behind. The rebels would
soon find them and know he had been there.

All day he alternately walked and ran. He was tired and
hungry and discouraged, but he didn't dare stop. The chase
was fast approaching a climax. It had become a grim, compelling game. When Fields arrived with that bloodhound, it
was going to be even grimmer.

That night Jeff came to a river. He saw the banks were high
and steep. Entering the water from a ford downstream, he

waded to a sandy place directly below the highest bank, where he crawled out and lay beneath some willow bushes, covering himself up in the warm sand almost at the water's edge. The last thing he remembered was the whippoorwills.

When he awoke the sun was shining brightly. Sleepily he raked the sand off himself and found that his feet and legs were still wet. But he felt refreshed.

A stick broke on the bank above him. Jeff caught his breath. There sat a big, dark-skinned rebel on a gray horse. With him were the same two black dogs Jeff had seen yesterday in the hazel clump. Jeff heard voices and knew the searchers had arrived in force.

Cautiously, he eased first one foot, then the other into the river. Then he lowered his whole body into it until only his nose and forehead stuck out. The water was cold but he didn't care. He hoped the willow leaves would hide him. Trembling with cold and fear, he lay perfectly still in the opaque water, watching them hunt for him.

They had plenty of men to do the hunting. Soon the tops of both riverbanks were black with Indians and rebel soldiers, mounted and on foot. The Indians looked like Creeks. In the hot sunshine their greased faces glistened. They were poking into the brush piles with their rifles and shotguns. Jeff was thankful that the bank behind him was so steep that they could not get down. With a feeling of annoyance, he thought of his pistol in his waistband. The water had ruined the loads. Now he had no weapon but his knife.

The rebels didn't give up. All afternoon Jeff lay in the water and watched them look for him. He didn't recognize any of them. It seemed there were more in the afternoon than there had been even in the morning, jabbering and eating with their fingers the cold beef they had brought along in their saddle-bags. The smell of the food was almost unendurable. He hadn't eaten in three whole days.

Jeff stayed in the water until after sundown. Gradually

everything became quieter. When the wolves started howling savagely close by, he thought he had never heard a sweeter sound. It meant the rebels had gone.

The moon was up. Jeff set his course by the North Star. Each morning early before he went to sleep, he located the north star in the heavens, then marked its direction with several stones or sticks, so if it was cloudy when he started walking each night, he could stay on his course without getting lost. He had got the idea from Heifer, whose last act before crawling into his bunk had always been to turn the tongue of the commissary wagon toward the North Star, so that if it were overcast next morning and they were in unfamiliar country, they would take the right direction.

The hunger cramps and the fatigue hit him at the same time. Wanting only to get away, he hadn't particularly noticed the cramps before. But now they struck like the blade of a hot bowie knife held against his stomach, and he had to walk more slowly. He was chilled to the bone. He wondered how long it would be before Fields and the bloodhound overtook him? He had never seen a bloodhound but he had heard his father speak of what wonderful noses they had and how, back in Kentucky, the sheriffs and marshals used them to track down criminals. Jeff knew his rambling trail would be easy to follow. That Texas hound would sniff it up at a gallop.

He smelled pine trees ahead. When he awoke, a cool north breeze was blowing on him, carrying the clean, strong smell of the pines. Chilled, Jeff blew upon his hands. It was late September. There would soon be frost in these mountains.

He stood, weak and stiff and hungry. There was no sound save the scolding bark of a buck squirrel and the high, thin, buglelike notes of an ivory-billed woodpecker. He began walking again.

Once he surprised a small, short-eared owl dozing on the limb of a sycamore. Flushing it with a stick, he watched it flap away through vertical streaks of sunshine that leaked in through the tops of the pines. He saw a wolf, a catamount, and even a small brown bear waddling up a draw. There were so many wild animals prowling about that he concluded the rebels weren't around and therefore it might be safe to travel in the daytime.

Every step he took, he saw birds and flowers and occasionally an animal he had never seen in his life before. He wished Noah were here to help identify them. He wished Noah were here with a couple of big, strong horses, a knapsack full of food, and about a gallon of hot Union coffee.

Then he thought of Heifer and the commissary wagon back at Boggy. It was breakfast time in the rebel camp. The rebel range was full of fat beeves and the flour had come up from Texas. Heifer would be turning the pink T-bones in his Dutch ovens, searing them to hold the juices in. Then he would take his gouch hook and lift the lids to see if his sourdough biscuits were browning properly. The light, tightly packed "dough gods," as Hooley called them, stood seven inches high. Jeff's mouth watered.

Ahead of him loomed the mountains, rounded, pine-covered. He was sure he couldn't climb the first one.

He braced and began to labor up the rise, concentrating on each step and thinking of Pete Millholland and his words, "You can always go farther than you think you can." It was funny how a fellow could lie moldering in his grave and still his words could go right on helping people.

He paused to eat a cluster of wild grapes, greedily swallowing some of the seeds. The tart, reddish-purple juice tasted good but there wasn't enough of it. It was cool in the shade beneath the pines. A flock of wild turkeys arose with a thunder of wings.

At noon he came to a wide road with deep ruts made by wagons. He knew it was the road running east from Perryville to Fort Smith. It was an important landmark and he felt a little encouraged, knowing he was roughly halfway to the fort.

His head throbbed. Black spots came before his eyes. He knew now what hunger meant, what that line in the Lord's Prayer meant that he had repeated a thousand times without thinking, "Give us this day our daily bread." He lay down in the sunshine to rest but each time it was a little harder to get up. He thought, *One of these times I'm not going to get up.*

Ahead, the Limestone Mountains looked still higher and more rugged. Sighing with despair, he walked down into the valley between the two ranges. It was growing dark.

A strange sound came to his ears, a strange domestic sound that had no business existing in the vast wilderness of green timber rolling endlessly over one round-domed hill after another. It was the sound of a spinning wheel. The sound died away, and Jeff smiled sadly. In his delirium, his ears were playing him tricks.

Then he heard it again, a steady, mechanical humming, and all at once he came upon a small shanty set in a dogwood thicket a hundred yards away. He lay down in the brush to watch.

Presently a woman in a blue dress came out the door carrying a piggin of shelled corn. She had black hair. Going to a small steel mill fastened to a big oak, she ground the corn in the mill, then took it back inside. Soon gray smoke began to spiral out of the fireplace chimney.

Two men walked up. Each was heavily armed and carried his rifle into the house with him. Jeff didn't see a horse on the place. Sighing, he guessed it didn't make any difference. He doubted if he had strength enough now to mount a horse, let alone catch one. He didn't even have a bridle.

He smelled corn bread baking and beef roasting in the fireplace, and again the hunger cramps grabbed him, twisting cruelly at his vitals. His appetite became so savage that it took all his will power not to rush into the house and snatch the food away from them. Afraid their dogs might scent him and raise an alarm, he backed through a brier patch, cutting his hands on the brambles, and circled the place widely. Doggedly he kept plodding forward. He was so tired now that he took his knife and cut himself a thick willow stick, using it for a cane.

Just before dusk the country grew flatter and gold-washed with autumnal wild flowers. He came to a wide river with cottonwood and black willow growing along its sandy shore. Jeff knew it was the Canadian River. Cautiously he scanned both its banks. The gray current rippled gently as it flowed in lazy loops and whirls among the sand bars. He might have to swim across.

Taking off his clothing, he waded tentatively into the shallows. The water was warm. It rose to his waist, and his feet touched sand and flat stones on the bottom. He got across safely, waded out, and slipped into his ragged pants and shirt. Very weak now, he started walking slowly northward, then pulled up, staring incredulously.

Several buildings loomed ghostlike in the woodsy gloom ahead. The place seemed empty and uninhabited. It was dark and cool beneath the trees.

He felt faint. Staggering inside the nearest building, he lay down on the dusty plank floor. He was sure he had come to the end of his rope. If he had to die, this would be as good a place as any. What a fool he had been not to show himself at that shanty he had passed in the afternoon.

The floor was covered with old paper. The room smelled musty. Apparently it had once been occupied by rebel soldiers. On the floor he found an old voucher dated "North Fork Town, August 7, 1863." It was signed by General Douglas H. Cooper. Was this North Fork Town? He was too tired to care.

He tried to sleep, but packs of snarling wolves kept entering the deserted town. It sounded as if they were chasing other creatures out. In the morning he was awakened by a wild hog squealing in terror. He hobbled out to investigate and found

a pack of wolves had killed it and had part of its intestines
out on the ground.

Yelling and waving his stick, Jeff drove them off. The
young ones ran away, but the old ones sat only a few yards
distant, hungrily watching him. With his knife he peeled the
skin off the hog's flanks and hewed off most of both hams. He
carried the meat back into the house, leaving the rest for the
wolves.

He ransacked the house and finally found two dry matches.
By that time the wolves had devoured the remains of the hog
and were gone. Carefully he gathered dry twigs, grass, and
leaves. His hand trembled so badly when he struck the first
match that he dropped it on the ground and it went out.

Muttering a prayer, he scratched the last match on a small
rock. With a loud crackle, the yellow flame flared up. Exultantly Jeff touched it to the grass. Soon he had a fire going.

With his knife he sliced off a slab of the pink ham. Using
two green sticks, he suspended it over the fire. Maddened by
the smell of the cooking meat and the hiss of the juice dropping
into the flames, he cut off a bite of the half-cooked meat and
began to chew it. At first it had no taste; then the saliva came
back into his mouth, and he gulped it down.

It felt like a rock in his stomach. He cut himself another
piece and gorged it down, too, unable to control himself. He
kept cutting up the hams and shoulders, barbecuing them as
fast as he could.

For three days Jeff lay around, cooking and eating the ham
and recovering enough of his strength to start north again.
Each day he practiced walking, touring the abandoned town.
On the morning of the fourth day, he set out, a willow stick in
his hand, striding northeastward along a wide highway whose
dimly marked ruts were all grown over with green Bermuda.
He knew it must be the Texas Road. It seemed odd to see the
big thoroughfare so silent and deserted. He guessed he walked
six miles that morning.

In late afternoon of the following day he passed a small creek. Horse skeletons lay on the ground and broken-down wagons without wheels. The place looked familiar; Jeff recognized Elk Creek, scene of the Battle of Honey Springs in which Bostwick had died.

For the first time since he had left Boggy Depot, he began to think he was going to make it. With every step he took, he felt a little stronger. He couldn't be more than twenty miles from Fort Gibson now. He wondered how the dun was and if they had taken good care of him. He thought of Noah and Bill Earle and Stuart Mitchell and David Gardner and suddenly found himself wanting very much to see them all.

He moved off the broad Texas Road, where he could easily be seen, and began to walk in the brush. Ahead, he could faintly smell willows and water and mud; he knew he was nearing the Arkansas River.

He was walking through a green patch of tamarisk and sand-bar willow when he first heard the baying of the hound. The sound came from far behind him in almost exactly the direction he had been traveling, a long, low, melancholy moaning that swelled into a deep, sobbing roar, filling the air like a hunting horn. The hills and hollows back of Jeff rang with its weird howling.

Terror cramped his stomach muscles. He quickened his stride. He knew it was the Texas bloodhound Fields had gone to Preston after.

He threw away his stick and began running. A feeling of bitterness and disaster surged over him. He was trapped almost at the fort's threshold. The hound would lead the rebels to him long before he reached the river. *This time they've got me sure,* he said to himself. *They may not even bother to take me back to Boggy. This may be my last fifteen minutes on earth.*

His breath began to snag in his throat, and he slowed to a fast walk.

Long bars of light from the sinking sun fell across his path.

The hound sounded much closer now. It yelped and whimpered eagerly as the trail grew hot and it realized it was close upon the quarry it had been so long pursuing.

Jeff felt the sweat running down his nose, and his tired feet chafing in his broken shoes. The hound was coming faster and faster. Suddenly it broke into a long, full-throated roar of triumph, and he knew it had sighted him.

His skinny ribs heaved like bellows under his torn blouse. Pouring out the last of his fading energy, he ran twenty more faltering steps, then staggered and fell headlong into a small depression. He couldn't get up. Panting in utter exhaustion, he turned over on one elbow and waited for them, his heart thumping wildly.

A thin, continuous patter of racing feet approached over the hard, smooth sand. There was a loud snuffling. Then the tall grass above him swished and parted.

A big liver-colored hound thrust its ugly head through the grass. Its forehead was pitted with long, deep wrinkles wet with perspiration. It had low-hanging jowls and its long ears hung down like cabbage leaves. When it opened its mouth to pant, its long, pink tongue dropped almost to the ground. Bracing itself with its front feet, it regarded Jeff solemnly.

Staring at the dog, Jeff felt no horror of it. Its sad face reminded him of an old man, rather than a monster.

The hound peered at Jeff and then back over its shoulder as if to say to its followers, "He's here." But Jeff heard no sounds of approaching horsemen. Apparently the hound had outrun its handlers.

The closer he looked at it, the more it seemed like any other dog except for its terribly homely face. He felt a flash of hope.

He had never seen a dog he didn't like, nor one he couldn't pet. He crawled to his knees, tottering dizzily. Holding out one hand, he talked kindly to the hideous-looking animal. Its long tail began to wag back and forth, sweeping the sand behind it in a smooth half circle and sending the small twigs flying.

Jeff got one foot under him and stood weakly.

The dog walked slowly up and sniffed loudly at Jeff's clothing, satisfying itself that Jeff was the scent it had been following for miles. He felt the suckling pressure of its nose on his legs and ankles. It sounded as if it had rollers in its nose.

He reached behind its ears and rubbed its head gently. Its police spirit fading, the hound forgot duty completely. It sat down, permitting him to fondle it at will.

Jeff examined its collar and saw the name Sully engraved on a tiny brass plate. It was the Texas hound, all right. But where were Fields and the rebels?

He tottered out of the depression and looked and listened to the south. Although he saw nothing, he could faintly hear cursing and shouts somewhere in the gathering dusk behind him. He didn't wait to hear more. Reaching into his shirt, he pulled out the last of his barbecued ham and gave it to the hound. The animal sniffed curiously at it, then bolted it down.

Jeff whistled coaxingly and held out his hand. "Come on, Sully," he invited, using his most persuasive tones.

Without hesitation the dog began to follow him. Jeff was elated. As long as he had the bloodhound, its rebel masters were going to have a hard time finding his trail in the dark. He was careful to stay on the grass and out of the soft sand, where his footprints would be easily visible. Plodding along steadily, boy and dog vanished into the river canebrakes. . . .

Next morning, an hour after sunrise, a squadron of Union cavalry riding patrol five miles below Fort Gibson saw them emerging out of the river mists. The lieutenant in charge, a medium-sized fellow with a big Roman nose, pulled his mount to a stop. Pushing his hat back on his shaggy, blond head, he stared incredulously.

"Looks like a man walkin'. But what in Sam Hill's that with him? Mebbe we better go see."

They came cantering up, and the lieutenant, riding at the

head of the column, hoisted his fist, halting the patrol. The boy was all skin and bones and dirt. And where in the world had he found the sad-faced hound that accompanied him?

Jeff saw their blue uniforms with the yellow braid down the side of the trousers. For a moment he feasted his eyes upon them. Pants and blouses all the same color. Sabers and carbines and metal canteens. Every man dressed and equipped alike and riding a thousand-pound horse. No patches, nor ponies, nor shotguns, nor clay jugs. His eyes misted over. They were the prettiest sight he had ever seen in his life.

Wearily he shoved his heels together and saluted. The hound sat down beside him.

"Sir, I'm Private Bussey. I'm just getting back from being fourteen months overdue on a scout. I have some very important information. Please take me to General Blunt at once."

The lieutenant looked queerly at him. "General Blunt ain't assigned here now. He was transferred back to Kansas a year ago. Colonel Wattles is in charge at the fort. We can take you to him, I reckon."

When he heard the lieutenant's voice, Jeff's mouth popped open and his bloodshot eyes lighted up with recognition.

"Sir, you're Lieutenant Orff, aren't you? Don't you know me, Lieutenant? Remember stopping the rebel charge with your Spencer that day we were returning from the scout across the Arkansas?"

Orff gaped. "Gosh all fishhooks! It's Bussey!"

He spoke so loudly, the whole patrol heard him. A bay horse turned out of the column. The tall cavalryman astride it rode alongside Jeff.

"Waw!" he growled commandingly to his horse. Climbing off, he picked Jeff up bodily and with a mighty swoop of his wide shoulders, swung him easily into the saddle. Then he mounted behind.

"Howdy, youngster," he drawled. "Where ya been all this time?"

Jeff grabbed at him with both hands and held on weakly. "Noah!" he blurted. He had never felt so glad in his life.

They moved off at a swinging gallop. Jeff craned his neck around, anxiously watching the hound behind him.

"Noah, don't let 'em lose my new dog. He wouldn't dare go back to Texas now. They'd stand him up before a firing squad and shoot him full of holes. Is he coming?"

Noah looked back over his shoulder.

"He shore is. Like the heel flies was after him. Runs easy, too. Looks like he could go all day without a drink. He seems to think he's yore dog, all right. Ugly as galvanized sin, ain't he? Where'd you take up with something as raunchy-lookin' as that?"

Jeff grinned. "It's a long story," he said.

☆ 25

Linn County, Kansas, 1865

Jeff rode north up the military road. It was a cloudy morning in June, 1865. The war was over, and they were going home.

It was hard to get used to being out of the army. He had traveled so widely, learned so much, and had so many things happen to him that it seemed he had been gone fifteen years instead of nearly four. He wanted very much to see his family. And he wanted very much to see Kansas, now that peace had finally come.

They came to the crossing of a small creek spilling noisily across the road. The dun's ears flattened warily. After last night's rains everything was fresh and cool. The road was muddy, and puddles stood in the weed-grown fields. The sky was dappled with big, cottony thunderheads drifting lazily northward, speckling the wet, green earth with great moving shadows.

Steering with his knees, Jeff urged the dun into the shallow, brown torrent. The horse was in good condition. Blunt's orders to the grooms at Fort Gibson had been plain on that score after Leemon Jones had faithfully delivered every word of Jeff's message.

"Some rain," said John Chadwick.

"Regular ole frog-strangler," said David Gardner.

"It rained so hard I didn't know whether it was lightnin' at the thunder or thunderin' at the lightnin'," said Bill Earle.

Mounted, they followed Jeff into the stream. The four of them had been mustered out. They planned to stay that night with Bill's Aunt Phoebe, who lived half a mile over the Missouri state line on the road to Neosho. Bill called her his "Confederate aunt" because her slaves had never left her when she offered them their freedom. Her two-story home had been one of the few spared by rival raiders during the war.

A mourning dove cooed from a roadside elm. Its pensive song seemed a lament for the waste and ruin Jeff saw everywhere.

All the way north from Fort Gibson he had been shocked by the destruction. When they had hiked down the same road as infantry with Weer in '62, the Cherokee farms had been prosperous and well-kept herds of cattle and droves of hogs grazed on the rich tribal pasturage. But now everything was changed.

Fire-blackened chimneys thrust themselves, gray and stark, against the June sky. To Jeff, they seemed like gravestones marking the spots where happy families had once lived. He remembered the fine orchards, the radiant lawns, the white-washed plank fences, and the broad valleys filled with tasseling corn he had seen three years before.

Houses, barns, outbuildings, corrals—all had been burned. The splendid shade trees were now lifeless stumps. Fences were torn down, wells had caved in, farming tools had been carried off, every hoof and horn swept away. The fields were dense with weeds growing higher than the corn ever had.

Occasionally they passed places where a house still stood, lonely and eyeless, its windows and doors gone, and the frames and sills torn out. Sometimes they saw the former owners had returned and were camped in the yard, bravely beginning the long, slow rehabilitation of their property.

Jeff watched with pity their rude efforts to work the soil with crudely sharpened sticks or with a solitary horse or plow that would pass as a loan over an entire neighborhood for a whole season. The Union Cherokee soldiers hadn't been mustered out until May 31, too late to plant corn.

Even Colonel Phillips had resigned his commission. In a short speech to his men, he had thanked them for their bravery and their loyalty. "God bless you all," he had concluded. "I am now going home and help Nellie peel peaches."

Jeff thought of the rebel Cherokee families down on Red River. The war was over for them, too, but he knew they couldn't return to their ravaged homes in the Cherokee country until the peace treaty had been made. And that might take months.

Sighing, he wondered if the Jackmans' big home near Briartown had been burned? He hoped not. His association with the rebels had taught him a tolerance and sympathy for the defeated side that he would keep all his life. He thought the South had been wrong to start the war, but now that it was over and the Union restored, he didn't want to see the rebels punished unreasonably. He hoped the country would be united again, bigger and stronger than ever, North and South.

Just before sundown they turned off the road and trotted down a long cedar lane to the home of Bill's Aunt Phoebe. It was the finest home Jeff had seen since he had left the Jackmans.

A Negro man met them at the main gate. He was carrying a pair of shears, several large towels, and a big, square bar of homemade lye soap. He looked with fear at their weapons and their blue uniforms.

"Mistus say ah'm to take y'all gennelmens to the springhouse fo a bath an' clean-up. Then yo to come to de house fo suppah."

Bill blushed, looking around apologetically at the others. "Aunt Phoebe's cranky about dirt and graybacks. She means all right, but she was born with her hands on her hips."

Jeff didn't mind. As usual, he was hungry enough to eat his own saddle blanket. He noticed that Aunt Phoebe's phobia for cleanliness included her servants. The Negro's curly hair was slicked down neatly, his black shoes were shined, and his clothing was neat. He smelled nice and clean. Lots cleaner than they smelled after their long ride in the sticky heat, he knew. They dismounted.

The Negro's eyes bugged whitely when he saw the fierce-looking bloodhound standing gravely beside Jeff.

"Is dat de houn dat chased one ob yo gennelmans all de way fum Red Rivah to de fote?"

They all laughed. The story of Jeff's long flight on foot from the Watie headquarters and of the renowned Texas bloodhound had been told hundreds of times all up and down the Texas Road.

"He don' look lak no bloodhoun'. He too ugly."

Bill Earle turned toward the dog. "Sure he's a bloodhound, ain't you, Sully? Bleed for the man, Sully."

But the hound seemed to know he was being teased. Staring at them with his mournful eyes, he stood closer to Jeff. Jeff reached down and stroked his long ears.

The Negro led them into the springhouse, a large room of blackjack logs that had been built over a live spring in the floor. It was cool there. The clear, cold water bubbled out of a short length of hickory log that had been bored by an extension auger to make a pipe. The place was almost nice enough to live in. The walls were stained a grayish white. There were chairs, a table, and a large cabinet built from sassafras saplings. Everything was scrupulously clean.

They stripped. With his shears, the Negro clipped each head carefully for lice. Then they bathed with the lye soap, toweled themselves, and donned clean gray cotton drawers, blouses, pants, and socks. Jeff felt clean and strange in the borrowed garments. Another Negro fed and rubbed down their horses and gave Jeff some beef for Sully. Missing his blue blouse, Jeff looked out the window and saw the first Negro hold it up and stare at the three yellow stripes on the shoulder before hanging it on a stone fence to air.

Jeff was going home a sergeant. He had found the promotion waiting for him the day he rode back to the fort. Blunt had seen to it personally after Leemon Jones arrived. As he stuffed his borrowed blouse into his pants, Jeff thought about how he had joined up at sixteen, wanting to be a soldier, to see battle and savor adventure.

Well, he had got what he wanted and more. Although he was barely twenty he had served the Union as an infantryman, cavalryman and scout, with two hours as an impromptu artilleryman at the Battle of Prairie Grove thrown in. And during his service with the South, he had been both a cavalryman and a teamster. He had lain ill several months in a rebel home, narrowly escaped a rebel firing squad, had nearly starved to death, been trailed one hundred miles by a bloodhound and fallen head over heels in love. Few men in either army had lived the war so fully.

Bill's aunt, tall and austere, met them at the door. Jeff had never seen a more meticulous woman. Nothing had a chance to be out of place in her parlor. If you laid something down, she picked up after you in your presence. She sent a Negro girl out onto the Bermuda lawn with a dustpan to scoop up the quid of tobacco John Chadwick had spat out.

But she set a good table. After supper they went into the parlor.

There Aunt Phoebe thawed a little. Bill sang several religious hymns while she accompanied him on an organ. She pumped with her foot and fingered the keys with long, flowing gestures of her hands and wrists.

One of the songs was "Amazing Grace" and with a stab of melancholy, Jeff's thoughts went back to Boggy Depot, and he heard Heifer humming the same tune in his broken, sobbing voice as he pounded out his steaks with the butt of his double-barreled pistol.

When they changed back into their own clothing next morning and got ready to leave, Bill elected to stay behind and rest up a week before going on to his home in northern Kansas.

Jeff thanked Aunt Phoebe. Then he shook hands with Bill, feeling kind of foolish. Bill promised to come and visit the Bussey homestead after he got settled.

"What are you going to do when you get home, go back to school at Bluemont?" Jeff asked.

"Heck no! I'm gonna git me a rockin' chair an' sit in it an' rest. After I rest about six months I might even rock a little. You goin' to school, Jeff?"

Jeff nodded. "I hear they're opening the new university next year at Lawrence. That's where I'm heading. It's only about sixty miles from home."

He put his foot in the stirrup and swung up on the dun's back. The bloodhound got up from where he had been lying on the grass and looked at Jeff with doleful expectancy. Jeff glanced once more at Bill and raised his hand.

As they rode off down the cedar kite track, Jeff swallowed

a couple of times. It was hard to leave a comrade you had eaten with, bunked with, and fought with so long. It reminded Jeff of his parting with Noah. Noah had gotten his discharge in May and returned to his home in Illinois.

With a lump in his throat, Jeff had taken Noah by the hand and thanked him for all he had done. He told Noah that he would never forget him and made him promise to stop at Sugar Mound and see him the first time he came through Kansas on one of his long hikes as a tramp printer.

"I'll come by an' see you, youngster. But I won't be walkin'." Noah pointed over his shoulder. Jeff saw the bay bridled and saddled and tied to a cannon wheel. "Old Cold Jaw here is gonna be my locomotion from now on. Now that I've finally learned how to stay on him, he's so gentle, I can stake him to a hairpin." Noah had bought the bay from the government the same way Jeff had purchased the dun, for seventy-five dollars taken out of his pay.

Jeff had found Leemon Jones, too, when he got back to the fort. The Negro boy had decided to stay in the North and join the First Kansas Colored Infantry, a Union Negro regiment trained at Baxter Springs, Kansas. He had seen some hard fighting and been shot through the shoulder during a skirmish at a hay camp near Flat Rock. When the war ended, he intended to homestead a farm somewhere in Kansas and bring his old mother to live with him.

Clardy never returned. After Jeff told Colonel Wattles about the repeating rifles, the colonel rushed a full report by courier to Fort Scott. It was telegraphed to Leavenworth, St. Louis, and Washington, and the illegal traffic through Kansas stopped. No one knew what had become of Clardy. He was nowhere to be found.

When Jeff didn't return from his scout with Bostwick, General Blunt personally wrote his parents, sending them Jeff's personal belongings, including the Medal of Honor he had won at Prairie Grove. Later, when Jeff turned up at the fort,

Colonel Wattles wrote again to Jeff's father, detailing the important service he had rendered the nation.

When Jeff and David and John crossed the Kansas state line just southeast of Baxter Springs, their excitement grew. They arrived first at the timbered boundary of the Gardner farm, and David stared unbelievingly from beneath his heavy white eyebrows at the corn growing in the thin, rocky soil. The rows were straight, and the crop looked good. A sleek, fat cow grazed in a pasture with a new calf gamboling at her side. Farther on they saw a small patch of wheat and a garden heavy with tomatoes. Apparently there had been plenty of rain.

As they rode up to the house a small black dog charged them, barking shrilly at the bloodhound. Jeff had never seen it before. He felt a vague alarm, wondering if David's mother had moved.

But when David called, the redheaded Gardner brood poured out of the house into the yard, and Jeff was surprised to see how much they had grown. Both girls were taller than their mother, but they had her plain, homely face and freckles. David got down off his horse.

"It's David!" Mrs. Gardner cried and ran forward to throw both arms around his neck. She was so glad to see him that she began pounding him with both fists. Recognizing Jeff and John, she greeted them, too.

Bashful and smiling, the two girls stepped forward to be kissed. David pecked them both dutifully on the cheek. A muscular, red-haired lad of ten ran up from the new barn built of poles and straw. There was mud on his bare feet and awe and excitement in his face.

David grinned. "Hello, Bobby. Well, I didn't git killed after all. An' my bones ain't bleachin' on no prairie."

Bobby stood there with his mouth open, staring first at his brother and then at the gaunt, sad-faced bloodhound.

A stranger followed Bobby from the barn, carrying a pitchfork. He was small in stature. To Jeff, he looked like an old gray rooster whose tail feathers had been draggled by the rain. His black hair was sprinkled with gray. Timidly he stood in the background, as though reluctant to intrude upon David's homecoming.

Beaming, Mrs. Gardner turned to David. "David, this is yore new pappy."

Then Jeff knew why the corn rows were so straight.

He and John rode on. As they angled off to the Chadwick farm, John straightened in the saddle, watching for familiar landmarks. Grown and heavily bearded, he stood six foot two and weighed 210 pounds, easily the biggest man in his company.

"Think my old man'll still try to whop me fer joinin' up?" he laughed.

At the same woodpile where he had thrown down the armful of blackjack logs when he left for Leavenworth with Jeff, he stopped his horse. Crawling off, he tied him to the saw rack. Grinning mischievously, he stooped and picked up an armload of logs and carried them toward the house. His father and mother came to the door, staring at him as though he was a stranger.

"Howdy, Pa," he said. "Well, I finally got back with the wood."

Then they recognized him. Elated, they rushed forward to greet him, chattering joyfully.

Now Jeff rode alone. The dun nodded his head patiently up and down as he walked down the center of the narrow road, sweat running off his flanks. The bloodhound trotted along in the brush, his long, intelligent nose whuffing and snorting loudly as he read the roadside trail like a newspaper. If the hound had been able to talk, Jeff was sure it could have told him the identity of every creature that had passed that way for a week.

It was late afternoon. With sweet nostalgia he drank in the

green Kansas countryside, the fragrance of the alfalfa and
sweet clover, the pastures blued over with wildflowers, the
creeks and ponds shining like glass in the setting sun, the
quail whistling cheerfully from the corn. He felt good clear
through about it all. No more violence and crime in Kansas.
No more trouble with the Missourians. The land was calm
and peaceful at last. Jeff was proud he had helped bring it
about.

Impatient, he wanted to shake up the reins and gallop the
dun on in, but he knew the horse was tired. In his saddlebags
were a pair of prunella shoes for his mother to wear to church,
a bolt of blue cotton cloth, and a skein of silk. For his sisters
there were shawls and shell side combs. For his father, several
twists of tobacco, a satin vest, and a new pair of calfskin boots.
He had purchased it all from the sutler's store at Fort Gibson.

He passed the spot where he had thrown rocks at Ring the
morning the dog had tried to follow him to Fort Leavenworth.
He knew the house was just around the corner. He smelled
smoke and saw a thin gray wisp curling above the trees; he
knew it came from his mother's fireplace, and a fresh wave of
homesickness washed over him.

As the road leaned familiarly to the left, he caught his first
view of his father's house. It looked different. He saw that an
extra room had been built off the west side. A new rail fence
ran around the yard. The trees looked twice as tall as when
he had left four years before. But the corral fence of peeled
cottonwood logs was still there.

As he trotted up, a big gray dog with a white ring around
his neck leaped up from the shade of the parked carryall and,
with a low growl, trotted out springy-legged to smell noses
with the bloodhound. Jeff's heart jumped exultantly. It was
Ring.

"Ring," he called, "don't you know me?"

When Ring heard Jeff's voice, he cocked his ears and forgot

all about the hound. In two bounds he was at Jeff's stirrup, wild with excitement.

Whining eagerly and springing up on his hind legs, the dog took sky hops almost as high as the saddle, trying to reach Jeff. The dun snorted and shied to one side. Jeff quieted him and dismounted. Before he could tie the horse, Ring sprang upon him. Laughing happily, Jeff pulled the big dog's ears and scratched his back. Finally he tied the horse by the woodpile and walked across the chip-strewn yard to the house.

A girl came out the back door, her mouth parted in surprise. She wore a simple cotton gown of purple. She was slim and shapely, with a couple of cinnamon-colored freckles high on the bridge of her nose. Jeff grinned at her. She had sure grown up but she didn't fool him any. After seeing David's sisters, he was prepared.

"Jeff!" she shouted and ran to meet him. Throwing both arms around his middle, she hid her brown head under his arm. Her cry aroused the whole house.

Jeff gave her a big squeeze and kissed her on top of her warm, clean-smelling head. "How are you, Bess?"

She gasped and, looking up at him, giggled. "Why, Jeff, don't you know me? I'm Mary. Bess is married. She lives over by the trading post with her husband. They're coming to visit us tomorrow." Now it was Jeff's turn to look surprised.

Jeff embraced his mother and father. They looked fine. His mother was crying. She said it wasn't Jeff at all, he had grown so much.

His father gazed at him with quiet pride and satisfaction. Mary claimed it was a miracle he hadn't been shot, considering all he had been through.

Jeff laughed. "A running target is hard to hit, Sis. I was too small for their rough sights."

And so, Jeff came home. . . .

Later, after he had helped his father do the feeding and

milking, they had supper in the firelit kitchen. He told them the whole story. When he had finished it was very late. His mother arose and quietly left the room. Returning, she handed Jeff a letter.

"It's for you. It came by army courier to Sugar Mound and was sent by a Colonel Matthews. He was in Doaksville in the Choctaw Indian Nation receiving the surrender of the Confederate Indian forces. He said a Captain Washbourne handed him the letter personally to give to you."

Jeff's heart gave a glad leap when he saw Lucy's name written in small, neat letters in the upper left-hand corner. Moving nearer the fireplace, he tossed a handful of dry chips on the coals and carefully slit the envelope open. He pulled out the two folded pages of ruled paper torn from a record book and began to read:

> Boggy Depot, C.S.A.,
> May 27, 1865.

My dear Jeff:

You cannot imagine how thankful I was to learn you got back safely to Fort Gibson. When I heard you were on foot and our soldiers were close on your trail, I had no breath to speak. I thought of you all alone out there in the hills and how you could never be rid of the awful fear of being captured and executed. I don't know how you did it with the whole country after you.

You must have done a great deal of praying as well as running. I couldn't run for you but I prayed hard for you every day. Once I heard that the hounds had run you down and mangled you terribly. Another time I heard you were dead. We do not know what to believe here any more, there is so much rumor.

Our refugee home is a log house eleven miles west of Boggy Depot, near Blue River. When I heard after the dance that something went wrong and they were after

you, I told my father everything. He knew about the
rifles. He told me about having one of our men sing a
certain song across the river to signal when we had the
gold ready to buy the contraband rifles. Father had just
returned from Texas. He went to Boggy Depot and talked
to General Watie. The general promised to let us know
when you were taken. When they got me up in the middle
of the night to tell me they had lost the hound and you
had escaped, my pulses throbbed and then almost ceased
to throb at all. I knew before I answered the door that
you were dead. Thank God I was wrong.

The war is over here, and I am glad. General Watie
gave nearly all our boys a furlough in March so they
could help their families put in a crop.

Boggy Depot is desolate. The streets are quiet. We had
already lost our homes and property. Now we have lost
the war. It is so dreary in town that one feels it is almost
sacreligious to laugh. Everybody here is worrying about
what kind of terms we will get in the peace treaty.

I am wearing my last calico frock, and it is mended in
many places. Most of my nice dresses were left behind in
the trunk at Tahlequah. We have learned to make fine-
flavored coffee from roasted okra seeds, and now everybody is planting long rows of okra along the edges of their
cornfields. Before our cow died we churned every day
but we didn't drink the precious buttermilk. We made
biscuits of it instead. Tonight we have nothing to eat, so
I am going to bed early and fill up on sleep.

I saw Hooley Pogue taking a walk around the hospital
block the other day. He was the raggedest, shabbiest, most
patched-up little fellow I ever saw. When I told him I
was going to write to you, he said tell you to keep the
hound. He said, "If that hound ever shows up here again,
Fields will have him court-martialed." Hooley's wound is
almost healed. He told Father and me about you holding

him on his horse all the way back from Pheasant Bluff.
I told him and Father how you were forced into our army
by Bostwick's remark. Mother had already told Father
how good you were to us at Tahlequah. I think he would
have tried to help you even if they had caught you.

Hooley introduced us to Mr. Hobbs, the cook. He
looked so lonely I felt sorry for him. We heard later he
went back to his ranch in Texas and that he gave your
pony and saddle to the youngest Jackman girl.

We all want to return to our homes but Father says we
cannot until late this year or early in 1866, after the
treaty is made. Father is going to work driving freight
wagons. Mother plans to run a boardinghouse at Fort
Gibson, catering to the Union officers there. After feeding
that polite Wisconsin major at our home in 1862, she has
decided that many of your officers are nice people.

I almost forgot to tell you about Clardy. When they
didn't catch you, he was afraid to go north. Meanwhile
some of his followers became intoxicated and our people
found out what his real name was and that he was the
one who had ordered Lee's execution. A few days later
he was found stabbed to death and his twelve thousand
dollars gone. Some say he was slain in revenge, others
think his own companions murdered him. Hooley Pogue
said, "I'll bet he's in hell pumping thunder at three cents
a clap."

We are excited to hear that our Methodist conference
will soon start up again. Now that the war is over and a
minister is coming, nearly everybody here plans to get
married.

Remember the plans you and I made under the redbud
tree at Boggy? Jeff, please don't make me wait too long.
I've said "No" three times in the last two weeks. Soon I'll
be the only unmarried girl in the refugee country.

Your dog Dixie is with us. She is the family watchdog and pet.

We all love her very much. I hope you don't want her back too soon. She is all I have to remember you by.

You should have seen me milk the cow before we lost her. Mother said I did it almost as well as Jed, our slave who ran away. I do most of the cooking when we have anything to cook. I am learning to weave and spin. You already know how well I sew. Except when I grow angry and stick my finger with the needle.

Jeff, when are you coming to see me? I wish with all my heart that you were here tonight. I don't think it would be safe for you to come now. Wait until we get back to Fort Gibson, then it will be perfectly safe. Please write to me here at Boggy. Please write the day after you receive this. I think of you every day and every night. Do you ever think of me?

> Ever yours affectionately,
> Lucy Washbourne.

Jeff laid the letter on the sandstone hearth. He sighed deeply. What did she mean, asking him if he ever thought of her? Corn! He thought about her all the time.

Lately he had begun worrying about her, too. In a few short months she would go with her family to Fort Gibson and be courted by all those ardent Union officers flocking around her mother's table.

A frown puckered his face. He was going to have do something about it right away. He almost wished she lived at Fort Gibson now so he could start back first thing in the morning. If he ever lost that girl, he'd never get over it.

His mother put him on a shuck mattress in the new room. The floor was made of split logs. There was a rag rug on it. He could smell the fragrance of the newly hewn hickory. The walls were plastered with clay and felt smooth to the touch. Through the open south window, a cool breeze was blowing, gently stirring the red cotton curtains Mary had made. Truly, it was a fine room.

But Jeff couldn't rest in it. After reading Lucy's letter, his heart kept going back to her and to the fine people on the defeated side who would have to wait another year before they could return to their homes and start making a new life for themselves. From somewhere on the warm night wind, he kept hearing a rowdy banjo tune picked by flying rebel fingers back at Boggy, and tasting Heifer's yeasty "dough gods," and feeling the water of the muddy Arkansas rise to his armpits as he rode again with Watie at Pheasant Bluff. And his regret came like pain.

Restless, he climbed through the open window to keep from awakening his family and spread his blankets on the Bermuda outside. Sleeping outdoors on the ground was a habit he would have for many years.

He settled back comfortably upon the blanket. The Kansas sky was spangled with blazing stars. They shone so brightly that he imagined he could almost hear the crackle of their fires. Down in the corral a cowbell tinkled faintly. He felt a slight movement at his side and saw that Ring had joined him and was lying close by, his head upon his forepaws.

Reaching over with his hand, Jeff gave the big dog a couple of pats. Then he closed his eyes. Soon he began to breathe deeply and regularly.

ABOUT THE AUTHOR

HAROLD KEITH grew up near the Cherokee country he describes in *Rifles for Watie*. A native Oklahoman, he was educated at Northwestern State Teachers College at Alva and at the University of Oklahoma, where he was a long distance runner.

While traveling in eastern Oklahoma doing research on his master's thesis in history, Mr. Keith found a great deal of fresh, unused material about the Civil War in the Indian country. Deciding that he might someday write a historical novel about it, he interviewed twenty-two Civil War veterans then living in Oklahoma and Arkansas; and much of the background of *Rifles for Watie* came from the notebooks he filled at that time. The actual writing of this book took five years. Mr. Keith is married and has a son and daughter.